BAREFOOT
IN THE
STUBBLE FIELDS

by
Mary Frailey Calland

To my mother, whose quiet heroism inspired this book, for giving of her time, her remarkable intelligence, and her very heart.

Acknowledgements

The idea for this story came from a conversation at my mother's kitchen table, and evolved over the course of seven years into the book you hold in your hands today. During that time, many people contributed their thoughts, their expertise and their support, and I would like to say thank you to them now:

First and foremost, to my husband, Dean, who has always believed in me and to whom I owe this opportunity to do what I love.

To my parents, Henry and Margaret Frailey, who offered their time, their scrapbooks and their stories of courtship during the war years.

To Richard Jackman and John Jackman, my talented uncles, whose generous sharing of their memories of what it was like to grow up on an Iowa farm during the Depression added immeasurably to my understanding of the time, and to my knowledge of, and appreciation for, them.

To my sister, Anne Martinez, who read and reread large portions of my manuscript, for having the courage to give me her invaluable honest critique, and the trust that we would remain on speaking terms.

To my children, Mat, Emmie, Rosie, Grace and Mike, who were unstinting with their hugs, words of encouragement and their computer expertise.

To my niece, Brennan Martinez, the model for the cover of this book, for braving the stubble and the burrs in her bare feet in order to provide me with such a poignant cover picture.

To my extended family, who enthusiastically offered their encouragement, even when they weren't sure what I was doing or why it was taking so long.

To the staffs of the Saint Mary's College Archives, the

Emmetsburg Library in Emmetsburg, Iowa, the Sioux City Public Library and the Sioux City Historical Society. The good work these people do goes too often unheralded, but without them the fascinating details of our history would be lost to us forever.

To Elizabeth Collins, Mindy Wilke and Deborah Courtney, my patient editors, for their painstaking review and invaluable suggestions.

And, finally, a very large thank you to Elizabeth and Bob Collins and all the folks at Gardenia Press, for giving new writers a chance.

Part 1

Chapter 1

September 1931

The Boru Democrat, Boru, Iowa,
Monday, September 7, 1931

One of the saddest deaths we have been called upon to chronicle is that of Mrs. Terrence Fahey, age 36, which occurred in her home northwest of the city early Thursday morning. Here a young wife and mother was called from earthly scenes, leaving a heartbroken husband and six children. Death came at the birth of a baby boy who did not survive his mother.

Boru had no better, truer wife and mother than Elizabeth Brennan Fahey. She was an exemplary Christian woman and her virtues were numerous. On January 19, 1915, she was united in marriage to Terrence Fahey, the youngest son of one of Boru's first settlers. They built a fine farm home in this county, and lived a loving and companionable life, until God called her to so untimely a death, a martyr to the great and mysterious cause of Divine Creation.

Funeral services were held at St. Thomas church at 10:00 Saturday morning. Burial was in St. John's Cemetery. The Democrat extends heartfelt sympathy to the sorrowing husband and the six motherless children, some of whom are too young to realize the irreparable loss they have sustained.

The night they took her away was cold. Maggie Fahey, six years old, pulled her wool church coat up around her shoulders and burrowed deeper into the backseat of the car. The cushions smelled faintly of the farm and the cigarettes her father was so fond of smoking, and, once again, she had to fight back the urge to cry. Careful not to make a sound, she lay there staring at the back of her father's head as he drove, replaying in her mind the conversation, only partially overheard from her bedroom above the front parlor, which had resulted in this silent car ride through the dark Iowa night.

Her father's raised voice was what first caught Maggie's attention, his tone one she had never heard before and didn't understand. She shimmied out of the protective cocoon of her bed covers, to which she had retreated immediately after dinner, and tiptoed across the room she shared with her two older sisters. Holding her breath, Maggie cracked the door slightly, and pressed her ear to the opening.

"I can take care of my own family."

"Terrence, be reasonable."

Maggie recognized the loud, commanding voice of her Uncle John. "You can't be workin' the fields and lookin' after all these children, too. The girls have their hands full taking care of little Michael and this house, not to mention you and the boys."

"We'll manage. I'll find some woman to come in from town."

"And supposin' you did find someone, how would you pay her? You're behind on your bills as it is. Look, it's not just you. Times have been tough for all the farmers, and it'll get worse before it gets better. Our helpin' out would give you one less worry and one less mouth to feed. You know that Nora and I have more than we need — "

"I'm well aware of your financial situation, John."

Maggie knew now that her father was angry, for a little bit of an Irish brogue had crept into his voice.

"I only meant that business at the stockyards hasn't been as affected by the drop in prices. And you've so much to deal with, with Elizabeth, God rest her soul, gone just these few weeks — "

Her Aunt Nora's soft voice interrupted and Maggie had to

strain to hear her words.

"Terrence, I know that you and the children miss Elizabeth terribly. We miss her, too. Now, the older children, they can at least understand about her dying, and little Michael is too young to know, thanks be to God. But Maggie, she's just turned six. She needs someone to look after her and comfort her. Sure, Kit and Bid have offered to help, but they've their own families to care for. I could look after Maggie full time. You know I always prayed for a little one of my own, and since our Patrick died. . . . Well, I know I'll never replace her dear mother, but I think that having Maggie with us for a little while might be a help to her. And it would mean so much to me."

Uncle John's voice broke in again.

"She'd have her own room and there are friends her age close by. And Blessed Sacrament School in Sioux City is excellent."

"The school she goes to right here is fine."

"I'm sure it is. I just meant that, we'd do our best by her, Terrence. I love your sister and this is somethin' she wants to do — we both want to do — for Maggie and for you."

"This is my family. I'll not have my children separated."

Again, Maggie heard her aunt's quiet voice.

"We're her family, too, Terrence. We love her and only want what's best for her. I wish we could put things back to how they were when Elizabeth was alive, but we can't. Please, let me at least help by caring for her little girl until things settle down. I'd love her as my own."

Maggie waited, heart pounding, through a long silence. When she heard her father's footsteps trudging up the stairs, she dove for the bed, just making it before he gave a soft knock and stuck his head into the room.

"Hello, Magpie." That was his pet name for her, a gentle tease at her shyness. He came to sit next to where Maggie lay, pretending to play with the little blue and pink quilted dog her mother had given her for her last birthday.

"And how's Patches this evening?"

"Fine."

"Ah, that's grand, that's grand." Her father paused for a moment, distracted. He rubbed his calloused palms together and cleared his throat. "Maggie, I want to talk to you about something. Remember last summer when you went to visit your Aunt Nora and Uncle John in Sioux City?"

She nodded.

"You liked visiting them, didn't you? They have that pretty red brick house with the garden. And there's an ice cream parlor right down the street. Well, they would like you to come and spend a long visit with them." She made no response. "You know, it's hard for Daddy to spend as much time with you as I'd like, what with the corn harvest overdue, and Anna and Elly and the boys have school and their chores and, of course, taking care of little Michael. So we ... your aunt and uncle and myself ... we thought it might be fun for you to stay with them awhile."

"I want to stay here."

"I know, but I think this would be better for you. You'd have new friends to play with and get to go to a new school. And Aunt Nora told me she'd like to take you shopping for a pretty new dress — "

"I don't want a new dress. I want to stay here." Maggie's blue eyes began to fill with tears.

"I know, Maggie, but I have to do what's best for you even if it's hard. It will just be for a little while, then you'll be back home with all of us."

"No, Daddy, please," she begged, her voice rising. "I want to stay home."

"Now, Margaret, I'll have no carrying on."

"Daddy, please!" she wailed. "I'll be good. Don't make me go, Daddy." She crushed her stuffed dog to her chest, burying her face in its calico coat. Then, in a voice filled with loss and confusion, she cried out, "Momma, I want my Momma!"

In the midst of her sobbing, she heard her father reply in a strange voice, "So do I, little one, so do I."

Maggie looked up at him, and through her tears, was shocked to see her own pain and grief mirrored in her father's face. Her invincible father, so tall and strong, sat by her side, head down, shoulders slumped, and, as she watched in wonder, a single tear zigzagged down his furrowed, sunburned cheek. She had never seen him cry before, not on the afternoon he told her that her mother and her new baby brother had gone to heaven, not on that long, awful day when their pale bodies had lain side by side in the casket downstairs in the parlor, not even on that foggy morning when the casket was lowered into the ground in the small cemetery on the edge of town.

Stronger than her own grief, there arose in her young heart the urge to comfort and protect the father she so loved. She slipped her arms around his waist and buried her head in his chest, willing her own crying to stop for his sake.

They sat there with their arms around each other for a long time. Finally, taking a deep breath, Maggie managed to whisper, "It's all right, Daddy. I'll go." In response, her father hugged her a little bit harder, kissed the top of her head, and left the room.

A few minutes later, thirteen-year-old Anna came into the bedroom, smiling and determined. Their mother's suitcase was in her hand.

"Dad tells me you're going to stay with Aunt Nora and Uncle John for a little while. Aren't you the lucky one?" At the mournful look on her sister's face, Anna continued with exaggerated cheerfulness.

"I'm to help you pack a few things for the trip. Let's see. You'll be wanting your good dress and some play clothes. And, of course, your nightgown. You can take your stuffed dog and some of your books, too. The children at Blessed Sacrament wear uniforms. Aunt Nora will buy you that, so you needn't worry about school clothes." She chattered on, carefully packing Maggie's clothes, underwear and socks into the suitcase.

"Here, why don't you put this on for the trip," she said, handing Maggie her Sunday dress and underslip. "And you'll be needing your good coat to go with it."

Without a word, Maggie unbuttoned her overalls, took off her shirt, and slid the starchy white slip over her head. Her blue cotton dress with the white lace trim followed. Gently, Anna turned her around so she could button up the back. While Maggie struggled with her socks and shoes, Anna transferred the last of the clothing from the dresser to the suitcase.

Ready to go, Maggie stood, eyes downcast, before her big sister.

"There, now. You look fine. You'll just need one more thing." Anna reached into her pocket, pulling out her own blue silk hair ribbon, her favorite one that she only wore to church and special occasions. She slipped the ribbon around Maggie's neck, drew it around the top of her wavy, auburn hair, and tied it up into a bow. Maggie looked up at Anna, her lip trembling with the effort of holding back her tears.

"Don't you worry, Maggie," Anna said, taking her gently by the shoulders, meeting her gaze. "Everything's going to be all right. You'll be back home before you know it."

Just then, their father knocked on the door.

"Are you ready, girls?" he called in a soft voice.

Anna took Maggie's hand and gave it a squeeze. "We're ready, Dad."

Down the stairs they went, Maggie holding tight to her sister's hand, their father following close behind. At the bottom of the stairs, waiting by the entrance to the parlor, stood Maggie's two older brothers, eleven-year-old James and ten-year-old Patrick, and her eight-year-old sister, Elly. To their right, just inside the front door, stood her Aunt Nora and Uncle John.

Maggie had always liked her Aunt Nora, though it was hard for her to believe that this pretty woman could really be her father's sister. At forty-one, Aunt Nora was five years older than her father, but looked much younger. She had a soft, round face. Her dark chestnut hair was short and curly, and she always looked as if she'd just come from the beauty parlor. By contrast, her father's face was thin and chiseled from years of farming, and his light brown hair was fine and wispy. But, they both had the same twinkling blue eyes and quick wit, displayed readily only when amongst family or close friends. They shared a special emotional bond, as well. Terrence, being the youngest of eleven children, had been almost beyond the purview of his mother, and it was Nora, by age and predilection, who had watched over him.

Whenever Aunt Nora and Uncle John visited the farm on their way to some livestock convention or another, Maggie, her sisters, and in truth, her mother, too, loved to look at the pretty *city* dresses and hats that Aunt Nora would bring along. Sometimes, if she promised to be careful, Aunt Nora would even let Maggie play with some of her jewelry.

Today, however, Aunt Nora was dressed in somber fashion, as befitted a house of mourning, in a dark blue suit with a matching cloche hat, the only ornamentation, a small circular pin of semi-precious stones affixed to her lapel. She was tall for a woman, but few realized this since standing next to her 6'4" husband, she looked quite petite.

Uncle John was a robust man, still muscled and athletic at forty-three, with a booming voice and a quick laugh. His thinning, brown hair was beginning to go gray at the temples, but his clear blue eyes were as keen as ever, taking in everything and everyone from behind his rimless glasses. Uncle John wasn't much taller than Maggie's father, but his massive build and boisterous personality made him seem twice as large. Since adolescence he had been called *Big John Owen*, a nickname that described his ambition and take-charge attitude as much as it did his size. Maggie had always looked forward to his visits, which usually included a surreptitious treat of candy, viewing him with a mixture of fascination and awe.

But, now, standing there by the front door in his dark gray wool suit, holding his felt fedora in his hands, Uncle John looked unfamiliar and frightening. Maggie, so determined to be brave, buried her face in her sister's skirt and again began to cry.

Quickly, Aunt Nora was at her side.

"Oh, Maggie. Don't cry. Everything's going to be all right. We'll have a wonderful time together, you'll see." As the little girl continued to weep, Nora looked beseechingly from her brother to her husband. John stepped forward and placed his hand on his wife's shoulder, but said nothing.

Sitting down on the step next to Maggie, Terrence stroked her hair. Then he gently took her by the shoulders, turning her around to face him. The sight of her tear-stained, freckled face, still so baby-like, tore at his heart. He took a deep breath.

"Maggie. Maggie, darlin', listen to me. Remember what we talked about? This is just for a little while. Your aunt and uncle will take good care of you. Now, be a good girl, and dry your tears."

Without looking at John, Terrence said, "I'll have Maggie ride along in the car with me until she feels a little calmer. Then, when she's ready, she can ride with you." He stood and lifted Maggie into his arms. She wrapped her arms around his neck as if she never intended to let go, the stuffed dog dangling from her right hand. "Anna, you watch over your brothers and sisters until I get back."

"Yes, Dad. Goodbye, Maggie," Anna managed, handing Maggie's coat to her father.

"Bye, Maggie." Elly's voice was faint. Maggie's brothers stood with their hands in their pockets, their eyes downcast. She heard their muttered goodbyes as her father pushed open the screen door with his shoulder, and carried her down the front steps to the side of the house where his own car was parked.

Setting her down with care on the backseat, her father said, "You sit there for a moment, Maggie. I need to talk to your aunt and uncle." He tucked Patches into her arms, folded her coat around her, and closed the door.

Maggie could hear his muffled footsteps as he walked across the soft dirt of the driveway.

Nora and John stood by their car. Nora spoke first.

"Oh, Terrence, I'm sorry this is upsetting her so."

"Well, Nora, she's had a hard time of it. She's always been a shy, serious little thing, but since her mother died, she hardly speaks at all, except to family. Elizabeth always knew what to do with her, with all the children. I've tried, but ... I just don't know if I — " His voice caught and Nora placed her hand on his arm. With an effort, he steadied himself. "Well, you may be right. Having her spend some time with you may be the best thing."

"Are you sure you're up for a long drive?" John asked. "She may not settle down for quite a while, and you've had a rough time of it yourself these past days."

"I'll be fine," Terrence answered. He got into his own car and shut the door.

That was how it came to be that Maggie found herself lying on the backseat of her father's car on a late summer's night while the miles unraveled between her and home. She didn't understand the reasons her father had given for sending her to live with her aunt and uncle. All she knew was that her mother was dead, her father was sad and angry, and now she was being sent away.

Was that it? Maggie wondered, fighting a sudden wave of nausea. Was it her fault? She remembered how her father had yelled at her the day the doctor came, telling her she was making too much noise and to go outside to play. Not long after, her father came out of the house, then drove away without a word. And her mother and the baby were dead. Was that it, then? Had they died because of her?

Quickly, Maggie closed her eyes tight in an effort to banish the horrible thought from her mind. She lay there, confused and frightened. Despite the presence of her father in the front seat, she felt very much alone.

They must have been driving for quite some time, for Maggie suddenly realized that she could see the first stars through the windows of the car. She knew that her father, true to his word, would drive her the whole way to Sioux City if he had to.

Though desperate to stay with him, she didn't want to be the cause of any more pain or trouble, so she concentrated all of her efforts on pretending to be asleep. A couple of times, her father turned his head to check on her, but each time Maggie was able to shut her eyes before he could catch her watching him.

Maggie felt the car slow and heard the muffled sound of the wheels as they pulled over onto the dirt shoulder of the highway. Her father turned off the engine. He just sat there for what seemed like a long time. Maggie was very tempted to open her eyes to look at him, but she knew that if she did, she would start crying again. Then he would have to keep driving. So, she stayed very still and waited.

After what seemed like a long time, Maggie heard the driver's door open and close, followed soon by the sound of her own door opening. She felt a rush of cold night air and heard the chirping of crickets as her father leaned over her. Ever so gently, he bundled her up into his arms. She managed to remain limp. He laid her down inside her uncle's car, and though it was bigger and smelled different, she still didn't move. She felt something brush her cheek just before the door closed.

Bits of hushed conversation carried to her inside the car.

" ... so little. . . . "

" ... doing the right thing. . . ."

" ... back for the holidays. . . ."

" ... take care of her. . . ."

The car doors opened. She smelled perfume and felt the sagging of the shocks as her aunt and uncle got into the car. Panic rose inside her, but she fought it back down. She knew she'd been very brave not to let her father see how sad she was. She'd continue to be brave so she wouldn't make him cry anymore. For that reason, she refused to allow herself to look out the back window as her uncle eased the car out onto the paved road. She didn't see the figure of her father, thin and still, standing beside the old car, the glow of his cigarette receding as the darkness of the corn fields closed around him.

Chapter 2

October 1931

Sioux City, Iowa grew up around the confluence of the Big Sioux, the Floyd and the Missouri rivers. An area of rich grazing land, it was surrounded by fertile loess hills and steep bluffs carved by ancient winds. From its start as a fur trading post, Sioux City took advantage of its geographic position on the Missouri River to provide the pioneers of the sparsely populated Western prairie with a lifeline to the culture and goods of the East. But, it was with the coming of the railroad in 1898 that Sioux City truly began to prosper as an agricultural, transportation and marketing center.

The railroad enabled farmers from Iowa, South Dakota, Nebraska, Montana and Minnesota to economically ship their cattle, hogs and sheep to the stockyards in Sioux City. There, the livestock was sold to meat packing firms, large and small. The meat packers, in turn, used the railroads to ship the processed meat to consumers around the country. As a result, Sioux City soon established itself as one of the premier meat packing centers in the world. By the 1920s, more than 300 train carloads of livestock were being unloaded at the Sioux City stockyards each day, the majority of them destined for one of "The Big Three" meat packers - Armour, Swift and Cudahy - whose large meat packing plants were located just across the Floyd River from the stockyards.

Between the farmers and the meat packers stood the commission men. These men worked for independent livestock commission firms, and traveled throughout the surrounding states, contracting with farmers and ranchers to sell their livestock at the best possible price. It took an

*experienced eye and a keen business mind to judge both
the animal and the market correctly, but, for a smart
man with a talent for judging livestock, there was money
to be made.*

John Owen had come to Sioux City in 1910. As a small
boy on his father's farm in Boru, Iowa, he had been fascinated
by the expertise demonstrated by the commission men who
came to the farm to contract to sell his father's hogs and cattle at market.

Young John would shadow these men as they surveyed the
stock, asking questions about how weight and worth were
determined, and what happened to the livestock once it was
shipped out. Despite the fact that he'd never finished grade
school, John showed himself to be an uncanny judge of animals
and a whiz with numbers. He soon was able to estimate the
correct weight at which a hog or cow would *dress out*, figuring
in his head the price it would bring as quickly as the commission men could compute it on paper. His talent and shrewd
mind didn't go unnoticed. Just before his twenty-second birthday, he was offered a job with the Grant Livestock Commission
Company based in Sioux City, Iowa.

John soon discovered that the life of travel, along with the
fraternity found with the other commission men, suited him
well. He worked hard, listened and learned, and established a
reputation for honesty and fair dealing among both the farmers and the representatives of the meat packers. He rose quickly
within the company.

For three years, John worked and saved his money. When
he felt financially ready, he returned to Boru to ask for the
hand of Nora Fahey, his childhood sweetheart and the
youngest daughter of the formidable R. J. Fahey, one of the
town's founding fathers. With a skeptical eye toward the
eager young man in the fancy new suit and shiny black car,
who was, after all, just little Johnny Owen from up the river,
old R.J. Fahey yielded to his daughter's pleadings, giving his

grudging permission. John and Nora married six months later and moved to Twenty-seventh Street in Sioux City into a house that John had had built just for Nora. The beautiful, two-story, red brick house had white trim, green shutters, a sun porch for Nora's piano, and lots of room for the many children that they both hoped to have.

That was eighteen years and many heartaches ago.

Maggie awakened in the morning to the sensation of sunlight and a gentle breeze on her face. But, even before the last mists of sleep had cleared, she realized that the sounds were wrong. She couldn't hear the cows or chickens or her father's voice as he scolded his team, Dan and Ruby, into harness for the day's plowing. Instead, she heard automobiles, the clanging of what she later learned was the milk truck, and the pealing of numerous church bells, some near, some distant, calling worshipers to early Mass. From within the room, there was only silence.

Maggie opened her eyes. She was lying in a four-poster bed in a large room with white and pink flowered wallpaper. Someone had dressed her in her cotton nightgown and had draped her clothes from the night before over a rocking chair in the corner. Across the room, there was a vase of pale pink, late blooming roses reflected in the mirror of an immense, dark dresser. Next to the dresser was her mother's suitcase.

With a rush, it all came back to her, and Maggie's stomach constricted as if she had received a physical blow. She squeezed her eyes shut quickly, willing it to be a dream, so that when she opened them again she would be in her room at the farmhouse, hearing her sisters' quiet snoring, the thundering of her brothers down the stairs, and the cries of little Michael for his breakfast. But, even before she reopened her eyes to find it so, the unnatural quiet coupled with the scent from the roses told her that her presence in the bedroom of her aunt and uncle's house was real; home was the dream.

Maggie drew back the chenille blanket that covered her

and hung her feet over the side of the bed. As quietly as possible, she slid down to the hardwood floor, padded across the room, and turned the glass doorknob. Through the crack in the door, she could see a long hallway carpeted in an oriental runner, at the end of which was a huge grandfather clock and the beginning of a curved stairway. Gathering her courage, she tiptoed down the hallway to where the wall ended and the railing of the stairway began. Maggie peered through the balustrades. Below her was a spacious foyer with a gray slate floor. In the middle of the foyer there was a round, marble-topped table and, on the table, a bowl of large, white flowers. From earlier visits to her aunt and uncle's house, Maggie remembered that off this entrance was the dining room, and from that direction she could hear the faint sounds of silverware on dishes and muffled conversation.

"Well, what have we here?"

Startled, Maggie looked up. A tall, blonde-haired girl with a strange accent stood over her, a pile of freshly washed towels in her arms.

"You must be little Maggie, yah? Mrs. Owen said you'd probably be up soon. I'll yust let her know you're awake." Before Maggie could say a word, the girl trotted down the stairs, disappearing into the dining room.

"Oh, thank you, Kirsten," she heard her Aunt Nora say.

"Maggie?" Aunt Nora, dressed in a pale gray dress with pearl buttons, came around the corner and began to ascend the stairs, a hopeful smile on her face. "Maggie, dear. You're awake. I've been waiting for you."

Maggie drew back a bit when her aunt knelt down beside her, but Nora managed to keep her smile in place. "How did you sleep, sweetheart?"

"Fine."

"Are you hungry?"

Maggie shrugged.

"Why don't you come downstairs with me. We'll get you something to eat, then we can have a nice talk."

Maggie took her aunt's hand and followed her down the wide staircase. There was a place already set for her at the polished mahogany table in the dining room. Aunt Nora guided her to a chair, then took a seat at the place across from her where a half-empty teacup waited.

"I'm sorry that your Uncle John couldn't be here when you got up this morning, but he had to be at the stockyards early. He said to tell you that he'd be home to see you at supper tonight."

Just then, the swinging door from the kitchen opened and a plump, gray-haired woman entered, wearing a starched white apron over an expansive floral dress.

"Oh, Louise. Your timing is perfect. Louise, I'd like you to meet my niece, Maggie."

Louise smiled at Maggie.

"Louise is our housekeeper and the best cook in Sioux City. She and Kirsten keep this house running."

"Oh, Mrs. Owen, you flatter me. But, I have to admit, I did just take some cinnamon rolls out of the oven that smell awfully good. Maybe Maggie would be willing to try one for me to let me know how they taste?"

Maggie realized she was very hungry. She stole a quick glance at Louise and replied in a soft voice, "Yes, ma'am."

Aunt Nora mouthed a silent *Thank you* to Louise over the top of Maggie's head. Louise nodded knowingly and headed off to the kitchen to get the rolls.

Maggie studied the room, wide-eyed, over the rim of the glass of milk Louise brought her along with the cinnamon rolls.

The walls were painted a pale green and were trimmed with cream-colored plaster molding where they met the high ceiling. There were floor length lace curtains on the large, double-paned windows facing the street which were, in turn, framed by heavier damask curtains in a muted floral with matching tiebacks. On the adjacent wall was a large, gilt-framed mirror centered on a sideboard that sported a silver tea service. The wall opposite the windows was taken up by the swinging door to the kitchen and a large hutch that matched the dining table, filled with crystal and china. An exotic plant in an oriental pot stood in one corner and on the wall just behind Aunt Nora's head was an oil painting of a horse race. Above the table hung a large, electrified, glass chandelier.

Aunt Nora sipped her tea while she waited for Maggie to finish her examination of her surroundings. When she did, Nora smiled, putting down her cup.

"Well, Maggie. I thought after breakfast you and I might head downtown and do a little shopping. I have a few errands to run and thought maybe we could get you some new clothes and some things for your room here. Then perhaps we can have lunch at the Warrior Hotel. Would you like that?"

Maggie, who had no idea what all of this would entail, answered hesitantly, "Yes, Aunt Nora."

"Good. Well, then. If you're finished, let's go upstairs and get you cleaned up. We can be on our way in no time."

As Aunt Nora had hoped, the sights and sounds of Sioux City temporarily distracted Maggie from her new living situation. The excitement of the streetcar ride downtown would have been enough, but the sheer number of cars, wagons, people and buildings they saw along the way caused Maggie to gasp and point. How tall was the tallest building in Sioux City? Were those real Indians she saw on that street corner? Where were all these people going? Was that man in the cowboy hat a real cowboy? Aunt Nora laughed and tried valiantly to provide answers to all of the questions that burst from the previously silent little girl.

When they got off the trolley at Martin's Department Store, Maggie marveled at its size and the seemingly limitless selection of items; they had five different styles of white cotton gloves for little girls alone. Aunt Nora helped her pick out two nice pairs, along with new underwear and socks, a new dress and matching hat. When Maggie stopped to admire an elaborately dressed doll with a china face and real hair, Aunt Nora placed

it in her arms. Maggie watched in amazement as their purchases piled up on the counter.

After stops at a few more stores, they went to the hotel
for lunch. Maggie had never tasted anything as wonderful
as the chocolate mousse her aunt ordered for her for dessert.
She couldn't wait to get home to tell her family about everything she had seen ... only she couldn't tell them, because she
wasn't going home.

Maggie was subdued on the streetcar ride back to Twenty-
seventh Street, the new doll almost forgotten in her lap. She
seemed oblivious to the bustle of the city that had so enthralled
her just a few hours before, and upon entering the house, she
complied at once with Aunt Nora's suggestion that she go
upstairs for a nap.

She must have slept for quite a while, for the next thing
Maggie knew, she was jolted awake by her uncle's unmistakable
voice.

"Nora? Nora! Where is everyone?"

"John, sh! Maggie's taking a nap."

"Oh, sorry. I guess it'll take me a while to get used to havin'
a little one in the house. How was she today?"

"Quiet, for the most part. Everything is still so new and
strange to her. But, she did seem to enjoy going into town with
me this morning. I'm afraid I might have overdone it a little,
though. She's been asleep for over three hours. I'd better go
check on her."

Nora slowly opened the door to Maggie's room and peeked
in. Maggie lay on the bed, her eyes scrunched up tight, clutching her calico dog to her chest. The new china doll lay face
down at the foot of the bed.

Nora sighed. Well, what had she expected? This was all so
new to Maggie. Patience. Nora had to be patient. Tiptoeing over
to the bed, she gave Maggie's shoulder a gentle shake.

"Hey, sleepy head. Time to get up. It's almost time for supper."

Maggie gave an exaggerated yawn and stretched.

"Your Uncle John is home, Maggie. Let's comb your hair and wash your face. Then we'll go downstairs together to say hello."

Inadvertently, Nora's eyes flicked toward the china doll. "Maybe you could show him some of the new things you got today."

Maggie looked at her Aunt Nora as if she'd suggested a trip to the dentist, but then she murmured, "All right."

"Well, there she is." John put down his newspaper and his cigar as Maggie and her aunt entered the parlor. As he often did, he had showered at the Livestock Exchange Building before coming home, and was now dressed smartly in a blue, three-piece suit. He remained seated so as not to frighten Maggie, and Nora was pleased to see that her husband was attempting to modulate his voice and manner. "Maggie, I understand that you and your aunt had quite an outing this morning. And, who's this pretty lady you're holdin' in your arms?"

Maggie held up the doll for her uncle to see.

"Why, she's almost as pretty as you are, except that you have two dimples and she only has one." He gave her a big smile. "Oh, I almost forgot." Stepping over to the hall table, he picked up two bundles wrapped in tissue. "Flowers for my best girls." With a little bow, he gave a small bouquet of flowers to Nora, then turned and gave a single yellow rose to Maggie.

"Oh, John. How sweet. They smell heavenly."

Maggie held the rose up to her own nose and gave it a tentative sniff. The fragrance was indeed wonderful, and Maggie, a little unsettled, yet pleased at this unexpected attention from her uncle, looked up at him — way up.

"Thank you, Uncle John," she said.

"You're quite welcome, Maggie." Uncle John bent down toward her, and added in earnest, "I'm very glad you're here." He gazed at his little niece for a long moment. Then, embarrassed, he straightened and cleared his throat.

"Well, what does a hard-workin' man have to do around here to get a meal? Louise!" he bellowed. "Louise, where's my supper?" He strode off toward the kitchen to harass the long-suffering cook.

Nora shook her head and rolled her eyes at this, but Maggie saw that she was smiling.

After supper, while Kirsten was clearing away the plates, Nora turned to Maggie. "How would you like to telephone home and let your father know how you're doing?"

Home! Maggie tried to imagine what her family would be doing right now. Her father and the older boys had probably finished up the chores by now. They would have lit the kerosene lamps and settled in to listen to the radio while the girls cleaned up the supper dishes and got Michael ready for bed. She felt a sharp pang of longing.

"Could I?" Maggie asked, full of excitement.

"Yes, you *may*. In fact, your uncle is placing the call right now."

Maggie followed her aunt to the little alcove beneath the stairs where the telephone sat on a low table. Uncle John was already seated in the chair beside it, speaking into the receiver.

"Yes, I'll take care of it. Oh, here she is now, Terrence. I'll put her on."

He handed the phone to Maggie, then discreetly disappeared into his study. Maggie held the big, black receiver in both hands and her voice trembled a little when she spoke.

"Daddy?"

"Hello, Maggie. How are you?"

"Fine."

"Uncle John tells me that you and Aunt Nora had a fun day together; that you went shopping and out to lunch?"

"Uh huh."

"That's grand, that's grand. There's a lot to see and do in Sioux City. You'll have a wonderful time with your aunt and uncle."

"I guess so. I miss you, Daddy."

"I know, Maggie. I miss you, too. But, it'll be Christmas before you know it and you'll be back here to celebrate with all of us."

"Christmas?" Maggie's voice rose in panic. This was the first time anyone had mentioned when she would be returning to the farm. Harvest time was not yet over and the leaves on the trees had barely begun to change color. Christmas seemed very far away indeed.

"Yes, Maggie. That's when you'll have your vacation from school. I know it seems a long way off now, but with school and your new friends, the time will fly by, you'll see. Wait, now. Your brother James wants to say hello."

Her brothers and sisters got on the phone one by one. Maggie could almost see them there in the kitchen, the shorter ones standing on the little step stool that enabled them to reach the mouthpiece of the wall phone. None of them seemed to know what to say, and after a quick *hello-how-are-you*, they passed on the phone to the next person. The sound of their voices made Maggie more homesick than ever, in addition to the realization that she would not see any of them for what appeared to be a very long time.

"Maggie? This is Daddy again. We'd better hang up now. Don't want to run up your uncle's telephone bill. You be good for your aunt and remember to say your prayers tonight. I'll be saying one for you, too. Goodbye, now, Magpie. I'll talk to you soon."

"Goodbye, Daddy."

Through her tears, Maggie fumbled with the phone as she tried to hang up. Quickly, her aunt was at her side. She took the receiver from Maggie and placed it in its cradle, admonishing herself in silence for her poor judgment. The phone call had obviously upset Maggie more than it had helped her. But, then again, maybe the sooner Maggie understood and accepted her situation, the better. Knowing the right thing to do was so hard. Nora sat down in the chair, lifted Maggie onto her lap, and put her arms around her.

"There, there. It'll be all right."

Maggie held herself rigid. She didn't want to be here in this place with this woman. Aunt Nora smelled of powder and perfume, not the homey smells of baking, laundry soap and lemon that had been her mother. She wanted her mother. She wanted to go home. But, her mother was gone, and she wouldn't be going home any time soon.

Unable to hold it in any longer, Maggie gave a shuddering breath. She leaned into Aunt Nora's soft body and began to sob.

Nora guided Maggie's head onto her shoulder and rocked her. For a long time, the two of them sat that way, swaying slowly to an ancient rhythm. To Maggie, it seemed ages since she had experienced the solace and security of a woman's arms, and her spirit was soothed by the memory of another's loving embrace.

Nora, with the little girl clinging to her for comfort, felt a slight easing of the emptiness within herself as well.

When Maggie's crying had at last tapered off to sniffles, Nora produced a handkerchief from the pocket of her skirt.

"Better?" she asked after Maggie wiped her eyes and nose. "You know, I've found that sometimes the best thing you can do in a tough situation is to have a good cry — and a really big dish of ice cream." A flicker of a smile crossed Maggie's face. "Why don't you and I go into the kitchen and see what Louise might have hidden in the icebox?"

"All right," said Maggie, sliding off of her aunt's lap. She hesitated. "Aunt Nora?"

"Yes, dear."

"Do you think Uncle John would like some, too?"

Nora smiled.

"Yes, Maggie. I think he'd like that very much."

They went, hand in hand, to find Uncle John.

"Hello, Maggie. I'm Sister Annunciata. I'll be your teacher this year. I'm so glad you're going to be joining us here at

Blessed Sacrament."

Maggie peered up at the young Dominican nun. Sister Annunciata's face was as soft and pretty as her voice, and her smile seemed kind. With her long, brown robes and veil, Maggie thought she looked just like the picture of the Blessed Mother on the holy card that Father Fitzgerald had given her one Sunday back in Boru.

"Now, don't you worry. I know it's a little scary to come to a new school. I felt that way when I first came here not so long ago. But, I promise I'll be right there with you the whole time. We'll get through this together, you'll see, and before you know it, you'll be as happy here as I am." Sister smiled. "Now, why don't we go meet your classmates?" Maggie took Sister Annunciata's outstretched hand.

Maggie's new black shoes made tap-tapping sounds on the tile floor as she accompanied Sister down the long hallway. On either side, there were wooden doors with frosted glass windows and transoms. Once or twice, she thought she heard the faint sounds of children's voices raised in recitation coming from behind them. But, mainly, it was just Maggie and the Sister, walking, walking.

They came to a door with a large number *1* on it. Sister Annunciata stopped and turned to Maggie.

"Well, here we are. First Grade. Ready?"

Maggie, taking a deep breath, nodded, and Sister gave her hand a little squeeze.

The hallway had been so quiet that Maggie was amazed when Sister opened the door to reveal a large, window-lined classroom filled with students working diligently at their desks. All of the girls wore dark blue uniforms with long-sleeved, white cotton blouses like the one Aunt Nora had dressed her in this morning. The boys wore dark blue pants with white shirts and blue ties. There were more students in this one first grade classroom than there had been in the entire eight grades attending Walnut School #4, the one room schoolhouse back in Boru. As she and Sister Annunciata entered the room, every single one of the children looked up at her and stared. Maggie drew back, but Sister kept a firm grip on her hand, walking with her to the front of the room.

"Boys and girls. I would like you to meet a new student who will be joining our First Grade class. Her name is Margaret Alice Fahey, but she goes by *Maggie*. She is from a town to the northeast of us and has come to spend some time with her aunt and uncle here in Sioux City. I hope that you'll all try to make her feel welcome here at Blessed Sacrament. Now, please say hello to Maggie."

"Hello, Maggie," they chimed in unison.

"Maggie, why don't you take that empty desk there in the second row. You'll find paper, pencils, and the textbook we're working on in the desk. We were just about to begin practicing our alphabet."

Head down, Maggie made her way to the desk Sister had indicated and sank into the seat. She could still feel the curious eyes of her classmates on her.

The morning passed in a blur of letters and lessons. Maggie found comfort in the fact that she was no further behind nor ahead in her schooling than her classmates.

When lunchtime came, Sister Annunciata assigned a tall, dark-haired girl named Patricia to eat lunch with Maggie.

"Hi," Patricia said, standing in front of Maggie's desk.

"Hi." Maggie's voice was a whisper.

Having exhausted their conversational skills for the moment, Patricia sat down at the desk next to Maggie, and the two girls began unwrapping their lunches.

Patricia broke the silence. "You want my pickle?"

Maggie jumped. "What?"

"Do you want my pickle? My mother gave me a pickle and I don't really like them very much."

"Oh. No thanks."

Again, the two sat in silence. Maggie reached into her lunch bag and pulled out something wrapped in waxed paper. She hesitated, then turned to Patricia.

"Would you like a cookie?"

"What kind?"

"Oatmeal. With raisins. My aunt made them."

"Sure. Thanks." Patricia smiled, taking the cookie from Maggie. Her brown eyes were warm and friendly. "Who's your aunt?" she asked, a few cookie crumbs falling unnoticed onto the front of her school uniform.

"Aunt Nora. Mrs. Owen."

"Mrs. Owen who lives in the big, red house on Twenty-seventh Street, the one with the green shutters?"

"Yes."

"Why, I know her. She's in the Ladies' Sodality with my mother. They make pies and stuff for the Church Sociables. I only live a couple of blocks away from you. On Twenty-fifth Street. I'm Patricia, Patricia Maloney. But you can just call me Patty."

As Patty chattered on, Maggie listened politely, glad to have the company of this gregarious girl to shield her from the inquisitive looks of the other children. Patty seemed nice, and Maggie began to feel a little less scared. Perhaps it wouldn't be so bad here after all, with Sister Annunciata, and now Patty here to help her. If she worked hard and did well, it would be Christmas before she knew it. Then she'd be going home to the farm. Yes, perhaps she could make the best of things until then.

Sister Annunciata monitored the lunch period as she went about putting the afternoon lessons on the chalkboard. She was pleased to see that, as she had hoped, Maggie seemed to respond to the irrepressible Patty. Though saying very little herself — a strong child it was who could get a word in edgewise when Patty Maloney was in full sail — Maggie seemed more at ease than she had been all morning.

Sister clapped her hands. "Line up for recess, children."

She watched with apprehension as Maggie followed Patty out to the playground. They put their heads together for a moment, then began to pick the dandelions that grew along the playground fence. After a few minutes, some of the other girls joined them. Sister gave a sigh of relief.

After six years of teaching first grade, Sister Annunciata had become accustomed to dealing with the homesickness and fears that plagued children of this age in their first school experience. Unfortunately, since the stock market crash of '29, Maggie's situation wasn't all that unusual. Hard economic times made it necessary for many parents to send their children to live with relatives who were in a better financial position to care for them, and the transition from farm to city, or vice versa, was often difficult. But, there was something particularly heartrending about the predicament of this little, freckled farm girl with the big blue eyes, upturned nose and serious expression. To lose one's mother so young, then suddenly find oneself in a new school in a new town, living with dimly remembered relatives . . . .

Sister Annunciata crossed herself, saying a quick prayer that the angels might watch over this little girl who found herself so alone in a strange, uncertain world.

"We need some more. Maggie, you go get some from over there," Patty instructed, indicating a group of dandelions as yet unharvested by eager hands. The girls had decided to make dandelion chains during recess and Patty, as usual, had taken charge of the project.

Maggie ran over to the metal fence that bordered the sidewalk next to the street. Kneeling, she picked the dandelions one by one, careful to tear off the stems as close to the ground as possible so that they'd be nice and long for threading.

"Hey, you."

Startled, Maggie looked up. Directly across the street from Blessed Sacrament's playground was the playground for the Bryant Public School, similarly enclosed by a metal fence. At that fence stood three older boys, fourth graders at least, their fingers entwined through the mesh of the fence. They were staring at her.

"What yah doin,' prayin'?" jeered the shortest of the three, brushing his stringy brown hair out of his eyes. His two companions laughed. Maggie, despite the two fences and the roadway between them, felt threatened and hastily gathered up her flowers to leave.

"Hey! He asked you a question. You too good to answer?" demanded one of the other boys.

"Leave her alone, Henry Miller." Patty had appeared at Maggie's side, a scowl on her face and an unfinished flower chain dangling from her hand.

"Well, if it isn't *Fatty Baloney*. Look out, guys. The little *Catlicker* might throw her daisies at you."

"What'd you call me?" Patty demanded.

"*Catlicker*. You go to a *Catlick* school, don't you?" The boys laughed and began to chant, "Catlickers, Catlickers, Catlickers—"

"Oh, yeah?" Patty retorted, not to be outdone. "Well, you go to a *Puplick* school, so that makes you *Puplickers*."

The small group of Blessed Sacrament boys and girls that had gathered behind Patty immediately took up the cry. "Puplickers, Puplickers, Puplickers—"

The two camps continued to taunt each other from the safety of their respective fences until teachers from both schools, hearing the commotion, came scurrying over to break it up.

As they sat at their desks fifteen minutes later, laboring over copying the phrase, *I will not insult the children from the public school*, the required ten times, Maggie whispered to Patty.

"Why were those boys making fun of us?"

"Because they're jerks, especially that Henry Miller. They're just jealous because we're Catholic and they're not."

Sister Agatha, the vice principal, cleared her throat in a threatening manner, and the two girls returned to their task.

Still, Maggie wasn't satisfied with Patty's explanation. She didn't think that the boys sounded jealous. They sounded as if they thought that they were somehow better than the Blessed Sacrament school kids, as if there was something wrong with being Catholic. Maggie frowned.

Back in Boru, almost everyone attended the same, one-room school down the road. There were plenty of fights over who won the foot races at recess or who took someone else's lunch, but no one fought over religion. But then, almost everyone Maggie knew in Boru was Catholic. Being Catholic here in Sioux City must mean something different.

Maggie sighed. There were a lot of things about Sioux City that were different. She wondered if she'd ever get used to it.

But she didn't have to get used to it, Maggie thought suddenly, raising her head. She just had to hold on until she could go home.

Sister Agatha cleared her throat again, looking pointedly at Maggie. Maggie bent back to her work. But she couldn't keep from smiling.

Chapter 3

December 1931

Deck the halls with boughs of holly,
Fa la la la la, la la la la
'Tis the season to be jolly,
Fa la la la la, la la la la
— traditional Yuletide song

"They're here! They're here!" The screen door slammed and Elly clattered down the wooden front steps of the farmhouse. The black Ford had barely come to a stop when Maggie pushed open the heavy car door, tumbling out of it straight into the arms of her sister.

Anna, balancing little Michael on her hip, was next out of the house, followed closely by James and Patrick whose feigned nonchalance was undermined by the big grins on their faces. They all crowded around Maggie, talking and laughing, and she stood in the midst of them, beaming. The door slammed again, and she heard her father's voice.

"Maggie."

There he was at last, standing quietly apart from the swirl of children, dressed in his shirtsleeves despite the December cold. He looked older, frailer somehow. But he was there.

"Daddy!" Maggie leapt into his arms. Terrence hugged her tightly for a long moment, murmuring, "My sweet girl, my sweet girl," into her soft hair. He set her down in front of him.

"How are you, my little Magpie? Let me look at you. You've grown! And, how pretty you look in your purple coat and hat. Have you been a good girl for your aunt and uncle?"

"Indeed, she has," answered John, stepping from behind the car, carrying the bags he had gotten out of the trunk. Nora stood beside him, her arms full of brightly wrapped presents.

"John. Nora." Terrence shook John's hand and gave his sister a hug. "How was your trip over?"

"Pretty good, considerin' the snow," John answered. "But nowhere near fast enough for little Maggie here. She's talked about nothin' but seeing you and the children for weeks."

"Well, we're glad you're here, all of you. Come. Let's go inside by the fire where it's warm. Anna and Elly have been busy baking all morning, and I've got a little hot cider waiting for you. Come."

They entered the welcome warmth of the farmhouse. Anna took her aunt and uncle's coats and hung them in the closet by the front door while Maggie looked about in excitement. The house appeared smaller and somewhat shabbier than she'd remembered, but it was neat as a pin with the wonderful aroma of baked cookies filling the air. And, oh, the decorations! Every windowsill bore a candle that would be lighted at dusk to shine the way for the Holy Family. The creche, minus the figure of the Baby, was in its place of honor on the fireplace mantle, complete with some straw from the barn, *courtesy of Dan and Ruby*, as her father liked to say. Her mother's Chickering piano, lovingly polished, filled one corner of the parlor. On it there was a paper snowman that Elly made at school. A pine tree, which their neighbor Mr. Curran brought all the way from Mason City, stood in its accustomed place to the left of the fireplace. The children had decorated it with popcorn strings, paper decorations made at school, and their mother's precious spun glass ornaments. Maggie reached up to touch one of the glass icicles, marveling at how it magically transformed the glow of the fire into little rainbows of light. Just like every Christmas she could remember.

At the familiar creak of the kitchen door opening, Maggie turned in happy anticipation. Her joyous greeting died on her lips as Anna, dressed in an oversized apron, entered the room, carrying a tray laden with cups of steaming cider. Maggie felt the familiar ache in the pit of her stomach. Quickly, she pushed the sad thoughts down and away. She was back with her family in her own home. This was what she'd dreamed about and prayed for these past three months. But it wasn't enough.

The adults settled around the fire, talking of the weather, the farm and the stockyards. James and Patrick volunteered to bring in the rest of the refreshments. They disappeared into the kitchen, little Michael at their heels.

"Dad, I'll take Maggie upstairs and help her unpack."

"You do that, Anna. Thank you."

"I'll help, too!" Elly chirped. Terrence sent them off with a wave of his hand.

The three girls bolted up the stairs.

While Elly and Anna chattered on about friends and school, and oohed and aahed over each new article of clothing they pulled out of the suitcase, Maggie gazed in puzzlement at the bedroom. Something was different. The same pictures hung on the walls, the worn rag rug was still on the floor, and the two beds and the dresser had not been moved. But, she could tell that her sisters' possessions, having found their way to shelves and drawers that once belonged to Maggie, had been pushed aside in haste to make room for her. This was her room as she'd remembered it, and yet, it wasn't really hers anymore.

"Oh, Maggie! Where did you get this?" Maggie turned and saw that Elly was staring in rapture at the fancy new doll that had been packed with care at the bottom of the suitcase.

"Aunt Nora bought it for me."

"Oh, you're so lucky. Can I hold it?"

"Sure."

Elly cradled the doll in her arms.

"It looks so real," she said in wonder, stroking the curly brown hair.

Watching her sister admire the doll, Maggie felt an inexplicable wave of guilt. The feeling became stronger when she saw Anna linger a moment to stroke the soft wool of one of Maggie's new sweaters before placing it in the dresser drawer.

"I'm hungry," Maggie announced abruptly. "Let's go

downstairs."

With reluctance, Elly laid the doll on the bed, and the three of them headed to the kitchen.

And not a moment too soon, for, with the girls occupied and the adults engrossed in conversation in the parlor, James, Patrick and Michael were well into the cookies that Anna and Elly baked for dessert. Anna shrieked and grabbed a broom, chasing them, mouths full, out of the kitchen. James winked at Maggie as he jammed a last cookie into his pocket before scooting out the door. Maggie followed them, laughing, enjoying the chaos of home after the quiet order of her aunt and uncle's house.

But, the laughter died when they saw the somber faces of the adults in the parlor. Chastened in the face of their father's continued grief, the boys put on their coats, gloves and boots and headed out to do the afternoon milking. The girls returned to the kitchen to start supper.

Anna had planned a special meal for Maggie's homecoming, and with Elly's help, had set a beautiful table using their mother's fanciest lace tablecloth, and her best dishes and glassware. Anna bustled back and forth from kitchen to table, wanting everything to be perfect, and if the chicken was a little dry and the biscuits a bit overdone, no one seemed to notice. Even the boys were on their best behavior. At the end of the meal, Anna, tired and somewhat disheveled, accepted their compliments — and the boys' offer to do the dishes — with obvious pleasure.

In the morning, Aunt Nora tied an apron around her waist. As her first act, she banished Anna from the kitchen, taking over the cooking, cleaning and laundry duties herself. Anna, in charge these past three months, resisted at first, but soon allowed herself to enjoy the luxury of having a grown woman around to handle the running of the household. Before long, she was engaged in the whispered intrigues and clandestine gift wrapping that occupied her brothers and sisters on this day before Christmas, free, for a while at least, to act like the thirteen-year-old girl she really was.

The sun made a brief appearance on Christmas morning, the first Christmas since their mother's death, as if it, too, was determined to present a brave face to the world. The family dressed in their best clothes and, as they did every year, drove along the snow-packed river road to attend early Christmas Mass at St. Thomas Church in Boru. But, this time, the telling of the Christmas story, with its message of joy and the promise of new life, seemed only to serve as a painful reminder of the tragic death in childbirth of their own mother and her infant son. Their father, whose clear tenor could always be heard over the congregation, stood silent with his head bowed during the sacred hymns.

After Mass, friends and neighbors stopped to talk and wish the family a blessed Christmas, expressing their particular pleasure in seeing Nora and John who, after all, had grown up among them. They were all solicitous and kind, but no one spoke directly of Elizabeth, not wishing to intrude upon the family's privacy or draw possible unwanted attention to the loss that was still so fresh. An occasional, quiet *God bless you, Terrence,* or a lingering handshake, were the only acknowledgments of the grief that hovered over the family, which sympathies their father accepted with a quiet nod.

At last, they returned to the farmhouse to eat breakfast and exchange gifts. Nora and John tried to keep the mood light and happy, particularly for the sake of the younger children, but each tradition repeated or neglected brought back bittersweet memories of the previous Christmas, so full of happiness and hope.

Maggie's father sat in silence during the festivities, thanking the children with a wan smile for the small handmade gifts they gave him. Then he resumed his reverie of smoking and staring into the fire. Only little Michael seemed able to take full enjoyment from the day. His antics and squeals of delight provided the family with their only real respite from their somber thoughts.

So, it was with no small relief that the Fahey family's Christmas celebration came to a close for that year.

Maggie had assumed that once she came home for Christmas, she was home to stay. During the course of the holiday she learned that it was not to be. Although no one sat her down and told her so directly, as the days wore on it became obvious from a word spoken here, a reference made there, that she was expected to return with her aunt and uncle to finish the second semester at school. Maggie was devastated. She longed to ask why she, of all the children, was being sent away, and when she would be coming home for good. But, she said nothing. She'd been taught not to question her elders. She also held a child's belief that speaking aloud one's worst fear would make it come true. Maggie preferred the uncertainty of her current situation to the finality of an answer she could not bear to hear.

On the day after Christmas, Nora and John prepared to drive to Des Moines to visit friends and see to some stockyard business. The five-day trip had been planned in part so that Maggie could spend at least a few days alone with her family before it was time to leave.

Nora's eyes were bright with tears as she hugged Maggie goodbye. John just patted Maggie on the head. Then he shook Terrence's hand and assured him they would return on New Year's Day to take Maggie back to Sioux City.

Maggie clutched her coat around her as she waved her uncle's car down the drive and watched it turn south toward the highway. As the noise of the car receded, it was replaced by the quiet winter sounds of the farm. Maggie suddenly felt shy standing alone with the father she had not seen for more than three months.

"Well, it's time to be feeding the animals. Come along, Maggie."

Happy to have a mission, Maggie followed her father along the snow-packed path to the barn.

"Watch out for second base," her father cautioned, side

stepping a large cow patty that lay in their path. When they reached the horse barn, he lifted the wooden latch of the door and held it open for Maggie. Stepping through the doorway, she was enveloped by the warm, pungent odor of the horses and the stored hay. Three large heads turned in their direction, Dan and Ruby, her father's reliable team, and Trixie, the saddle horse. Her father climbed the ladder to the hayloft and gathered up a large mound of hay with a pitchfork.

"Stand aside, now."

Once he was sure she was clear, Maggie's father tossed the hay onto the barn floor. Descending the ladder, he scooped up a small amount of the dried grass and placed it in her arms.

"Give this to Dan. Then come back, and I'll give you another armful for Ruby."

Maggie staggered a little under the weight of the hay, so light in her father's arms. The stalks tickled her nose, but she managed to leave only a small trail on the way to Dan's stall. The old plow horse stood resting on three legs, tied by a rope and halter to a ring on the wall. He appeared to Maggie to have grown much larger in the time she'd been away. She hesitated for a moment at the end of the stall, but when he turned to look at her with his gentle brown eyes, she made her way along his side, dropping the hay in front of his bewhiskered chin. Dan lowered his heavy head and snuffled at the sweet grass, his soft, loose lips making quiet flap, flapping noises as he maneuvered the wisps of hay into the path of his large, yellow teeth. Maggie reached out and stroked the soft hair of his neck. The soothing goodness of these animals, their smells and sounds and rhythms, this at least had not changed. People came and went without reason or explanation, but the animals followed the same pattern, season after season, year after year. They were the constant, like the land.

For the first time since she returned home, Maggie felt at peace.

Ruby nickered loudly from the next stall.

"Oh, Ruby. I'm sorry. I'm coming." Maggie smiled and

hurried off to get the impatient mare her share of the morning's rations.

Leaving her family at the end of the Christmas holiday, while difficult, did not cause Maggie the wrenching pain of the first time. At least this time, she knew what to expect. There were even things to look forward to — seeing her friends and Sister Annunciata, baking cookies with Louise, and listening to Kirsten's funny stories of the *horrors* of growing up with her six brothers on a farm in Minnesota. Maggie also had to admit that she'd come to enjoy the frequent shopping trips, luncheons and outings to the museum and library that were just a part of life at her aunt and uncle's house.

There was something else, however. Something she dared to tell no one. When Maggie was at the farm, she couldn't deny the loss of her mother. As much as she wanted to be there, it had ceased to be the home she remembered. Though no one spoke of it, grief lurked in the corners, ready to pounce if you dared to play, dared to laugh, dared to forget. Most of all, grief was a physical thing that weighed upon her father, making his shoulders sag and his hair turn prematurely gray. Maggie loved her father with all her heart, but since her mother's death, he had changed. His smiles were rare, and he never laughed anymore. Just speaking seemed to require enormous effort. Try though she may, there didn't seem to be anything she could do to make him feel better. In fact, most of the time, he didn't even seem to notice she was there.

But, in Sioux City, Maggie could pretend. She could pretend nothing had changed, and that she was only physically separated from her mother and from her family. They were there, just as they had always been, talking and laughing in the warm kitchen of the white farmhouse, waiting for her. Maggie knew it was just a fantasy, and she didn't dare tell anyone about it, but it comforted her. And she clung to it in desperation on those nights when it was very dark and she was very alone.

So it was with mixed emotions that Maggie hugged her

family goodbye on that cold first day of 1932 and climbed into the backseat of the car behind Aunt Nora and Uncle John. She was quiet for the first part of the drive back to Sioux City. After a time, however, in response to her aunt and uncle's gentle urging, she began to relate, with increasing enthusiasm, all she had done while they'd been gone.

"James dared him, so Patrick rode a cow around the pen — standing up! It was really funny, but Daddy got so mad he made James and Patrick clean out the whole cow barn. Anna says that when she's older, she's going to learn to fly an airplane like Amelia Earhart. Elly said that Aunt Kit is teaching her how to embroider, and that if I asked her, she'd probably teach me, too. And, on Saturday night, Daddy took us into town and gave us each a penny to spend on candy at the General Store, even though Aunt Bid told him it would rot our teeth. Oh, and James is teaching me to spit, and twice Dad let me steer the tractor — "

John and Nora laughed as the stories spilled from the little girl's mouth. But as Maggie continued to prattle on about the escapades of the past week, and repeat in worshipful tones everything her father had said or done, Nora became more and more quiet. Concerned, John glanced over at his wife. She was sitting very still, staring straight ahead, her hands clasped so tight in her lap that the knuckles were white. John reached over and patted her knee. Nora turned, giving him a faint smile, but the look in her eyes filled his heart with fear.

Chapter 4

January 1932

We got more wheat, more corn, more food, more cotton, more money in the banks, more everything in the world than any nation that ever lived ever had, yet we are starving to death. We are the first nation in the history of the world to go to the poorhouse in an automobile.
—Will Rogers, radio broadcast, 1931

Readjusting to the genteel atmosphere of her aunt and uncle's house took Maggie some time. Here there were no boys sliding down the banister, cows getting loose, or chickens being chased through the kitchen by a mischievous two-year-old. The transition was eased somewhat, however, by the presence of the implacable Patty Maloney.

From that first day when Sister Annunciata assigned Patty to sit with Maggie at lunch, Patty took it as her solemn duty to show Maggie the ins and outs of life in Sioux City. Precocious, if not wise, beyond her seven years, Patty possessed a natural talent for leadership. She was forever organizing the neighborhood children into teams for stickball, kick the can or less peaceful pursuits. If there were flowers missing from a garden, a window broken, or a treasured Victorian doll that had been given an impromptu flapper haircut, everyone in the neighborhood looked to Patty first.

Patty's parents, having long despaired of exerting any real control over their youngest daughter, were thrilled at Patty's friendship with *that sweet, quiet little Maggie.* Aunt Nora and Uncle John were not. Every so often, they would encourage Maggie to cultivate some *other* friends, to little avail. Despite their concern, however, they recognized the fact that, with Patty around, Maggie was a little less lonely.

Still, Maggie's world revolved around her twice-monthly phone calls home. That was how she learned that Michael's cat had kittens, that Elly was spending Wednesday afternoons in town taking piano lessons from Aunt Kit, and that her father tied a clothesline from the house to the barn because Patrick had almost gotten lost in a blizzard just trying to go out to milk the cows. Maggie loved hearing all their news. But each time she hung up the phone, she felt just a little farther away.

On a school holiday in early February, Uncle John invited Maggie and Aunt Nora to come down to the stockyards to meet him for lunch in the cafeteria of the Livestock Exchange Building. Maggie couldn't wait. She loved the stockyards. One of her earliest memories was of a summer visit to Sioux City when she was four. Her mother had taken her to the yards to see Uncle John at work. They found him in a swirl of dust out in the holding pens, riding atop the biggest, reddest horse she had ever seen, wielding a long cane like a pointer to select the cattle he wanted. When Uncle John spied them watching from the fence, he rode over and lifted Maggie up onto the front of his saddle. She had never been up so high. She was scared, but excited. She felt like a princess in one of Anna's storybooks about knights and castles.

There would be no riding around the pens today, though. The weather, cold since long before Christmas, had turned bitter. Even Maggie's warmest coat, hat, and gloves, combined with the valiant efforts of the heater in Aunt Nora's car, could not keep out the chill.

They left the house a little early so that Aunt Nora could first run an errand across the river in South Sioux City, Nebraska. At the entrance to the Combination Bridge over the Missouri River, Aunt Nora handed five cents to the toll taker, then rolled up the window as fast as she could. They were almost halfway across the bridge, when Maggie saw something startling.

"Aunt Nora, look. There are cars on the river!"

Down below on the frozen surface of the Missouri, there

were a number of cars and small trucks, headed in both directions, inching their way across the ice between what was Sioux
City, Iowa on the east bank and South Sioux City, Nebraska on
the west. Looking behind them, Maggie could see the tracks
where the cars had come down the steep embankment to the
river and, looking ahead to the other side, the tracks that would
lead them up onto solid ground again.

"What are they doing?" Maggie said. "Aren't they afraid
they'll fall through the ice? Why aren't they using the bridge?"

"Some people can't afford to pay the toll to cross the bridge.
They wait until the river is frozen, and drive across it instead."

"But, it's only five cents."

"Five cents will buy a loaf of bread. You see, Maggie, there's
something going on right now called a 'Depression.' It's very
complicated to understand, even for grown-ups, but what it
means is that there are a lot of people who are out of work and
can't find jobs. They have very little money, so they do whatever they have to do to save the money they have, even if it
might mean doing something a little dangerous."

"Like driving over the ice?"

"Like driving over the ice."

They reached the Nebraska shore, and Maggie's view
was blocked by the bridge girders, but she couldn't shake the
image of those people risking an icy death in the river to
save a five-cent toll.

She wore her coat all through lunch with her uncle.

Maggie came home from school on Wednesday, March
second, and plunked her books down on the kitchen table. She
was surprised to find that neither Aunt Nora nor Louise was
there to greet her. Grabbing a piece of homemade nut bread
from the plate on the table, she followed the sound of the radio
coming from the parlor. There she found her aunt and the cook
with their chairs pulled up close to the radio set, worried expressions on their faces. So intent were they on the voice emanat-
ing from the radio that neither of them noticed Maggie standing

in the doorway.

> *"... police in Hopewell have recovered a homemade ladder and a ransom note pinned to the windowsill demanding $50,000 for the baby's safe return. Again, the twenty-month-old son of world famous aviator, Charles A. Lindbergh, has been kidnapped. A massive manhunt has begun. . . ."*

"Aunt Nora. What does 'kidnapped' mean?"

The two women jumped. Nora snapped off the radio.

"Maggie! We didn't hear you come in."

"What's going on?"

"Oh, just something that happened far away from here."

Nora stood and repositioned the chairs while Louise attacked the top of the radio with her feather duster.

"Did you have a good day at school today?"

"Yes. But what did the man say about a baby?"

"It's nothing for you to worry about. Come. Let's get you some milk to go with that bread."

Aunt Nora put her arm around Maggie's shoulder to guide her from the room. All of a sudden, she stopped and wrapped her niece in a tight embrace.

"Aunt Nora! You're squishing my bread."

"Oh, I'm sorry, honey." Aunt Nora, her eyes bright, released the squirming little girl. "I guess I'm just glad to see you."

Despite the attempts of many parents to shield their children from news of the tragedy, the kidnapping of the Lindbergh baby was the talk of school, and indeed, the whole country, by the next day. All of the classes at Blessed Sacrament included a special petition in their morning prayers for his safe recovery. While not the first kidnapping to have occurred in America, the notoriety of this *Crime of the Century* brought the terror into the nation's homes as had no other. This glimpse of evil and the profound effect it had on even the adults in their world, both titillated and frightened the children. On the playground,

Maggie's friends whispered to each other of the horrors and dangers of *kidnapping*, wondering aloud what it would be like never to see their parents or home again. Maggie just turned away and said nothing.

Spring was a long time coming that year. By the end of April, however, the land seemed to have shaken off the last of the winter chill. Warm breezes blew, and the stark lines of the trees and fields around Sioux City were softened by tender, green growth.

Maggie and her classmates were scheduled to make their First Holy Communion on the second Saturday in May. Aunt Nora shopped for some beautiful white fabric, lace and netting to make Maggie's dress and veil, and she and Louise worked long hours on it. When it was finished, Maggie thought it the most beautiful dress she had ever seen.

Everything would've been perfect if her father could have been there, but he was in the middle of the spring planting and couldn't leave the fields to make the trip to Sioux City. He did send a gift to Maggie for her special day with instructions that it be given to her before they left for the church. Maggie was getting dressed when Aunt Nora brought her the small brown package, tied with twine. Together they read the accompanying note.

"To My Darling Maggie: Wish I could be with you. Here is a picture of the special angel that will be watching over you today and always. Love, Daddy."

Maggie unwrapped the present. Inside was a framed picture of a little girl. She was dressed in a lace-trimmed dress of pale linen, and wore a necklace of beads around her neck. She had a round face, a little bow mouth and wore her hair in brown ringlets that hung to her shoulders. Maggie did not know who the little girl was, but something about her large blue, deep-set eyes looked familiar. Aunt Nora came up behind her.

"That's a picture of your mother, Maggie. It looks to have been taken when she was just about your age. You look very much like her, you know."

Maggie stared at the photograph, trying to compare it to her mother's face as she remembered it, but the image danced just out of reach.

"Let's put that over here, shall we?" Aunt Nora took the picture from her and placed it face down on the dresser. "We have to get going if you're going to be on time for the ceremony. Now, let's pin on your veil." With great care, Aunt Nora removed the white veil with the delicately beaded headdress from its hanger, and placed it on Maggie's head, attaching it with some hairpins.

"There. What do you think?"

Careful not to knock the veil askew, Maggie turned toward the mirror. There she saw a pretty little girl, her auburn hair curled and combed, looking radiant in a white dress and veil. And that little girl stared back at her with the same eyes that were in the photograph. Maggie smiled.

On the third Thursday in June, it was Nora's turn to host the monthly meeting of her book club. She had planned a fancy luncheon for the seven ladies coming over to discuss *All Quiet On The Western Front*. She, Louise and Kirsten were in a flurry of washing, ironing, polishing and cooking.

John arrived home for lunch at twelve noon. He was nearly run over by Kirsten, carrying a freshly ironed linen tablecloth to the dining room. In the kitchen, he discovered an assembly line of silver trays filled with artfully arranged sandwiches, cookies, and cakes. Checking to be sure Louise's back was turned, he reached out to sample one of the elaborate concoctions. Like a shot, Louise whisked the tray to safety.

"Mr. Owen, you get away from those sandwiches. You know those are for the ladies."

Nora, her arms full of just-picked flowers, came in from the garden.

"John, what are you doing here? I told you this wasn't a good day for you to come home for lunch. My book club will be here in half an hour, and we're trying to get ready. Go sit in the den and read your newspaper awhile."

"What? And be trapped inside when the invasion begins? No, thank you."

"Well, go for a walk then." She began arranging the tulips, peonies and irises in a large cloisonné vase. "Just get out from underfoot."

Just then, Maggie skipped into the kitchen.

"Maggie! I thought you were going over to Patty's to play and have lunch," Aunt Nora said in dismay.

"I was, but Patty's father said she wasn't allowed out of her room today. Something about making doll clothes from her mother's evening gown. So now I have nothing to do. I thought maybe I could come back and help you. Ooh, can I try one of those?" she asked, eyeing a petit four.

"No, you may not. John? " Nora threw him a desperate look.

"Maggie, I've a great idea. Since it's clear we'll not be gettin' anythin' to eat around here today, why don't you come with me down to the stockyards? It's about time you learned what I do for a livin'. Then afterwards, we'll have lunch in the cafeteria."

He received a grateful smile from both his niece and his wife.

Uncle John drove down Seventh Street, over the railroad tracks, and turned right onto the road that ran between the Floyd River and the stockyards. Maggie knelt on the seat of the car, leaning her head out the window. The cattle pens were laid out in a giant grid that seemed to go on forever, an end-less sea of motion and noise. The smell of cows and dust brought with it bittersweet thoughts of the farm.

"Most of the cattle come in early in the week, so the pens aren't too full today," Uncle John commented as he sped along the road. "Look there. See that red building in the middle of the yards? That's the Exchange Building. My office is on the top floor of the tower."

The Livestock Exchange Building was a brick, three-story Romanesque structure with a rounded turret on one end. The various livestock commission companies had their offices there, literally overseeing the buying and selling that went on in the yards below.

In a swirl of dust, Uncle John swept into a parking space in front of the building. Taking Maggie by the hand, he led her up the steps of the main entrance into the lobby. She gaped about her in wonder. High above her head was a pressed tin ceiling, at her feet, a floor of thousands of small gray and black hexagonal tiles. The walls were paneled in wood, and a wide stairway with a carved oak banister led to the floors above. Hallways branched off to the left and right, filled with men in suits, farmers in overalls, dust-covered cowboys and officious looking secretaries bustling about on important business. Many of them called hello to Uncle John as they passed.

Maggie followed her uncle up the wooden stairs, scuffed and worn by the tread of many boots. When they reached the third floor, he turned right, stopping in front of a door with a frosted glass window. On it was printed *Grant Live Stock Commission Company*. Below it in smaller letters, *John K. Owen, President*.

"After you, your highness."

Maggie stepped through the doorway into a room that served as a combination office and waiting room. To the right was a grouping of leather chairs flanked by end tables and lamps. A coffee table held various cattle industry reports, recent issues of *The Cattleman* magazine, and one very large glass ashtray. At a desk on the other side of the room sat a thin, middle-aged woman wearing a white blouse with a navy blue ribbon tied in a bow at the collar. She stopped typing, peering at them over the top of her eyeglasses.

"Maggie, I'd like you to meet the person who really runs this office. This is Miss Branch, my secretary, the only person on the face of the earth who knows where anythin' is in those file cabinets over there. I'd be lost without her."

Miss Branch ignored his flattery.

"How nice to finally meet you, Maggie. Your uncle has told me so much about you."

Maggie returned her smile.

"Miss Branch, if you need us, Maggie and I will be conductin' important commission business in my office."

"Yes, Mr. Owen."

John led Maggie through a second door into the inner office. This was his domain, a man's place filled with wood, brass, and leather, smelling of cigars and cattle. He strode to the massive carved oak desk and skimmed the messages that Miss Branch had arranged in chronological order on the leather blotter. Picking up one of the slips of paper, he frowned.

"I just need to make one quick phone call."

John picked up the black desk phone and dialed. As he waited for his party to answer, he sat back in his large leather swivel chair, tapping his fingers on the armrest.

Maggie hopped up into one of the smaller chairs positioned in front of the desk, and sat there, swinging her legs. As her uncle talked, she began a close, clockwise examination of the rest of the office. On the wall behind her uncle's head hung an oversized calendar from the Great Northern Railroad Company featuring bright-colored paintings of the fierce looking *Great Indian Chiefs of the West*. A big olive-green stuffed armchair was tucked into one corner of the room, next to a brass pedestal ashtray. In the other corner was a coat rack made of bent wood on which hung a long leather whip and a rumpled raincoat. On the wall in between was an oil painting depicting a stampede of wild-eyed cattle and horses. Looking to the left, she squinted into the bright afternoon light streaming through the large, uncurtained turret windows.

Curious, Maggie slipped down off her chair. Placing her hands on the edge of the lower sill, she stood on tiptoe and peered through the center pane. There, spread below her, was a panoramic view of the swirling stockyards. Cattle milled about in the dust and heat while wiry men danced along the boards atop the pens, throwing down hay or filling the drinking troughs with water. At the edge of the yards, a cattle car was unloading its stock, the yard hands using long poles to guide the travel weary animals into the appropriate enclosures. Men on horseback rode back and forth in the alleyways between the pens, checking on the number and condition of the various herds, and making preliminary selections for their buyers. All the while, just beyond, the packing plants whirred and chugged and turned the little Floyd River pink with their refuse.

Uncle John joined her at the window.

"Do you see those railroad tracks over there on the west side of the yards?" he asked, bending down close to her. "Farmers and ranchers from all over this part of the country send their cattle to us by train to be sold. The trains bring the cattle cars right up there along the river, unhitch, then the stockyard uses its own switchin' trains to maneuver the cars right up next to the pens. See? They're getting ready to unload some cattle right now. They'll come down those chutes there right into the pens, about ten to fifteen to a pen."

Maggie looked out over the great expanse of animals.

"How do you know who owns which cows?"

"Well, that's a very good question, Maggie. The western cattle are branded or tagged with their owner's mark. Cattle from farms closer to Sioux City are kept track of on a tally sheet when they're loaded onto the train. A record's made of whose cows are in what car. Then, when they're unloaded, they're placed directly into the pens of the commission company that's been hired to sell them. Now, my company, the Grant Commission Company, has a big group of pens startin' over there in the left-hand corner." He pointed. "Each commission man has his own *alley* of pens that hold the cattle that he's been hired to sell. Would you like to see mine?"

Maggie nodded with enthusiasm.

Uncle John grabbed the whip from the coat rack, and marched out of his office.

"Miss Branch, I'll be down in the pens with Maggie for the next half hour or so. I'd like to get her opinion on some of the stock."

"Yes, Mr. Owen. Have fun, Maggie."

It was not necessary to go back down to the ground level to view the cattle pens. An elevated walkway connected the Exchange Building with the stockyards and ran along its entire length a few feet above the top of the enclosures. As they walked along, Uncle John talked, using his whip as a pointer as he described the various cattle in the pens on either side.

"Most of the cattle we sell here at the stockyards are Aberdeen-Angus, Herefords or Shorthorns. They've the largest ratio of flesh-to-bone."

Maggie gave her uncle a puzzled look.

"That means they have more meat. Buyers from the meat packers come, take a look at them, and make a bid. My job is to get the best possible price I can for the ranchers and farmers I represent. Then, for negotiatin' the deal, I get paid by the owner a percentage of the total price paid for each cow."

Maggie looked up at him again in total confusion. Uncle John smiled.

"You'll have to forgive me, Maggie. This is the first tour I've ever given to a six-year-old."

"Almost seven," she corrected him.

"Yes. Well. Let's see if I can make it a little clearer for you."

He pointed down to a pen that held five dozing steers.

"If I sold each cow in this pen right here for, say, a dollar apiece, how much would the owner get for all five?"

He waited while Maggie counted. "Five dollars?"

"Very good. Then if the owner turned around and paid me a penny for each cow I sold for him, how much would I get?"

Maggie thought hard.

"Five cents?"

"Right, again. So out of a total sale of five dollars, the owner keeps four dollars and ninety-five cents, and I get five cents. That's how a commission man makes his money. And why you should be payin' close attention when the good Sisters teach you your sums."

Maggie nodded, though she didn't really understand how her

uncle could make a living on a penny a cow. They walked on.

"Now, most of the cattle will be bought by buyers from one of the big meat packin' plants over there." Uncle John again used his whip to indicate the three large factories visible just across the Floyd River. "There's Armour, Cudahy and Swift. We call them *The Big Three*. The rest go to smaller packers or are sold as feeder cattle." He tapped on the railing of a pen with his whip. "These cows here are feeder cattle."

Maggie looked down to see the upturned faces of some placid, white-faced Herefords, staring at her with their liquid brown eyes.

"You can see that they're a bit younger, a bit scrawnier. Farmers come to the yards to buy them, fatten them up for a few months, then bring them back to sell, hopefully at a higher price than the one they originally paid for them. Dependin' on the cost of the grain it takes to feed them, you can make a nice profit with feeder cattle."

As a farm girl, Maggie understood and accepted the ultimate fate of the stockyard cattle. Still, she was relieved to hear that the sweet-faced cattle in the pens below had at least a little more time left to enjoy being cows.

They had walked only about a quarter of the length of the yards, but Uncle John stopped and turned.

"I think that's enough information for one day. Let's head down to the cafeteria for some lunch." He chuckled. "Maybe after that, it'll be safe for us to return home."

Maggie trotted along beside him, lost in thought. She'd had no idea her uncle was such an important person. He had an office and a secretary, and he had to know all about cows and numbers. And everyone at the yards tipped their hat to him and called him *Mr. Owen*. Despite all this, he acted like he really enjoyed her company. He took the time to explain things to her, which made her feel very grown up. She realized with surprise that she would miss him a little when she went home to Boru.

"Maggie, that's an excellent report card. We're very proud of you."

Seated between her aunt and uncle on the davenport in the

parlor, Maggie lowered her eyes and blushed with pleasure at her uncle's praise. Her first year of school had ended, and despite a late start, she had received six A's and one B, with no conduct or deportment marks against her.

"Yes, a grand effort all the way 'round," Uncle John continued. "You've earned some time off. So, Maggie, what do you and Patty have planned for this summer? Spendin' all day at the ice cream parlor, I suppose."

Maggie looked up at him with a puzzled expression. What did he mean? School was over. She was going home. Had he forgotten? That must be it. Things were so busy at the stockyards, he had just forgotten.

"Uncle John, school's over. I'm supposed to go home, now. Remember?"

"Oh, yes, you'll be going to the farm in just a few weeks," Aunt Nora assured her. "Your uncle just needs to finish up some things at the stockyard first. Then he'll be free to drive us over. Until then, I've arranged with Miss Sanders for you to begin piano lessons. Remember, you said you wanted to learn how to play? In fact, there's a man coming over to tune our piano this afternoon so it will be ready for you."

A few weeks? Maggie felt the ground shift beneath her feet. But, her family was expecting her home. Her daddy would be waiting for her.

As if reading her mind, Uncle John added, "We've talked everythin' over with your father. He knows when you'll be arrivin', and he's lookin' forward to seein' you. So, it's all set."

Daddy knew about this? A succession of emotions played across Maggie's face: confusion, disappointment, then resignation. Once again, her expectations had been disregarded, swept away in the wake of adult plans and agendas. She tried not to let her chin quiver. She knew from experience that further protests would be futile. There was nothing for it but to go along and make the best of things.

In the meantime, it *was* true that she had wanted to learn to play the piano like her mother. And it *would* be fun to join in on a few of the activities that Patty and her other friends had been planning for the summer. Maggie guessed she could wait a little longer before going home.

"All right," she said.

"Good." John clapped his hands together. "Now, go change out of your uniform. The three of us are goin' downtown for a special dinner to celebrate your wonderful report card. Off with you now."

Partially mollified by the promise of an outing, Maggie headed up the stairs, unaware of the worried look that passed between her aunt and uncle.

Once Maggie was out of earshot, Nora turned to her husband in dismay.

"Oh, John. Am I being awful to keep her here? I know she wants to go home, but I'm worried about her. There's really just Anna to take care of her there, and she's still needing a mother herself. And I do think it has helped Maggie to be here with us. She was so forlorn when she first arrived. Now, look at her. You can see by her grade card how bright she is. Sister Annunciata told me she shows exceptional promise, particularly in her reading and writing skills. And she's made so many friends here. I'm just afraid that once she's back at the farm, she'll forget everything and ... everyone."

John put his arm around her.

"No, of course you're not awful. You only want what's best for Maggie. Terrence knows that. Otherwise, he wouldn't have agreed to let her return to us at the end of the summer."

"Well, I'm not so sure he was happy with that decision."

"Perhaps not, but he realizes it's the right one. He knows what good care you're takin' of Maggie, and that she can learn and do things here that she can't back at the farm. And, though he may not want to admit it, Terrence is just not ready to take Maggie back full time yet. For one thing, he's strugglin' financially. You know he had to sell the car last month to pay his bills. God forbid he should accept my help."

"He's a proud man, John. Like you."

"Humph," John retorted. "The main problem is, he's still not quite himself … mentally. You know that yourself from talkin' to him, when you can get him to talk."

"John, he's still grieving."

"Well, all I know is, if it weren't for Anna, James and Patrick keepin' the farm goin', I don't know where he'd be. It's a good thing your sisters in Boru have been willin' to spend so much time lookin' after Elly and little Michael."

"Still, he does seem better … ever since his dream."

"Ah, yes. His *dream.*" John aimed a skeptical look at his wife. "Nora, you don't really believe his story that Elizabeth came back and spoke to him, do you?"

Nora hesitated. "I don't know, John. Anything is possible. They loved each other so very much. That would be just like Elizabeth to tell Terrence to pull himself together and take care of those children. She was always so strong and practical. Who's to say she didn't come back?"

John, adopting a gentler tone, put a comforting hand on Nora's shoulder. "It's just wishful thinkin' on Terrence's part, Nora. He misses her so much that he dreams her into bein'. No, I'm afraid it just shows that Terrence needs more time to get his mind and his life back on track. Keepin' Maggie's visit to the farm a short one will be best for all concerned just now."

Nora nodded, but the troubled look did not leave her face.

That night, Maggie dreamt that she was in a small boat on a river. It was dark and she was trying to row to shore. Someone was waiting for her. She knew if she could just get there, she would be safe. She rowed with all her might, but the current was too strong, pulling her farther and farther downstream. She kept trying to call to the person on the shore, but she couldn't make herself heard over the noise of the wind and the water.

Suddenly, strong arms grabbed her.

"Maggie. Maggie! Wake up. You're havin' a nightmare. Maggie!"

Maggie opened her eyes to see her uncle's worried face staring down at her. If she hadn't been so frightened, she might have laughed at his comical appearance. His hair was sticking out in all directions, his nightshirt was rumpled, and without his glasses he had to squint to see her properly.

"Oh, Uncle John," she sobbed, "I was so scared. I kept calling and calling, but no one could hear me."

"Sh. There, there. It's all right now. It was just a bad dream. Too much chocolate cake for dessert, I suspect. Go back to sleep now."

Uncle John held her in his arms until she stopped trembling and drifted back to sleep. Laying her down, he tucked the blanket underneath her chin. He stroked her hair one last time, saying a silent prayer of thanks that she did not seem to remember, nor had his sleeping wife heard, the word Maggie had called out in her terror — *Momma*.

Chapter 5

July 1932

Let's call a "Farmer's Holiday"
A Holiday let's hold
We'll eat our wheat and ham and eggs
And let them eat their gold.
                    —Iowa Union Farmer, 1932

Aunt Nora and Uncle John drove Maggie to the farm in the middle of July. As they left the outskirts of Sioux City, the rolling bluffs of the Missouri River valley quickly gave way to the higher, flatter terrain of northwestern Iowa. Maggie watched with growing excitement as the very land itself seemed to unfurl, stretching its eager limbs toward the horizon after too long a time confined within the ordered, paved streets of the city. From the open window she breathed in the smells of new mown hay and turned earth, realizing how much she'd missed the sight of these wide-open fields of gold and green. She couldn't wait to get home.

After about two and a half hours, Uncle John turned north off the highway onto the dirt road that paralleled the west bank of the West Fork of the Des Moines River. A trailing dust cloud marked their progress as they sped along. Frilly white Queen Anne's Lace bobbed in the breeze made by their passing car, and Maggie caught the scent of the wild roses that gathered in tangled masses at the edges of the fields. A ring-necked pheasant scurried across the road up ahead, and the few sloughs they passed were alive with ducks, curlews, cranes and geese, all taking advantage of what little water remained in these shallow depressions.

Maggie, up on her knees now, hung out the window, looking for familiar landmarks. There! Off to the right on a slight rise was the group of sheltering trees that marked the location of Curran's farmhouse. Mr. and Mrs. Curran were Maggie's parents' closest friends. She'd slept at their house the night after her mother died. So long ago. Only yesterday. Maggie banished the memory. Squinting into the wind, she searched. Just a mile farther, around the next bend, was the farm. Home.

The Fahey farm consisted of 240 acres of workable land, planted mostly in corn and oats. The white clapboard farmhouse stood in a small grove of black walnut trees about thirty yards back from the road on a gentle bluff above the river. Ordered as a *kit home* from Sears-Roebuck during a period of relative prosperity for farmers at the time of the Great War, it was a traditional American four square with two main stories and a third floor attic tucked under the eaves. A covered front porch faced the road and the fields beyond. Just behind the house, forming a loose courtyard, were the horse barn, cow barn, corncrib, and a granary, their once vibrant red paint beginning to fade and peel. From there, the land sloped down to the heavily wooded bank of the West Fork of the Des Moines River.

As they rounded the turn, the farmhouse flashed white beneath the sheltering shade of Maggie's favorite tree, a big walnut with a thick horizontal limb just perfect for a tire swing.

"There it is!" she squealed. And there in the swing, acting as sentinel, was Elly, who gave a whoop and a holler when Uncle John's car pulled into view.

Aunt Nora and Uncle John had arranged to spend a few days at the farm so they could visit with relatives and friends in town. But this was only part of the reason for their stay. They were concerned about Terrence's emotional and mental state. By the third day, however, they felt satisfied that Terrence was coming to terms with the loss of his dear Elizabeth. Although he remained quiet and somewhat withdrawn, he had resumed his duties toward the children and the farm. Grief still overwhelmed him at times, but the routines and demands of everyday life were beginning to cover over the wound.

But now other troubles threatened the fragile security of his family.

The morning that Nora and John were to leave, Terrence asked John to accompany him on a short walk around the farm. They made an odd twosome skirting the edge of the cornfield. John, with his broad-shouldered linen suit, rimless glasses and wide flushed face, had the look of a prosperous Irish politician. Beside him in blue denim overalls, Terrence looked as thin and sharp as a plow blade, his narrow frame reduced by hard work and the elements to pure muscle, sinew, and determination.

In silence, they walked along through air that vibrated with the heat and the electric hum of the locusts. The summer had been hot and dry, and the fields and pastures were turning brown from the lack of moisture. What little rain had fallen barely dampened the uppermost layer of the soil, then had evaporated within hours. Terrence stooped to examine one of the stunted corn stalks that stood stoically beneath the withering Iowa sun.

"'Knee high by the Fourth of July'," he muttered to himself, shaking his head. He stood and squinted up at the sun. "Looks like it'll go over 100 degrees again today."

John nodded, waiting for his brother-in-law to come around to the real reason for this stroll in the midday heat. At last, Terrence spoke.

"They foreclosed on another farm last week, John. The McNulty's place."

"McNulty's? Why that's some of the best farm land around here."

Terrence snorted.

"Doesn't matter when it costs twice as much to grow your corn as you can sell it for at market. It's already down around fourteen cents a bushel."

"Which bank held the mortgage?"

"First Bank of Iowa. Same as mine. But it doesn't matter. They're all foreclosing." He kicked at a clod of dirt in his path. It exploded into a mini dust cloud.

"You know, that land has belonged to the McNulty's since they first came out here in '70. Three generations have farmed it — honest, hardworking people. Good neighbors. And all that time, they've paid their debts, maybe a little late in the hard times, but they always paid. But with prices the way they are now, no matter what you do, you just keep getting farther and farther behind. What little money they'd put away went to doctor bills for the baby." Terrence spit into the dust at his feet. "James sold off everything he could to try to meet the mortgage payments — first the hogs, then the cows and horses — but he barely got ten cents on the dollar. No one's got any money to buy with. In the end, there was nothing more he could do."

"It's a terrible time for the farmers, said John.

"Terrible, indeed. I went over to help him pack up. It was the only thing I could think to do for him. There was a small crowd there, mostly locals, but a few out-of-towners. The man from the bank was auctioning off everything they had left — the tractor, the chickens, even their household things. James, Theresa and the kids just stood off to one side and watched. Ah, it was awful. Everything they worked for — gone. Just like that." He closed his eyes for a moment, pressing the fingers of one hand hard against his forehead as if to stop the painful pictures from coming. "A terrible time indeed."

"What's James goin' to do?"

"I don't know. He said he's got a brother outside of Chicago who's agreed to take them in for awhile. But, God, John, that farm was his life. It's all he knows."

They came to the end of the row and rested their arms on the post and rail fence that separated the field from the farm buildings. In the distance, they could see the older boys over by the barn, their heads under the hood of the old Chevy truck, tinkering with the engine. Maggie and Elly were tossing feed to the chickens that were, in turn, being chased by Michael. Nora and Anna were behind the house, hanging wash on the line to dry. The scene was, at first glance, idyllic. But a closer study revealed that the house and barn needed painting, the children's clothes were worn and patched, and the grass and fields were too brown for this early in the summer.

"How are things by you, Terrence?" John's voice was quiet.

For a long moment, the only sound was the faint cackling of the chickens as they scurried to get out of little Michael's reach. Then, without turning to look at his brother-in-law, Terrence spoke.

"John, I'm up against it. You know how the market is. The price I'm getting for my hogs is the lowest I've ever gotten. Corn and oat prices continue to fall. Milk, cream — low and going lower. But the cost of everything we need to buy keeps going up and up, not to mention taxes and credit payments." He paused. "You hear about the Iowa Farmers Union convention last May in Des Moines?"

John nodded.

"They've been trying to talk the farmers into going on strike, telling them to keep their stock and produce away from the markets to drive up the price." Terrence removed his hat from his head, wiped his sweaty brow on his forearm and set the hat firmly back in place. "That may be fine for some, but if I can't sell what I grow, I can't live. I may be able to feed my family for a while on vegetables, chickens and milk from the cows, if this drought doesn't take it all. But, I gotta have money to buy clothes for the kids and make repairs to the machinery." He paused. "And I'm four months behind on the mortgage."

Neither man looked at the other. They'd grown up together in the same small farming town, played together as boys, competed with each other as young men. They were proud, raised to value independence and self-reliance, and to respect it in others. Only the most desperate of circumstances could have brought them to this moment, and it was almost as painful for John to witness his brother-in-law's need as it was for Terrence to acknowledge it.

"Will you accept my help, Terrence?"

Terrence continued to peer out over the parched field of

corn. He felt ashamed, angry and relieved, all at once. Having to accept help from anyone, even his sister's husband — especially his sister's husband — was almost more than his pride could stand. How he longed to say, *Thanks all the same, John. I can do it on my own.* But that morning at McNulty's farm had forced him to see what he had refused to see for so long. They could not, any of them, do it on their own. There were forces at work that would not yield to hard work and determination. And pride would not keep a roof over his children's heads.

With a mixture of gratitude and humiliation, Terrence turned to his brother-in-law.

"Yes, John. I will."

No more was said. Together, they headed toward the house to join the rest of the family.

During that first week, Maggie jumped into the farm chores with the zeal of someone who is not required to perform them every day. She hauled water and feed for the animals, gathered eggs, carried water on wash day, and even endured the dreadful job of having to handpick the worms off Anna's prized tomato plants.

Despite the daily round of chores, Maggie loved it at the farm. There was always something to do and someone to do it with. With her father and older brothers off working in the fields and Anna busy with the housework, the garden and the chickens, no one had the time to keep too close a watch over the younger children. As a result, as long as they got their work done, Elly, Maggie and Michael were pretty much free to do what they wanted. They made wonderful, secret caves in the straw pile by the cow barn, or played cowboys and Indians, taking turns holding Michael captive. When it got too hot, they'd strip down to their underwear and go swimming in the river, swinging out over the deeper water on a rope swing suspended from one of the trees that arched over the river bank. Sometimes they would go horseback riding, riding double or

even triple on Trixie, although exactly where they went and
how fast was pretty much up to Trixie. If they got hungry,
they'd pick the blackberries that grew down by the river and try
to cajole Anna into making a pie out of the few they hadn't
already eaten. Or maybe they'd shell the walnuts that fell from
the huge, old trees that shaded the farm, eating the sweet meat
until their stomachs ached and their hands were black from the
effort. At night, they'd catch hapless fireflies and wear them
on their fingers as short-lived, glowing rings.

But, what Maggie liked best of all were those late summer
evenings when the work was done, the supper dishes put away
and the corn stalks in the near field stood dark against the fading light. Then she would sit at her father's feet on the front
porch and beg him to tell her stories about the old times. Often,
he was too tired from the day's work, and would shush her
away. But sometimes he would agree to tell *just one, now, just
one*. He'd sit on the porch swing, setting it into motion with
just the slightest flexing of his foot, and smoke as he talked. A
lilt would come into his voice, and soon, even the older children would draw near, hypnotized by the melodic sound of it
and the vibrant pictures it painted in the darkness.

"Your grandfather, R. J. Fahey, was one of the first people
to settle this area of the country. He was just a lad of 14 when
he left Kilkenny with his two brothers for a new life in America.
That was just after the famine years in Ireland. They came by
ship to Canada, it being cheaper to get passage there than to
New York. They landed at Grosse Island near Montreal, a place
of great suffering. Thousands died there of disease and sick-
ness. But, your grandfather and his brothers were young and
strong. They made their way across the border into the United
States.

"They did odd jobs and such, saving what little money they
could. Then, one day, they heard of free land in a place called
Iowa, rich land for growing with plenty of water. Your grandfather and his brothers joined with seven other Irish families and
traveled by ox team to this area. That was in 1856. People

called them the 'Irish Colony.' Your grandfather chose the land where we sit right now because it was close to the river, with a good view of the surrounding countryside. It also had a fine stand of trees for building and firewood. He built a log and sod cabin at first, then later, a fine house.

"Life was hard in the beginning. The soil was rich, but difficult to plow because of the thick roots of the prairie grass. The grass grew so high, higher than my head is now, that they had to stake the cattle when they grazed or they'd never find them again. That first winter, provisions ran low. Your grandfather and some of the other settlers walked to Fort Dodge for supplies, a distance of some ninety miles, in the bitter cold and deep snow, wearing snow shoes."

"What about the Indians?" This was Elly's favorite part of the story.

"Well, the Indians lived all around here, hunting and trapping. Sioux Indians, mostly, fierce and warlike. They weren't too happy, as you might imagine, with these new pioneers coming onto the land, but there was no real trouble in the beginning. If they bothered the settlers at all, it was usually just to ask for food. One day, while your grandfather was out hunting, a group of them pulled their canoes right up on the bank of the river below the cabin, right down there where you girls were swimming today. They came up to the cabin door, demanding something to eat. Scared your grandmother near to death. But she gave them some biscuits and dried meat, and they went away.

"But then, in 1857, a Sioux Chief by the name of Inkpadutah, an altogether disagreeable fellow, led a band of Sioux up to a settlement at Spirit Lake, massacring more than forty men, women and children. That's only thirty-five miles from here. They say he was avenging the murder of his brother and his family by white men. The army from Fort Dodge and the settlers put an expedition together, but they never did catch him. He might be out there still." Terrence paused, and the tip of his cigarette glowed brightly for a moment in the darkness.

"Just five years later came news of a general Sioux uprising under Chief Little Crow. They nearly took the town of New Ulm, just over the border there in Minnesota. Well, enough was enough. The good people of Iowa formed the Northern Border Brigade to protect the settlers. Your grandfather was one of the first ones to volunteer."

"Did he kill any Indians, Daddy?" Michael asked, wide-eyed.

"Well, once the Indians heard that your grandfather was protecting the area, they headed out west where it was safer. So, that was the end of the troubles. And, that's enough story-telling for tonight. The cows will be expecting you early in the morning. You'd best be getting your sleep, now."

He sent them off to bed to hide under their covers, listening for sounds of the fierce Chief Inkpadutah lurking outside their windows.

"God help us. It's Mrs. Burns and the Widow Reilly. Is there to be no peace on a man's one day of rest?"

Maggie, lying on her stomach on the floor, looked up from the book she was reading.

"Oh, no," groaned James, putting down his magazine.

"What's the matter?" asked Maggie.

"You'll see," said Elly, rolling her eyes.

Turning from the sight of the two elderly ladies climbing from their car, Terrence surveyed the wreckage of his home. Playing cards, books, newspapers and children were strewn about the parlor, the front entry was a jumble of shoes and boots, and the open door to the kitchen showed the remains of Sunday dinner, still waiting to be cleared from the table.

"Ah, they'll be reporting me to the County Agency for sure when they see this place. Children, quick! Pick up, pick up! Our only hope is that Mrs. Burns' arthritis will slow her down, poor woman. James, take that mess from the entry and hide it on the back porch. Anna, go put on some tea, and see if you can get a layer of dirt off Michael's face. And close that kitchen door. Maggie, empty the ashtray and put the footstool over that stain on the rug. Patrick, Elly, get those newspapers and cards out of sight. And, everybody, make yourselves presentable."

Elly was stuffing the last of the newspapers under a couch cushion when a tapping came at the door. Terrence took one last look around, then, with a resigned sigh, opened the door.

"Why, Mrs. Burns. What a lovely surprise."

Mrs. Patricia Burns was beloved by the entire community as one of the original founders. She had come to Boru as a sixteen year-old bride in the early 1860's. Her family was from the same county in Ireland — County Mayo — as Terrence's mother, and the two had become close friends. In those hard early years, while the men carved farms out of the thick Iowa sod, the few women who had come with them turned to each other for comfort and companionship. They shared conversation, recipes and home remedies, and helped to deliver, and sometimes bury, each other's children. They clung to each other during those first long, lonely years on the prairie, forming a bond that lasted a lifetime. Terrence had known Mrs. Burns since he was a little boy. He revered her as a beloved link to his own parents.

Now in her late 80's, the diminutive Mrs. Burns was fragile and hard of hearing. She peered up at Terrence through her thick glasses, smiling an almost toothless smile.

"Ah, Terrence. How are you, dear? It does me heart good to see you. You look so like your Da, God rest him. I hope we're not bothering you. Edna thought I needed to get out for a bit of fresh air, and suggested that we pay you a wee visit."

A tall, severe looking woman dressed in black loomed in the doorway.

"Oh, now, Patty dear, you know it was your idea we come calling." She spoke to Terrence in a loud whisper. "The poor dear forgets so. She insisted that we come check on you, Terrence, to see how you were getting on since… well … you know." She stopped her scrutiny of the room long enough to give Terrence a look of exaggerated concern.

Terrence forced a smile.

"Hello, Mrs. Reilly."

Mrs. Edna Reilly was what Terrence referred to as a *professional widow*. After twenty-two years, she still dressed in black and always referred to her late husband as *my dear departed Johnny*. In truth, Edna's marriage to the 40ish John Reilly had been a hasty affair, arranged by his sister, Maddy, who had tired of cooking and cleaning for him. Maddy had convinced Edna, with whom she had worked as a maid at a boarding house in Chicago, that her brother was a wonderful catch. At twenty-seven, Edna was fast approaching spinsterhood, and she agreed to marry the *prosperous businessman*, sight unseen. She and John Reilly were wed in St. Thomas Church after a two-week engagement.

Edna soon discovered that John's business consisted of sweeping up and stocking the shelves as a clerk at the general store, and that he was quite content with his lot. She began to nag him without mercy, demanding that he make something of himself. John obliged by making himself scarce, spending more and more time in the blissful camaraderie of the local saloon. One night, just five weeks after they were married, he tripped on his way home from the bar, hitting his head on a lamppost. He was killed instantly.

Edna threw herself into the role of the grieving widow. To make ends meet, she took a job selling sundries at the general store, where she spent her time regaling the customers with stories of her *dear departed Johnny*, and sticking her nose into everyone's business.

When old Mrs. Burns, herself a widow, suffered the first of a number of small strokes four years ago, Edna appointed herself as Mrs. Burns' unofficial caretaker. This was, undoubtedly, a service to Mrs. Burns, but it also provided Mrs. Reilly with an entrée to places where she might not otherwise have been so welcomed. Now, whenever Mrs. Reilly felt the need for a little gossip, she would drag Mrs. Burns visiting.

"Well, why don't you two ladies come in and sit down,"

Terrence said, stepping aside. "Mrs. Burns, I think you'd be most comfortable in this chair over here."

Mrs. Burns took the arm he offered, and lowered herself into the faded-floral upholstered chair that had been Elizabeth's favorite.

"Now, don't bother about me. I'll just take this little chair over here." Mrs. Reilly walked over to a wooden ladderback chair, brushed off the seat with her gloved hand, and sat down with an ill-concealed grimace of discomfort.

Maggie saw the little muscle in the side of her father's cheek begin to twitch. Gripping the back of Mrs. Burns' chair, he called to the children who were lurking about the edges of the room.

"Children, come say hello to Mrs. Burns and Mrs. Reilly."

One by one, the children lined up to say their greetings. As she got closer, Maggie became mesmerized by the large, fleshy wart over Mrs. Reilly's left eyebrow, so much so that Patrick, standing behind her, had to nudge her to get her to say hello. By this time, Anna and Michael had returned from the kitchen with the tea.

"Ah, Terrence," sighed Mrs. Burns, holding Anna's hand for a moment. "This one is the image of your dear mother when I first met her those many years ago." She looked at three-year-old Michael and smiled. "And if it isn't little Terrence all over again, as I live and breathe. And as much of a scamp, I'll wager."

James stepped forward and made a little bow.

"Ladies, I'm so sorry that I'm unable to stay and enjoy your visit, but the cows are not yet up from the far pasture, and I promised Dad I'd bring them in."

"Yes, indeed. As it should be. You must tend to the livestock first." Mrs. Burns nodded her approval.

James knew that his father would not contradict him in front of their guests. He would pay for it later, but it was worth it to avoid participating in the custom that was to come. Smiling, he headed for the door while his father and the stranded Patrick glared after him.

"Well, ladies," Terrence said as the door closed, "Can I offer you some tea?" As Terrence bent over Mrs. Burns' cup, he saw Patrick out of the corner of his eye, attempting to slip out of the room.

"And now," he announced in a loud voice, "I believe the children would like to provide us with a little entertainment. Patrick. Why don't you go first? A little something on the clarinet?"

Patrick grimaced. He walked over to fetch the clarinet from where it sat in its case atop the piano, both testimonies to happier, more prosperous times. With great pain and a modicum amount of talent, he played a dispirited version of *Yankee Doodle Dandy*. The two ladies dutifully applauded.

"Thank you, Patrick, for that moving rendition." Terrence glowered at his middle son. "Girls, have you something for our guests?"

Anna sat down at the piano while Maggie and Elly reluctantly took up their positions side by side in the middle of the parlor. As Anna began to play an Irish reel, the two girls, arms at their sides, performed in unison the steps their mother had taught them. Feet fluttering and legs kicking high, they danced and turned, the only movement above their waists being their bouncing hair. Mrs. Reilly tapped her foot and Mrs. Burns thumped her cane on the floor in time with the music. When the song finished, the girls bowed, huffing and puffing, to their delighted guests.

The only one of the children who seemed to look forward to this command performance was little Michael. When it was his turn, he strode to the center of the room, hands clasped behind his back, an earnest look on his face.

"*Bed In Summah*," he bellowed, "by Wobert Wouis Stevenson.

'In winter I get up at night
And dwess by yewow candle-wight.
In summah, quite the other way,
I haf to go to bed by day...'"

When he finished, Michael beamed a triumphant smile at his stunned audience.

"Now the chickens won't lay for a week," whispered Elly. Maggie tried to stifle a giggle.

"My goodness," said Mrs. Reilly when she had recovered herself. "Well, Michael, you may want to consider a career as a stage actor when you grow up."

"Or a hog caller," said Patrick. Michael gave him a dirty look.

"Well, I thought it was just lovely," exclaimed Mrs. Burns, clasping her hands together. "I could hear every word. Really, all of you children were wonderful. Terrence, you must be so proud of them."

"Yes, Terrence, you've done a remarkable job with them." Mrs. Reilly clucked in sympathy. "Such a burden you were left with. And now, with the farm doing so poorly, too. Not just your farm, mind you, but all the farms. Of course, everyone knows your sisters have been a great help to you, God bless them. Especially Nora, caring for Maggie full time like she does. Still, it must be nice to have them all back together like this. How much longer are you planning to leave Maggie with Nora and John?" Mrs. Reilly's inquisitive eyes belied the casual tone of her question.

Terrence's scowl was ill-concealed. "Children, time for chores."

"But, Dad — "

"Now."

The children trooped out of the house and wandered in the direction of the barn. They had already completed their chores before dinner, and it was too early to do the milking. But it was clear now was not the time to argue the point with their father. They were milling about, uncertain of what to do, when they heard the front door open.

Mrs. Reilly, her face red, stomped down the front steps. Without a word to the children, she got into the waiting car and slammed the door. In a few moments, Mrs. Burns appeared, hanging onto their father's arm. They descended the steps together, chatting amiably. Terrence helped her into the car, then bent down and kissed the old woman on the cheek with great tenderness. She reached up and held his chin in her wrinkled hand for just a moment, her eyes wistful.

No sooner had Terrence shut the door then the car lurched out of the farmyard, leaving a cloud of dust through which the children could just see Mrs. Burns waving goodbye. Mrs. Reilly was scowling straight ahead.

Every morning after finishing the early chores, Maggie's father would listen to the grain prices on the radio while he ate breakfast. If the price was good or cash was running low, he would order the boys to shovel some of the oats from the granary into the bed of the truck. Then, he would drive it over to the grain elevator in Osgood to sell it.

Maggie liked to ride along on these trips for the diversion and because, sometimes, her father would let them visit the little store at the base of the elevator. There, they were allowed to buy one candy bar to share amongst all the children — a great treat, even if Anna and James, by virtue of age, always claimed the coveted end pieces that had the most chocolate. So, when, just three weeks after her return to the farm, Maggie saw James and Patrick shoveling oats into the truck, she asked and was given permission to go along.

As with anything of any height in Iowa, you could see the grain elevator from a long way off. The one at Osgood was particularly distinctive. It had a giant picture of the Quaker Oats man in wig and colonial clothing painted on the side of it. A natural gathering spot for the farmers, it was a place where they could socialize and share information about crops, weather and prices. This particular morning, however, there seemed to be more trucks than usual parked at the elevator, some empty, some still full of grain. About a dozen farmers, all of them from nearby farms, stood listening to a short, husky man in overalls standing on the running board of a truck, waving a stack of handbills.

As Maggie's father pulled over to the side and turned off the engine, a man separated himself from the edge of the crowd. He came to the driver's side window.

"Hello, Terrence."

"Mornin', Henry. What's going on?"

"Just a wee bit o' treason." He gave a pained smile. "Did you hear what the price is today?"

"Yeah. Thirteen cents a bushel."

"No. They've dropped it again, to twelve cents."

"Twelve cents! Sweet Mother of God," Maggie's father swore under his breath.

The man nodded in agreement, then jerked his head in the direction of the man on the running board. "That's Patrick Elliot from over near Spencer. He's trying to get people to organize, telling them they should hold their grain and livestock back from the market. Try to drive the price back up."

"You kids stay here," Terrence instructed as he opened the door to the truck and stepped down. He walked with the man over to where the others were gathered. Maggie slid over next to the open truck window to better hear what was being said. Angry voices called out from the crowd.

"I planted twenty more acres this year and I'm getting even less for the whole lot than I did last year."

"It's the same thing over at the stockyards. Hog prices are so low you don't get back half of what you put into raisin' 'em."

The crowd grumbled their agreement.

"How do they expect us to live?"

"I have to have cash if I'm going to pay my bills."

"The bank's breathing down my neck."

"What are we supposed to do?"

The man on the running board held up his hands for silence.

"We can strike, that's what. Like the automobile workers in Detroit. A lot of farmers in our part of the state have gotten together and formed a group called the Farmer's Holiday Association. They're saying we should just shut down our farms for a while — take a *holiday*, like the *bank holidays*. Let people go without corn and hogs and milk for a while, and they'll start paying a decent price for 'em."

"But, what am I supposed to do with the crops I got settin' ready to harvest? I can't just let 'em rot in the field."

"You might have to."

"That's easy for you to say, Patrick Elliot. You own your farm free and clear. I've got mortgage payments to make, and kids to feed and clothe."

"Well, you won't be able to take care of 'em for long at twelve cents a bushel, that's for sure."

"Patrick." It was Mr. O'Neil who owned the farm just up the river from the Fahey's. "This Farmer's Holiday Association you're talkin' about. Isn't that the group led by that Reno fella from the Iowa Farmers Union?"

"That's right. Milo Reno is the President of the Association."

"I heard about him. Some of his group's been stoppin' farmers on the way to market, letting their hogs loose and dumping their milk in the road."

The farmers grumbling grew louder.

"Anybody tries to stop my truck and they'll be looking at the business end of my shotgun!" yelled an angry voice.

Elliot held his hands up for quiet.

"I know it sounds desperate, but these are desperate times. You work harder and harder and grow more and more — and for what? President Hoover says *Prosperity is just around the corner.* For who? Not for the farmer! The price of corn and hogs keeps going down while the price of everything else keeps going up. All of you know people who've lost their farms because they can't pay their mortgages or taxes. I dare say most of you are in pretty bad financial straits yourselves. Are you just going to sit there until you lose your farms, too? The time to act is now, and we've got to act together!"

"He's right," shouted someone from the middle of the crowd. "If we don't stick together, we're all going to lose our farms, one by one."

"Nobody's going to tell me whether I can or can't sell my corn, " came a heated reply.

The angry voices continued. Maggie's father, having heard enough, returned to the truck.

"What's going on, Daddy?" Maggie asked as he got in and started the engine.

"Just crazy talk, Maggie. You kids hop out — but stay right here." His voice was stern.

"But, Dad," Maggie protested as she climbed down from the truck, "Can't we go into the store?"

"No." Her father pulled the door shut. "Just stay put."

Maggie folded her arms across her chest and stood in the dust next to her brothers, watching while her father drove their truck onto the huge scale next to the elevator. He got out and stood next to the grain office manager while the man recorded the weight of the fully loaded truck, then watched carefully while the oats were loaded into the elevator, and the truck re-weighed, empty. With a pencil and a small pad, the manager computed the difference between the two weights, multiplied it by the going price for a bushel of grain that day, and showed the final tally to Maggie's father. Maggie's father looked at the figures, then began to say something to the grain office man-ager. The man just shrugged his shoulders. Finally, jamming his hands into his pockets, Maggie's father followed the man-ager into the grain office.

Maggie's father emerged a few moments later, counting the money he held in his hand. With a shake of his head, he folded the bills and put them in the pocket of his overalls. He was walking back to the truck when he spied one of the Farmer's Holiday Association handbills on the ground. He hesitated. Then he picked it up and stuffed it into the same pocket in which he had put the money from the sale of the oats.

Taking their cue from their grim-faced father, no one talked on the ride home. Just as they pulled into the driveway leading to the house, their father spoke.

"Maggie, I don't think you should come along on these trips to the elevator anymore."

"Why not?"

"It takes most of the morning, and I think your sister Anna could use your help at home. I already have the boys to help me."

"But, Daddy...!"

"No, Maggie. I want you to stay home from now on."

Maggie suspected that her father's sudden decision had nothing to do with helping Anna and everything to do with this morning's trouble at the grain elevator. She pouted as pointedly as possible, but her father, deep in thought, didn't seem to notice. Her only hope was that he'd forget his decision by the next trip.

But, come the next trip to the elevator, she was left home. Her father drove off with just Patrick and James – and a shotgun carefully hidden under the front seat.

On the nineteenth of August, 1932, Maggie turned seven years old. Anna and Elly cut up an old flowered apron and made her some little clothes to fit her doll. Her father and the boys made a doll-sized wooden table and chair. Aunt Nora and Uncle John sent a teddy bear, two new picture books and a miniature china tea set with pink flowers. Anna cooked all of her favorite foods for dinner. Then, with great ceremony, she carried out a slightly lopsided angel food cake with seven lighted candles. Maggie's brothers and sisters broke into an off-key rendition of *Happy Birthday,* which made her smile. Her smile broadened when her father joined in, in his clear, beautiful tenor. It was the first time she had heard him sing since her mother died. She closed her eyes, wished as hard as she could, and blew out the candles.

On a lazy Sunday afternoon a few weeks later, Maggie and Elly walked into the parlor, fresh from drying the dinner dishes. Their father sat smoking in his favorite chair, his head inclined toward the old Majestic radio, the most recent issue of *Wallace's Farmer* open on his lap. A rich, mellow voice, with a touch of an Irish brogue, issued from the set. Elly groaned.

"Oh, no. It's the Radio Priest. So much for listening to *Uncle Don*."

"Sh!" their father hushed them, straining to hear. *Listen Up* with Father Charles Coughlin was his favorite radio program. The charismatic priest from a small Detroit parish had become a national sensation with his weekly radio sermons championing the downtrodden. Millions now tuned in each Sunday to listen to his impassioned exhortations on the evils of big business, and the failure of the Hoover Administration to bring the country out of the Depression. He was pro-labor, pro-farmer and pro-Franklin Delano Roosevelt in the upcoming presidential election. Many of the struggling and dispossessed of the country agreed with him.

"… I am a simple Catholic priest endeavoring to inject Christianity into the fabric of an economic system woven upon the loom of the greedy," intoned the hypnotic voice.

"Come on, Maggie," Elly said with an exaggerated sigh. "I guess we'll have to find something else to do."

"I'll find something else for you to do if you don't shush. I can't hear what the good Father is saying," their father snapped.

Maggie and Elly scurried outside. They decided to amuse themselves by jumping rope. They tied one end of the rope to the porch post outside the kitchen door, and took turns spinning and jumping. Each smack of the rope on the packed dirt of the side yard kicked up a little puff of dust so that, every few minutes, they had to stop, hacking and coughing, to let the air clear.

Michael came out and sat on the step. After watching for a while, he called out, "Maggie?"

"Nine, ten … yes? … twelve, thirteen — "

"Are you kidnapped?"

Maggie stopped so fast the rope hit her in the head.

"What?"

"Are you kidnapped?"

"Michael, why would you say a dumb fool thing like that?" said Elly.

"Well, Uncle John and Aunt Nora came and took you away, just like the Limbert baby."

"*Lindbergh*. And Aunt Nora and Uncle John didn't kidnap Maggie. Maggie's just staying with them for a while. Besides, kidnappers don't give the person they kidnap back. Come on, Maggie. It's still your turn."

Maggie missed after just a few tries. She switched places with Elly. Just then, their father came out of the kitchen and sat down on the steps.

"Watch me, Daddy!" cried Elly. "Look what I can do." Maggie spun the rope for her, and Elly turned a circle while jumping on one foot.

"That's fine, Elly, that's fine. Now, how about going in and giving Anna a hand. You, too, Michael. I want to talk to Maggie."

"Yes, Dad." Elly threw a quizzical look at her sister, and headed into the house with Michael. Maggie began to wind up the jump rope.

"Maggie, come up here and sit by me."

She joined her father on the step. He took a few more puffs on his cigarette, then reached over and patted her hand.

"It sure has been nice having you back home, Maggie. We missed you when you were away at your aunt and uncle's. Was everything all right for you there?"

"Yes, Daddy."

"What about school? Did you like it?"

"It was all right."

"Well, your grade report was certainly good. Did you make some friends there?"

"Yes." Maggie's tone was wary.

"That's grand." Terrence sat quietly for a few moments, smoking and flicking the ashes from his cigarette. He looked out at the mended and patched boards on the corn crib, the rust patches beginning to show on the old Farmall tractor parked next to the barn, and the stunted fields of corn, beyond. Maggie waited.

"Maggie, I don't expect you to understand this, but these are hard times we're going through right now. Hard times. It's called a Depression."

The Depression. That word, again.

"What it means is that if I'm to hold onto this farm, I've got to put in long days and even nights in the fields, so I can't be here to take care of you younger children. Once school starts, Anna and the boys will have class work to do in addition to their chores, so they won't be able to do it. And I can't afford to pay someone to come in."

Maggie felt a queasy feeling in the pit of her stomach.

"Last year Elly spent a lot of time with Aunt Kit, and Aunt Bid watched Michael for me off and on. Well, even though they have their hands full with their own families, they've offered to help me out again, God bless them." Terrence stood and walked over to tighten a loose strand of chicken wire on the fence that surrounded Anna's vegetable garden. He continued speaking without turning around.

"The way of it is, Maggie, Aunt Nora and Uncle John would dearly love to have you back with them while you go to school, and I just don't see any other way right now but to have you go back to Sioux City. I didn't say anything about it earlier, because I was hoping I could figure something out."

Maggie said nothing. She'd allowed herself to believe that she was home to stay, that her father wanted her there. But she'd been wrong — again. The ground beneath her feet had shifted once more. The disappointment was painfully, bitterly familiar.

"Maggie, it's not what I want, believe me, but it's what has to be. If there were any other way — " Terrence turned to look at her. He stopped in mid-sentence.

Maggie had pulled herself into a tight ball, head down, her knees hugged close to her chest. She made not a sound, but the dust by her bare feet was speckled with tears.

Terrence thought his heart would break at the sight, and the frustration and anger that seemed his constant companions these days threatened to overwhelm him. He fought to maintain control, clenching his jaw so hard that the muscles twitched. He'd been over it and over it in his mind. There was just no other way. If he lost the farm, he would lose everything — his livelihood, his children — and he'd have broken his promise to Elizabeth to keep the children together. Besides, as hard as it was, this would just be a temporary thing, just until he could get the farm back on its feet. Then they'd all be together again. It would all work out. He would make it all work out. And, somehow, he would make it up to Maggie.

Terrence threw down the stub of his cigarette and ground it out with his shoe.

"Aunt Nora and Uncle John will be here to pick you up at the end of next week," he said in a quiet voice. As he stepped around her little form on the stair, he paused, reaching out as if to stroke her hair. But his hand hovered in midair.

"I'm sorry, Maggie," he whispered. Then he walked quickly into the house, the screen door banging shut behind him.

Chapter 6

September 1932

The only thing to vote for in this election is justice for agriculture. With Roosevelt the farmers have a chance, with Hoover none. I shall vote for Roosevelt.
        —*Henry A. Wallace,*
        Editor of Wallace's Farmer-Homestead,
        1932 (later Secretary of Agriculture
        under FDR)

John set his valise down on the floor with a thud, tossing his hat and newspaper onto the table in the front hall. He was glad to be home. The last five days had been spent visiting farms and ranches throughout Nebraska and South Dakota, and everywhere the story was the same. What people were calling the worst economic depression in the nation's history was taking its toll on the cattlemen and farmers. A surplus of cattle and hogs, combined with the decreased demand precipitated by the current money crisis, had driven prices down so low that, even with cheap grain prices, it cost more to feed the animals than the farmers and ranchers could get for them at market. As a consequence, they were desperate to sell their animals before things got worse. They were flooding the market with livestock, which was driving the price down even further. He and the rest of the commission men were having a very difficult time getting anything resembling a decent return for the owners whose interests they represented.

John took off his glasses and rubbed his tired eyes. It wasn't just the livestock producers who were suffering. He knew firsthand from talking to Terrence just how bad things were for the farmers who depended on corn and oats for their cash crop. Affairs were in an awful state when a man couldn't get a decent price for what he raised or grew when so many people were practically starving. Always before, these tough, self-sufficient farmers had been able to ride out the hard times, living on credit, working harder, and just doing without until times got better. But this Depression was different – longer, deeper, pervading all areas of society. Farms were failing in record numbers, and there appeared to be no end in sight.

Things had become so desperate that many of these same stubbornly independent farmers were now beginning to organize, rallying behind the Farmer's Holiday Association's instruction to *Stay At Home - Buy Nothing - Sell Nothing*. And taking action against those who went against them.

John glanced down at the *Sioux City Journal* on the table. The front page was filled with news of the striking farmers. *5000 Farmers In Parade. Milk Producers Near Mitchell Send Ultimatum*. John had seen for himself the picket lines and blockades on the highways outside of town. Just last month, there'd been a *Milk War* in Sioux City. Blockading dairy farmers, angered at the low prices being paid by the milk dealers, had confiscated, given away, or dumped into the streets truckloads of milk bound for Sioux City dairies. What a shame, he thought. Farmers trying to stay alive by selling their produce, pitted against other farmers trying to stay alive by preventing them from selling.

Other tactics were being used, as well. In many parts of the state, *penny auctions* were successfully blocking the attempts of banks to foreclose on defaulting farmers. John, the son of a farmer himself, had to chuckle at the ingenuity of these strong-willed men of the land. When it became known that a farm had been foreclosed upon and was coming up for sale, farmers would come from miles around. They let it be known, sometimes by the not so subtle tactic of hanging a noose from a nearby tree, that no bids higher than a few dollars would be acceptable. In this way, mortgages of hundreds and even thousands of dollars were satisfied for as little as two dollars. The winning bidders would then return the farms to their original owners. Auctioneers and sheriffs could only stand by helplessly.

Although one could not condone breaking the law, it was hard not to sympathize with the farmers' desperate plight. If a solution was not found soon, many feared a revolution was at hand. John sighed. Perhaps Roosevelt, if he won in November, could turn things around with his *new deal*. He hoped so — and soon.

The sound of laughter interrupted his grim thoughts. John followed it toward the kitchen, stopping in the doorway. There at the sink stood his wife and his niece, chattering away as they washed dishes. Maggie stood on a chair with one of Louise' aprons tied around her waist, attempting to dry a dripping spoon, while Nora, up to her elbows in soapy water, was scrubbing away at a dirty mixing bowl. Scattered about the kitchen counter and the floor was evidence of the flour, sugar, butter, fruit, cinnamon, and eggs that had gone into making the apple pie that now sat cooling on a rack near the open window.

"Good heavens! What army marched through here today?"

"John, you're home! We didn't hear you come in." Nora turned to him with a beatific smile on her face. "Maggie and I have been baking."

"Yes, I can see that."

"Well, it's Louise' day off, and Maggie and I thought it might be fun to try our hand at a pie without her looking over our shoulders."

"It came out really good, Uncle John," said Maggie.

"Really *well*, dear," her aunt corrected.

"Really well. We're going to have it for dessert tonight."

"Just give us a few minutes here to clean up, John. The rest of the supper is ready and we should be able to sit down to eat in about fifteen minutes."

John left them to their task and headed to the study. Seeing his wife so relaxed and happy should have filled him with joy. Instead, he felt troubled. He walked over to the sideboard and opened a bottle of bootleg whiskey, a gift from a cattleman with relatives over the Canadian border. He poured himself a small amount and sat down in one of the chairs facing the fireplace, staring with unseeing eyes into the cold ashes.

After the death of their infant son ten years ago, and the doctor's sad determination that Nora could bear no more children, John had watched his pretty, vivacious young wife succumb to a grief so overwhelming he feared for her sanity. He would never forget the anguished conversation that took place just before her operation.

John had knelt by Nora's hospital bed, holding her hand and stroking her hair, trying without success to comfort her.

"Oh, John, I'm so sorry, I'm so sorry." The tears had streamed down the sides of Nora's cheeks and dampened her hair.

"Sh, Nora, there's nothin' to be sorry for."

"No, I've failed you. I've lost our little baby, and now I'll never be able to give you any more. All our dreams of a family together — " Her body shook with her sobs.

"Nora, it's not your fault. These things just happen sometimes. The doctor said so. What's important is that you're all right. I just want you to be well."

She didn't seem to hear him.

"I've failed you. I've failed us both. I'll never be able to give you the family you wanted. I'll never know what it's like to be a mother. I'll never know — "

Her voice and her sobs tapered off as the sedative took hold. She drifted into an uneasy sleep. John wiped the last of the tears from her cheeks, pressing her cool hand to his lips. From his pocket he took a white rosary and folded it into her other hand.

"Mr. Owen? We need to prepare you wife for surgery, now."

John stepped aside as the nurse and an orderly pulled a curtain around Nora's bed. He had never felt so helpless and alone.

Nora's physical recovery from the hysterectomy was unremarkable, but she sank into a long, deep depression. She refused to talk or eat, and spent almost all of her time sleeping. She seemed to have lost the will to live. Weeks passed with no change. John began to worry that she might never recover. But, at long last, through prayer, the loving support of her husband and some unknown inner strength of her own, she was able to turn away from the tempting oblivion of the darkness that beckoned her.

After six weeks, Nora returned with John to the house on Twenty-seventh Street, reconciled to living a life much different from the one she'd planned.

As soon as her strength returned, Nora threw herself into activities. She volunteered at the hospital and the church, and joined the Women's Club, the monthly Book Club and the Ladies' Sodality. She took frequent trips, with and without John, often driving the new green Ford V-8 coupe that he had bought her as a coming home present from the hospital. Always careful with his own spending, John lavished gifts on his wife, denying her nothing that he thought might make her happy. Nora redecorated the house from top to bottom, spending countless hours deciding between different shades of paint and fabric. She planned each day's menu down to the last detail, insisting on the choicest meat, the ripest fruit and the freshest vegetables, and supervised the preparation of all the food. She became known for her lovely luncheons and exquisite dinner parties, which she orchestrated right down to the rose-shaped pads of butter at each place. She personally selected John's wardrobe, making sure he had the appropriate dress for the many conferences and meetings he was required to attend. Nora channeled all of her energies into making everything around her as perfect as possible. But, there was one thing she could not achieve, one empty place no amount of activity could fill.

Until Maggie came. With Maggie's arrival in their home, John witnessed a gradual easing of the sadness that had gripped his wife. More and more he saw glimmers of the old Nora as she laughed with Maggie over a silly radio program or sat with Maggie nestled in her lap to read a bedtime story. Nora helped

Maggie with her school work, fussed over her hair and clothing, and made sure that Maggie practiced her piano lessons each week. Maggie's need gave renewed purpose to Nora's life, putting a light back in her eyes that her husband had thought extinguished forever. John was torn between relief at seeing Nora take joy in life again, and fear at her growing attachment to this little girl who was, after all, her brother's child. With trepidation, he watched her feelings for Maggie grow, but he hadn't the heart to deny her that which had brought her happiness for the first time since their little boy had died.

Still, John knew it could not last forever. At some point, Terrence would come to take his daughter back. When that happened, John feared it would be more than his wife could take. Even now, when Maggie would ask about going home, or when they left her at the farm for an extended visit, the haunted look would return to Nora's eyes, and John knew that she was struggling with both the memories of the loss of their son, and her fear of losing yet another child that she had allowed herself to love.

John gripped the glass in his hand. It was so unfair. When Nora had offered to help her brother by taking in Maggie, her motivation had been pure and genuine. She hadn't meant to grow so attached to the little girl. Was Nora now to be punished for allowing herself to feel again? Didn't she deserve some happiness after the hell she'd been through?

And, what about him? John had to admit that he, too, had come to care about Maggie more than he'd ever intended — her blue eyes that looked up at him so trustingly, her laughter that filled the house, her quick mind that absorbed everything as she trotted around after him at the stockyards. He'd already lost a son and could have no other children, and the little girl had touched his heart. Yes, it would be very hard for him, too, when Maggie left. His main concern, however, was what her leaving would do to Nora.

At that moment, John made a vow to himself. Right or wrong, he would not allow his beloved wife to slip back into that well of despair from which he feared, this time, she would not have the strength to return. He would do whatever it took to protect her — and, yes, himself — from ever having to experience that kind of pain again.

John lifted his glass and drained it.

"Has it started?" asked Nora as she hurried into the parlor where John was adjusting the dials of the radio. Maggie trailed behind her.

"Yes. They're just about to do the swearin' in."

"Sister Placide told us that it's very bad to swear," Maggie scolded as she plopped down in her usual place on the rug in front of the radio.

Not only was it too rainy and cold to play outside on this March day of 1933, but Maggie's usual Saturday radio programs had been preempted for the President's inauguration. She was not happy.

"No, Maggie," her aunt explained. "A *swearing in* means that Mr. Roosevelt is going to take office as our new President today.

"Sh. It's startin'." Uncle John turned up the volume, and the crackling voice of the new President filled the room.

"I, Franklin Delano Roosevelt, do solemnly swear to uphold — "

"He talks funny."

"Maggie, sh!" Uncle John continued to fuss with the dials.

The President's voice, clearer now, thundered on, interrupted at intervals by the cheers and applause of the crowd in attendance.

" ... let me assert my firm belief that the only thing we have to fear is fear itself.

"This nation asks for action, and action now. Our greatest primary task is to put people to work.... [The task] can be helped by preventing realistically the tragedy of the growing loss through foreclosure of our small homes and our farms —

"For the trust reposed in me I will return the courage and the devotion that befit the time. I can do no less."

When the broadcast finished, Aunt Nora spoke first.

"Well, he certainly is an electrifying speaker. He makes you feel as if he could do anything he sets his mind to."

"Yes. And the people are behind him." John shook his head in wonder. "I never thought I'd live to see the day Iowa would go Democratic. But the farmers believe in FDR. Now we'll just have to wait and see if he can deliver on some of those promises he's made." He chuckled. "Well, at the very least, he's going to repeal Prohibition. That should cheer people up."

"John." Nora frowned, nodding toward Maggie.

"What was the President talking about, Uncle John?"

"Well, it's kind of complicated, Maggie, but he was talking about makin' some laws to try to help the poor people and the people out of work and the farmers — "

"Like my Daddy?"

"Yes, like your Daddy."

"Oh, goody. Then my Daddy will have enough money to pay someone to take care of me, and I'll be able to go home for good." Maggie smiled from ear to ear.

For a long moment, the only sound in the room was the happy voices of the radio chorus singing the praises of *Beechnut Gum*. Then, with a sympathetic look at his wife's bowed head, Uncle John spoke.

"Well, Maggie. There are a lot of problems the President will have to solve before things get better. I guess we'll just have to wait and see."

"I'm going to say a prayer for Mr. Roosevelt."

"That would be a very nice thing to do, Maggie." Aunt Nora's smile was wan. "Yes," said Uncle John. "The whole country could use our prayers right now."

But, for many of the farmers of Iowa and the surrounding states, prayer and patience were no longer enough. Disastrously low prices and high costs threatened them with the loss of their livelihoods and their homes. In desperation, more and more of them were turning to violence. Bloodshed had already

occurred in February of 1933, when some non-striking farmers had tried to run a Farmer's Holiday Association blockade
outside of Sioux City. The resulting gun battle left five
wounded and one dead. On March 24th, an attorney in the
southwestern part of the state was held hostage by a group of
farmers when he tried to serve an eviction notice on a farm outside the town of Harlan. On April 27th, farmers in Primghar,
Iowa invaded the courthouse to block a sheriff's sale of a
neighbor's farm. Overpowering the club-wielding deputies,
they persuaded the attorney for the mortgage holder to accept
a token settlement of the debt. For good measure, they took
the attorney, the sheriff and his deputies outside, and forced
them to kneel and kiss the American Flag. Then, flush with success, they set out to stop some foreclosure hearings in the
nearby town of LeMars.

Maggie and her uncle knew nothing of this most recent
development just to the northeast of them as they drove down
Highway 140 on that same warm April afternoon. As a treat,
John had taken Maggie along on his sales trip. They'd spent the
morning at a farm near Alton, where Maggie spent the time
playing with the farm dog's new litter of puppies while John
assessed the worth of the farmer's herd of Hereford cattle.
Then, while the mob from Primghar was driving in a caravan
toward LeMars, John and Maggie were at a farm in Remson,
about ten miles to the east. An hour later, business concluded
at last, Uncle John turned the black Ford west onto Route 3,
heading for Sioux City. Maggie dozed lightly on the front seat
next to him.

They were just a few miles east of LeMars when Maggie
felt the car slow. Blinking awake, she sat up and looked out the
window to find more than twenty-five cars and farm trucks
pulled over on both sides of the road up ahead.

"What's going on, Uncle John? Is it a fair?" she asked, her
voice hopeful.

"I don't think so, Maggie."

Uncle John slowed the car to a crawl. As they drew closer,

they could see a large group of close to 200 men, some of them carrying clubs and farms tools, yelling and waving their fists. An older man wearing a suit was being dragged to the front of the mob. They shoved and slapped him as he passed, throwing handfuls of dirt at his head. Someone threw a rope around a telephone pole while two other men hauled the unfortunate victim up onto an overturned crate. They pulled the noose tight around his neck. He stood there, above the heads of the other men, his eyeglasses askew and his clothing disheveled. Even from a distance, Maggie could see the frightened look on his face.

Uncle John pulled the Ford over to the side of the road just beyond the line of cars and turned off the engine. He turned to Maggie, speaking to her in as stern a voice as she had ever heard him use.

"Maggie, I want you to roll up the windows and lock the door. No matter what happens, do not leave this car. Do you understand?"

"Yes, Sir."

Maggie, her heart pounding, watched as her uncle got out of the car and walked over to the edge of the crowd. Despite his warning, she rolled down the window a few inches, pressing her ear to the opening to hear what was going on.

"You're in our courtroom now, Bradley," shouted a stocky man in worn coveralls, his face red with anger and excitement.

"Yeah. Not so high and mighty now, are ya, Judge? You've been doing the bank's dirty work, kicking men and women and little babies off their land. Well, now we're kicking back!" yelled another.

"You sign those foreclosure orders and you're a dead man," threatened a third. The crowd roared its approval.

A tall, red haired man near the front of the crowd motioned for silence. He seemed to be some kind of leader, and the mob quieted. He turned to the judge, who was struggling to keep his precarious balance on the crate, and spoke in a loud clear voice so all could hear.

"Well, Judge, what's it gonna be? You let our people stay on their farms, we set you free. You don't and, well — " He gave a playful tug on the rope around the trembling man's neck. The crowd snickered and jeered.

"You tell 'im, Red!"

The judge licked his lips a few times in an effort to get his dry mouth to work. Then, in a voice choked by fear and the pressure of the rope around his neck, he replied with what dignity he could muster.

"I can only promise that I will do the fair thing to all men to the best of my knowledge."

This declaration was met with angry catcalls from the crowd. Red shook his head in disgust. He looked out over the angry farmers as if for guidance as cries of *Hoist him up!* filled the air.

"Hold on, now. Hold on!" A familiar voice rang out over the throng. Maggie realized with a sinking heart that it was Uncle John. All heads turned toward the big man striding toward the front of the mob. John stopped between Red and the judge.

"Who are you, friend?" Red asked, his eyes narrowing. "I don't recall seeing you around before."

"The name's John Owen from Sioux City."

"You a farmer?"

"No. Commission man."

Red snorted.

"Well, Mr. Commission Man. I suggest you head on back to Sioux City. This business doesn't concern you."

"It concerns me if a man's life is at stake. I sympathize with what you men are goin' through, but this isn't the way to go about it."

"Oh, you sympathize, do you?" A man in a battered fedora shook a pitchfork in John's face. "Are your kids going without food or decent clothes? Does your wife cry herself to sleep every night with worry? Are you about to be driven off the land your grandfather and father worked and sweated over?"

John kept his voice firm and steady. "No, God have mercy,

but I know many who are. It's cruel and it's wrong. But killin's not the answer. I'm tellin' you, you don't want to be doin' this thing."

The crowd's grumbling grew louder. They began to close in around him.

"Get out of the way, Mick," someone shouted. When John stood his ground, they began to shove him. Then one of them took a swing at him, knocking his hat off.

"Uncle John!"

The child's scream, shrill and unexpected, cut through the noise of the crowd. Stunned, the men stepped aside as Maggie, tears streaming down her face, pushed her way through the crowd. She threw her arms around her uncle's waist.

"Don't you hurt him! Don't you hurt him!" she shrieked at the now silent farmers.

"Maggie! I told you to stay in the car!" Uncle John admonished her, scooping her up into the relative safety of his arms. The men looked from the distraught little girl to each other, then lowered their eyes to the ground. For a long moment, the only noise was the sound of the Maggie's weeping.

Red reached down, picked up John's hat, and handed it to him.

"I think you'd better take your little girl home," he said in a quiet voice.

He and John exchanged a long look. John nodded. As he turned to leave, the crowd parted for him without resistance.

Red looked back at the judge, almost forgotten in the unexpected turn of events. He considered him carefully for a moment, then turned to face the crowd.

"Well, I think we've made our point," Red announced in a loud voice. "Take the rope off him," he instructed the men on either side. With reluctance, they complied. The judge, still standing atop the crate, brought his trembling hands up to touch the raw skin of his neck.

"Judge," Red continued, "I hope you'll remember this little warning the next time you're called upon to decide whether to deprive innocent people of their homes and livelihoods. But, just in case, we'll give you one more little reminder." He gave a menacing smile. "Hold him."

Two men grabbed the judge's arms. Red brought his face up close to the older man's. The judge, pale and shaking, met his gaze. Suddenly, Red winked. He reached out and undid the judge's belt. With the help of a few others from the crowd, he pulled off the judge's pants, leaving him standing in his underwear. The crowd laughed derisively.

"Perhaps now, your Honor, you'll understand what it's like to lose the clothes off your back."

Red flung the pants into the crowd. The farmers, hooting and cheering, tossed the pants back and forth until, tiring of the game, they threw them into the ditch by the side of the road.

At last, the mob began to disperse, getting into their cars and trucks, and driving off the way they'd come. They left the judge to find his own way back to town.

With Maggie safe in the car, Uncle John, too, pulled back out onto the highway. Maggie, her stuttered breathing slowing, looked out the back window to see the forlorn figure of the judge sitting all alone on the crate in his underwear, his head in his hands.

"Uncle John, don't you think we should help him?"

She looked over at her uncle, and was surprised to see a little smile tug at the corner of his mouth.

"No, he'll be all right now. And the walk to town will do him good." His face became stern again. "Now, young lady, about what happened just now. You did a very foolish thing leaving the car when I told you not to. There's no tellin' what a mob like that will do. What you did was disobedient, foolhardy … and quite brave." He reached over and patted her knee. "Fortunately, it all turned out for the best, so I see no need in worryin' your Aunt over the matter. Agreed?"

"Agreed."

Exhausted, Maggie leaned her head on her uncle's shoulder and closed her eyes. John put his arm around the sleeping child, glancing down at her in wonder.

The front page of the *Sioux City Journal* the next day carried the story of the near-lynching near LeMars, although there was no mention of the presence of a little girl. This assault on a district judge, together with continuing trouble at foreclosure sales in northwestern Iowa, was enough to move the Governor to declare martial law in three counties. This successfully calmed the situation. Martial law was lifted six weeks later.

Finally, on May 12, 1933, the federal government responded. With the urging and support of Agricultural Secretary Henry Wallace, himself an Iowan, Congress passed and the new President signed into law the Farm Relief Act. This Act, in turn, created the Farm Credit Administration, which provided relief for farmers in the form of mortgages at lower rates, and the Agricultural Adjustment Administration, or AAA, which sought to raise farm prices through government subsidized scarcity. Some time would pass, however, before any beneficial effects of these programs would be felt by the farmers. Still, as the Farm Relief Act began to be implemented, protest waned. Although not universally popular or successful, Roosevelt's farm programs gave the farmers something that had been in short supply – hope. And that hope was beginning to grow.

At the beginning of June, Maggie's father timed a hog-selling trip to Sioux City to coincide with Maggie's first piano recital. His plan was to conduct his business at the stockyards, attend the recital, spend the night at Nora and John's house, then return to Boru after morning Mass. Maggie was so excited about seeing her father and Elly, who had been allowed to come with him, that she could barely sleep the night before.

Early Saturday morning, Maggie took up her position on the front porch. The minutes dragged by, but at last, the old farm truck rattled up to the house. Maggie flew off the porch and leapt up onto the running board.

"Daddy! Elly!"

"Well, if it isn't the great pianist. Now, wait a minute. Let me at least get out of the truck." Her father chuckled.

"Oh, Daddy, I thought you'd never get here," Maggie exclaimed, hugging him around the waist. "Come on," she urged, tugging on his arm. "Let's go see Aunt Nora. Come on, Elly." She led the way up the front walk.

"Wow. I forgot it was so big," Elly exclaimed, looking up at the house.

"Close your mouth, Elly, before you swallow a fly," said her father.

"Terrence. Elly. You made it." Aunt Nora, wearing a pretty, flowered dress, opened the front door. She gave Elly a kiss on the cheek, then reached out to hug her little brother.

"Careful, now. I smell like the yards," Terrence cautioned, stepping back.

"Ah. As if I'm not used to that with John," she replied, hugging him anyway. "Speaking of whom, did you see him down there?"

"No. I didn't know he was there this morning. But, I was over at the hog pens the whole time, anyway."

"How'd you do with the hogs?"

Terrence shrugged. "The price is up a little from last month. Still, it's less than half of what we were getting five years ago."

Nora clucked in sympathy.

"Well, you're done with it now. Come on in and have some cool lemonade and some cookies. We've some time to relax yet before we need to get ready for the big performance."

The piano recital was scheduled for two o'clock at the house of Maggie's piano teacher, Miss Sanders. Maggie wore the new pink dress that Aunt Nora had bought her for the occasion and a small corsage that Uncle John had given her to wear *for good luck*. Holding her father's hand, she joined the others in Uncle John's car for the drive over to the recital.

Miss Sanders' baby grand piano had been polished and tuned, and her parlor rearranged to accommodate five rows of chairs for the performers and their families. Punch and cookies had been placed on a side table for the reception after the recital, and the teacher's many cats shut away in an upstairs bedroom.

Maggie sat with the other nine students scheduled to perform that day, furtively wiping her sweaty palms on the skirt of her dress as she waited her turn. At last, Miss Sanders introduced her and the piece she was to perform. Maggie made her way on shaky legs to the piano, seating herself on the bench. Taking a deep breath, she raised her hands to play.

The notes sounded loud in the hushed quiet of the room, and Maggie felt a moment of panic. But, so often had she practiced the piece, her fingers seemed to know what to do without her help. Before she knew it, she was playing the final notes of *The Elf and the Fairy*. With a sigh of relief, she stood and curtsied to the applauding audience as she had been taught. She broke into a shy smile when she saw the pleased expressions on the faces of her father, sister, aunt and uncle.

"Well done, Maggie," Miss Sanders whispered to her as she guided her back to her seat.

Her father leaned over and patted her knee.

"You play just like your mother," he whispered, his eyes bright.

Maggie beamed.

To celebrate her musical debut, Louise cooked Maggie's favorite foods for supper. Afterward, Aunt Nora announced that she was taking the girls on the trolley to see an early evening movie at the Orpheum Theater downtown.

"Are you sure you won't change your minds?" she asked her husband. "Everyone says *Duck Soup* is the funniest Marx Brothers movie yet."

"No, you ladies go on ahead," John answered. "Terrence and I have some business to discuss. We'll see you after the movie."

"All right." Nora kissed her husband on the cheek.

"Goodbye, Terrence. Don't let John keep you cooped up inside on this beautiful evening talking hog prices."

"Come on, Aunt Nora. We're going to miss the serial!" Elly and Maggie tugged their aunt in the direction of the door. With a helpless wave of her free hand, Nora allowed the giggling girls to steer her out of the house and off down the sidewalk.

"Come on, Terrence. We'll be more comfortable in the study."

John's study was more like him than any other room in the house. Paneled in dark wood with an oriental rug on the floor, it smelled of tobacco and furniture polish. An enormous roll-top desk with a swivel chair took up most of one wall. The other walls were lined with books on a wide variety of subjects. Two overstuffed brown leather chairs faced a stone fireplace and between them sat a large round table bearing an ashtray with the inscription, *Sioux City Stockyards*, and the most recent editions of the *Chicago Tribune*, the *Des Moines Star*, the *Sioux City Journal* and the *Sioux City Tribune*. Here and there were framed photographs of John with some clients, or John and Nora at various livestock conventions and horse races. A crystal decanter and matching glasses sat on a cherry table beneath the window facing out to Twenty-seventh Street.

John took a seat in one of the armchairs and motioned Terrence into the other.

"Cigarette?"

Terrence accepted the cigarette and light proffered by John, then settled back into the comfort of the leather chair.

"Drink?"

"No, thanks." Terrence blew a soft spiral of smoke into the air. He smiled in amusement at this brother-in-law. "So, John. What is it you'd like to discuss that's so important it has you waiting on me hand and foot?"

Chagrined, John began.

"Well, Terrence, I've always felt that the best way to handle things is head on, so I'll say it to you plain. Nora and I would like Maggie to continue livin' with us."

Terrence smiled. "That's very nice of you, John, but I can't let you do that. You and Nora have been very good to me and to Maggie. I'm not forgetting how you took her in just after Elizabeth died, and me not quite myself. Well I know that without your help, I'd have lost the farm by now." Terrence flicked the ashes from his cigarette into the ashtray. "But, things are beginning to improve, what with the AAA setting farm prices and all. I'm not saying it'll be easy — the drought is hitting us all pretty hard. But things are moving in the right direction. In fact, I think it's time we became a real family again. It's been over a year and a half since Maggie left. It's time she came home for good. I'm ready for it, and I know it's what Elizabeth would have wanted."

"I don't think you understand." John stood and walked to the table by the window. He poured himself a glass of whiskey from the crystal decanter. Taking a sip, he stared for a moment at the quiet tree-lined streets. Then, without turning around, he began to speak.

"Terrence, I never told you or anyone else in the family just how sick Nora was after our baby, Patrick, died. Not so much physically — although it was a long recovery — but mentally and emotionally. She had a very bad time. The loss of the baby was one thing, but when the doctor told her she could have no more — "

"John, I'm not sure this is something you should be telling — "

"Please!" John whirled around to face Terrence. "You need to know this. Maybe then you'll understand why — " He stopped. With an effort, he composed himself.

Terrence, startled, considered his brother-in-law warily.

"Go on."

John turned back to the window, slowly twirling the amber liquid in his glass.

"Your sister was so overcome with grief that I feared for her sanity. She retreated into her own little world. The doctors had a name for it. *Catatonia*. But they had no idea how to treat it, or how long it would last. For weeks she wouldn't speak. She didn't seem to see or hear anythin' going on around her. I thought I'd lost her. But, at last, slowly, she began to get better. After two months, I was able to bring her home. But she was never quite the same. It was as if a part of her had died. Until Maggie came."

He turned to face Terrence.

"Maggie made Nora come alive again. Little by little, she returned to the Nora I knew and loved. I know I should have put a stop to it. I could see how deeply she was becomin' involved. But for the first time in such a long time, she was happy, truly happy. Surely, you can see that, after all she had been through, I couldn't deny her that."

John returned to his chair and set down his glass. He leaned toward Terrence, his expression solemn.

"I'm asking you to try to understand, Terrence. Nora loves Maggie as much as if she were her own. She's already lost one child. I don't think she could survive it if she lost Maggie, too."

Terrence stared at John, sure that he must be misunderstanding what his brother-in-law was saying. Then, in measured tones, he responded.

"She's not hers to lose, John. She's my daughter."

"I know, Terrence. And because she's your daughter, I'm askin' you to think about what's best for her, too. Let her stay here with us, permanently. I'm not askin' just for Nora's sake, but for Maggie's, too. She's thrived here, you said so yourself. And the cold fact of it is, Nora and I can give her so much more than you're able to give her — private schooling, travel, music lessons, even college. She's such a bright little girl. It would be wrong to deny her those opportunities."

Terrence leapt to his feet, upsetting his chair in the process.

"Have you lost your mind, man? Do you know what you're saying? This is not some stray kitten we're talking about. You can't just decide to keep her. This is my daughter, *my* daughter, and she has a father and a family, and that's where she belongs!" He righted the chair with a bang.

Now, John, too, was on his feet.

"And what kind of a father have you been? For months after Elizabeth died you were so consumed by grief you practically abandoned your own children. Your three youngest were scattered amongst the relatives while young Anna and the boys were left to try to keep the farm goin'."

"How dare you!" Terrence sputtered in his anger. "You have no idea what it's like to lose someone you love as much as I loved Elizabeth, how the pain of it overwhelms you so that you pray to God you'll die yourself. It was only *because* of the children, *our* children, that I was able to go on."

John sat back down in his chair, weighing his response with care.

"That's where you're wrong, Terrence. I do know, because that is exactly how I feel about Nora. And I did lose her. But, praised be to God, with Maggie's help, I got her back." He looked Terrence straight in the eye. "I'll not risk losin' her again."

John paused for a moment, then reached out his hands.

"Terrence, I'm beggin' you. You couldn't save Elizabeth, but you can save Nora. And Maggie. Leave the little girl with us. Please."

Terrence' expression was incredulous.

"You've no right to ask me to make such a choice. No right!" His eyes narrowed. "Does Nora know what you're about?"

"No. Of course not. She'd never ask you to make such a sacrifice. But, if you could see the look in her eyes when Maggie talks about going home for good ... I've see that look before. I can't sit by and watch my wife go through that agony again. God forgive me, I can't and I won't."

Recognizing the pain in his brother-in-law's voice, Terrence' anger abated somewhat.

"John. I'm sorry for your troubles. Truly I am. But what you're asking is impossible. I love my sister very much, but I'll not sacrifice my daughter for her. I'm sorry, but that's the end of it." He snubbed out his forgotten cigarette in the ashtray.

"No, Terrence. There's one more thing to consider."

John crossed to the desk. He removed a brown, file folder from the top drawer, hesitated, then handed it to Terrence. The label on the file read, *Mortgage, Parcel 329, Boru, Iowa. Fahey, Terrence J.* Inside the file was a deed and some receipts for mortgage payments made for the last several months on the farm in Boru. There were also a number of letters and official looking documents signed by both Mr. John T. Owen and the First Bank of Iowa.

"You're welcome to read it, Terrence, but I can give you the gist.

"When I sat down with the loan officers at the First Bank of Iowa to make arrangements for takin' over payment of your mortgage last summer, I discovered that you had paid down all but $4,500 of the principal you owed. Given the large number of farmers defaultin' on their loans and the small amount brought in by foreclosure sales, the bank was happy to accept my offer to purchase the mortgage from them."

Terrence looked up quickly from the papers, a dark fear tugging at his heart. "You know, of course, that I will pay you back as soon as I possibly can."

"I've never doubted that for a minute, Terrence. I know that your word is your bond. So is mine."

John folded his arms across his chest. He spoke in a voice devoid of emotion.

"Listen carefully to what I am about to say. The next payment on your mortgage is due in a week. As holder of that mortgage, I have the legal right to demand immediate payment. If payment is not made, I am again within my legal rights to foreclose. You would lose the farm and your livelihood. If that were to happen, you and the children would have no choice but to ask your relatives to take you in. They're good people. They'd do it no matter the personal hardship to them. But, because there are so many of you, it's certain you and the children would have to be separated, perhaps for a very long time."

Terrence was stunned into silence. The enormity of what his brother-in-law was doing hit him like a blow. He stared down at the papers in his hand while the strength seemed to drain from his body. He opened and closed his mouth as if gasping for air. When at last he spoke, it was in a low, hard voice.

"John, I didn't think you capable of this."

John did not reply. He just stared at Terrence, his expression unreadable.

"You do realize what you're doing," Terrence said. "You're asking me to sacrifice Maggie, or lose the farm and the other five children as well."

"I'm sorry, Terrence." John's voice was cold. "I hoped it wouldn't come to this. But I'm only doin' what I feel I must do to protect my wife. And, in the end, I think it will be best for Maggie, too."

"You bastard."

Terrence threw the file at John. Fists clenched, he headed for the door. For the first time in his life, he understood what it meant to be in a murderous rage.

"Terrence."

Terrence stopped but did not turn around.

"There are two more things you should know. First, I think it would be best if Nora and I formally adopt Maggie so there'll be no more fears on Nora's part that Maggie will be taken away. You will, of course, be able to see her whenever you want. Second, if you ever breathe a word of this conversation to Nora, Maggie or anyone else, I'll foreclose immediately. You have my word."

Terrence turned. His eyes were filled with hatred and contempt. John felt the chill to his very soul.

"May you burn in hell for the evil you do this day, John Owen."

Not until he heard the front door slam did John allow himself to hang his head.

Maggie lay awake in her bed for a long time that night. Something bad had happened while she and her sister were at the movies. They returned to find their father sitting on the porch, with a set to his jaw that he only got when he was very upset. Uncle John stood at the front door. Neither man spoke, but the very air was filled with anger as if harsh words spoken hung there still, only Maggie was unable to read them.

Her father announced that he had some unexpected business back at the farm and that they would be unable to spend the night as originally planned. He kissed Maggie on the cheek and gave a perfunctory hug to Aunt Nora. He did not even say goodbye to Uncle John.

As her father strode down the front walkway, a protesting Elly trotting to keep up, Maggie caught the questioning look her aunt gave her uncle. The three of them stood watching the battered old truck rumble away. Then Aunt Nora informed Maggie that she *looked tired,* and sent her to bed early. Now, lying there in the dark, Maggie could still hear the troubled droning of their voices in the parlor below.

Maggie did not know what the problem had been about, but she sensed that it somehow involved her. She thought hard. Had she done something to anger her father? Her uncle?

Maggie rolled over onto her side. Today had started out so happy. She had played well at her first recital, and everyone had been so proud of her. But, then it had all been spoiled, and she didn't know why. She must have done something wrong to cause her father to leave. She thought back over everything she had said and done since her father had arrived, but she couldn't come up with an answer. Maybe he was angry that she'd gone off to the movies without him. Maybe he thought she liked being with Aunt Nora better than him. Why else would he have gone away and left her?

But, she knew why. She'd always known why. All of a sudden, the guilt and loneliness that were never far away rose up, stronger than ever, threatening to overwhelm her. Maggie curled herself into a tight ball, unsure of whether she was keeping the terror in or keeping it out.

At breakfast the next morning, nothing was said about her father's hasty departure. Maggie wanted to ask. But she'd been taught that you didn't pry into other people's business, even if those people were family. Especially if they were family.

Days passed and things slowly returned to normal. Except that now it was Aunt Nora who placed the Sunday phone calls to her father.

To her great relief, Maggie was still allowed to make her scheduled visit to the farm in July. Her father was out in the field when Uncle John dropped her off. By the time he returned to the house, her uncle's car was just a dust cloud in the distance. Her father's greeting was warm, and he hugged her to his sweaty overalls. Maggie was relieved. He did not seem to be angry with her anymore. Walking toward the house with his arm around her shoulder, she decided that whatever the problem had been, everything was going to be fine now.

Chapter 7

August 1933

*Threshing day. To the farmer, it was the culmination
of months of hard work - plowing, planting, cultivating
and praying for good weather; the day when the oats in the
field were harvested and stored in the grain bin, providing food for the animals and security for the farmer for one
more year. Threshing day brought the entire farming community together in an ancient harvest ritual of coopera-
tion and dependence that was repeated at each of the farms
in the area until everyone's crop was in. To the adults and
older children, it meant long hours and backbreaking
work, both in the field and in the kitchen. But it brought
with it the satisfaction of a year's labor come to fruition.*

*To a seven-year-old girl, however, threshing day was
filled with excitement, delicious food and the chance to
get together with friends and neighbors. In fact, only the
tap of reindeer hooves on the roof at Christmas was awaited
with more eagerness than the sound of the big steam tractor pulling the threshing machine, clanking and clanging,
into the farmyard.*

The sun was not yet up when Maggie awakened that morning, the first week of August. She squinted at the clock. 5:22
A.M. Rubbing the sleep from her eyes, she tiptoed to the window to discover the source of the noise that had disturbed her
sleep. She drew aside the curtains and peered through the pre-
dawn darkness just in time to see old Mr. Nolan climb down
from his tractor and walk toward the house. There, hitched
behind the tractor, crouched the hulking, metal threshing
machine.

"Elly. Elly! Wake up! The thresher man's here!"

Elly groaned and rolled over. Glancing over at the bed next to hers, Maggie saw that Anna was already up and gone. Hurrying into her pants and shirt, Maggie made a quick pass at her hair with her fingers. Then, she bounded down the stairs into a kitchen filled with people, noise and the wonderful aromas of freshly baked pies and breads.

Tradition dictated that the woman of the house was in command on threshing day. But, deeming the job too big for Anna, Terrence's sisters, Katherine and Bridget, or Kit and Bid as the family called them, had taken charge of the day's major meal. The two sisters had arrived from town just before 5:00 A.M., laden with homemade jellies and relishes as well as pies, cakes and bread baked the night before. Already they had a ham in the oven, a pot of potatoes boiling on the stove, and were in the process of cutting up so many chickens for frying that Maggie wondered if there were any survivors left in the barnyard. Anna was stationed over a large pot, peeling potatoes, her lips pressed into a thin line at this invasion of *her* kitchen. James shuttled in and out with armloads of wood to keep the stove stoked. Four-year-old Michael, lured by the smell of rarely enjoyed treats, sat at the kitchen table eating cold cereal, but hopeful of wheedling something tastier out of his busy aunts.

"Well, hello, sleepyhead. There's cornflakes on the table. Eat. We've got a full day ahead of us."

With a gory knife, Aunt Bid motioned to the opened box sitting in front of Michael. Maggie helped herself to a bowl full, adding a little milk and a lot more sugar than the distracted women would have ordinarily allowed. Breakfast on such a morning was a perfunctory affair, but no one minded given the elaborate feast to come. Maggie settled herself out of the way at the end of the table to eat and observe the intricate choreography of a farm kitchen on threshing day.

The two women before her were a study in contrasts. Aunt Kit, the oldest of *The Big Aunts*, as the children called them, was tall and thin like Maggie's dad with the same piercing blue eyes.

Her brown hair, which she wore in a low bun, was faded and streaked with gray, and her hands were wrinkled from years of hard work. But she was strong, with a quick wit and a quicker temper. Even her sisters, all grown women with families of their own, deferred to Kit's take charge attitude.

Aunt Bid, on the other hand, was short and round with the dark, curly hair of the Brennan side of the family. Where Kit's humor was often sarcastic, Bid's was gentle. Her laugh was open and generous, and her calm, easygoing ways had served to soothe many a minor family flare-up. She was the favorite of all of the nieces and nephews. Maggie remembered her Dad once saying that, for day-to-day living, Bid was a joy to have around. But in a crisis, you wanted Kit.

Despite their differences, or maybe because of them, Kit and Bid worked together like an old team of plow horses — one driving, one steadying — comfortable and efficient in harness together.

"Nugget, hand me the big mixing bowl," instructed Aunt Kit as she prepared to make-up the batter for the fried chicken.

"Aunt Bid," asked Maggie, her mouth full of corn flakes. "Why do people call you *Nugget*?"

Aunt Bid smiled as she brought her knife down with a frightening whack onto the wooden cutting board, expertly severing another chicken wing. "Oh, it's a nickname I got when I was a little girl, even younger than you. You see, when they discovered gold in South Dakota — in the late 1870's, wasn't it, Kit — lots of the men from around Boru, including my uncle, your Great Uncle Sean, went off to the gold fields to make their fortune. Well, he wasn't exactly rich when he returned —" Aunt Kit snorted. "But he did bring back some gold nuggets for us to see."

"Were they real gold?" Michael asked, his eyes big with wonder.

"Yes. Not pure, mind you, but real gold just the same. So bright and shiny they were. Anyway, Uncle Sean gave me one to keep. After that, whenever anyone would return from the gold fields, I'd ask if I might have a small gold nugget. In a few years, I had quite a collection. And a new nickname."

"Do you still have the nuggets?" asked Maggie.

"Oh, I suppose I have them tucked away somewhere. They're not worth much now, but to me at the time, they were the most beautiful things in the world."

Just then, Elly shuffled into the kitchen.

"How nice of you to join us, your highness," Aunt Kit greeted her. "I was about to have the butler bring your breakfast up on a tray."

"'Morning, Aunt Kit, Aunt Bid," Elly mumbled, resting her sleepy head on her hand. "What's for breakfast?"

"Cornflakes, which will be waiting for you when you come back in from feeding the hogs and the chickens."

"Awww! Aunt Kit!"

"Don't 'Aunt Kit' me. It's not the animals' fault that you decided to lounge in bed this morning. James and Patrick have already finished milking the cows, and Anna's been helping here in the kitchen for almost an hour. Now, off with you. You, too, Maggie. And take Michael with you."

As the three of them trudged toward the door, Aunt Bid turned and produced three warm rolls from the pocket of her apron. She slipped them to Elly with a wink.

"Wait."

They froze, sure they had been discovered, but Aunt Kit, up to her elbows in flour from the dough she was kneading, merely jerked her head toward the bucket on the floor by Anna's feet.

"Add those peelings to the hogs' slop. And be sure to give fresh water to the chickens. It looks to be a hot one today."

The sun was already peeking up over the trees by the river as the children set about their tasks, annoyed at having to do regular chores on such a day. The girls hurried to dump a mixture of corncobs and potato peelings into the pigs' trough while Michael sloshed water into some pans for the chickens and fairly pelted the indignant birds with corn kernels.

A little after six o'clock, neighbors and friends began to

arrive, bringing their own teams and wagons to help with the threshing. While the men and older boys gathered in the yard to divvy up jobs, the women and girls headed into the house to help with the endless round of cooking, baking, frying, serving and dishwashing that would go on until late afternoon.

Every so often, Maggie would find an excuse to go in or out of the house by way of the front door so she could sneak a peak at old Mr. Nolan. Mr. Nolan had had one arm severed in a threshing accident years ago, and his empty, pinned-up sleeve was a source of gruesome fascination to all the children. As owner of the only threshing machine in the area, he sat in a rocker on the front porch like a king upon his throne, oblivious to the hubbub taking place around him, drawing alternately on the cigarette and the cup of coffee he held deftly in his one good hand. Mr. Nolan had spent the previous Monday at the Connelly's farm, Tuesday and Wednesday at the Hagans, and planned to spend the better part of this day here before moving on to the younger O'Neil's place just before evening. He sat and sipped and waited patiently for his part in the day's drama to begin.

Maggie had caught only glimpses of her father and older brothers that morning. They were busy seeing to the disposition of the teams of horses and wagons that would be used to bring the grain to the thresher that day. The entire job needed to be completed before evening, and all must be in readiness if they were to finish on time.

Preparations for the threshing had actually begun two weeks before when Maggie's father had hitched Dan and Ruby up to the grain binder and headed out to the thirty-four acres they had planted in oats this year. The binder was a complicated-looking contraption that mechanically cut and tied the bundles of oats, a job that used to require many man-hours of backbreaking labor to do by hand. When the binder spit the tied bundles of oats out onto the ground, Maggie's brothers, following behind on foot, gathered them up into vertical shocks, about eight bundles to a shock. Then they placed one or two more bundles on top as a cap to shed the rain. The shocks had been left standing in the fields to dry since that time. Now, they were ready for the thresher.

"Can I have your attention, please? Gather 'round, gather 'round." Her father's clear voice rang out over the snorting of the horses, the creaking of the wagons and the conversation of the men. "I think we're all here now and we're about ready to start. You all have your assignments. Does each man know his place?" The question was a rhetorical one. Everyone present had performed his part many times. "Mr. Nolan. Are you ready, sir?"

Mr. Nolan rose from his chair on the front porch.

"I am."

"Grand. Well then, gentlemen, let's get to work."

The men broke for their wagons. Terrence, James and Patrick climbed up onto the seat of the lead hayrack. With a slap of the reins and a *Get up, there,* Terrence set the horses moving, and the procession of eight wagons and hayracks rumbled out of the barnyard. Watching, Maggie thought they looked like pioneers heading westward to find their fortune. Only, today, that fortune lay in the oat field across the road.

Every man and boy on the threshing crew had a specific job to do. The less skilled or strenuous jobs, such as driving the bundle wagons back and forth from the fields, or greasing the belts and oil cups on the thresher to keep it running smoothly, were given to the younger boys or older men. The jobs that required more skill, strength or stamina were given to men with more experience.

When the wagons arrived at the oat field, the *field pitchers* jumped down, grabbed their pitchforks and began tossing the cut bundles of oats into the nearest wagon; grain ends in, butt ends out. The driver arranged the bundles into a tight, balanced load. As soon as each wagon was full, it was driven off to the thresher, and an empty one took its place, maintaining an efficient, continuous circuit from field to thresher at all times.

The threshing machine was set up a short distance from

the barn. Fifteen feet high, it looked like some prehistoric monster made of metal, gears, belts and chutes. At one end was the feeder, a long, metal tray containing a slatted conveyor belt. This fed the bundles up into the whirring separator where the heads of the oat grain were separated from the shaft. The cleaned oats slid down a chute on one side of the thresher and the straw was blown up out of a tall, angled chute, called a *wind-stacker*, on the other side. The whole thing was run by a series of belts ultimately powered by a larger belt attached to Mr. Nolan's big steam tractor, which served as a stationary power source. It was a noisy operation with lathered horses whinnying and snorting, wagons rattling in and out, grain whooshing down the chute and men shouting to be heard over the ceaseless chugging of the giant machine. All the while, the air around the thresher was filled with oat dust and bits of straw from the stacker.

"Bring 'em up! Bring 'em up!" Mr. Nolan yelled as the bundle-filled wagons arrived from the field, guiding them into place on either side of the feeder. A *bundle-pitcher* would then position himself in each wagon and begin placing the oat bundles onto the feeder. This required some skill as the bundles had to be fed in head first and not too fast or the thresher would choke. If this happened, the whole process would come to a grinding halt while the separator man cleaned out the machine. Then, for as long as it took, the roar of the machinery would be replaced by the sound of Mr. Nolan ranting about the *eejits* who were destroying his fine equipment. Maggie's father was considered to be one of the best bundle-pitchers on the crew, both for his skill and his ability to withstand Ed Nolan's tirades.

The cleaned oats that came out of the chute on the side of the thresher were collected in yet another wagon. When full, this wagon was driven over to the grain bin to be unloaded. The unloading was made easier by use of a belt-driven elevator that carried the grain from the wagon up to the top of the bin. This elevator needed to be fed by a *spike-scooper*, a strong man standing in the grain wagon who was able to shovel left or right handed as needed.

The straw that came out of the wind-stacker on the other side of the thresher automatically formed a straw pile downwind. This straw pile, which was often over twelve feet tall and twice as wide, needed to be shaped in such a way that it would not collapse, yet would be able to shed rain water. It took two men skilled with a pitchfork to create this agrarian skyscraper. First, they decided how big the straw stack was to be by outlining the dimensions in the dirt at the place designated by the owner of the farm. As the first of the straw came flying out of the wind-stacker, they used their pitchforks to form it into a solid base. Then, as the threshing progressed, they worked their way around and around the stack, standing atop the straw itself, until they had formed a carefully shaped mountain. As the last bit of straw came out of the chute, they shaped the top of the stack so that it would shed the rain.

All of this hot, dusty work was performed beneath a relentless Iowa sun. The younger children were kept busy running water out to the men and animals in the fields either on foot, or, if they were lucky, on horseback.

By noon, the men were ravenously hungry and ready for a break. Since it was important that the thresher be kept running without stop to get the job done, they ate in shifts. Now, the ladies went into high gear.

Having cooked and baked all morning, the women and girls prepared to serve the tired crew. Large, oilcloth-covered plank tables and mismatched chairs from half a dozen households had been set up end to end beneath the shade of the big walnut trees in front of the house. While the men stripped to the waist and washed the dust, sweat and bits of grain and straw from their bodies at the pump out back, the women began to bring out the first of the food. Jugs of lemonade and water kept cool in the springhouse, baskets of rolls and cornbread, fresh butter and homemade jellies, jams, and relishes were set out on each table. One call was all it took for the hungry men to take their places. But before anything was touched, heads were bowed in thanksgiving for the food before them as well as the future sustenance represented by the crop being gathered that day.

Then it began. With the possible exception of Thanksgiving dinner, the noontime meal on threshing day was the culinary highlight of the year. For each of the seven or so days that it took to complete the threshing run of all of the neighboring farms, those in attendance would eat a fabulous midday meal put together by the host wife with the help of the other neighborhood women. A not-so-subtle rivalry existed between the ladies of the various households as to who could put out the best spread for the threshing crew. Aunt Kit and Aunt Bid rose to the challenge. Out from the kitchen came platters of ham and fried chicken, bowls of peas and beans from the garden, potatoes, boiled and mashed, swimming in butter, potato salad, fresh tomatoes and, of course, homemade pies and cakes.

The children were put to work serving the food and clearing the table. Sometimes they were able to snatch a roll here or a piece of cake there, but they had to be fast. Maggie found that no sooner did she place a serving of food on the table than the bowl would be empty and the men clamoring for more. But she didn't really mind. Bustling back and forth between table and kitchen, she was able to observe and listen to everything that happened.

While pouring lemonade, she saw how fifteen-year-old Althea McKay, under the pretense of serving the fried chicken, let her arm brush against that of Johnny Tyrell – and the smile he gave her in return. So engrossed were they in each other they did not notice when old Mr. Behan, seated right next to Johnny, removed his set of false teeth from his mouth, setting them on the table next to his now empty plate.

Maggie was filling Mr. Curran's glass when Aunt Kit came out from the kitchen with a basket of her famous honey rolls, each one the size of a small loaf of bread.

"Kit, you make the best rolls in the county," purred Mr. Curran, reaching for one of the still warm buns.

"Oh, these didn't come out near as well as they usually do," Aunt Kit protested, but a little smile flickered at the corners of her mouth.

When Maggie returned to the kitchen with the empty pitcher, a small group of women stood lined up at the sink, washing the platters, bowls and dishes as fast as they were brought in. All hands were busy, but the air was filled with stories and laughter as the women enjoyed this respite from the usual isolation of farm life.

Maggie shouldered her way out of the kitchen door carrying another pitcher of lemonade. She headed to where James, Patrick and some of the older boys were grouped at the end of the nearest table. As she drew near, she could hear Willie Hagan's voice over the others.

". . . and there was old Sweeney, well into his cups, sitting with his back against the wall, not two doors down from the Church, when, who should come along but the good Father Fitzgerald himself. 'Drunk again, Sweeney,' says Father Fitzgerald in disgust when he sees him. 'Ah, so am I, Father. So am I,' says Sweeney, quick as a wink. You should have seen the look on Father Fitz' face!"

Amidst the laughter, Willie noticed Maggie and held up his empty glass.

"Well, Maggie. Haven't seen you in a while. So, how do you like living high on the hog in Sioux City?"

"I don't live in Sioux City," Maggie replied, sloshing a little of the lemonade over the side of the glass. "I'm just visiting."

"Pretty long *visit* if you ask me."

"Nobody asked you." James' stern voice stilled the laughter.

"Take it easy, James. I didn't mean anything by it."

James glared at Willie across the table. "Maggie, why don't you go see if Dad needs anything?"

Maggie was glad to get away. The older boys' jokes were always a little too mean, their play a little too rough.

She moved over to the long plank table where the older men had gathered. They were as strong, most of them, as the younger men, but the affects of time and weather showed in their hard lean frames and their faces as furrowed as the fields they plowed. Lifelong neighbors, these men had shared much, the good times and the bad, and took joy in the simple blessings of family and the land. They talked and smoked, resting for a moment before resuming the day's hard work

Mr. Curran had pushed away from the table and was slowly fanning his face with his hat. At a lull in the conversation, he spoke.

"Terrence, I understand that that seamstress, Miss Stephens, stopped here after she left our place last week."

"Yes. I paid her to do some mending the girls couldn't handle," her father answered, holding out his glass for Maggie to fill.

"She's a pleasant looking woman," Mr. Curran observed. "Magic with a needle. And I understand she's a good cook, too." He paused. "A man could do worse."

"True, true," the others at the table nodded their heads in agreement.

Terrence made no comment. He just took another bite of his apple pie.

Maggie turned to serve the next table, but her attention was riveted on the conversation behind her. For a few moments, no one spoke.

"It's been two years, Terrence," Mr. Curran said at last. "Have you thought about marrying again, providing a mother for your children?"

Maggie's father wiped his mouth with his napkin and placed it on the table. With a solemn expression, he considered his old friend.

"I am married," he replied. He said it without anger or recrimination. Just a statement of fact. Then he pushed his chair out from the table and stood up. "Think I'll head back now."

The men stared after him in wonder.

When both shifts had finished eating and returned to the fields, it was time to wash the dishes, pack up the tables and chairs, and load them into the wagons. Later, they'd be taken to O'Neil's to be set up for the next day's threshing meal.

Despite the August heat, the men kept up a steady pace throughout the long afternoon. By the time the last of the bundles had been fed into the thresher and the last of the grain shoveled into the bin, the setting sun was throwing long shadows over the barnyard. The threshing machine, which had throbbed like some manic heart since early morning, went quiet at last. Eddie Nolan hitched it up to the tractor and, with a wave of his hand, rumbled off down the road to spend the night at O'Neil's before beginning the process all over again in the morning.

One by one the weary neighbors left. There were cows to be milked and chores to be done at home before they could turn in for a much-needed rest. Tomorrow's threshing would begin just as early as today's.

Maggie slumped down on the front porch step to watch them go. Her aunts were the last to leave. They hugged her father good-bye and climbed into their car with their empty pie tins and baskets. As they drove away, the first cool breeze of the evening blew through the barnyard, bringing with it the comforting fragrance of new oats in the bin.

For a long moment, Terrence stood facing the road, reveling in the quiet and solitude. The oat yield had been disappointing, but, still, not as bad as it might have been given the continuing drought conditions. There was enough to feed the stock, and maybe even a little left over to sell at the grain elevator for some much needed cash. He began to do the calculations in his head — the debt at the general store, the cost of tarpaper and shingles to repair the barn roof, shoes for the horses. If the market price would rise just a little bit, he might even have enough for new shoes for Michael and Patrick. Maybe enough to —

Suddenly, his eyes grew hard and the euphoria of that golden harvest day evaporated like the morning mist before the August sun.

No. It would not be enough. It would never be enough. The anger and shame welled up inside him. Not enough to pay off his brother-in-law and tell him to go to hell. Not enough to put his family back together. And, he admitted, not enough to give Maggie half of the advantages and opportunities that John and Nora could give her.

Suddenly, Terrence felt exhausted, even beyond the day's efforts. He looked up at the sky streaked with the gold and pinks of a summer sunset.

Ah, Elizabeth, *cushla mo croide*. How did I let it come to this? Forgive me, he prayed silently. Forgive me.

At last, Terrence turned toward the house. He stopped short when he spied Maggie half-asleep on the step, grateful that she could not read his thoughts just now. He walked over to her and crouched down.

"Well, little Magpie," he said. "Determined to be the last one standing? Up to bed with you, now. You've put in a full day."

"What about the cows?"

He chuckled. "The boys have already taken care of the cows. Whatever else needs to be done, I'll do. You go on up to bed before you fall down."

Maggie dragged herself up the stairs that she had descended with so much excitement — how many hours ago? Though it was just past 8:00 P.M., she fell into bed without even bothering to undress. She was asleep in an instant.

That night she dreamt that she saw her father dancing in a newly mown field with a beautiful lady. She was wearing a flowing white dress with a white veil trimmed in bits of real gold.

Chapter 8

September 1933

I watched this flood of people who had been once well-to-do, judging by their clothing. People used to steady work, coming in vain with their stories of five children, no work, savings gone.
        —*"School for Bums" by Mary Heaton Vorse,
        published in* The New Republic,
        April 29, 1931

Maggie stood on the chair in her bedroom as Aunt Nora, kneeling on the floor, pinned the hem of her school uniform.

"There," Aunt Nora mumbled. She removed the extra straight pins from her mouth and stuck them into the red pincushion she wore on a band on her wrist. "I think we can get one more year's worth of use out of this uniform. I swear you've grown a foot since last year. What did they feed you out at the farm this summer?"

"Potatoes and tomatoes. Lots of 'em. James always says, 'We ain't got much, but what we got, we got plenty of'."

Aunt Nora chuckled. "Well, if you keep growing at this rate, Maggie, you'll be taller than Uncle John by the end of the year!"

"Did I hear my name bein' bandied about?" John stuck his head in the half-opened door.

"Oh, come in, John. We're all finished here." Aunt Nora helped Maggie pull the prickly uniform over her head. Maggie, clad in her slip, jumped down from the chair.

Seeing the uniform, Uncle John smiled.

"Well, Maggie, I see it's that time of year again."

She made a face.

"Oh, now, you'll like third grade. Think of all the new

things you'll learn. Besides, be glad you have the chance to go to school."

Maggie looked at her uncle in disbelief.

"Glad? Why?"

"Because it helps you in everythin' you want to do in life. I had to quit school after the sixth grade to help my father on the farm. Many's the time now that I feel the lack of it." He bent down to pick up a stray pin that had fallen to the floor. He handed it to Nora, then cleared his throat.

"Since we're talkin' about school," he said, "there's somethin' that's going to be a little different this year. Well, from now on, really."

Aunt Nora hesitated for just the barest of moments as she put away her sewing kit.

"Your father and your aunt and me, we were talkin' about your education. We decided it would be best if you continued your schoolin' here in Sioux City, with you doin' so well and all. That means you'll be finishin' out grade school at Blessed Sacrament, then goin' to Cathedral High School after that. And, you'll be livin' here most of the time with Aunt Nora and me. So, we … all of us … thought it might make things easier if you were to use *Owen* as your last name instead of *Fahey*. You know, on your papers at school and such. That way there'd be no question as to who was responsible for you, or where you lived." He cleared his throat again. "In fact, your father has agreed to let Aunt Nora and me formally adopt you so the name change will be legal, and there'll be no confusion."

Maggie frowned. Adopt her? She had only a vague notion of what that meant. She'd seen a Shirley Temple movie once where Shirley was very happy because some nice people had adopted her and she got to live with them forever. But, in the movie, Shirley had no parents or family at all.

Uncle John hurried on.

"Of course, this doesn't change anythin' about your visits to the farm or your time with your family. It just means that now, well, we're your family, too."

Maggie picked up her worn calico dog from her bed, hugging it to her chest, as the anxiety rose inside her. Something was not right. There was more to this name change business, something she didn't understand. A thousand questions leapt to mind. She asked the only one whose answer she dared hear.

"So ... what name do I put on my papers at school?"

"Margaret Alice Owen," Aunt Nora replied, sounding relieved. "I've already spoken to the Sisters, and that's the name they'll be using when they call on you from now on."

"And, if you'd like," Uncle John added, "you can call your aunt, *Mother* or *Mother Nora* since now she's ... well, since she'll be takin' care of you now." His voice trailed off at the look of disapproval he got from Nora. Neither of them saw the flash of anger in Maggie's eyes.

No! Maggie bristled. Aunt Nora was *not* her mother. She had a mother — in heaven — and a father who loved her. But, if he loved her, why did he agree to let them adopt her and change her name? Why?

She wanted to scream it out, to make them tell her. But she just looked down at the ground and said nothing. Hers was a world in which children did not ask and adults did not explain; a world in which painful questions went unanswered and silent wounds did not heal.

"Well, let's not worry about all of that right now," Aunt Nora said breezily as she gathered up the last of her sewing items. "Maggie, you go ahead and get dressed for supper. I'm going to get Kirsten started on this hem. John, could you help me carry these things downstairs?"

The door closed. Maggie was alone. She didn't move for a long time. Then, still clutching the dog, she crossed to the full-length mirror on her closet door. Did it show? She stared at her reflection — the same freckles across the same upturned nose, the same wavy auburn hair, the same deep-set blue eyes. No, she didn't look any different. But Maggie knew in her heart that at the moment of Uncle John's announcement, she'd been changed forever. A last, vital connection to her family had been severed. Now, there was nothing left, not even her name. She was truly alone.

Maggie sank to the floor and buried her face into the little dog's worn coat, crying hot, silent tears into the faded calico.

In the weeks that followed, Nora and John watched Maggie with growing concern. Any attempts to involve her in preparations for school, social outings or trips to the stockyards were met with polite refusal. Maggie even turned down invitations from her friends, preferring to stay in her room, reading. Nora fretted at Maggie's continued seclusion, but John counseled patience, allowing the little girl time to work things out for herself.

When the first day of school arrived, Nora packed Maggie a special lunch, kissed her on the dutifully proffered cheek, and watched, her heart aching, as she trudged off down the sidewalk.

Maggie walked up the school steps with a knot in her stomach. Coming to school this year should've been easy. As a third grader she knew her classmates, the routine and most of the teachers. Everything was familiar to her. Everything, except herself.

Upon entering the classroom, Maggie smiled and waved at friends not seen since early in the summer, but didn't engage in the mass squealing and giggling that took place as the little girls grabbed each other by the shoulders and jumped about in their excitement.

"Maggie! Where've you been? I called you a million times." Patty plunked down in the seat next to Maggie.

"Oh, I've just been real busy ... getting ready for school and everything."

"Well, I was calling to tell you I found out we're not going to have Sister Miriam as our teacher this year. They switched her to fifth grade. We're going to have — "

"Children! I would like it quiet in here immediately."

Maggie gulped. Sister Aquinas. As if things weren't bad

enough.

Sister Aquinas was a far cry from the beautiful, soft-spoken Sister Annunciata who had been Maggie's first grade teacher, or even the grandmotherly Sister Cecilia who taught second grade. Sister Aquinas had the voice and build of an army drill sergeant, dark, piercing eyes and a double chin that she attempted, without success, to keep tucked inside her wimple. Rumors circulated among the students that before she became a nun, she'd been a gun moll with Al Capone's gang, and had even done some jail time. But Maggie was pretty sure it wasn't true.

Sister Aquinas began to call the roll, directing the children to their assigned seats. Maggie stood, lost in thought. All of a sudden, she realized that the droning baritone had ceased. The classroom was hushed.

"Margaret Alice Owen!" Sister repeated louder, peering over her glasses at Maggie.

"Oh! Present," Maggie replied in a thin voice. There was a surprised buzzing from the children in the classroom. Patty, standing in front of her, turned and gave her a puzzled look.

"Quiet!" Sister Aquinas barked. The room snapped to attention. "Margaret, take your seat over there." She continued with the roll. "Maria Pacelli, Jimmy Patterson, Timothy Reilly — "

Maggie, red-faced, stared down at her desk. She hadn't told anyone about her name change, not even Patty. Now Sister Aquinas had announced it to the whole world. She knew her friends would be full of questions at recess. And she had no idea what to say.

Sure enough, as soon as the bell rang, she was surrounded by a cluster of girls.

"Maggie, why did Sister call you Margaret *Owen?*" asked Tina Higgins.

"Yeah. I thought your name was *Fahey,*" chimed someone else. The other girls nodded, waiting for her response.

Maggie feigned indifference.

"My daddy and my uncle just wanted me to use *Owen* while I'm going here to school. Just so everyone knows who takes care of me."

"You mean your daddy isn't going to take care of you anymore?" Tina persisted.

"Of course he is, stupid." Patty turned on Tina. "He's still her father. The Owens just take care of Maggie while she's in Sioux City. She goes home every summer, you know."

Tina bristled. "Well, my Mom said that Maggie's daddy had too many kids to take care of, so he gave her to Mr. and Mrs. Owen to keep. So there."

"Yeah? Well your Mom's just an old busybody."

"Oh! I'm telling Sister what you said."

"You do and you'll be sorry." Patty curled her hand into a fist.

"I'm not afraid of you." Tina backed slowly toward the door. "Besides, what do I care what silly old name Maggie wants to use. It's no skin off my nose." Turning to the girls beside her, Tina announced with as much bravado as she could muster, "Come on. Let's go out to the playground."

After they'd gone, Patty turned to Maggie.

"Maggie? You wanna go outside and play or something?"

"In a minute. I ... I need to straighten up my desk first."

"Okay." With a last sympathetic look at Maggie's bowed head, Patty shuffled out the door.

Almost at once, Maggie regretted her decision to linger, for she saw, too late, that Sister Aquinas was bearing down on her.

"Maggie, I'd like a word with you."

"Yes, Sister."

Sister Aquinas grabbed the chair of the desk in front of Maggie, turned it around, and lowered her large frame onto it. Her brown robes flowed over and around the small chair, giving the impression that she was suspended in mid-air. Maggie steeled herself for a scolding.

"Maggie, do you know who Abraham Lincoln is?"

Maggie looked up in surprise. "Why ... yes, Sister. He was the President who freed the slaves."

"Yes, that's right. But, I'll bet you didn't know that he was also a devoted father and husband. He and Mrs. Lincoln had five children whom they loved very much. Tragically, one of them died at birth. Another, a nine-year-old boy, died from an illness during the time that Mr. Lincoln was President. How do you think that made him feel?"

Maggie, trying in vain to discover the point of this impromptu history lesson, ventured, "Sad?"

"Yes, sad. Very sad. I'm sure it was very hard for Mr. Lincoln to go on performing his duties as President while he was grieving for his little boy. But, he didn't lose heart, nor did he lose sight of what had to be done to save our country. Instead of feeling sorry for himself, he focused on the things that were good in his life — his other children, his wife and the rightness of his cause. His philosophy was, *Most people are just about as happy as they make up their minds to be.*"

Sister Aquinas placed her coarse hand on Maggie's arm. Her voice remained brusque, but her eyes were kind.

"Maggie, a lot of bad things can and do happen to people, through no fault of their own. Some people rise above it. Some people don't. You have to decide which kind of person you want to be. I know you've been given a cross to bear, losing your mother and having to leave your home. But, you have a roof over your head, food to eat and an aunt and uncle who love you very much. You can spend your life feeling sorry for yourself and wishing after what's gone, or you can pray to the Lord for strength and look for the good things in life as it is. It's up to you."

Sister Aquinas stood up.

"Now, finish whatever it is you're doing and go out for recess. It's a beautiful day. Enjoy it." Sister smoothed her habit into place and lumbered out of the room.

Maggie's days resumed their familiar pattern of school, friends and piano lessons, almost as before. But there was still a reserve about her, a part of Maggie that resisted any attempts by her aunt and uncle to get too close. Nora worried they'd never regain the easy familiarity of those years before the adoption. She waited and prayed, wrestling with her fear – and her guilt.

Over breakfast one Saturday morning in late September, John told Nora he needed to run down to the stockyards for a few hours.

"Can I go, too?" asked Maggie without looking up from her cornflakes.

John and Nora's eyes met over the top of the little girl's head.

"Sure," John answered, trying to sound casual. "Go change out of your pajamas. I'll meet you at the car."

"Oh, John," said Nora in a hopeful voice after Maggie left the room.

John gave his wife's hand a squeeze.

"See," he said. "It's going to be all right."

Pulling up in front of the Livestock Exchange Building that morning, Maggie realized how much she'd missed the place.

"Well, look who's back."

"Hey, Maggie. Where ya been?'

"'Bout time ya showed up. The cows have been askin' for ya."

Maggie blushed at the warm welcome she got from the stockyard workers. She returned their greetings with a timid smile.

"I've got three phone calls to return this morning," Uncle John informed her after checking the notes on his desk. "Think you can find somethin' to do for an hour or so?"

"Sure. I think I'll go down to the pens."

Ever since she turned eight last August, Uncle John had allowed her to go to the pens by herself. When a train came in, Maggie would scamper down the elevated walkway connecting the Exchange Building to the pens to see the new stock. Each pen was skirted by a wide flat board that the handlers would walk to throw hay down to the cattle. Maggie could traverse the entire length of the stockyard balancing on these boards, her feet just inches above the heads of the placid cows. The Herefords were her favorite. She liked to talk to their upturned white faces as she tight-roped along.

Maggie was such a common sight around the pens that nobody paid her any mind. This cloak of invisibility enabled her to eavesdrop on the various groups of sellers and buyers clustered about the yards. The stockyards were a microcosm of the immigrant population who lived in the little country towns in and around Sioux City. Many of these towns were made up of tight-knit groups of first-and second-generation immigrants, each clinging to the customs and ways of their homelands. When these ethnic farmers came to Sioux City to buy and sell their livestock, Maggie liked to make a game of counting the number of different accents and languages she could hear in one day. One week, she'd heard cattle prices being discussed in German, Polish and Norwegian. She decided to see if she could top that record today.

As she reached the end of one pen, Maggie saw Mr. Branard, one of the commission men who worked with her Uncle John, leaning over the rail of a pen of Aberdeen cattle. Next to him was a wizened old farmer dressed in coveralls and a faded felt hat. The farmer smoked a dark wooden pipe as he watched the cattle being separated by one of the men on horseback. Mr. Branard looked up and saw her.

"Hello, Maggie. Haven't seen you in a while. Where've you been?"

"Hi, Mr. Branard." Maggie sat down on the rail of the pen.

"Mr. Swenson, this here's Maggie Owen, stockyards mascot and champion fence walker."

The man considered Maggie over the bowl of his pipe.

"You are John Owen's little girl, yah?"

Maggie, unwilling to explain the particulars of her situation to a total stranger, just nodded.

Mr. Swenson grunted in approval.

"Gut man. Honest. Get you fair deal."

The man watched while the last of the cattle were selected, puffing silently on his pipe. Then he shook Mr. Branard's hand, tipped his hat to Maggie and walked away. Mr. Branard walked over to Maggie.

"That man just paid your uncle a big compliment. He's from Orange City, about sixty miles northeast of here. They're a tight bunch up there, Scandinavians, the lot of 'em. Strictly Lutherans. They don't take much to outsiders. But your uncle's business has always been welcome there, though he's as Irish as Paddy's pig — and a Catholic to boot. That's what comes from fair dealin'. The name *Owen* stands for something around here."

Mr. Branard jiggled the latch on the gate of the pen to make sure it was secure. "Well, I'll see ya."

He tipped his hat to Maggie and headed off down the row of pens.

Maggie remained behind, deep in thought.

At exactly 7:45 A.M. on a Monday morning in early October, Maggie sat down at the keyboard of the piano on the sun porch. There was just enough time to get in her half hour of practice and make it to school by 8:30 A.M. The tedium of these early morning practices was relieved only by the thought of the annoyance she was causing Jimmy Keaton, the ten-year-old boy who lived in the house across the alley, and whose bedroom window had the misfortune of opening onto the same side of the house as the sun porch. As Jimmy's behavior toward her in school this past week had been particularly odious, Maggie decided to serenade him this morning with a rousing rendition of Czerny's exercises.

She'd just finished the second run-through when she heard the sound of the ice truck pulling into the alley.

"Oh, the card!" Leaping from the piano bench, Maggie ran to the window by the back door and propped up the numbered cardboard card that signaled to the iceman that a delivery was desired. She rotated the card so that the number 20 showed right side up at the top, the number of pounds of ice Aunt Nora had asked her to request.

"Whew! Made it!" Maggie breathed a sigh of relief. The last time she'd forgotten to put the card in the window, the milk had gone bad before they could get more ice brought in. She hadn't been allowed to play with her friends after school for a whole week.

Maggie watched out the window as the iceman opened the back door of his truck and chiseled off a precise hunk of ice with his pick. Then, using a huge pair of tongs, he grabbed the heavy chunk and lifted it onto the piece of burlap protecting his shoulders.

"Iceman!" he sang out as he made his way up the back steps of the house.

"I'll get it," Maggie called to her aunt who was still getting dressed upstairs. She opened the back door and stepped aside.

"Hello, Mr. Tolliver."

"Well, hello there, Maggie. How are you this morning? I heard you doing your scales as I drove up."

"Yes. They're finger limbering exercises." Maggie rolled her eyes. "Mrs. Sanders says I'm supposed to do them for ten minutes every day before I actually start playing."

"Well, I'm sure the neighbors look forward to it. Say, open up that bottom drawer, will you?"

Maggie opened the lower compartment of the icebox, and Mr. Tolliver slid the large chunk of ice inside.

"There. That ought to do it. Now, you be sure to check that drip tray when you get home from school. It's supposed to get mighty hot today, even if it is October."

"I will, Mr. Tolliver. Thanks." Maggie handed him the money her uncle had left to pay for the ice. Mr. Tolliver tipped his hat and went out the door.

With a glance at the clock, Maggie headed back to the piano. No sooner had her hands touched the keys, however, than she heard a knock at the back door. "I'll never get my practicing done at this rate," Maggie muttered, returning to the kitchen.

"Did you forget something, Mr. — "

Maggie's voice trailed off as she swung open the door to find, not Mr. Tolliver, but a younger man dressed in a thin shabby coat, frayed pants and badly scuffed dress shoes. He held his hat in one hand and was attempting to smooth his unruly hair into place with the other. He avoided Maggie's eyes as he spoke.

"Excuse me, Miss … I heard the music." He cleared his throat. "I was wondering if I might speak to the lady of the house?"

"Who is it, Maggie?"

Aunt Nora came into the kitchen, buttoning the cuff of her blouse. Maggie stepped to the side, revealing the gaunt, unshaven stranger at the door.

"Excuse me, Ma'am. I don't mean to bother you. My name is Reynolds. Peter Reynolds. I was wondering if you might have some work you need to have done … in exchange for some food?"

Aunt Nora considered the man for a moment.

"Why, yes. How fortunate that you came by when you did. I offered to drive our parish priest on his calls this morning, but I didn't have a chance to get the car washed. It would be very helpful if you could wash it for me."

"But, Aunt Nora — "

"Maggie, it's not polite to interrupt."

"But — "

"In a minute, dear." Aunt Nora gave Maggie one of her *we'll-discuss-this-later* smiles. Maggie snapped her mouth shut. Turning back to the stranger, Aunt Nora continued in a business-like tone.

"It's the Ford parked in the driveway on the other side of the house. There should be rags and a bucket just inside the garage door. You'll find a water spigot there, too."

"Thank you, Ma'am." The man backed out the door and

disappeared in the direction of the garage.

As soon as the door closed, Maggie turned an accusing face toward her Aunt.

"But, Aunt Nora, you just got the car washed yesterday."

"I know that, Maggie, but it's been very windy, and the car is dusty."

Aunt Nora opened the icebox and took out some eggs and the ham left over from the previous night's dinner. She set them on the stove to cook, then went to the pantry, returning with some bread, rolls, fruit and a very large piece of pie.

"Who is that man?" Maggie asked, as her aunt turned on the oven and slipped the rolls inside to warm.

"Just someone a little down on their luck," she replied, bending down to take a big crock of butter out of the icebox. "Maggie, set a place at the table, will you, please? And see what's keeping Kirsten."

"Another one, is it?" Kirsten yawned as she made her way into the kitchen. At the reproachful look she received from Aunt Nora, she came wide-awake. She hurried to the stove to take over preparation of the eggs and ham.

Maggie stared in amazement at the table her aunt had prepared for their unexpected guest. There were rolls and nut bread, apple slices with cinnamon, sweet butter, marmalade and a large pitcher of buttermilk. There was much more there than one person could possibly eat at a sitting, and she saw that her aunt had already begun to prepare a sack for leftovers.

After about thirty minutes, Mr. Reynolds rapped on the back door. In the process of washing the car, he'd obviously attempted to remove some of the dust of the road from his own person, and looked a bit more presentable than he had on first arriving.

"I've finished the car, Ma'am."

"Well, let's have a look. Come along, Maggie."

Maggie followed Aunt Nora and Mr. Reynolds to the driveway. The car had been cleaned and buffed, the bucket put back in the garage and the rags rinsed and hung on Aunt Nora's clothesline to dry. Her aunt circled the car, running her hand along the hood, inspecting for dirt and grime.

"A fine job, Mr. Reynolds," she said, nodding her head. "You've earned your breakfast. Please, follow me."

Aunt Nora led the way toward the kitchen. Mr. Reynolds stopped at the door.

"I'll just eat out here on the stoop, Ma'am."

"You'll do nothing of the kind." Aunt Nora motioned him inside.

The kitchen smelled of ham cooking and coffee brewing. At the sight of the feast before him, Mr. Reynolds just stood there, his eyes filling with tears.

"God bless you, Ma'am," he managed at last. "You're a saintly woman."

"Go on with you," said Aunt Nora. "You've done me a service. I couldn't show up at the rectory in a dirty car, could I? Now, sit down and eat before your food gets cold."

Aunt Nora indicated the place Maggie had set at the table, then turned toward the stove to oversee Kirsten's preparation of the man's plate of food. In doing so, she caught a glimpse of the clock above the kitchen window.

"Good heavens, Maggie. Look at the time! You'll have to run if you want to escape Sister Aquinas' wrath this morning. Off with you, now. Hurry!"

Maggie took the school steps two at a time. She managed to slide into her place at her desk just as the school bell rang.

The first subject to be covered that day was religion.

"Who can tell me what the Gospel was about on Sunday?" Sister Aquinas' eyes raked the room while twenty-six heads attempted to duck out of sight.

"Anyone? No one?" Her bushy eyebrows became one as she frowned. A tentative hand went up in the third row. "Elizabeth, yes?"

"It was something about sheep and goats."

Sister Aquinas heaved a great sigh.

"Sheep and goats? Jesus talks about who will be saved and

who will burn in the eternal fires of hell and all you can remember is sheep and goats?" She looked up to the ceiling. "Give me strength, Lord."

Sister Aquinas walked to the front of the room and picked up a bible from her desk. "I will read to you from the Gospel of Saint Matthew *if* you will be so kind as to listen this time."

Then he will separate them into two groups, as a shepherd separates sheep from goats. The sheep he will place on his right hand, the goats on his left. The king will say to those on his right: 'Come. You have my Father's blessing! Inherit the kingdom prepared for you from the creation of the world. For I was hungry and you gave me food, I was thirsty and you gave me drink. I was a stranger and you welcomed me, naked and you clothed me. I was ill and you comforted me, in prison and you came to visit me.' Then the just will ask him: 'Lord, when did we see you hungry and feed you or see you thirsty and give you drink? When did we welcome you away from home or clothe you in your nakedness? When did we visit you when you were ill or in prison?' The king will answer them: 'I assure you, as often as you did it for one of my least brothers, you did it for me.'

"Oh!"

All heads turned toward the little girl whose outcry had interrupted the lesson. "Maggie? Maggie Owen! Are you all right?" asked Sister Aquinas in alarm.

"What?" Maggie started.

"Are you ill? You're as pale as a ghost."

"Oh, no, Sister. I'm fine."

"Are you sure?"

"Yes, Sister."

Sister Aquinas pressed her hand to her ample bosom to still her pounding heart.

"Well, I want no further outbursts in my classroom, then."

She continued on with the lesson, casting an occasional quizzical glance at Maggie, whose face now wore a beatific expression.

As soon as school let out, Maggie ran all the way home to tell her aunt just who it was she'd fed at her kitchen table that morning. And, while a part of Maggie remained closed off, from that day on, she began to look on her aunt with a new appreciation.

The rains came in the spring of 1934. Day after day the skies opened. The farmers, at first grateful for the life-giving water after the long drought, were soon eyeing the rain laden clouds with apprehension. The downpour was too much, too fast for the land to absorb, and the farmers watched helplessly while what was left of their precious topsoil ran off in ever deepening, muddy streams.

Thursday, the seventh of June, found Maggie at the parlor window, head in hand, watching the rivulets of water stutter their way down the glass. School had been over for a week, but the constant rain had kept her confined indoors. She was now desperately bored. Aunt Nora sat in the floral armchair across from her, doing some needlework while her favorite classical piano program played on the radio. Over the soft music, Maggie could hear the tick, tick of the grandfather clock at the top of the stairs, counting out the seconds with excruciating deliberateness. She sighed the world-weary sigh of an eight-year-old trapped in the house on a rainy day.

Uncle John walked into the room.

"I'm off to check out things at the yards," he announced, slipping on his raincoat.

"Oh, John. Do you think that's wise?" Nora asked, looking up from her tatting. "The radio reports say the Floyd is already awfully high."

"It'll be fine, Nora. The Floyd splashes over its banks almost every spring. At the worst, some cows will get their feet wet, but that's why I need to get down there. We might need to move a few of them to higher ground."

Maggie jumped to her feet.

"Can I go, too?" she asked excitedly.

"Oh, no, young lady." Aunt Nora was emphatic. "The last thing the men need down there right now is a little girl running around. Besides, it's bound to be a sea of mud with all this rain."

"Oh, please, Aunt Nora. I promise I'll be careful. I'll stay right with Uncle John and I won't cause any trouble. And, I'll stay out of the mud. Please? I'll go crazy if I have to stay inside all day."

"It's okay with me," Uncle John offered, slipping on his boots. "I don't plan to be there long."

"I don't know, Maggie. I don't think it's such a good idea — " Aunt Nora began.

"But, I'm so bored!" Maggie began to pout. Suddenly, her face took on a look of great innocence. "Well, I guess I could always invite Patty over to play, instead."

"Ow!" Aunt Nora sucked on the finger she had stabbed with her needle. "On second thought, it would probably be good for you to get out of the house for awhile and get a little exercise. All right, you may go. *If* you promise to listen to your uncle and stay out of the way."

"I promise."

"Take your raincoat and your boots. And try not to come home smelling like a wet cow, the both of you."

Liberated, John and Maggie splashed their way out to the garage and climbed into the car. With the windshield wipers beating double-time, Uncle John peered through the cleared half-moon of the windshield as he drove, narrowly missing a few raincoat-clad figures that dashed across the downtown streets.

When Maggie and her uncle reached the road that ran between the pens and the Floyd River, she couldn't believe her eyes. The Floyd, usually little more than a stream, had become a roiling, brown river, more than ten times its normal size.

"Hmm," frowned Uncle John. "Looks like we *are* going to

have some floodin'.'"

Instead of parking near the Exchange Building, Uncle John parked the car on some higher ground near the Armour plant, *Just to be on the safe side.* They walked down the hill and over the little bridge that spanned the Floyd. The rank smell of river mud filled the air. Through the heavy downpour, Maggie could see rats, snakes and other small animals scrambling out of the water onto the apparent safety of the riverbank. She shivered, clinging tighter to her uncle under the safety of his umbrella.

The new shipment of cattle had not yet come in for the week, so the stockyard pens were only half full of sodden steers, huddled together for comfort in the dreary gloom. What few handlers were about had taken shelter under whatever cover they could find. Uncle John stopped to speak to one of them. The man assured him that the cows were in no immediate danger and that, despite its ominous appearance, the level of the Floyd had actually dropped a bit in the last few hours.

Uncle John and Maggie trudged on to the Exchange Building. With most of the commission men out on buying trips, the building was almost empty. They went to Uncle John's office where he began working his way through his in-basket, while Maggie attempted to draw the picture of Red Cloud, the Indian chief featured for the month of March on the calendar behind his desk. Every so often, however, Uncle John would walk over to the bay window and look out through the gray sheets of rain to the pens and the angry river beyond.

Almost an hour had passed, when there came the sound of people running through the hallways. Bill Young from the Midwest Livestock Commission Company office down the hall stuck his head in the office door.

"Hey, John. If you've got your car parked down below, you'd better move it. The Floyd's going over."

The three of them hurried to the bay window. Looking northeast in the direction of the Swift, Cudahy and Armour plants, they could see that the Floyd River had indeed begun to spill over its banks, and was creeping towards the road that ran between it and the pens.

"Bill, round up all the boys you can find and tell them to be ready to open the pens if the water gets too deep."

Uncle John grabbed his raincoat and hat from the rack in his office. Maggie reached for hers.

"No, Maggie. If the river does fill the pens, it'll spook the cattle. That's no place for a little girl to be. Besides, your aunt would have my head if I let you go down there. You stay right here. Understand?" He stopped. "I mean it this time."

Uncle John shrugged his way into his coat, jammed his hat on his head and disappeared out the door.

Maggie, disappointed, returned to her vantage point at the window. Within moments, her uncle emerged from the entrance below with a group of men. They were all shrouded in raincoats and hats, but Maggie could pick out her uncle's head above the others. The men hurried to the pens, joining a group of stockyard workers already gathered there. One of the men climbed up onto the narrow horizontal board atop the nearest pen and peered through the gloom to the river beyond. Suddenly, he began pointing and gesturing wildly. Maggie looked in the direction he indicated. The Floyd River, now a widening, swirling, debris-filled current, had reached the road and was bearing down on the pens.

The rain streamed from their hat brims as the men huddled together for a brief conference. Then they fanned out, running from pen to pen, opening latches and swinging wide the gates in order to free the cattle before the waters reached them. The cows, their eyes wide and nostrils flaring, were too frightened to move, crowding together in whatever part of the pen was farthest from the approaching flood. The men went in after them, shouting and cracking their whips in an attempt to drive the terrified beasts out. And all the time, the water drew closer.

Just as the pens closest to the road were being emptied, the water reached them. The cattle began to bellow in fear, plunging about. Soon, the water was so deep in some parts of the yard that the cattle had to swim in their pens. Those that had been freed formed a long line of bobbing heads, splashing and swimming against the current toward the high ground beyond the railroad tracks. The water continued to rise, yet still only about half of the pens had been opened.

Maggie tried to pick out the figure of her uncle, but the confusion and the driving rain made it difficult to identify him among the desperate men working below. Suddenly, she saw a man pull himself up onto the board atop a fence and run toward the pens in the deepest water, those belonging to the Grant Livestock Commission Company. He stopped next to a pen filled with swimming cattle, the water there only a few feet below the board on which he stood. He threw off his hat, coat and glasses, and began tugging off his boots. Maggie realized who the man was just as he jumped into the muddy water.

"Uncle John!" she screamed through the glass.

The cold, chest high current slammed her uncle against the far side of the pen. For a brief moment, he clung to the rails of the enclosure, trying to regain his senses, while the frightened cattle thrashed and spun all around him. Then, with great effort, he began to make his way, hand over hand, along the fence. He reached the gate of the pen only to find that the latch was under two feet of churning, brown water. Without hesitation, he dove and disappeared under the swirling flood. Maggie held her breath, fearing her uncle would be hit by the sharp hooves of the frantic cattle swimming overhead. After what seemed an eternity, his head emerged from the water. Gasping for air, he pushed on the gate with all his might. In slow motion, it swung open through the current. Then, again working hand over hand, he maneuvered himself behind the rapidly tiring cows. Yelling and slapping the water, he turned them in the direction of the open gate. They swam out, joining the stream of cows heading for high ground.

Maggie's relief was short-lived as she realized that her uncle was preparing to do the same thing in the next pen. Again and again she watched him jump into ever-deepening water, opening gates and driving the hapless cattle out of their pens toward safety. At last, he reached the end of the alley. With great effort, he hauled himself up onto the walkway and lay there, exhausted. After a few moments, he struggled to his feet, retrieved his coat, hat and boots, put on his glasses and staggered toward the Exchange Building.

Maggie left her post at the window and rushed to the door of the elevated walkway. She got there just as her uncle entered carrying his boots. She stopped and stared. He was soaked from head to toe, his hair, face and clothing streaked with river mud and manure, his glasses splashed with rainwater. He had a bruise on his cheek from where some cow's hoof had left its mark. His wet, filthy socks left a trail behind him.

At the sight of her, Uncle John gave a tired little smile.

"Well, Maggie, looks like we'll be stayin' here till the water goes down. Good thing, too, for I don't think your aunt would let me in the house. If ever anyone looked and smelled like a wet cow, it's me."

Maggie threw her arms around her uncle, holding on for dear life.

Three days passed before Maggie, her uncle and the other men were able to return home. After telephoning their families to tell them they were safe, they stockpiled some food from the Exchange Building cafeteria and settled back to wait for the floodwaters to recede. Maggie was asleep on the couch in Uncle John's outer office when, at 10 P.M. on Friday night, the Floyd gave a last mighty heave, carrying away the concrete bridge that spanned the channel near the hog chutes at the southeast part of the yards. By Saturday noon, the flood had crested. By evening, the waters began to recede.

Late Sunday morning, the flood retreated enough that Maggie and her uncle were able to begin the slow, slippery trek home, walking along the mud-covered road they'd driven just three days before. Maggie looked around in disbelief at the devastation. The wooden fences of the cattle pens lay broken and askew, or had been swept away entirely. Dead steers, trapped against the fences by the strength of the current and drowned, lay rotting in the sun. Over by the railroad tracks, freight cars were overturned, the tracks themselves twisted by the powerful floodwaters. And everywhere was the overpowering stench of the river mud.

When at last they made it up to Seventh Street and across the bridge, a tearful Aunt Nora greeted them with hugs, kisses and a relieved, half-hearted scolding.

The people of Sioux City gathered to survey the damage. Large numbers of livestock had been lost, but the numbers would've been much greater had it not been for the efforts of the men at the stockyards that day. Clean up, repairs and the round-up of loose cattle began at once. They never did recover them all, however. Uncle John told Maggie that he suspected some of them had ended up in some hungry family's stew pot.

Not long after, the rains stopped. Hopes evaporated with the precious moisture, and the farmers of Iowa steeled themselves for another summer of drought and Depression.

Chapter 9

July 1934

Back in nineteen twenty-seven
I had a little farm and I called it heaven
Prices up and the rain came down
I hauled my crops all into town
Got the money ... bought clothes and groceries ...
Fed the kids ... and raised a big family
But the rain quit and the wind got high
Black old dust storm filled the sky.
Talking Dust Bowl Blues
      —Woody Guthrie

As the car pulled up in front of the farmhouse, Maggie's stomach flip-flopped. This was her third summer at the farm since going to stay with Aunt Nora and Uncle John, but her first time returning as an *Owen*. Did her brothers and sisters know of the adoption? What would they say? How would they act? Nervous, Maggie got out of her uncle's car.

"It's Maggie! Maggie's here!

Michael dropped the rake he'd been using in the kitchen garden and came running, Elly close on his heels. Anna's smiling face appeared at the kitchen window. She emerged, wiping her hands on her apron, just as James and Patrick trotted over from the cow barn. Maggie breathed a sigh of relief. If they knew of the adoption, it didn't appear to have affected their feelings toward her.

Suddenly, she saw her uncle stiffen. She turned in the direction of his gaze.

Terrence stepped out from the shadow of the horse barn. He made no move to cross to the chattering group. He just stood there, wiping the harness oil from his hands onto an old rag.

"Daddy," she said softly.

The voices around her stilled. Terrence stared at her for just a moment. Then he dropped to one knee and opened his arms.

"Welcome back, Magpie."

Maggie ran into his embrace. He hugged her, kissing the top of her head. With his arm around her shoulder, he walked her back to the others, halting in front of his brother-in-law. Terrence made no move to extend his hand nor did John proffer his. Glancing from her husband to her brother, Nora stepped forward.

"Hello, Terrence," she said, her voice filled with apprehension.

Although she and Terrence had spoken on the phone numerous times in the year since that fateful confrontation in John's study, they'd never discussed what had really happened that night to convince Terrence to allow the adoption — Terrence, because he'd promised not to tell; Nora, because she didn't know — and didn't want to.

Now at this, their first face-to-face meeting since that night, she feared his reaction. She hesitated, then leaned over, giving him a peck on the cheek.

"Hello, Nora. How are you?" Terrence's tone was reserved, but not without warmth. He relinquished his hold on Maggie to hug his big sister. Elly took this opportunity to grab Maggie's arm.

"Come see my new kittens." She dragged Maggie up onto the porch to peek at the mewing kittens nestled in a cardboard box.

While John, assisted by James and Patrick, carried Maggie's things into the house, Nora spoke with her brother, asking about family and friends. She stopped when John emerged from the house, the screen door banging behind him.

"Well, I guess it's time to go. Now, you be sure to call us if there's any problem."

"There won't be any problem, Nora," said Terrence.

"I know. It's just that I think Maggie might be coming down

with a cold."

"She'll be fine."

"Of course she will, of course she will." Nora fiddled with the chain of the gold locket she was wearing. "Well, I guess we'd best be off."

Maggie hugged her aunt and uncle goodbye, mindful of her father watching her.

"You be good, now." Aunt Nora smiled at her through teary eyes.

"I will."

"And call us if you need anything."

"Come, Nora." Uncle John put his arm around his wife's shoulder, gently steering her toward the car. He helped her in, shut her door for her and walked around to the driver's side. Then, just before getting in himself, he gave Maggie a wink. She smiled back, feeling an unexpected pang as the engine roared to life.

"Don't forget to write me," she called after them as they drove away.

Maggie turned around to find her father's hard eyes following the dust cloud made by the retreating car. He stood with his hands balled in his pockets and a scowl on his face. Becoming aware of her stare, Terrence looked down at Maggie. His expression softened. Squinting up at the sun for a moment, he removed a handkerchief from his back pocket and wiped the back of his neck.

"Too hot to work the horses in this heat. Good a time as any for a break." Looking at Maggie again, he smiled. "Well, young lady. You're going to have a hard time swimming in those fancy duds. Hurry up and get changed."

The other children cheered at this unexpected break from the day's routine. Maggie let out the breath she'd been holding and ran into the house to put on old clothes.

Dawn had just broken when Maggie came down to breakfast the next day, eager to explore the farm. Anna was already shuffling around the kitchen, lighting the wood stove in preparation for the day's baking. As Maggie munched on her corn flakes, she pestered her older sister with questions: What new animals had been born since her last visit? Could they go swimming in the river again after lunch? If they caught any fish, could they have them for dinner? Would they be going into town this Saturday?

In mild exasperation, Anna turned from the batter she was mixing.

"Maggie, why don't you go out to the barn and see if you can give Dad a hand with the milking?"

"Okay."

Maggie slid down from her chair and skipped out the kitchen door. Halfway to the cow barn, she heard singing. She stopped in the doorway of the barn to watch and listen. Her father, seated on a stool beside one of the cows, was chanting his way through the Latin Mass, tugging at the cow's teats in time to the music. The cow stood chewing her cud, flicking her ears back and forth as if enjoying the a cappella concert. When he turned to replace the full milk pail with an empty one, he spied Maggie in the doorway. He gave her a sheepish smile.

"Don't stop, Daddy. I like it when you sing. I think the cows like it, too."

"Yes, well, the cows are an attentive audience, but they're no good on the responses." He stood up from the stool, motioning her to sit. "Here. Do you think you remember how to do this?"

"I think so." Maggie sat on the stool and gingerly took one of the cow's warm teats in her fingers.

"There, now. Make sure the bucket's underneath. That's right. Now, it's not so much a squeeze as a stroke. Slow and firm, now."

Maggie did as she was instructed. She was rewarded by the tinny sound of a stream of milk hitting the bottom of the bucket.

"I did it!"

"Ah, you're a natural. Mind you don't tell your brothers,

or they'll be making you do all the milking from now on. You keep on. I'll get started on the next one."

They worked together, side by side, for some time, her father singing and Maggie joining in on the *Sanctus*, the *Agnus Dei* and a few of the *et cum spiritu tuo's*. By the time she finished milking her cow, her father had finished with two more.

"I don't think I'll ever be as fast as you are, Daddy," Maggie exclaimed, flexing her tired fingers.

"Oh, now. It just takes practice. You'll be beating us all before you know it."

"That's what Uncle John always says, *Practice makes perfect*."

She regretted it the minute the words came out of her mouth. Her father's genial expression turned stony. Without a word, he picked up the full bucket from in front of her, setting it with the others.

"Maggie, go tell James I want him out here right now to carry this milk to the separator. And tell him to be quick about it. It won't keep long in this heat."

"Yes, Daddy," she replied in a small voice.

He took a pair of work gloves and a hammer from a shelf on the wall. "I'm going to check on the fence around the hog pen. You'd best go in and see what you can do to help your sister."

Without meeting her eyes, he walked out of the barn.

Maggie, still sitting on the little stool, buried her face in the cow's soft side.

"Hello, there, Elly." Mr. O'Neil, their neighbor to the north, leaned out of the window of his truck. "Hey, Maggie. Heard you were back."

"Hi, Mr. O'Neil." Elly set down her pan of chicken feed, and climbed onto the running board of the truck. Maggie nodded, but hung back.

"I was just in town picking up my mail and saw there was some there for your father. Thought I'd drop it by."

"Thank you," said Elly, taking the small bundle he handed out the window.

"You're welcome. Tell your Dad I said hello, now, hear?"

As the truck pulled away, Maggie and Elly examined the items of mail. There wasn't much, mostly bills. Their father had canceled his subscriptions to *Wallace's Farmer* and the local newspaper as unjustifiable extravagances in these hard times. Then Elly spied a small envelope with familiar handwriting addressed to Maggie.

"Maggie. You got a letter."

Elly knew what a letter from Aunt Nora or Uncle John meant. Sure enough, as Maggie opened the letter, out fell a shiny coin.

"Oh, Maggie. A silver dollar!" Elly exclaimed, scooping it out of the dust. "You're rich. What are you going to do with it?"

Maggie, embarrassed, hesitated. "I don't know."

"I've got an idea. It's so hot, why don't we go buy some Koolade?

Koolade was the Fahey children's favorite drink, but at five cents a package, it was a luxury seldom enjoyed anymore.

"But, we can't right now," Maggie said. "Dad's in the field with James and Patrick, and Anna won't be back from Curran's for at least an hour and a half."

"Sure we can. Let's just saddle up Trixie and ride to the store in Graettinger. It's only four miles. We can make it there and back before anyone comes home."

A glass of Koolade would taste awfully good, Maggie thought.

"Okay."

"I'm going, too, or I'm tellin.'" Michael stood before them, hands on hips.

Elly gave an exasperated sigh. "Well, we can't leave him here by himself. I guess we'll have to take him."

Within minutes, Elly had a bridle on the reluctant Trixie, and the three children shinnied up onto the mare's broad back.

Off they went at a plodding walk, the horse's hooves kicking up little clouds of dust. Past the empty, one-room schoolhouse, on up the road they traveled in a zigzag pattern, Elly trying without success to keep Trixie from nibbling the dried blades of grass that grew on either side of the road. Six little bare feet hammered at the mare's sides in an attempt to get her to move faster, but Trixie kept to her meandering pace through the shimmering heat of the July morning.

When at last they reached the little store in Graettinger, it took them only moments to agree on buying the strawberry flavor. They scrambled back aboard Trixie with their treasure and turned for home. The mare was much more cooperative now that she was headed for the barn, even managing a slow jog once or twice. They made it back in half the time.

While Maggie put the mare away, Elly and Michael got a pitcher from the kitchen cupboard and filled it with fresh water from the pump. Maggie joined them, and they poured the pale pink crystals into the water, watching in awe as the liquid turned crimson.

"Shouldn't we add more water so it will last?" Maggie asked as Elly stirred sugar into the mixture with a spoon.

On those few occasions when the children were able to cajole their father into buying some Koolade, they'd learned to make it stretch as far as possible. They'd mix up a pitcher, drink it down half way, then refill it with water, repeating this process until the liquid left in the pitcher had just the faintest tinge of its original color and flavor.

"No. We'd better just drink it all right away. We don't want Dad to find out we spent the money, even if it was your money."

"It was Uncle John's money," Maggie corrected.

"All the more reason," Elly answered, continuing to stir.

"Let's just drink it!" said Michael.

Elly filled up three tall glasses with the bright red beverage. The children gulped it down without stopping.

Lowering her glass at last, Maggie stared at Michael in horror.

"Oh, no! Look at your lips! And your tongue! Yours too, Elly." All three of the children's mouths were stained scarlet from the sugary concoction.

"Now they're sure to find out," Maggie wailed, already dreading having to explain to her father where they got the money.

"Don't panic," said Elly. "I know. We'll just each a bunch of blackberries. That'll hide the stain. I'll clean everything up here while you two go pick some. Hurry, before Anna gets back."

That night at supper, three children sat with their heads bowed over their untouched plates of food.

"Well, how many blackberries did you eat?" Terrence asked in exasperation.

"I don't know," Elly moaned.

"I swear, one of you is dumber than the next. Well, I don't want you getting sick all over the table. Up to bed, all of you."

Michael, Elly and Maggie crawled up the stairs to their beds, their stomachs aching, but their secret safe.

Anna stood on the little back porch off the kitchen, sweat dripping from her brow, up to her elbows in hot, soapy water and wet clothes. During the summer months, she liked to start the washing right after breakfast to take advantage of what little coolness might still be in the air, but on this hot August morning the heat was already oppressive at 8:00 A.M.

Wiping her forehead on her rolled-up shirtsleeve, Anna gave the pants she was holding a few last good scrubs on the washboard. Then she fed the heavy, dripping garment through the wringer, turning the crank to squeeze out as much of the soapy water as possible before plunging it into the rinse water.

"More rinse water," she hollered.

"Coming, coming. Keep your shirt on," grumbled Elly, staggering up the back steps with a full bucket. For the last hour, she and Maggie had been hauling fresh water from the pump outside to be poured into the rinse tub or heated on the stove for the washtub. Then, when it got dirty, the water in both tubs had to be emptied — onto the kitchen garden, for each drop was precious — and replaced with clean water. The work was hard, and the girls were hot and tired.

Elly went back for more water just as Maggie shouldered her way through the kitchen door with another bucket of steaming water from the stove. While she poured it into the washtub, Anna stopped her scrubbing, pressing both hands to her aching back.

"Goodness, it's hot. Maggie, finish scrubbing this shirt for me, would you?" Anna arched her back to try to get the kink out of it. "I swear, this washing will be the death of me yet."

Grabbing the shirt with both hands, Maggie began rubbing it up and down along the washboard. "Boy, I hate scrubbing clothes. I wish we had a washing machine like Aunt Nora's," she grunted through her efforts. "It has a motor and scrubs the clothes all by itself."

"Well, Miss High-And-Mighty, we don't. And we don't have a maid, either, so you'll just have to scrub the clothes like the rest of us," Anna snapped, brushing the hair from her eyes with her forearm.

Maggie's face turned as red as her rough, soapy hands. Dropping her head, she mumbled, "Oh, Anna. I just meant — "

Anna sighed.

"I know. Don't mind me. I always get a little short-tempered on laundry day." She picked up the bucket, handing it to Maggie. "Go get some more water, okay?"

Elly passed Maggie on the way back from the pump.

"What's the matter with Maggie?" she asked, pouring another bucket into the rinse tub.

"Oh, nothing. She's just trying to adjust to being back with the peasants."

"Peasants? What peasants?"

"Never mind." Anna jerked her head toward the empty bucket. "More," she barked.

"Boy. Nobody ever tells me anything."

Elly slammed the screen door on her way out.

By 10:00 A.M., they'd finished with the laundry. Maggie was standing on an overturned bucket, pinning the last of the damp socks to the clothesline, when she heard Michael's excited cries from down near the spring house.

"Anna! Anna! Here comes another one!"

Michael was running for the house for all he was worth, pointing toward the southwest. Maggie turned and saw a huge, black cloud boiling on the horizon. It was not a rainstorm, but an enormous cloud of dust, *black blizzards* their dad called them, comprised of topsoil blown from fields maybe hundreds of miles away. These storms filled the air with stinging, blinding particles of dust, making it hard to see or breathe. When they were over, they left everything covered with a fine layer of grit.

There'd been many such storms this dry summer. The Fahey children had learned the hard way that, unless they acted at once, all of the hours of hard work that had gone into washing the clothes, cleaning the house or oiling the machinery would be undone within a matter of minutes. They sprang into action.

Anna flew out of the house.

"Dust storm!" she yelled, running for the clothesline. "Elly! Maggie! Quick. Get that laundry down and into the house."

Their father, who had also spied the oncoming dust cloud, came roaring into the farmyard with the tractor in high gear.

"Get the animals!" he yelled as he hurried to put the tractor away in the barn.

Maggie threw all of the wet laundry into the basket Elly was holding. Then she joined Michael and Anna as they chased whatever chickens, cows and pigs they could find into the nearest shelter. From the field by the river came the sound of shouting and the rumble of the fast approaching hay wagon. James was standing up in the driver's seat, yelling and slapping the reins over the backs of the startled Dan and Ruby, who thundered into the farmyard at what was for them unprecedented speed. Patrick, who'd been clinging to the back of the wagon for dear life, fell to the ground in a heap.

"James, you're going to kill those horses," his dad shouted, "and your brother, too. Patrick, unhitch the team and put them in the barn. But walk them around inside until they cool down or they'll get colic. James, help me with the cows."

Suddenly, there came a shriek that could be heard even over the rising wind.

"My tomatoes! Oh, cover my poor tomatoes!" Anna ran like one possessed toward her precious plants, clutching an armful of burlap sacks. Maggie and Elly rushed to help her cover the tender vegetation as the cloud moved ever closer.

At last, with the wind increasing and the first grains of dust beginning to sting their faces, their dad yelled, "Everyone! Into the house!"

They stumbled in through the back door, stamping and coughing. Still, there was more to be done to ward off the storm. Anna hurried to the sink and began wetting the strips of rags she'd stacked there. Well drilled, the rest of the children took them and ran throughout the house, closing the windows and doors, and stuffing the damp rags against each sill and doorjamb in an attempt to seal out the dust. This accomplished, all they could do was sit and wait.

The family gathered in the kitchen, listening to the howling of the wind and the ticking of the fine particles of dirt against the house. In silence they read, played cards or sat lost in their own thoughts.

"You know," commented their father, his voice jarring in the quiet, "the papers say that the dust storms in Oklahoma and Kansas are much worse than the ones in Iowa. They say that sometimes the cattle get so buried in the stuff that they suffocate, and people get lost and wander around till they die."

"A cheery thought," remarked Anna.

They fell silent again. Then, little by little, the storm lessened. Terrence stood and peered out the brightening window.

Satisfied, he opened the kitchen door.

"Looks like we got away with just a little storm this time. Boys, let's go let the animals out and get back to work. Girls, you start the clean-up in here."

As they left, their shoes left footprints in the dirt that had managed to sift under the door. Anna ran her finger along the half-inch or so of powdery dust that, despite their best efforts, now lined the windowsills.

"I don't know why I ever bother to clean this place," she grumbled. "Well, come on, girls. Grab a rag or a broom."

Sweeping the dust from the back steps, Maggie succumbed to a fit of sneezing. If this was just a small dust storm, she thought, her eyes watering, what must it be like in Oklahoma and Kansas?

At the sound of the telephone, Maggie popped her head up from the book she was reading. She waited. Their phone was on a party line, and every farm on it had a distinctive set of rings that let them, and everyone else on the same line, know that they were receiving a call. One long ring. Two short. Another long. The call was for them! She scrambled up onto the step stool below the phone, took the receiver off the hook and spoke into the mouthpiece.

"Hello. Fahey's. Maggie speaking."

"Hello, Maggie. This is Mrs. Curran. Is Anna home?"

"No, Mrs. Curran. She went into town with Daddy."

"Oh. Well, is there anyone there who could drive the wagon over? I was doing my baking today and I made way too much. I was hoping your family might take a couple of these berry pies off my hands. I'd hate to have them go to waste."

"Patrick is here. He could have the horses hitched up in no time. That is, if you really want us to," Maggie replied, trying to keep the excitement out of her voice. Anna was so overwhelmed with housework that she lacked the energy or inclination to make treats like pies. Besides, no one could make a pie like Mrs. Curran.

"You'd be doing me a favor. I'll see you in a little bit, then. 'Bye."

Maggie ran to the barn to tell her brother of their good fortune.

"Pie? Great!" Patrick leaned his pitchfork against the horse stall. "But, Dad would have a fit if we went empty handed. Go down to the root cellar and get one of those jars of green beans Anna put away. I hate those things anyway. We can give one of them to Mrs. Curran by way of thanks. I'll hitch up the team."

In no time, Patrick and Maggie were on their way. As they bounced along, the sound of the wagon wheels muffled by the thick dust of the road, Maggie noticed something strange. They were traveling along one of their father's cornfields, only there was no corn. Just tall weeds and grasses.

"Patrick," Maggie asked, "how come there's no corn in this field?"

"Oh, that's one of the government fields," he replied.

"What's a *government field*?"

"It's land that the government pays the farmer not to grow any crops on."

"Why would they do that?"

"So the prices will go up. You see," he explained, "when there's lots of corn, the price the farmer can get for it is low. Not enough to live on. But, when corn is scarce, people are willing to pay a lot more for it. Corn prices have been really low for the last few years, and with this Depression on, the farmers are hurtin'. So, the government is trying to force the price back up by reducing the amount of corn that's grown. Our teacher said it's called *supply and demand*."

"I don't get it."

"I don't either, really," he admitted. "But, Dad says if it wasn't for the money the government pays him not to grow corn, he'd have a hard time making ends meet."

"Seems like a waste of land."

"Not a total waste," he said, slapping the reins over the horses' backs to get them to hurry along. "We can still cut the stuff that's growing there now and use it for bedding for the animals." He chuckled. "People call it *Roosevelt Hay*."

The Depression. It sure makes people – and the government – do strange things, Maggie thought. But, as they rounded the turn to Curran's farm, her mind turned to something much more important. Mrs. Curran's berry pies.

Maggie had put off the hated job of cleaning the disks of the cream separator as long as possible. Now, with dinner finished and night closing in, she could delay no longer. Sitting down on the side porch outside the kitchen door to take advantage of whatever breeze there might be on this hot, August night, she began the painstaking job of dismantling the apparatus and cleaning each of the ninety discs so they'd be ready for the morning milking. She'd been at the task for about fifteen minutes when loud voices from the kitchen caught her attention.

"Please, Dad. Just this one time. I haven't had anything new in so long. It's on sale. Only five dollars. And Elly could wear it after me."

"Anna, we've no money to be spending on fancy party dresses."

"It's not fancy. It's just new. And we have the egg money. I got a good price this week. There's a little left over for extras."

"Extras?" her fathered responded in an incredulous tone. "When the tractor's being held together with baling twine and the grace of the Almighty, and we've a bill at the general store as long as your arm?"

Maggie heard dishes being tossed into the sink with an ominous clatter.

"You found the money when James wanted a new pair of pants."

"*Needed* a new pair of pants — for working in the fields. A necessity. Not such fluff as a party dress."

"Well, maybe we could borrow the money from ... someone. Just this once?"

There was a long pause. When her father finally spoke, his voice was angry.

"Have you learned nothing these past years, Anna? You've seen your friends and neighbors kicked out of their homes because they couldn't pay back the money they borrowed. Did it mean nothing to you?" His voice began to rise. "Debt has been the curse of this country — and this family. It buries you deeper and deeper till there's no way out of it. Then they come and take away everything you've worked so hard for, everything that's dear to you. No. There'll be no more borrowing in this family!" He slammed his fist on the table. "And for such foolishness as a dress."

The banging of the pots and pans grew louder.

"You're not being fair," Anna insisted.

Her father snorted.

"Fair, is it? And where did you get the idea that life is fair? Is it fair that the rains don't come or that, even when they do, the prices for what a man raises are so low it's all he can do to keep a roof over his family's head? Is that fair?"

"No, but it's also not fair that I'm seventeen years old and every time I go to a dance in town, I have to wear the same worn-out old dress. No boy is ever going to take a second look at me in that horrible thing."

"Ah, so it's the boys you're after. Well, you'd be better off concentrating on your duties here at home than worrying about boys."

"Sure. Be an old maid, and stay here and look after you, James and Patrick for the rest of my life. That'd suit you just fine."

"Keep a civil tongue in your head, Anna," her father snapped. "You're not the only one who's had to go through tough times."

"No. But, I'm the only one who's had to do it in that hideous old dress!"

Anna slammed a pot into the sink, and ran out the kitchen door. She hurried past Maggie, sobbing into her apron.

Maggie watched her disappear around the corner of the horse barn. A moment later, her father burst out onto the stoop, his face red in the porch light. He stood there, scowling after his eldest daughter. Suddenly, he became aware of a presence in the shadows. He whipped his head around to find Maggie staring up at him, a dripping disk in her hand. Their eyes met, and in the split second before he turned away, she saw the anger in her father's eyes give way to something else. He lowered his head and went back into the house, the screen door closing behind him with a soft bang.

The weather continued hot and dry, punctuated by the occasional dust storm. Summers without rain were of no real worry to the younger farm children who remembered no other way. They coped by taking more frequent dips in the river. But their parents fretted and worried, toiling under a merciless sun, their desperation increasing as their crops failed and their bills mounted.

One afternoon, Maggie was out in the farmyard drawing pictures in the dirt with a stick when Anna opened the kitchen door.

"Elly. Elly!"

"She's down playing in the river," said Maggie.

"That lazy good-for-nothing," Anna snapped. "She knew I wanted her to take some water out to Dad and the boys. As if I don't have enough to do."

"I'll do it," Maggie offered, an eager expression on her face.

Anna hesitated.

"Well, all right. They're cutting and shocking the oats in the field just across the road. There's a bucket right there by the pump. Don't forget to take a cup, too."

Happy to be useful, Maggie filled the bucket with as much water as she could manage to carry. She could see her father and brothers about a third of the way across the field. Her father was driving the binding machine, while her brothers arranged the

bundled oats it spit out into tall shocks to dry. They weren't so
far away, Maggie thought. A short walk, really. No need to go
to all the trouble of locating her shoes, which she hadn't seen
for a few days, anyway. She lugged the heavy water bucket
across the road and made her way into the field.

About the time she crossed the fifth row of stubble Maggie
realized her mistake. The plowed ground made footing uneven,
and the water sloshing in the bucket kept knocking her off balance causing her to step on bits of sharp oat stubble protrud-
ing out of the ground. By the time she reached the spot where
her father and brothers were working, her feet were cut and
bleeding.

"Jesus, Mary, and Joseph!" exclaimed her father from atop
the binder, yanking on the reins. Dan and Ruby came to an
abrupt halt, tossing their heads in protest. "Don't you have
more sense than to walk barefoot through a stubble field?
Haven't we got enough worries without you cutting your feet
to ribbons?"

Maggie just stood there with tears in her eyes, her embarrassment greater than her pain.

With an exasperated sigh, her father climbed down from
the binder. His sweat-stained shirt clung to him as he knelt to
examine Maggie's lacerated feet. He shook his head, but his
voice was softer when he said, "James, carry her back to the
house and have Anna put something on those cuts."

"Yes, Dad."

James scooped Maggie up into his arms and headed for the
house.

"And, hurry back," their father shouted after him. "There's
a lot more work to be done on this sorry field, and we've precious little light left. We can't spend all day taking care of someone who won't use the good sense God gave her."

"Don't worry, Maggie," James consoled her as he picked
his way back across the cut rows of oats. "I once spent the
better part of a half an hour trying to get the horses to back
up with a drag. You should have heard Dad that time."

Maggie had no idea what a drag was or whether you could or could not back up with one, but she knew her brother was trying to make her feel better. Still, she felt miserable. She'd just wanted to prove she could be of help. Instead, she'd acted like some stupid city kid. And made her father angry.

When her dad trudged in from the barn that evening, Maggie watched in trepidation as he hung his hat on the peg by the door and slumped into his chair at the supper table. He bent over his plate, mumbled grace, and ate without speaking, except for the occasional grunted question to one of the children about whether this or that chore had been completed. He said nothing about Maggie's mistake or even inquired about her bandaged feet. She finished her meal in miserable silence.

One night not long after, Maggie was awakened from her sleep by a strange tapping against her window. So long had it been since she'd heard it, that it took her awhile to realize that it was the sound of raindrops against the glass. She slid out of bed, careful not to awaken Elly and Anna. Peering out the window through the pre-dawn gloom, she was met by a strange sight. There in the center of the barnyard was her father in his nightshirt, his arms outstretched and his face raised to the heavens, turning a slow circle as the raindrops pelted down upon him. She left her bedroom, hurried down the stairs and out the front door.

"Daddy?" she called from the porch. Her father just stood there in the rain, face upturned and eyes closed.

"Glory be to God." he exclaimed, a blissful look on his face. "Glory be to God."

"Daddy!" she called a little louder.

He turned then, and gave her a big smile. He sat down on the porch step, gathering her onto his soggy lap.

"Oh, Maggie. Isn't it wonderful? Rain!"

He hugged her. Maggie, now almost as wet as he was, could not have been happier. They sat together, listening to the rain and watching the morning sky lighten, each grateful for this cooling respite from the long, dry times.

The occasional rainstorm was not enough to undue months of burning heat, however. Soon Maggie's father and the rest of the farmers resumed their struggle, attempting to coax a decent crop out of land baked dry. The severe drought conditions which had so decimated Oklahoma and Kansas had spread to northwestern Iowa by the summer of 1934. The relentless sun and frequent dry winds robbed the land of its moisture, turning the fields brown and causing great fissures to open in the hard soil. What little rain did fall was not even enough to wash the dust from the leaves of the stunted cornstalks. The tragic irony was that now that government programs and controls had forced prices paid for farm produce to rise, the extended drought had left the farmers with very little crop to sell. Along with the rest of the beleaguered farmers, Maggie's father watched the sky for any sign of rain as the hope sown with the spring seeds began to dry up before his eyes.

After a long week of hard work, the farmers and their families looked forward to a Saturday night trip into town. They could shop, or at least window shop, visit with their friends and neighbors and take comfort in the fact that they were no worse off than anyone else. So, when Terrence suggested one Saturday that they drive into Boru after supper to go to confession and *have a look around*, the children finished their chores and were standing, dressed and ready to go, in record time.

Boru was built, as were so many of the towns, around the lifeline that was the railroad. On the north, the town was bordered by small, picturesque Lake Plover, with its picnic area and small boat dock. On every other side, Boru was surrounded by rich farmland. Depending on the season, you could stand at the edge of town and look out over newly-plowed soil so dark it was almost black, the brilliant green and gold of ripening crops, or a seamless blanket of white snow. The only things breaking the vista were the occasional homestead with its group of sheltering trees or, off in the distance, the water tower and grain elevator of a neighboring town.

Boru, itself, consisted of a main street, a town square and a few cross streets with churches, shops and businesses. At the head of the square stood the red brick courthouse, built by the early Irish founders, with a clock in its tower and a jail in the basement. Painted on the walls of its foyer was a large, gory mural of an ancient battle showing the legendary Irish hero, Brian Boru, for whom the town was named. Completing the square was the First Bank of Iowa, the post office, a drugstore, an ice cream parlor, some doctors' and lawyers' offices and the town's sole movie theater.

Boru had a Methodist Church and a small but thriving congregation of Lutherans, but most of the citizens of the town were Irish Catholic. The large gothic St. Thomas Church, which stood just off the main square, was built by Irish immigrants who had come to America to escape the devastation of the potato famine in Ireland. For these refugees, the Catholic Church was not just their religion, but their only link to a people and a homeland they would never see again. Now, nearly a century later, their descendants clung to it with a fierce devotion. The Church gave substance and structure to their lives, a force as nurturing and, sometimes, as harsh, as the land itself. In reality, these two things, the Church and the land, prescribed the daily existence of the people of Boru. *We're at the mercy of the cows and the liturgical calendar*, Patrick would mutter just out of hearing of his father as they rushed to finish the milking before heading into town for Mass on a Holy Day.

Sheltered in their Irish community, the children of Boru encountered little if any of the anti-Irish sentiment and *No Irish Need Apply* signs that had confronted their elders when they first came to this country. They did, however, inherit the clannishness and the natural wariness that had become part of the psyche of a people subjected to centuries of persecution under British rule. The people of Boru kept their troubles, as well as their triumphs, to themselves. Quick to help a neighbor, they were slow to accept help themselves. And, while they encouraged hard work and achievement, they looked with suspicion upon those who did *a little too well*, or were thought to have gotten *above themselves*. Boru was, at once, a safe and stifling place.

The town was already lively when the Fahey family arrived. Friends and neighbors strolled in front of Joyce's General Store, Flaherty's Pool Hall and McMahon's Dress Shop, women sat gossiping on benches in the main square while little children played at their feet, and a steady stream of people went in and out of the ice cream parlor.

Terrence parked the truck in one of the diagonal spaces in front of Jackman's Pharmacy on the main square. After a last minute check of their clothing, he led the children down the street and up the steps of St. Thomas' to make their weekly confession.

Afterwards, the family gathered outside, breathing a collective sigh of relief that their souls were clean and their consciences clear, for a little while, at least. Terrence reached into his pocket, pulling out six nickels. With great solemnity, he handed one to each of his children.

"There, now. Mind what you spend it on. And behave yourselves. It won't do for you to be havin' to confess at the end of the evening, too. Now, I'm off to Flaherty's to talk corn prices. James and Anna, you look after the younger ones."

"But — " Anna began.

"No *buts*. I want to leave here with the same number I came with. Now, we'll all meet back at the truck at 9:00 P.M. No later."

With that, their father strolled off in the direction of the pool hall, falling into step with some other men headed the same way.

Patrick was the first to move.

"Well, guess I'll go see who's around." He smiled at Anna and James. "It's comforting to know that the little ones are in such good hands." He sauntered off, whistling.

Anna and James exchanged desperate looks. James reached into his pocket.

"Okay, kids. Here's a nickel for an extra scoop of ice cream. Elly, you're in charge. See everyone stays out of trouble, and be back at the truck by 9:00. Got it?"

"I'm not a baby, James," Elly replied, sticking out her tongue.

"Just make sure you're back on time. Anna and I are going to go check on Patrick."

"Who do they think they're kidding?" Elly scoffed as the two older siblings hurried away. "Well, come on. Let's go take a look around."

The trio meandered down the sidewalk. In this small town, there was no concern for their safety. They knew almost everyone they saw — boys and girls from school, adult friends of their father's, aunts and uncles, distant and not-so-distant cousins. Skirting the line of people waiting beneath the lighted movie marquee to see *King Kong, starring Faye Wray*, they paused for just a moment to gaze at the toys displayed in the window of the general store, before cutting across the main square to reach the ice cream parlor. There they found Anna sitting at the counter, sharing a soda and a flirtatious smile with Terry Hagan. The look she gave them threatened to melt their ice cream, so they took their cones outside and sat on the curb, watching the passing parade of people.

Maggie was busy licking the drips that slid down the side of her cone when she heard Elly exclaim, "Uh, oh. Look who's coming."

The widow Reilly was headed right for them.

"Well, if it isn't the Fahey children."

"Hello, Mrs. Reilly," they replied in unison.

"Michael, one shouldn't talk with one's mouth full. Maggie, dear, I see you're making your annual visit to the farm. How are things in the big city?"

"Fine."

"Yes. A large city can be so mind-expanding. I myself

remember with great fondness my years in Chicago. Of course, I gave that all up to marry my dear departed Johnny. Now I'm content to stay in Boru to be near his memory."

The children just stared at her.

"It's funny," she went on, "but some people just can't seem to be happy in a small town. Your Uncle John, for instance. Big ideas, that one. Soon as he was able, he was off to find his fortune. Found it, too, I understand."

She looked at Maggie for confirmation, but Maggie said nothing.

"And your Aunt Nora," Mrs. Reilly continued, undeterred. "She fooled everyone else with her shy ways, but not me. When your uncle proposed to her, she shook the dust of this town from her feet and never looked back. Quite the fine lady, now. Busy, too, I gather, since she doesn't seem to have much time to come back and visit with family." She clucked in disapproval. "Of course, now she has her own little family to worry about, doesn't she?" She gave Maggie a meaningful look.

"What do you mean?" Elly frowned.

"Oh, my. I assumed you knew. Perhaps you should ask your father about it, dear. Well, I'd best be going home to get my rest. I always like to be early for morning Mass so I can say a rosary for my dear departed Johnny. Goodbye now, children. Give my regards to your poor, dear father." She rolled on down the street like a large black cloud.

"Maggie. Your ice cream is dripping all over your arm," Michael observed.

"Here," she said, thrusting it at her brother. "I don't want it anymore."

Elly looked at Maggie. "Maggie, what was she talking about?"

"I don't know," Maggie muttered. "Like Daddy said, she's just an old busybody. Come on. Let's get back to the truck."

At precisely 9:00, their father came strolling down the street, singing softly. James and Patrick trotted up from the direction of the train depot, smelling of cigarettes. Anna was the last to arrive, a dreamy look on her face.

"Are we all here, then?" said their father. "None of you need bail money? None of you ran off to join the circus? Well, better luck next week."

On the ride home, James, Patrick and Anna sprawled in the bed of the truck, lost in their imaginings of adventure and romance, youthful dreams that floated aloft through the gathering darkness to mix with the warm, sweetness of the summer night air. The younger children were squeezed into the cab with their father. He, too, seemed preoccupied. He drove in silence, the smoke from his cigarette curling up and out of the open car window. Elly leaned against his shoulder, her eyelids fluttering. Michael slouched against her, snoring softly with his mouth open. Only Maggie was fully awake, staring out the passenger window with unseeing eyes.

Maggie pulled the wooden door of the outhouse closed and latched it. Given the coolness of the evening and the fact that the outhouse had been moved to its present location only last week, it was not an unpleasant place to hide away, and it was the only place where she could be sure of privacy. Fully clothed, she sat on the toilet seat, rested her head in her hand, and tried to sort out the meaning of what happened that morning.

The day began as another in a series of hot, cloudless days. Elly and Maggie were assigned to gather the eggs for Anna to sell on her next trip into town. The heat had caused many of the chickens to seek out cool spots for laying, and the girls were having a difficult time locating their hiding places.

Having seen one of the Rhode Island Reds disappear into the horse barn, Maggie followed it. The interior of the barn was dim but for a single shaft of mote-filled light coming from the hayloft. Ruby and Dan were at work out in the fields, but Trixie stood dozing in the heat. The hushed quiet reminded Maggie of being in Church, and she spoke in a whisper as she assured the mare of her harmless intentions.

Starting near the door, Maggie worked her way around the

barn, searching for any temporary nests the chickens might have made. She found one White Leghorn lying in a hastily made bed of straw in the front corner of Dan's empty stall. She managed to relieve the chicken of two eggs without more than a quizzical look from the hen's beady eye. Maggie continued searching along the edge of the wall, carefully pushing aside the oat straw with her feet.

Suddenly, a pain like a knife shot through her bare foot. She screamed, dropping her basket of eggs, and fell to the floor. She clutched her right foot with both hands. A large, rust-covered nail had buried itself deep into the sole. Blood, crimson, then bright red, dripped onto the straw. At the sight of it, Maggie's cries turned to howls. Elly and Anna came on the run.

"Maggie! What happened?" Anna stood over her, holding the hoe she had been using in the kitchen garden, prepared to do battle with any varmint or foe.

Sobbing, Maggie attempted to lift her foot toward Anna.

"Oh, sweet Mother in heaven!" Anna grimaced. "Maggie, don't move." She ran from the barn, calling over her shoulder, "Elly, take Trixie and go get Dad. Then go get Mrs. Curran and ask her to come right away."

In a flash, Elly had Trixie out of her stall and was up on the startled mare's bare back. As the sound of the horse's hooves faded away, Anna returned with a bucket of fresh water, a bar of soap and a towel from the house. The bleeding had slowed somewhat, the nail acting as a plug. Maggie, with help on the way, had quieted a little, and just sat whimpering.

As gently as possible, Anna cleaned the blood and dirt from around the wound, leaving the nail in place.

"Don't you worry, Maggie. We'll have you fixed up in a jiffy."

Soon, they heard the sound of the tractor pulling into the barnyard. Their father hurried into the horse barn. Not far behind was Mrs. Curran with a bag full of bandages, towels and a bottle of iodine.

"Well now, let's see what we have here," Maggie's father said in a steady, calming voice.

Maggie gave a yelp as he examined her foot.

"Yep, that's pretty deep."

Her father washed the dirt of the fields from his hands with the soap and water Anna had brought, then wiped them on a towel.

"Anna, hold her leg still. Mrs. Curran, would you be so kind as to stand ready with a clean towel and water." He gave Maggie a serious look. "Now, Maggie, when I count three, I'm going to pull this out. It's going to hurt some, but it can't be helped, so I need you to be brave. Are you ready?"

Wide-eyed and tear-streaked, Maggie nodded. Her father, the perspiration showing on his forehead, gripped the head of the nail between his fingers.

"All right, then. One... two —"

Maggie shrieked as her father pulled the nail from her foot. Mrs. Curran applied immediate pressure with the towel. Her father examined the nail, covered with orange rust and bright red blood.

"It must have worked itself loose from one of the floor boards. We'll need to check the rest of them. Are you all right, Maggie?"

"You said you'd pull on *three*," she reproached him between sobs.

"Sorry, Magpie. I never was any good with numbers." He winked at her. "How does it feel now?"

The sharp pain of the nail had been replaced by a dull throbbing.

"Better, I guess," she sniffed.

"Good. It was pretty deep. That nail went straight in. I think we'd better get you to the doctor. We don't want you developing lockjaw."

"The doctor?!"

Everyone turned in surprise. Elly, still covered with dust from her wild ride, stood just inside the door to the barn, her hands on her hips.

"You said you hate the doctor. I step on nails and things all the time and you just brush the dirt off and tell me I'll be fine. But Maggie steps on a nail and you whisk her off to the doctor? Why's *she* so special?"

For a moment no one spoke. Maggie's father and Mrs. Curran exchanged quick looks. Anna busied herself with the bandages. Then Mrs. Curran rose.

"Come, Elly, let's put Trixie away."

She steered the indignant Elly outside to where the horse was tied, still blowing from her gallop. Without a word, Maggie's father finished bandaging her foot and carried her to the car.

The doctor cleaned and re-bandaged Maggie's foot. He gave her a tetanus shot, and sent her home with the hopeless admonition that she wear shoes next time.

When they returned to the house, Anna settled Maggie on the couch in the parlor, bringing her a blanket and a pillow to elevate her foot. Michael made her a glass of lemonade, and James and Patrick checked on her when they came in from the cultivating. Maggie would have enjoyed all the fuss except that Elly, after a half-hearted inquiry as to her condition, avoided her.

Humph! Maggie thought. She's just jealous because I'm getting all the attention. Well, too bad for her.

But, as Maggie lay there, Elly's question repeated itself over and over in her mind – *Why's* she *so special?* It wasn't so much what Elly said that bothered her, but the fact that no one — not her father nor Anna nor even Mrs. Curran — had answered her. They'd all just sat there, looking guilty. Increasingly troubled, Maggie had taken the first opportunity she could to escape to the outhouse to think.

The throbbing in her foot brought Maggie back to the present. She rested it on the Montgomery Ward catalog sitting within convenient reach on the floor. Dejected, she let her eyes wander over the walls of the outhouse. James, in one of his more jocular moods, had tacked a sign over the door — *Be It*

Ever So Humble, There's No Place Like Home.

Home. Exactly where was her home? Sioux City? She spent more of her time there, and she was pretty sure Aunt Nora and Uncle John loved her. They must to have wanted to adopt her. But they were not her real family.

The farm? Maggie swallowed hard. No. Not the farm. It was where her family was, but she was not really one of them anymore. Today had proved that. She was more like a favorite cousin, welcome, but still outside the family group. She was treated differently because she was different. Despite all of her efforts to fit in, to pretend it wasn't true, it was. And it always would be.

She didn't belong here and she didn't belong there, she realized with dreadful clarity. She didn't really belong anywhere.

Maggie felt the old terror begin to rise up inside her. She closed her eyes tight, shutting the thoughts away, far away into that place in her mind where she put all of the questions and memories too painful to deal with; a little room where hurt, loneliness and heartbreak could be kept at bay. Perhaps when she was older, she could bear to think about it. Perhaps, when she was older, she'd be brave enough to open that door.

Part 2

Chapter 10

July 1937

*The hopes of the Republic cannot forever tolerate either
undeserved poverty or self-serving wealth.*
—*Franklin Delano Roosevelt*

"Well, Miss Maggie. It's nice to see you back again."

The gray-haired porter smiled as he took Maggie's suitcase
from her aunt and lifted it onto the baggage cart.

"Hello, Mr. Julius. How've you been?" said Maggie. She
hung onto the brim of her straw hat to keep it from being
blown down the length of the train platform of Chicago's
Union Station by the hot, dusty July wind.

"I been just fine, riding this ol' train back and forth, wondering when Miss Maggie was comin' back to see me."

Julius Townsend had been a Pullman porter for thirty-two
years, the past ten of them on the Milwaukee Road line. Maggie
knew him from the many round trips she'd taken from Sioux
City to Chicago with her aunt and uncle.

"Now, Maggie," Aunt Nora instructed as Julius helped
Maggie up the temporary wooden steps to the passenger car,
"you mind your manners and listen to Mr. Julius. He'll make
sure you get your ticket punched, make up your berth and tell
you when it's time to go to the dining car."

"Yes, Ma'am."

"Do you have the money I gave you?"

"Right here," Maggie said, patting the small leather purse
at her side.

"And don't forget, Louise will be waiting for you at
the station in Sioux City."

"I won't forget."

"And if you have any trouble at all, you just ask Julius for help."

Maggie sighed

"I'll be fine. After all, I'm … "

"*Almost twelve*. I know. But *almost twelve* is not quite grown up, and this is your first time traveling alone — " Aunt Nora bit her lip. "Maybe I should go with you. They don't really need me to be at that stockyards dinner tonight."

"Now, don't you worry, Mrs. Owen," Mr. Julius reassured her. "I'll keep a close watch on your little girl."

"I'm not her little girl," Maggie said in a quiet but firm voice. "She's my aunt, not my mother."

"Sorry. I keep forgettin'," Julius apologized. Aunt Nora's face remained composed, but he saw the pain that flitted across her eyes.

"Thank you, Julius," said Aunt Nora, ignoring the awkward exchange. "I know you'll take good care of her."

"All aboard!" the conductor called. The last few lingering passengers scurried onto the train.

"Goodbye, Maggie," Aunt Nora called over the sound of the engine. "I'll see you tomorrow afternoon."

"Okay, Aunt Nora. Goodbye. Goodbye."

Maggie sat with an open book in her lap, watching the western outskirts of Chicago recede outside the window of the accelerating train.

The last few days had been fun. She and Aunt Nora had tagged along on Uncle John's business trip to the Union Stockyards. While he met with stockyard representatives, the two of them spent three wonderful days visiting museums, and shopping at the stores along Michigan Avenue. They'd all planned to return to Sioux City together today so Maggie wouldn't have to miss any more days of school, but Uncle John's business had taken longer than expected. After much pleading, Maggie had finally convinced her aunt and uncle to let her take the train home by herself.

Maggie loved to travel and learn about new places and

things. Living with her aunt and uncle these past six years had afforded her numerous opportunities to do just that. She often accompanied her uncle on buying trips to farms and ranches in Nebraska, South Dakota and Iowa. Her aunt took her on sight-seeing and shopping trips to Minneapolis and Chicago. They took vacations to Lake Okaboji. And they always took Maggie with them to the annual National Livestock Convention. She saw the Gateway Arch the year it was held in St. Louis, and took a boat trip around Lake Erie the year Cleveland was the host city. There were also less-well remembered excursions to Chicago, Omaha and Kansas City when she was younger. But, the most recent convention, just this past May in Louisville, Kentucky during Derby week, had been the best.

She and Aunt Nora spent weeks shopping for just the right clothes and Derby Day hats. They traveled on a special Derby train and stayed at the elegant Seelbach Hotel. There they dined amidst celebrities, roses and paintings of racehorses. The high-light, of course, was the race, itself. Maggie, seated between her aunt and uncle in a private box in the grandstand, had cheered War Admiral on to victory. She'd felt very cosmopol-itan and very grown up. Certainly grown up enough to travel on a train by herself.

Now, however, as the train clickety-clacked along, Maggie had to admit she was a little more nervous to be traveling on her own than she thought she would be. She was glad the train was not crowded, just a few people scattered about the car. She didn't want to have to share her seating compartment with anyone.

"Miss Maggie?"

Maggie started at the sound of the porter's voice near her ear. She returned his smile, glad to see his familiar face.

"Didn't mean to scare you," said Mr. Julius, "but it's almost eight o'clock. I thought you might like to go to the dining car for a little supper. While you're gone, I can make up the bed for you. Top bunk again?"

Maggie always preferred the top bunk, not because it was

cheaper, which it was, but because it was more fun.

"Yes, thank you, Mr. Julius."

She slid out of her seat and made her way down the aisle toward the dining car, staggering a bit with the motion of the train. With some difficulty, she pulled open the door, crossed the noisy, covered passageway between the cars and pushed open the door to the dining car. There, she hesitated. The dining car had three tables for four on one side of the aisle, and three tables for two on the other. A few of them were already occupied. A waiter came to her aid and escorted her to one of the smaller tables.

"May I get you a menu, Miss?" he asked, pulling out her chair for her.

"No, thank you," Maggie replied in what she thought a most sophisticated voice. "I'd just like a glass of ginger ale and an egg salad sandwich, please."

"Very well, Miss," the waiter answered, hiding a smile.

While he hurried off after her order, Maggie studied the elegant service on the table before her.

The Milwaukee Road took great care to ensure that its passengers on the *Hiawatha* traveled in elegant comfort. Each table was set with a white linen cloth and held a crystal vase of fresh flowers. There were silver salt and pepper cellars, and a sugar bowl with silver tongs. The linen napkins were trimmed with a band of red, with a red circle in the corner containing a silhouette of a swiftly running Indian and the scripted words *Hiawatha* in bold red letters. The plates were white with a blue inner circle on which was painted a stylized, speeding train with a bow and arrow superimposed over it. The tiny butter dish matched the dinner plate, and for just a moment, Maggie debated slipping it into her pocket as a souvenir. To distract herself from such larcenous thoughts, Maggie began studying the people around her.

At the table in the corner sat a young woman with four small children, step-staired in age, squeezed into the booth with her. She was thin and pale, with just a fringe of wispy brown hair showing below her wilted hat. Although her clothes were neatly pressed, they were faded and worn. The children were dressed in what Maggie was certain were probably their only good clothes, with their hair neatly combed and their faces clean. Under their mother's watchful eye, they squirmed but little, waiting to be served. When the waiter arrived, proffering a menu, the woman shook her head.

"Just water, please," she said in a quiet voice.

The waiter poured five glasses of water, bowed and went about his business. He pretended not to notice when the woman opened her straw bag and pulled out two butter sandwiches, which she divided between the four hungry children. The woman sipped at her water as they ate.

Watching them, Maggie felt the same pull of emotions that she experienced whenever she visited her brothers and sisters at the farm. She'd recognized early on that her life with her aunt and uncle was one of privilege, not to be talked about in front of her siblings. Hers was a world full of fancy clothes, exciting trips, concerts, museums, dinners at expensive restaurants and dance and piano lessons. If she wanted a cold soda from Toller's Drugstore, she never gave it a second thought. New shoes? Davidson's Department store had a wide selection. Such things were out of reach for her brothers and sisters, and Maggie felt guilty about the contrast between her life and theirs. Yet, at the same time, she was jealous of them. Her brothers and sisters had something she would never have. They had each other. She would gladly have given up all of her advantages to have that feeling of belonging. And *that* was something she had to keep from her aunt and uncle.

Troubled, Maggie turned her attention away from the little family, focusing instead on an older couple at the table just to her left. The woman was staring out the window, sipping her tea. The man was engrossed in his newspaper.

Maggie guessed the woman to be about sixty years old. She had silver hair and was dressed in a pale gray silk suit with a brocade collar. Her hat was a darker gray, with a large peacock feather tucked into the hatband. She wore pearl earrings, four strands of pearls around her crêpey neck and so many bracelets that she made a clacking noise each time she raised her teacup.

Her companion was a small man about the same age. He was going bald but attempting to conceal it by combing and shellacking a few long, grayish strands over his shiny pate. He was dressed in a three-piece tan summer suit and wore a blue patterned tie with a gold and diamond tie tack. He frowned down at his paper through rimless glasses, turning each page with apparent disgust.

"Hah!" the man exclaimed in delight.

"Good heavens, what is it, dear?" the woman asked.

"Roosevelt's little court-packing plan just got voted down by the Senate, 70-20."

"Oh, politics," the woman rolled her eyes. "You know I don't pay any attention to such things." She turned back toward the window.

"Well, you should. If Roosevelt had succeeded in loading up the Supreme Court with liberal judges, you would have seen a lot more of your family money being thrown away on his socialist New Deal programs.

"What I don't understand," he continued, "is how some-one with Roosevelt's upbringing, who has enjoyed all the ben-efits of his social class, could turn on big business and banking the way he did, blaming them for every no good bum who ever lost a job. Why, if it weren't for big business, there'd be no jobs."

"You're right, of course," his wife said. "Besides, lots of the rich have suffered, too. You remember Ann and Harold Glennings? When the stock market crashed, they had to sell their summer home in Rhode Island. You know, the one with the tennis courts and the beautiful pool? And they're never at the Club anymore." She sighed and shook her head. "With all of Roosevelt's make-work schemes, most of the little people are better off than they ever were. But I don't think people like the Glennings will ever recover."

"I, for one, don't think his programs have really helped anyone," her husband countered. "Just made a lot of people think they're entitled to a hand-out. Lazy people getting paid to do nothing, lazy farmers getting paid not to grow food. Paid with our tax money, I might add. I tell you, Roosevelt's destroying the work ethic of this country. Support the businessman. That's the way out of this Depression, not throwing money at a lot of good for nothing bums." He folded the newspaper and smacked it on the table for emphasis. "I'm just glad to see that there are still some of the right kind of people in government, and that they reigned in that power-hungry Roosevelt before it was too late."

"Well, I just wish they were more restrictive about letting the right kind of people on this train," the older woman said in a not-so-low voice, inclining her head to indicate the mother with her children at the back of the compartment. "Time was when that sort of person wouldn't be allowed in the dining car."

Just then, the wealthy woman noticed Maggie staring at her. Making a quick survey of the young girl's well-made, expensive clothing, she gave her an approving, inclusive smile.

Maggie quickly turned away, feeling the color rise in her face. The woman's obvious approval shamed and angered her. She was *not* one of them. How dare they think she was. And how dare they talk about President Roosevelt that way! Uncle John said he was a great man, that he'd done more to help the poor and the middle class than anyone in history. Uncle John had even worked with the local Democratic Party on Roosevelt's campaigns in 1932 and 1936. Her father was a loyal Roosevelt supporter, too. He had the President's picture, cut out of a newspaper, hanging in a frame in the parlor. That rich old couple was just snooty and mean and had no idea what they were talking about.

Suddenly, Maggie remembered the sixty acres of her father's good farmland that now stood in tall grass, acres that used to be green with growing corn. She realized with a sinking feeling that he was among those who received money from the government for letting their land sit idle. Yes, she rationalized, but only because he had to, not because —

"Here you go, Miss."

The waiter placed her food in front of her. Maggie discovered that her appetite was gone, and after a few bites, pushed the sandwich aside. She considered offering it to the woman and her children, but they'd already left the dining car. Wiping her mouth on the napkin, Maggie paid her bill and hurried from the table, anxious to be away from the self-righteous couple across the aisle.

She returned to her car to find that Mr. Julius had her sleeping berth ready. The two sets of seats, which faced each other, had been folded down into the lower berth, although Mr. Julius had not made it up since no one would be sleeping there tonight. The upper berth had been folded down from the ceiling, and made up with fresh clean sheets, two pillows and a warm wool blanket.

"How was your meal, Miss Maggie?" Mr. Julius arrived carrying the small ladder that would help her climb to the upper bunk.

"Fine, thank you."

"Here, now," he said, taking Maggie's overnight bag from her. "I'll just put this up here where you can reach it."

He set her bag in the little hammock-like shelf on the side of the upper bunk.

"There. Up you go." Mr. Julius stepped aside to let Maggie scramble up the ladder. "Now, if you need anything, you just call me. Good night, Miss Maggie."

Mr. Julius closed the heavy green curtain that closed the berth off from the corridor and went to see to the other passengers.

Maggie turned on the little light on the wall. She pulled her nightgown out of her bag, and shimmied out of her clothing. Most of the passengers changed into their nightclothes in the restroom while the porters made up their berths, but she was too shy to walk along the aisles in her robe.

When she completed the contortions necessary to get into her night clothes, Maggie said her prayers, flicked off the light and rolled over onto her stomach. Raising the shade on the window, she peered out into the darkness. Just the barest trace of moonlight lit the passing scenery. Every now and then, the lights of a far-off farmhouse would wink in the darkness. She tried to imagine who lived there and what their lives were like. Pretty much like life on her father's farm, she guessed — long days, hard work, praying for good weather and a decent price for a decent crop. Just trying to survive. She wondered how many of them accepted money for not growing anything. All because of the Depression.

The Depression. People talked about it all the time — on street corners, in the newspapers, on radio — how it started and how to fix it. The working people blamed the rich, the rich blamed the workers and everyone blamed the government for the fear and hopelessness that gripped the country. But Maggie knew when the Depression had really begun, the very day the darkness descended. The Depression had started the day her mother died. When she left the world, she took the light and the joy with her. And there was no way to fix that.

Again Maggie felt her anger rise at the smug, rich couple in the dining car. They had no idea how hard life was for that poor woman and her children, or for farmers like her father who fought every day for just the bare necessities of life. She knew because she saw it each time she visited the farm. With each passing year the buildings were a little more rundown, the clothes a little more threadbare and her father's shoulders a little more stooped. Yes, she knew. Which only deepened the sense of shame she felt for betraying him, for not having the courage to stand up and tell those rich people off. How oblivious and uncaring they were. While her father and the other farmers struggled, they rode in posh trains, dressed in their fancy clothes, dined on expensive dinners … just like her.

Maggie lay awake for a long time. It was 11 P.M. before she

succumbed to the gentle rocking of the train and drifted off to sleep.

"Miss Maggie." The voice came from just outside the curtain. "You asked me to wake you. Sioux City in fifteen minutes."

"What? Oh. Thank you, Mr. Julius."

Maggie sat up and rubbed her eyes. She pulled up the window shade to see the familiar sunlit fields of western Iowa rolling by her window. Changing into her clothes, she dragged a comb through her hair and swept the heavy curtains of the berth aside. Too impatient to wait for Mr. Julius to return with the ladder, she grabbed onto the curtain rod, stepped down onto the seat back of the lower berth and jumped to the floor.

By the time the train pulled into the station at Second and Pierce Street, Maggie was standing at the door, her bag at her side. She was relieved to see Louise, wearing her favorite fruit-encrusted hat, already waiting for her on the station platform.

Chapter 11

June 1939

Building The World Of Tomorrow
—theme of the 1939 World's Fair

The Mississippi River disappeared behind the bluffs around Davenport, giving way to the gently rolling land of eastern Iowa. From the open car window, Maggie breathed in the warm smell of summer rain coming towards them across the fields.

Fun though it had been, it was good to be coming to the end of their trip out east. The last ten days had been a whirl of new sights, smells and sounds. Maggie couldn't wait to tell her uncle and her friends all about it. She was glad she'd taken her aunt's advice and kept a journal of her experiences, for she wanted to remember it all. Her notes would also come in handy when she went to write the English paper on the Fair that Sister Bertrand had asked her to compose as part of the justification for excusing her from school. She opened that journal now, careful not to disturb her companions dozing beside her. She turned to the first page.

Friday, June 2nd

Left Sioux City this morning for the New York World's Fair. I'm so excited! Unfortunately, first we have to stop in Indiana to attend Theresa Powers' graduation from college. Mrs. Powers is one of Aunt Nora's best friends. They planned this trip together, so there's no way around it. Right after the graduation, Theresa, Mrs. Powers, her son, Lawrence — he's 16 and doesn't talk much — Aunt Nora and I will drive together to New York. We're driving Uncle John's car, the maroon Ford, because it's the biggest and we're hoping to bring back lots of souvenirs. Uncle John told us to be sure to leave enough room in the car for ourselves. Ha, ha.

I've been reading everything I can find about the Fair. The theme of it is *Building The World Of Tomorrow*. There are exhibits and rides and shows … I can't wait to get there!

Saturday, June 3rd

Arrived in South Bend, Indiana late last night and stayed at the La Salle Hotel in town. We got up early to take a walk around the Saint Mary's campus before the graduation ceremony. It's a pretty place with big stone buildings and huge old trees on the banks of a river. There were lots of girls running around, loading their trunks into cars and hugging and crying. The nuns here are members of the Holy Cross order. They wear black habits instead of brown like the Dominicans, and crinkly wimples that look like fans. I laughed when I first saw them, but Aunt Nora gave me *The Look*.

While Mrs. Powers and Lawrence helped Theresa get ready for the graduation ceremony, Aunt Nora and I took a drive around the University of Notre Dame, which is right across the highway. It's bigger than Saint Mary's and is an all boys school. I saw the Church and the football stadium and the golden dome with the statue of Our Lady on the top. When the sun shines on it, you can see it from almost everywhere.

The graduation ceremony was long — and boring! When it was finally over, we went back to Theresa's dormitory to help her pack. Theresa got mad because her mother only let her bring about half of the stuff she wanted and made her store the rest. It's the first time Lawrence smiled the whole trip. Right now, Theresa is sitting beside me, pouting.

Tonight, we'll stay in Massillon, Ohio with Mrs. Powers' sister.

Sunday, June 4th

Went to early Mass this morning, then got right on the road. Drove all day on the Lincoln Highway. As soon as we left Ohio, it got hillier and hillier. Just before lunch, we drove through the city of Pittsburgh. All up and down the river you could see big factories with tall stacks billowing dark smoke. The air was so dirty you could hardly see the sun. And people think the stockyards smell bad! Aunt Nora pointed out where two rivers — one is the Allegheny and the other is an Indian word I can't even pronounce, much less spell — come together to form the Ohio River. The Ohio doesn't look as big as the Missouri River to me, at least not here.

Once we got east of Pittsburgh, we really got up into the mountains. The skies started to clear, and I've never seen so many trees. It was very pretty, but I'm not that crazy about being up that high. I don't think I'd like living somewhere where you can never see the horizon.

We're staying in the Brunswick Hotel in Lancaster, Pennsylvania tonight. On the way into town, we passed a line of Amish people in horse drawn buggies. The men all have long beards, and both they and the boys wear wide-brimmed black hats; the women and girls wear plain dark dresses and bonnets. Aunt Nora says they don't believe in

using cars or electricity or anything like that, and
that they keep pretty much to themselves. She also
said they're pacifists, and that's something we could
use more of in this world.

Theresa seems to have cheered up somewhat. She
even talks to me occasionally. Lawrence still mostly
just grunts.

Tomorrow, we'll be at the Fair!

Monday, June 5th

What a day! We got in to New York City very late
last night, but there were still all kinds of people,
cars and taxis running around. Most of the shops
and restaurants were still open, too. Mrs. Powers
drove while Aunt Nora read the map. Between the
two of them we made it to our hotel with only a few
wrong turns. We're staying at the Taft Hotel near
the theater district. Our rooms are on the twelfth
floor, but you can't see very much out of the windows
because most of the buildings around us are even
higher. There are so many lights that you can't see
the stars.

This morning, we got up early, had breakfast in
the hotel restaurant and went straight to the Fair.
We drove over the Triborough Bridge that connects
Manhattan to Long Island where the Fair is. You
could see the Perisphere and the Trylon from a long
way off. They're bright white and look like a giant
snowball and a tall, skinny pyramid. Their pictures are
printed on everything from flags to the ticket stubs.

Even though we got there early, the parking lot
was almost full. We had to stand in line for twenty
minutes just to get our tickets to get in — they cost
seventy-five cents apiece! When we finally made it
through the main gate, it was like stepping into

another world.

The Fair is not like the county fairs I'm used to, or even like the old Corn Palace celebrations in Sioux City that Uncle John used to tell me about. It's enormous! There are buildings at the Fair representing almost all of the countries in the world, and a lot of the states and big industries. Poland's Pavilion has a golden tower, and Russia's has an enormous picture of *Uncle Joe* Stalin. But my favorite is Italy's — it has a huge waterfall that comes right down the front of the building! There are foods from all different countries and a lot of the people around us today were speaking different languages. I tried my French on a group of French tourists, but they just looked at me funny. So much for my pronunciation.

Everywhere you look at the Fair there are flowers and fountains and bands playing music. It would take weeks to see everything there is to see, and we only have a few days.

The first exhibit we went to was General Motor's *Futurama*. The lines for it were very long, but it was worth the wait. You sit in a special high-backed chair on a conveyor belt which circles slowly above a huge model of what the world might look like in the year 1960. Goodness, I'll be thirty-five years old by then! Sometimes the chair takes you in close and other times it pulls away — you feel like you're really flying over the landscape. As you look down, speakers built right into your chair explain to you what you're seeing. There were seven lane highways, trees under glass domes, sidewalks in the air and fantastic cities with huge skyscrapers. I thought it was really swell, but Aunt Nora wasn't pleased about the fact that there weren't any churches in these future cities.

When we were done, they gave each person a button that said, *I Have Seen The Future*. I think I'll give it to Sister Bertrand. That should help my grade.

Next, we went to the Ford exhibit. We got to ride in real cars on an elevated road around the outside of the building. They called it *The Road of Tomorrow*. We weren't really driving the cars, but it felt like it. I can't wait until I get my driver's license.

After lunch, Lawrence and Theresa wanted to go over to the Amusement Area, so Aunt Nora, Mrs. Powers and I walked down the main mall to the Borden exhibit. I wish my Dad could have been there. They actually put cows on a conveyor belt. The belt took them to a central platform where they hooked them up to a big machine called the *Rotolactor*. The Rotolactor milked them, electronically, five at a time! Then, they put the cows back on the conveyor belt and returned them to their stalls. Wouldn't that make quick work of milking in the morning!

There were so many other things — a giant statue of George Washington and free food at the Heinz exhibit. Aunt Nora wasn't feeling too well, so we came back a little early. She said she was just tired from all the excitement. I have to admit, I'm a little tired, too. But, I can't wait to get back to the Fair tomorrow.

Tuesday, June 6th

Today, we tried taking the train to the Fair. We took a bus to Grand Central Station and caught the special World's Fair train that lets you off at a beautiful station right on the fairgrounds. It ended up being much faster than going by car and trying to park.

First, we went inside the Perisphere and saw the *Democracity* exhibit. It showed another future city and had a very fancy light show, but, truthfully, my favorite part was riding the giant escalator that took you into the exhibit. When it was over, we stopped at the gift shop. Aunt Nora bought a snow globe for me with the Perisphere and the Trylon inside it.

In the RCA building they had something called *television*. It was like a very tiny movie screen. They said the pictures were being sent from the top of the Empire State building. On the first day of the Fair, they broadcast pictures of President Roosevelt and the Mayor of New York City at the official opening ceremony. They predict that someday, everyone will have a television in their home. Frankly, I don't see why anyone would want to look at a little tiny screen with black and white pictures when they could go to a movie theater and see a movie in color on a huge screen.

The Swift building was fun. We got to watch how they make frankfurters. Aunt Nora said she wouldn't be surprised if some of the meat they used came from the stockyards in Sioux City! That made me a little homesick.

At the Beechnut and Wrigley's exhibits, they were giving away free gum. I got some for Patty. I wanted to get some for my brothers and sisters, too, but then I'd have to explain where I got it.

One of the craziest things at the Fair was the Lifesavers Candy parachute jump ride. It was a huge metal tower with giant Lifesaver candies all over it. We didn't go on it, but you could see it from almost anywhere on the fairgrounds. People would sit in chairs attached to a parachute and be hauled to the top of the tower. Then they'd drop them. On the way down, the parachutes would open and they'd land safely. Lawrence was dying to go on it but his mother said, *Over my dead body!* She's not too happy with Lawrence and Theresa, anyway, since she found out there were *girly* shows over in the Amusement Area yesterday. I wonder if I should put that in my paper for Sister Bertrand?! Anyway, Mrs. Powers made Lawrence and Theresa stay with us all day today.

This was our last day at the Fair so we stayed until dark to see the fireworks. They were the best I've ever seen — so many colors. And the noise!

Got to get some sleep, now. Tomorrow, we're going to take a tour of New York City.

Wednesday, June 7th

I'm back in my bed in the hotel. We head back to Sioux City tomorrow. It's been a lot of fun, but I'm ready to go back.

Today we drove around New York City and saw the sights. We went to the top of the Empire State Building and looked out over the city. It's hard to believe that there are people living in all of those buildings. You could probably fit everyone in Boru into just one of them.

We saw Radio City Music Hall and the Statue of Liberty and had lunch at something called an *automat* where you choose your food from little glass window compartments. I don't think the food agreed with Aunt Nora 'cause she didn't feel too well afterward.

In the afternoon, we drove through Chinatown. On a lot of the shop doors and restaurants, there were signs that said, *Stop Japanese Aggression.* I asked Aunt Nora what that meant. She said the Japanese had invaded China and were causing all kinds of trouble. That must be why she didn't want to go in the Japanese Pavilion at the Fair.

One thing happened today that made me really mad. We were parked on Wall Street when a man came by and saw our Iowa license plate. *How's the corn out there?* he yelled, then headed off down the street, laughing. What a dope! If it weren't for the Iowa farmers, people like him wouldn't have anything to eat.

I'm glad I got to see New York and the Fair, but I'll take Iowa any day.

That was the last entry. Maggie closed her journal, laying it on her lap. Deep in thought, she watched the black clouds scudding over the cornfields outside the car window.

The World's Fair had been a magical place. They'd all been caught up in its vision of a future full of prosperity and peace. But all the way home, the newspapers and the radio had been filled with news of Hitler and ominous rumblings of the impending war in Europe.

Maggie leaned her head back against the car seat, closing her eyes. Going to the Fair reminded her of those hot summer nights at the farm when she, Elly and Michael, ignoring the thunder and flashes in the distance, would try to get in just one more joyous game of tag before the dark clouds reached them. Now it seemed that the storm was almost upon them. Maggie was as anxious as her fellow travelers to get home safely to loved ones, and prepare for a future that looked considerably less promising than the one they had glimpsed at the Fair.

Chapter 12

September 1940

*This is simply one more of those age old quarrels within
our family of nations – a quarrel arising from the errors
of the last war - from the failure of the victors of that war
to follow a consistent policy either of fairness or of force...as
long as America does not decay within, we need fear no
invasion of this country.*
    —*1939 radio address of Charles Lindbergh,
    speaking against U.S. intervention
    in World War II*

"Ladies! Ladies! Be careful on the terrazzo steps!"

Sister Dominic's warning did nothing to slow the herd of
uniformed girls clattering down the front steps of Cathedral
High School, thrilled to be finished with their first week of
school. They split off into groups of threes and fours, chattering about school and plans for the weekend. Maggie fell into
step with fellow sophomores, Sheila Nugent and Marie
LaRoche.

"What foreign language did you decide to sign up for,
Sheila?" Maggie asked, tugging at the hated celluloid collar of
her blue serge uniform.

"French. With Sister Beatrice."

"Me, too. How about you, Marie?"

"Not me," Marie sniffed. "My daddy said that since Hitler's
taken over France, there's no sense wasting your time learning
the language. I signed up for something I can really use —
Latin."

Just then, Patty Maloney skittered up along side.

"So, Maggie," she said in an all-knowing voice. "Do you

think he'll call this weekend?

"Who?"

"Who, indeed. You know very well 'who'."

"I don't. Tell, tell!" Sheila urged.

"Charlie Lewis," said Patty.

. "Charlie Lewis? The quarterback from the public school? Oooh, he's so handsome! Those gorgeous brown eyes. And those muscles!" Marie gushed.

"Patty, I don't know what you're talking about." Maggie shifted her heavy load of books to her other arm.

"The devil you don't! Mary Keely's brother, Gerry, told her that Charlie told him that he thought you were pretty and smart, and he wanted to know did you have a boyfriend or anything."

"Oh, really? Well, it seems to me that if Charlie Lewis wants to know something about me, he ought to ask me himself."

"Much good that would do him. It's easier to get the Sphinx to talk! What I want to know is, if he does call, will you go out with him?"

"That depends."

"Depends on what?"

"On whether or not he calls."

"Oh, Maggie Owen! Just see if I ever tell you anything again!" Patty stomped off in the direction of her house. Maggie knew she wasn't really mad. Even if she were, Patty couldn't hold a grudge any longer than she could keep a secret.

"Well, Maggie. See ya … and good luck!" Sheila and Maria turned off for home, giggling as they went.

Maggie frowned, continuing on toward her own house. She hated being the subject of the latest gossip. She couldn't imagine anything worse than having everyone know her business. Still, the idea that handsome, popular Charlie Lewis was interested in her was exciting — and a little scary. He was a senior, and it was quite unusual for a boy to cross the unseen yet formidable boundary of class years to date a sophomore. The fact that he went to Central and not Trinity, Cathedral's all-male companion school, made him that much more interesting and desirable. It didn't hurt, either, that he was 6'2" tall and looked like Tyrone Power. Maggie let her imagination run — going to the movies with Charlie, cheering him on at football games, being escorted on his arm to the senior dance in May . . .

"Who am I kidding?!" she admonished herself out loud. Even *if* Charlie was interested in her, and even *if* he did call to ask her out and even *if* she managed to stutter out some kind of a halfway decent reply, he would never get past Uncle John.

Uncle John always joked that Maggie could not begin dating until she was thirty, only she wasn't so sure he was kidding. And he always smiled and inclined his head toward her whenever the priest read Bishop Heelan's annual appeal for religious vocations from the pulpit.

On those few occasions when Uncle John did acknowledge the possibility that she might actually go out on a date someday, he expressed his firm desire that it should be with some *nice Irish boy from Trinity*. He'd have a fit if he knew she was interested in someone who not only wasn't Irish, he wasn't even Catholic. He couldn't see that she was a mature fifteen-year-old who could choose for herself. To him she would always be *little Maggie*. Her social life was doomed.

"Maggie. There's someone on the phone for you."

Maggie was lazing around the parlor, flipping through an old *Life* magazine while *Death Valley Days* played on the radio. The curious tone in her aunt's voice got her immediate attention.

"Hello?"

"Maggie? Hi. This is Charlie Lewis. I'm a friend of Gerry Keely's, Mary's brother."

"Yes, Charlie, I know who you are." Oh, dear. Did that sound too eager?

"Great. Well, Maggie. I've seen you around, at school and places, and I was wondering if you might like to go to a movie with me sometime. *The Philadelphia Story* is playing down at the Orpheum Theater. I've heard it's good and I thought, maybe if you're not busy tomorrow afternoon, you and I could go together."

"Tomorrow? Well, that's kind of soon. I'll have to check. Could you hold on a minute, please?" Maggie held the phone against her chest, hoping that Charlie wouldn't hear her heart pounding. Please, Aunt Nora, she thought, please say yes.

"Aunt Nora, would it be all right if I went to an afternoon movie tomorrow with a friend ... a boy ... a friend who's a boy?"

Aunt Nora, who had been close by dusting some spotless knick-knacks, managed not to smile.

"What's his name?"

"Charlie Lewis. He's a good friend of Gerry and Mary Keely's. His family lives in one of those houses next to Grandview Park."

"Does he go to school with Gerry?"

"No. He goes to Central."

"The public school?" She frowned. "Oh."

"Aunt Nora," Maggie protested in a stage whisper. "He's just asking me to go to the movies."

"Maggie, you know how your uncle feels about you dating boys outside your religion."

"Uncle John doesn't want me to date any boys, period. Please, Aunt Nora, Charlie's really nice and I'd really like to go. Please?"

"What movie are you planning to see?"

"*The Philadelphia Story.*" Maggie sensed a weakening. "It's been approved by the Legion of Decency," she added, hoping that the imprimatur of the Catholic Church's rating body would provide the necessary nudge.

Aunt Nora considered the desperate teenager in front of her. As it so happened, she and Mrs. Lewis had done some volunteer work together last year. She remembered her as a friendly, attractive woman. Mr. Lewis was some sort of executive at the American Popcorn Company in Sioux City, and he was active on the boards of many local charitable organizations. They seemed like nice people with good morals and reputations. John was on a buying trip until Tuesday night and it seemed silly to bother him about so insignificant a matter as an afternoon movie date. Besides, Maggie so obviously wanted to go. What harm could it do?

"Home by 6:00 P.M.?"

"Oh, thank you, Aunt Nora!" Maggie let out the breath she didn't know she had been holding. She composed herself. Then, in what she deemed to be her most sophisticated voice, she spoke into the phone.

"Charlie? A movie tomorrow would be fine. 2:30? Okay. See you then." She placed the receiver carefully back in its cradle, then let out a whoop.

"Oh, Aunt Nora. Thank you! Charlie's one of the most popular boys around. I can't believe he wants to go out with me!"

"Well, I certainly can. He's just lucky you said 'yes'."

Maggie smiled, but her pleased expression was soon replaced with one of horror.

"Oh, dear! What am I going to wear? There's absolutely nothing in my closet!" She bounded halfway up the stairs, then came to a sudden stop. Turning, she called over the railing to her aunt.

"Aunt Nora? Do you think perhaps we could keep this little trip to the movies a secret? Some people just might not understand and make more of it than it is."

Nora, who was already devising arguments to make to her husband, replied, "I think that would be very wise."

Charlie arrived at Maggie's door promptly at 2:30 P.M. looking fashionable in plain khaki pants, a blue cotton shirt and the brown and white saddle shoes that were so popular with all the college kids. He was in the parlor chatting with Aunt Nora when Maggie came down the stairs. Maggie thought she had never seen anyone look so handsome. After many hours of agonizing over what to wear, Maggie had chosen a blue polka dotted summer dress with short sleeves and a lace collar. At the last minute, she traded her ankle socks for stockings. They were hot for a late summer day in Sioux City, but she thought they made her look more sophisticated. Charlie's appreciative smile told her she'd made the right choice.

On the short walk to the streetcar, Charlie rambled on about the weather and mutual friends, requiring of Maggie only occasional one word replies. The streetcar arrived filled with movie-goers intent on finding relief from the heat in the air-conditioned comfort of the theater. Maggie and Charlie managed to squeeze onboard, but there were no empty seats. Grateful that further conversation was impossible, Maggie spent the short ride to the theater clinging to the overhead strap, her eyes just level with the third button on Charlie's shirt.

When they arrived at the theater, Charlie guided her to a pair of seats in the neutral area of the theater midway between the couples necking in the back and the younger kids seated in the first row. The movie must have been good because the audience alternately laughed and applauded, but all Maggie could think about was the fact that Charlie's arm was resting across the back of her seat.

When the movie let out, Charlie and Maggie stood for a moment beneath the fake icicles that adorned the theater's marquee, trying to decide what to do next. Almost everyone their age, as well as a fair number of the adults leaving the movie, recognized Charlie. They said hello to him as they passed, eyeing with great interest the young woman at his side. Maggie marveled at the ease with which Charlie handled all of this attention. She wondered again why this popular local hero had chosen her as his date.

"Brother, it's hot. How about heading over to Toller's for a soda? I could use something cold to drink."

"Yes, that'd be nice," Maggie agreed.

As they walked along together, Charlie, so talkative before the movie, said not a word. Maggie tried to think of a conversation starter.

"Well. What did you think of the movie?" she managed.

"What? Oh, the movie. I thought it was pretty good."

"Me, too. I love Jimmy Stewart and, of course, Cary Grant is so handsome."

"Yeah," Charlie replied and fell silent again.

"I … uh … I thought Katherine Hepburn looked beautiful. And she was very funny, too."

"Uh-huh."

Oh, dear, Maggie thought. What happened? He didn't seem to be having a very good time. He was probably regretting having asked her out. She bit her lip, trying to think of a gracious way to cut their date short.

"Charlie, we don't have to go for a soda. We can head back if you'd like."

"What? No. Oh, jeez, Maggie, I'm sorry. I'm being a jerk. It's just that, well, I had a little trouble enjoying the picture after watching those newsreels."

"The newsreels?"

"Yeah. All that war news, and the part about Roosevelt pushing for a peacetime draft." He shook his head. "He's just bound and determined to get us into the war."

Maggie thought back to the scenes of the bombed out cities and the refugees fleeing from the Nazis.

"But, don't you think we should try to help stop Hitler?"

"Why?" Charlie responded with unexpected vehemence. "What's he ever done to us?" At her startled expression, he softened his tone.

"Now, don't get me wrong. I think Hitler's a madman, with all his ranting and raving, but it's really none of our business. My father says that England and France brought this war on themselves because of the way they treated Germany after the last war. And he's not the only one who feels that way. Lots of people all over the country want to keep the U.S. out of the war. They've even formed a committee, *The America First Committee*. Charles Lindbergh's a member. So's that guy, Wood. You know, the guy who runs Sears, Roebuck? And they're right.

America should take care of itself first." Charlie's normally congenial expression had turned hard.

Maggie, taken aback, said nothing.

The drugstore was doing a brisk soda fountain business on this hot day. Charlie ordered their drinks and carried them to an empty booth by the window. Maggie sat in silence, staring down at her glass.

"Hey, now you're the one who's quiet. Even quieter than usual," Charlie teased. "Don't you like your soda?"

She blushed. "No, it's fine. I was just thinking about what you said, about Europe bringing this war on themselves? Maybe you're right … I wouldn't really know." She took a deep breath. "But, my Uncle John says that it's not just that the Nazis want to take revenge for losing the last war. They're trying to take over the whole world. Look at what they did to Poland and Norway. Hitler just marched in, took over and killed off anyone who tried to stop him. My uncle's no big fan of England's after the way they've treated Ireland all these years. But even he said that now, with France surrendering, Great Britain's the only thing preventing Hitler from taking over all of Europe. Don't you think we ought to help them?"

"Why?" Charlie responded. "Why do we always have to be the ones to save the world? We already bailed out Britain and France in 1918. My uncle died in the trenches in France helping them. Now they want us to come over and rescue them again?" He shook his head. "I don't want to die just because a bunch of Europeans get bored if they don't have a war to fight every twenty years. And that's who they'd be sending over there to fight, you know. Guys like me. I'll be twenty-one in just over two years. Just the right age for Roosevelt's draft."

Charlie's voice was bitter, and Maggie was surprised to see in his eyes not just anger, but fear.

Confused and upset, Maggie took a sip of her soda. This wasn't going well. Their first date and she'd made Charlie mad. He'd probably never want to go out with her again. That was bad enough. But, Charlie's words had also gotten her thinking.

He'd destroyed her illusion that the country was united in the belief that America should be the worldwide *Defender of Freedom*. And, he'd also made her realize that fighting for freedom was not just some romantic notion. Fighting for freedom meant that boys she knew were going to die. Boys like Charlie.

For a full minute, the only sound was the clinking of Charlie's spoon as he stirred his soda. At last, he lifted his head. A smile returned to his handsome face.

"Hey, let's not ruin a beautiful afternoon with gloomy talk about something that probably isn't even going to happen. Let's talk about something more cheerful, something really important. So. Who's Patty Maloney got on the line these days?"

Maggie laughed, grateful that he'd broken the tension and returned to his easy-going self. They began to talk, and as they did, the great issues of the day faded away. They were just a handsome young boy and a pretty young girl sharing a soda in a drugstore tucked into the heart of the freest nation on earth.

"Good evening, sir. I'm Charlie Lewis. I'm here to pick up Maggie."

"Good evenin', young man," said Maggie's uncle. "Won't you come in?"

Charlie, dressed in a blue blazer and a striped tie, stepped into the foyer. Under the older man's scrutiny, he stood shifting his weight from side to side.

"I'll be right down," Maggie called from upstairs.

"Why don't we wait for her in here?" said John, motioning Charlie toward the parlor.

John sat in the large wingback chair, leaving Charlie to perch on a dainty tufted Queen Ann chair. Pulling out a cigar, he cast an appraising eye over the young man.

"So, Maggie tells me you're the quarterback at Central."

"Yes, sir."

"How's the team look this year?"

"Strong, I think, sir," Charlie replied, beginning to relax.

"We lost a number of seniors last year to graduation, so time will tell how the new group performs."

"Well, Central always has a good team. Good material, good coachin' … and quite a good quarterback, I hear. Too bad, though. They could have used you at Trinity."

"Well, thank you, sir, but I couldn't have gone there."

"Oh, I'm sorry … bad grades?"

"No, sir. It's just that I'm not Catholic.

John paused in the middle of lighting his cigar.

"You're not?"

"No. My people are all Methodists. Except, of course, for Cousin Jerome. No one's sure what he is." Charlie's chuckle trailed off to an embarrassed silence at the expression on the older man's face.

At that moment, Nora swept into the room.

"Here she is!" she announced.

Both men stood and turned as Maggie entered the room behind her. She wore a full-skirted, below-the-knee, green tulle dress, just barely off the shoulder, with ruffles softening the neckline. The style complimented her willowy figure. Her long legs were shown off to great advantage in heels and silk stockings with the seams lined up perfectly in the back. She and her aunt had coaxed her dark auburn hair into an elaborate upsweep. With the addition of Nora's pearls and just a hint of make-up, Maggie looked at least eighteen years old. The effect was stunning.

John didn't know which he found more upsetting, the information he had just learned or the transformation of his little Maggie into the vision before him. Charlie found his tongue first.

"Wow, Maggie. You look sensational!"

Charlie leapt to her side to help her on with her coat. Maggie thanked him with a demure lowering of her eyelashes.

Nora, who'd been admiring the lovely young couple before her, suddenly noticed the thunderous look on her husband's face.

"Well, you two don't want to be late," she said, propelling them toward the door. "Charlie, you be sure to give our regards to your parents."

"I will Mrs. Owen, Mr. Owen. Goodbye and thank you."

No sooner had the door closed than the dam burst.

"Nora! Did you know that that young man is a Methodist?!"

"Yes, John. I believe Maggie mentioned something about that." She eased herself down onto the davenport, sinking back into the pillows.

"*Mentioned* somethin'? Nora, you know how I feel about Maggie datin' non-Catholics!" He began pacing back and forth across the parlor. "There are a lot of perfectly nice boys from Trinity she could be going out with. Why does she have to go out with this boy?"

"Because she likes Charlie, John. He's a very nice young man. This is only the third time they've gone out — "

John stopped in his tracks.

"The *third* time?"

"Just afternoon movies and soda fountain dates. Nothing serious. Tonight they're going to join his parents at the country club for an early dinner. Charlie has a 9 P.M. curfew for football. I think it'll be a nice opportunity for Maggie to meet some people outside her own circle. She can practice her social skills. Besides, I don't think they get around to the religious conversion ceremony until at least the fifth date."

"That's not funny, Nora."

"I'm sorry, John, but I wish you wouldn't worry so. Maggie is a very smart, very devout girl. She's in no danger of losing her faith because of a dinner-date with a Protestant."

"It's not her faith I'm worried about, it's her feelin's. Those country club types can be pretty cold. I just don't want her to get hurt."

"Oh, John. This isn't the 1920s, for heaven's sake. The Ku Klux Klan is not lurking in the bushes. Most of the people she'll see there tonight are friends of ours. The only thing they're going to say to Maggie is how beautiful she looks."

"That's another thing. Did you see the way she was dressed?"

"Yes, didn't she look wonderful?" Nora's expression turned wistful. "She's growing up so fast."

"Too fast, if you ask me."

Nora smiled up at him in sympathy.

"I know, John. It's hard for me to think of letting her go, too."

All of a sudden, John noticed how tired his wife looked. His frown changed to a look of concern. He sat down next to her on the sofa and put his arm around her. Nora rested her head on his shoulder.

"Well," he said, kissing the top of her head. "I guess it could be worse. He could be a Republican."

Nora hadn't the heart to tell him.

Maggie did a last check in the mirror of the ladies room of the Sioux City Country Club. She'd enjoyed driving through the city streets in Charlie's open convertible and, fortunately, not too much damage had been done to her hair. She'd been to the country club a few times for lunch with Aunt Nora and her friends, but this was the first time she'd ever been asked here on her own. And, to meet Charlie's parents! Well, she was as ready as she'd ever be. Taking a deep breath, she opened the door.

"There you are. All set?"

Charlie, who'd been leaning against the door jamb of the cloak room, straightened up, flashing her a brilliant smile. His effortless good looks made her heart flutter.

"All set." Maggie took his arm.

In the main dining room, Charlie guided her through a maze of white tablecloths and well-dressed people to a table where two older couples were engaged in animated conversation. As they approached, the men got to their feet.

"Son. We've been waiting for you," a man who looked like a shorter, grayer version of Charlie greeted them with enthusiasm. He motioned to the couple next to him. "You remember the Blairs?"

"Yes, of course. How nice to see you again." Charlie leaned across the table to shake Mr. Blair's hand, giving a polite nod to Mrs. Blair.

"And this must be Maggie," Mr. Lewis continued. "We've been looking forward to meeting you, young lady."

Maggie smiled as Charlie began the formal introductions.

"Maggie, these are my parents, Louise and George Lewis, and these are their friends, Mr. and Mrs. Blair. From New York."

"Why, Charlie, she's even prettier than you said."

Maggie blushed. Mrs. Lewis was a diminutive woman next to her burly husband and son, but there was no question that Charlie had gotten his warm smile from her. The arrival of a white-coated waiter saved Maggie from having to respond to her hostess' unexpected compliment

"Would you care for a beverage, Miss?"

"A ginger ale, please," said Maggie, taking the chair Charlie pulled out for her.

"Make that two," said Charlie.

"May I get anything for anyone else?"

"I think I'm ready for another," Mr. Lewis answered, surrendering his glass of bourbon-tinted ice cubes. "Leonard?"

"I'll join you."

"As will I," chimed in Mrs. Blair. "Another martini, please."

Mrs. Lewis shook her head no, and the waiter disappeared on his mission.

"Well, kids, I hope you don't mind. I took the liberty of ordering for you. With your curfew, Charlie, I figured that would give us all more time to talk and relax."

"That's fine. Thank you, Mr. Lewis," Maggie said.

"Well, Dad, how did the golf game go?" Charlie inquired.

"Must we talk about unpleasant things at dinner?" Mr. Lewis rolled his eyes.

"On the contrary, Charlie, your father played his usual skillful game of golf, holding back just enough to let me win by a few strokes, as a good businessman should," said Mr. Blair, chuckling as he lit his cigarette.

He was a small man, a little older than Mr. Lewis, with a receding hairline, pale blue eyes behind horn-rimmed glasses and a small, straight nose sunburned from the day's round of golf. He wore an expensive, dark three piece suit with a silk tie, and diamond cufflinks that caught the light each time he raised his cigarette to his lips.

"Held back my foot! That was one of the best rounds of golf I've ever played, Leonard, and you still beat me handily!"

"Charlie, do you play golf?" asked Mrs. Blair, idly fingering the pearl choker at her throat. Mrs. Blair was thin and long — long face, long nose, expensive rings on long fingers. She was dressed in a high-necked, lace encrusted off-white gown. Her pale, straight hair hung to her shoulders in a style more commonly seen on younger women. She reminded Maggie of something, but she couldn't quite think what.

"Just a little bit, Mrs. Blair. It's not really my game."

"Oh, I'd forgotten. Football's your first love, isn't it? How's your team doing this year, dear?"

"Central High's undefeated in its first four games," boasted Mr. Lewis.

"Central. Is that where you and Maggie met?" asked Mr. Blair.

"No," said Charlie. "We met through mutual friends. Maggie goes to Cathedral."

"Cathedral?" Mrs. Blair looked at Mrs. Lewis.

"Yes. Cathedral is the girls' Catholic High School here in the city," Mrs. Lewis explained.

"Oh." Mrs. Blair's eyebrows raised imperceptibly.

Just then, the waiter arrived with the drinks and the salad course. Maggie identified the salad fork as her aunt had taught her and began eating, careful not to drop anything in her lap. Determined to present herself as a well-mannered, mature young woman, she searched her mind for some appropriate topic of conversation. She remembered her aunt's advice, *Ask people about themselves. People love to talk about themselves.*

"What brings you to Sioux City, Mr. Blair?" she managed, her voice sounding strange to her ears.

"Oh, Mr. Lewis and I are old business associates."

"Mr. Blair owns movie houses all up and down the east coast, hundreds of them. That's a lot of popcorn!" Mr. Lewis chuckled at his own wit.

"What type of work does your father do, Maggie?" asked Mrs. Blair, pushing aside her salad after a few half-hearted bites.

"He's a farmer. He owns a farm about three hours northeast of Sioux City."

"A farmer?" Mrs. Blair brought her hand to her chest in alarm. "Oh, you poor dear! How has he fared through these difficult times? One hears such dreadful stories."

"Just fine, thank you," Maggie responded in a guarded tone.

"Maggie is living with her aunt and uncle here in Sioux City while she goes to school," Mr. Lewis explained. "Her uncle is John Owen. He owns the Grant Livestock Commission Company here in the city. Fairly influential in the community. Perhaps you've met him on one of your trips out here, Leonard?"

"Not likely. I don't spend a lot of time down at the pens."

Both he and Mrs. Blair seemed to find this quite amusing. Mr. and Mrs. Lewis exchanged a quick glance. Mrs. Lewis turned to Maggie.

"Charlie tells me that you play the piano, Maggie."

"Yes, Ma'am. I've been taking lessons since I was little."

"She's very good. I've heard her play," said Charlie, reaching for another roll.

"If I recall correctly, your aunt is also quite an accomplished pianist." Mrs. Lewis turned to the Blairs. "Maggie's aunt and I have done some charity work together. How is your aunt, Maggie? I'd heard she wasn't feeling well."

"She's fine, Mrs. Lewis. She asked me to send her regards."

"Speaking of piano," Mrs. Blair announced to no one

in particular, "last month when we were at the Met we heard a performance of Mozart's Sonata in D Major that was just, well, inspired is what it was."

She launched into a detailed, gesticulating description of the wonders of the Metropolitan Opera House. Mr. and Mrs. Lewis listened gamely, but Mr. Blair, with no effort to conceal his disinterest, concentrated on his drink.

As she droned on, Maggie realized what it was about Mrs. Blair that looked so familiar. In her jeweled choker, with her hair hanging on either side of her long face, she looked exactly like the picture of an Afghan hound that Maggie had seen in *Life* magazine a few months ago. Catching her inadvertent smile, Charlie gave Maggie a knowing look and rolled his eyes.

Mrs. Blair's monologue was interrupted when the waiter arrived with the main course.

"Ah, there's nothing like a good steak," exclaimed Mr. Blair. "One thing you people here in Sioux City do have is a first class steak. Rivals *Delmonico's*. I guess we have your uncle to thank for that, eh, Maggie?"

Maggie looked at the contents of her plate in dismay. At a loss, she began picking at the vegetables.

"Is there something wrong with your steak, Maggie?" asked Mrs. Lewis after a few minutes.

"Oh, no, Mrs. Lewis. It looks wonderful. It's just that … well … it's Friday."

For a moment, Mrs. Lewis just looked at her, uncomprehending. Then it came to her.

"Of course. How unthinking of us. George, will you please ask the waiter to come over and replace Maggie's steak with … what … a nice piece of fish, perhaps?" she looked to Maggie for guidance.

"That would be fine," Maggie answered in a quiet voice.

At the puzzled looks on the faces of her husband and the Blairs, Mrs. Lewis explained, "Catholics don't eat meat on Fridays. It's against their religion."

"Well, surely it wouldn't hurt to make an exception just

this once?" Mr. Lewis asked, a hint of irritation in his voice. "Shame to waste good meat."

"I'm sorry, I can't." Maggie wanted to crawl under the table.

"Well, no matter." He signaled for the waiter. "We'll take care of it right away."

"I'm sorry, Maggie. I forgot all about that." Charlie leaned toward her, contrite. Then he added. "But, if you're not going to eat that steak, may I have it?"

"Charlie, if I didn't know better, I'd think you'd planned this just so you could have an extra portion," his mother scolded. Her attempt at levity made Maggie feel a little better.

Charlie just smiled as he helped himself to Maggie's steak.

"No meat on Fridays? Of any kind?" asked Mr. Blair, incredulous.

Maggie shook her head.

"How odd," Mrs. Blair commented not quite to herself. "Rather like the Jews with all their funny little rules and limitations." Oblivious to Mrs. Lewis' frown, she continued. "What did you say your uncle's name was again, dear?"

"Owen. John Owen."

"Owen. We had a maid named Owen, once. That's an Irish name, isn't it?" asked Mrs. Blair.

"Yes," Maggie replied, icily. Mr. Lewis opened his mouth to speak, but not fast enough.

"Well, of course. That explains it, then. And the green dress. By the way, it looks wonderful on you, dear. So lovely with your hair." Mrs. Blair smiled at Maggie over the top of her martini glass.

Maggie felt her face flush. She struggled to swallow the food in her throat. The dress that had seemed so elegant and sophisticated when she descended the stairs at the start of the evening had now been reduced to a cheap ethnic joke.

"Eleanor ... " Mrs. Lewis began, but at a cautionary look from Mr. Lewis, she closed her mouth without saying anything further.

Charlie, with the sweet obliviousness granted only to babies, fools and seventeen year old boys, chose this moment to join the conversation.

"Actually, Mrs. Blair, Maggie's family name is Fahey."

"Oh, yes. I'd forgotten. Your real family is back on the farm. Then it's your aunt that is the blood relation. Is she your father's sister or your mother's sister?"

"Maggie's mother died when she was a little girl," Charlie informed them all with great solemnity. "Left six children behind."

Why didn't he just shut up? Maggie thought. Why didn't they both just shut up?

"Oh, dear. I'm so sorry," Mrs. Blair clucked, giving Maggie a look of pity. "But, then, of course, it's understandable. One can see how a father might not want to raise all those children on his own, even if he could manage it. How fortunate for you that your aunt and uncle were willing to take you in."

Maggie glared at Mrs. Blair. Charlie or no Charlie, she couldn't sit there one more minute. She removed her napkin from her lap and placed it alongside her plate.

"Charlie, I'm suddenly not feeling very well. Would you take me home please?"

"Now?" Charlie asked in surprise, his mouth full.

"Yes, Charlie. Now."

"Well, ... all right." He rose to pull out her chair.

"Mrs. Lewis. Mr. Lewis. Thank you for inviting me to dinner. Mr. and Mrs. Blair, it's been — " Maggie paused to steady her shaky voice, drawing on her anger for courage. "Actually, it's been a pretty horrible experience meeting you."

She turned on her heel and walked out.

Not until the valet brought the car and they were seated safely inside did Maggie allow the tears of humiliation to stream down her face.

"That mean, spiteful woman!"

"Mrs. Blair? That old bat? Is that why you left?"

"Yes, Mrs. Blair!" Maggie pulled a handkerchief from her

purse and began wiping angrily at her eyes.

"Maggie, the Blairs are snobs. Always have been. And Mrs. Blair is a lush. I just don't pay them any attention. Neither should you."

"Oh, I should just sit there and let them insult me and my family?"

"I'm sure they didn't realize they were insulting you."

Maggie looked at him incredulously. "Charlie, they made fun of my religion, my family, the way I dress — "

"Well, okay," Charlie amended, "maybe some of the things they said were a little off base."

"A little off base! Charlie, Mrs. Blair treated me like some poor, dumb mick just off the boat. And you just sat there and let her do it."

"Maggie, to be honest, when Mrs. Blair starts talking, I pretty much stop listening. I didn't hear half of what she was saying."

"Well, your parents did, and they never said a word." She gave Charlie an accusatory look. "Maybe that's because Mrs. Blair was just saying what they were thinking."

"Maggie, that's not fair. My parents aren't like that."

"No? Well I didn't exactly see them jumping in to defend me."

"Well, it's hard to get a word in edgewise with Mrs. Blair. Besides, it was a difficult situation. Mr. Blair is a big client of the company and they were my parents' guests tonight."

"And I was your guest."

Charlie sat in guilty silence. In a more apologetic tone, he continued.

"Gee, Maggie, I guess I just didn't realize you'd be so upset. Look. Some people are just prejudiced against Catholics — and the Irish. But, gosh, you name any group and there's going to be some other group that doesn't like them. You just can't let them get to you. They're not important. Me and my parents don't mind that you're Catholic."

"Don't mind?"

"You know what I mean."

"Can you honestly tell me that your parents didn't have a problem when you told them you were dating a Catholic girl?"

Charlie hesitated.

"Well, maybe a little at first. But once they knew how much I liked you — "

"See!"

"Hey, it's not like your uncle was real thrilled with you going out with me. He practically popped a blood vessel when I told him I was a Methodist."

Maggie knew Charlie was right, but she stubbornly defended her uncle.

"Well, it's just that he worries about me." Suddenly the realization hit her. "I guess he worries that I'll run into people like the Blairs," she said in a more subdued tone.

"Well, my parents worry about me, too. You being Irish Catholic doesn't matter to them, but they know that it does matter to some people, powerful people like the Blairs. People like that can make things difficult for me when I go to look for a job. I know it's not right, but it's the way things are."

The two rode in silence the rest of the way to Twenty-seventh Street. Charlie pulled over in front of Maggie's house and turned off the engine. For a long time, neither one looked at the other. At last, Charlie spoke.

"This isn't going to work, is it? Us, I mean?"

"No. I guess not."

Charlie took Maggie's hand.

"Damn." It was almost a whisper. "I just want you to know. If it were just the two of us . . ."

She raised her eyes to his. With a jolt, she realized just how young he really was, how young and how unsure of himself.

"But, it's not," she said gently. "And I don't think we're ready — either of us — to take on the whole world just yet."

Charlie leaned toward her and, placing his hand along the line of her jaw, gave her a soft, bittersweet kiss. Their first and last.

Chapter 13

December 1941

With confidence in our armed forces – with the unbounding determination of our people – we will gain the inevitable triumph – so help us God.
            —FDR's speech to Congress declaring war on Japan, December 8, 1941

That first Sunday of December dawned cold and gray without even a dusting of snow to entice the children of Sioux City out of their beds.

Half awake, Maggie listened to the church bells chime nine o'clock. She smiled, burrowing into the rumpled warmth of her blankets against the early morning chill of the room. Maggie couldn't remember the last time she'd slept in on a Sunday. Uncle John had agreed to fill in for someone as an usher at the 12:00 P.M. Mass today, otherwise, he would have had them all up and out into the winter gloom, seated in their accustomed pew by 6:45 A.M.

Maggie lounged for another half an hour before dragging herself from bed. She showered, dressed and headed downstairs. Because of the mandatory fast from midnight until Communion time of the Mass, Maggie bypassed the dark kitchen, going straight to the parlor. There she found her aunt and uncle seated in front of the fire, reading the *Sioux City Journal.* Aunt Nora smiled at her over the top of the paper, then returned to her perusal of an unusual recipe for banana bread. Uncle John, his brow knitted in a frown, was reading the news of the war in Europe. Without changing his expression, he nodded his welcome. Maggie reached for the funny papers, trying to ignore her rumbling stomach.

"Humph," Uncle John grunted after a few minutes.

"What are you *humph-ing* about now, John?" asked Nora without raising her eyes from her newspaper.

"This article, *Japanese Ambassador Negotiates With State Department.* I don't like the sound of it. They *negotiate* with us while they overrun China and Indochina. Sounds a little too much like the way Hitler *negotiated* with Chamberlain right before Germany invaded Poland."

"John, surely someone has to hold out for a better way of solving disputes short of bloodshed. You don't want the whole world involved in a war, do you?"

"Of course not. But, you don't get anywhere with a bully by making nice with him. Sometimes you just have to stand up for what you believe, and the devil take the hindmost."

"Fine talk for a Sunday morning." Nora sighed. "Look, it's less than three weeks till Christmas. Let's put aside the war talk for a little while, can't we? Maggie, how are things going for the school Christmas Concert?"

"All right, I guess. We're scheduled to sing three selections over KSCJ radio on Sunday afternoon, the twenty-first. Of course, one of them is a solo by the *great* Angela Cummings." Maggie made a face.

"Now, Maggie. Angela does has a lovely voice," Aunt Nora pointed out.

"Well, maybe, but ever since she got the lead in the school musical, she thinks she's Deanna Durbin. And, if that's not bad enough, they're making us wear our ugly school uniforms, too. I don't know how they expect us to sing in those celluloid collars."

"Well, look at the bright side," said Uncle John. "No one can see you on radio."

Maggie threw the funny papers at him.

Maggie stood at the back of the church, waiting for her uncle to finish up his duties as usher. Father Angelo, or as Maggie and her friends called him, *Father Much-Too-Slow*, had said the noon Mass today. He spoke with such deliberation that most of the congregation were jingling their pocket change in frustration by the Offertory. The Mass had taken almost an entire hour and a half.

Maggie fidgeted while Uncle John moved through the pews, collecting stray bulletins, offertory envelopes and the occasional glove. She checked her watch. 1:40 P.M. If she didn't get something to eat soon, she'd die of starvation.

Just then, she saw Aunt Nora leave her pew and go over to the small side shrine to St. Peregrine, the Patron Saint of the Sick. Lighting a candle, she knelt to pray. Maggie felt a sudden and deep sense of shame.

Three weeks ago, following months of increasing fatigue and amorphous pain, Uncle John had finally convinced Aunt Nora to see a doctor. The doctor, after a cursory examination, referred her at once to the specialists at the Mayo Clinic in Rochester, Minnesota. Nora was diagnosed as having an advanced case of breast cancer, now metastasized throughout her body. There was little to offer her in the way of treatment. All the doctors could do was prescribe various pain medications in an attempt to keep her as comfortable as possible.

John and Nora had not shared the doctors' diagnosis with Maggie, telling her only that her aunt was fatigued and needed a great deal of rest. But, Maggie could tell it was something serious by the look in her uncle's eyes, and by the spasms of pain that crossed her aunt's face when she thought Maggie wasn't looking.

Maggie pulled her rosary beads from her pocket, kissed the crucifix and began adding her prayers to those already streaming toward heaven.

As she counted her way through the decades, Maggie began to notice something odd. Although Mass had been over for fifteen minutes and there were no more Masses scheduled that day, people were beginning to drift back into the church. Some went directly to the Communion rail to kneel, others sat in the pews. A few of them were openly weeping. Aunt Nora, returning from her devotions, looked about in puzzlement. Spying

Mrs. Newton, one of the ladies from her book group, she went over and engaged her in whispered conversation.

"Oh, Lord help us!"

At her aunt's cry of alarm, Maggie rushed to her side. Nora's face was pale. Maggie, fearing she'd taken a sudden turn for the worse, grabbed her aunt's hand. It was icy cold.

"Aunt Nora! Are you all right?" said Maggie, helping her Aunt sit down.

"Oh, Maggie. They've gone and done it."

"Who? Done what?"

"The Japanese. They've attacked us. Bombed our ships. This morning. Someplace in Hawaii."

Maggie, too stunned to speak, made the sign of the cross. Suddenly, Uncle John appeared at their side. His expression was grim.

"Oh, John. Did you hear?"

"Yes, Nora. Father Angelo heard it on the radio as he was about to leave to make his sick calls. He came and told us."

"Does this mean we're at war?" Maggie asked in a tremulous voice.

"It would appear so," said her uncle. "Come. Let's go home."

Down the aisle they walked, John supporting his wife, Maggie following, while behind them the church continued to fill with stunned and frightened people.

Maggie tucked the ration book in her purse, shifting the package of ground chuck, wrapped in its heavy brown paper, into her other arm. She hated going to the butcher. Aunt Nora always insisted that she stand there and watch while the butcher ground the meat to be sure it was fresh and of the quality she ordered. Maggie felt sure the butcher must resent this close inspection. But Aunt Nora maintained that, with meat being rationed, it was more important than ever that they spend their stamps wisely and get exactly what they paid for.

Carrying the package by its string, Maggie began the

five-block walk toward home. She took little delight in the warm June breeze or the colorful flowers, for it seemed that in the front window of almost every house she passed, the houses of her childhood friends, there hung a banner with one or more blue stars, indicating that here was the home of a young soldier or sailor who was off fighting for his country's freedom. And, as of late, more and more of those blue stars had been replaced with a gold star, quietly announcing that the ultimate sacrifice had been made.

The spring had been a sad one. Singapore, the Philippines, Bataan and Corregidor had all fallen to the Japanese in rapid succession. So many of the boys from town had gone off to fight. Many had already been reported missing in action or killed — Gerry Keely, Henry Mueller and even Charlie Lewis. Poor Charlie. His worst fears had come true. Drafted early in 1942, his father's attempts to pull some strings and get him assigned to a naval base stateside had failed. In less than three months, Charlie found himself on the aircraft carrier, *Lexington*, headed for action in the Pacific. The *Lexington* was sunk on May 8th at the battle of the Coral Sea. Many of her crew, Charlie included, went down with her.

Maggie turned onto Twenty-seventh Street. There on the porch of the big white Victorian house on the corner was where George Whelan had taught her to jitterbug one hot summer night. The memory brought a bittersweet smile. George, three years older than Maggie, was never a romantic interest, but more of an older brother type who treated her to sodas at Toller's, and served as an agreeable, last minute escort whenever school dances loomed without a date.

George enlisted in the Navy the day after Pearl Harbor, eager to do his part in the war. Maggie felt her heart constrict. They received news of George's death just two weeks ago. He was killed at the Battle of Midway when the destroyer he was on, *The Hammon*, was sunk by a Japanese submarine. She, Aunt Nora and Uncle John had gone to comfort his stunned and grieving parents as soon as they heard, but it was all so strange and unreal. There was no body. No personal effects. George was just gone. All that was left was a gold star in the window.

Still, despite the tragedies, those of Maggie's friends who hadn't already been drafted or enlisted looked forward to the day they could join the fight. With reluctance, they'd heeded their parents' pleas to wait until after graduation to sign up, but they spent the majority of their remaining high school careers discussing the relative merits of the Army, Navy and Marines rather than Shakespeare, Ptolemy and Socrates.

Time seemed to accelerate as Maggie's senior year drew to a close. The parties, dances and graduation itself were filled with a special poignancy and urgency, for most of the young men were leaving for immediate enlistment in the armed forces. And everyone knew that some of them would not be coming back.

As more and more men headed off to war, life for the women left at home underwent significant change as well. Every week it seemed that another of Maggie's friends was getting married as the pending separation catapulted high school romances into marriages. Women everywhere were thrust into unfamiliar roles they could not have imagined a year before. Wives and mothers suddenly found themselves alone, left to assume the roles of mother, father and breadwinner. Women who had planned lives as secretaries, nurses or teachers, now, of necessity took over traditionally male jobs in factories, transportation, farming and government. These women soon discovered that not only did they like the work, they were good at it. They were proud to be doing their part for the war effort — and to be bringing home a paycheck each week.

Some women took part in the war effort in a more direct way, volunteering as nurses or joining the newly formed Women's Army Auxiliary Corps, called WAACs for short, or the Navy's Women Accepted for Voluntary Emergency Service, known as the WAVES. The WAACs drew a number of volunteers from Maggie's group of friends, since their Training Center was in nearby Fort Des Moines, Iowa. Maggie's sister, Anna, was in training there now.

As Maggie climbed the back steps to the kitchen of her house, she pondered the relative merits of her own options after graduation.

"Maggie, is that you?"

"Yes, Aunt Nora. It's me."

"Come on in to the sun porch. I've something to show you."

Aunt Nora spent more and more of her time on the sun porch now, wrapped in an afghan on the chaise lounge, resting and enjoying the warmth of the sun on her face. When Maggie entered the room, however, she found Aunt Nora more animated than she'd been in weeks.

"This came today." Nora beamed up at her, waving a piece of paper. She handed Maggie a letter addressed to Mr. and Mrs. John T. Owen. In the center of the top of the page was a blue shield with the words *Spes Unica,* the emblem of Saint Mary's College, South Bend, Indiana. Maggie hesitated.

"Read it, read it," Aunt Nora urged, almost giggling in her excitement.

June 18, 1942

Dear Mr. and Mrs. Owen:

It is with great pleasure that I inform you that your daughter, Margaret, has been accepted as a member of the freshmen class of Saint Mary's College for the upcoming fall.

Saint Mary's College is dedicated to the ideal of intelligent womanhood, achieved by the training of each girl's mind to the utmost of her potentialities.

We trust that Margaret will benefit from the unique religious, intellectual, social and physical environment of Saint Mary's, and look forward to welcoming her into the Saint Mary's family.

Sincerely,
Sister M. Madeleva, C.S.C.
President, Saint Mary's College

"Isn't it wonderful?" Aunt Nora gushed. "Oh, Maggie. I'm so proud of you. I can't wait to tell Uncle John."

Maggie frowned down at the letter.

"What is it, dear?" asked Aunt Nora, reaching for her hand. "Aren't you happy about being accepted?"

"Well, yes, but — " Maggie couldn't help but notice how frail her aunt's hand felt in hers. "I just wonder whether maybe I shouldn't wait another year or so. Going to college seems so, I don't know, so unimportant right now, with the war on. Most of my friends are enlisting right after school or going to work for the war effort. A lot of the girls got jobs with the Wincharger Corporation here in town making radio components. I thought maybe I could do that, too. Then I'd be around to help you and Uncle John. You know, just until you're feeling better."

With some difficulty, Aunt Nora moved over to make room on the chaise, patting the cushion for Maggie to sit down beside her.

"Maggie, listen to me. It's always been our dream, your Uncle John's and mine, that you would go to college. You are bright and talented, and we want you to make the most of those gifts. I admire the fact that you want to help out with the war effort, but there are lots of patriotic things you can do and still go to college. You can sell war bonds and help out with scrap and paper drives, just as you have been doing. You could even volunteer down at the USO. But, Maggie, going to college is an opportunity that few girls your age have. Don't let it pass you by. We'll need all of our bright young people to lead us when this war is over.

"Now, as for my illness." Nora's voice was calm and steady. "That's in God's hands, not ours. It's sweet of you to want to help, but your uncle and I can manage just fine. The doctors at the Mayo Clinic put me on a program of medicine and rest, and told me that it was important to keep my spirits up. So, you see, the best thing you can do for me would be to seize this wonderful opportunity. That would make me happier than anything else."

"I don't know — "

"Well, I do."

Aunt Nora again took Maggie's hand in hers.

"There's something else, Maggie. I want you to promise me that, no matter what happens, you will finish college and graduate. Even if ... circumstances change." She squeezed Maggie's hand. "Will you promise me that?"

Maggie looked into her aunt's eyes, frightened that they appeared to be fading a little with each passing day.

"Yes, Aunt Nora," she replied, her own eyes bright with tears. "I promise."

"Good. Then we'll speak no more of it."

Nora released Maggie's hand and sank back into the cushions.

"Now, would you please bring me my stationary and address book from the top drawer of my desk." Nora's eyes twinkled. "I've a little bragging to do."

She was asleep with a half-written letter on her lap when Uncle John came home, so Maggie gave him the news herself. He was thrilled, twirling Maggie around in a circle and declaring her acceptance to Saint Mary's *the best news since Doolittle's raid on Tokyo*. Maggie decided not to share her misgivings with him. She didn't want him to think she was ungrateful for the wonderful opportunity he and Aunt Nora had given her. And she didn't want him to know how very worried she was about her aunt's health.

They gathered around the old wooden table in the farm kitchen after supper, taking advantage of the faint breeze that wafted through the patched screen door on this sultry July night. As Maggie poured a pitcher of ice tea for her father, her brother and herself, she noted with satisfaction that the glasses sparkled, the table was scrubbed clean and her feet no longer stuck to the kitchen floor.

When Maggie arrived at the farm a week ago, the house

was already showing the effects of having been left at the mercy of two bachelor farmers for the three months since Elly had enrolled in nursing school and Anna had gone off to join the WAACs. Dust and grime covered almost every surface, the sink was full of dishes, a mountain of laundry stood by the wash tub and the cupboards were almost bare, save for the basic staples and a large number of boxes of chocolate pudding, Michael's favorite.

With a shake of her head, Maggie had rolled up her sleeves and plunged in. While her father and brother toiled in the fields, she scrubbed, washed and mended until the house fairly shown. Finished with those tasks, she drove into town and set about laying in a store of more nutritious food. Then she began to cook and bake as many different dishes as she knew how to make. Michael, now fourteen years old and always ravenous, was thrilled to have Maggie doing the cooking. He'd long ago tired of their bachelor's diet of eggs, bacon and store-bought bread. His rapture at learning that Maggie had used some of her precious ration stamps to buy sugar to bake a cake knew no bounds.

Now, with supper over and the temperature finally beginning to drop just a little, Maggie sank into the chair across from her father, taking a long sip of her iced tea.

"Great dinner, Maggie," said Michael, leaning back in his chair. "It's been a long time since we've had roast chicken."

"Glad you enjoyed it," Maggie responded with a pleased smile.

"Enjoyed it? He ate more than half the bird himself. I was hoping there'd be at least a little left for a nice sandwich for tomorrow," her father pouted.

"What can I say, Dad? I'm a growing boy." Michael helped himself to another glass of tea.

"What have you heard from anyone, Dad?" asked Maggie.

"Well, I got a quick letter from James. Heavily censored. He's *somewhere in Britain* flying bombers. Haven't heard from Patrick yet. The Navy's got him in training for some kind of destroyer or something." He snickered. "Imagine. Himself, who's never been on anything bigger than a raft on the West Fork of the Des Moines."

"When I get into the war I'm going to fly fighters off of one of those big aircraft carriers," Michael announced.

"If you get into the war, we're done for, for sure." Their father took a sip of his tea before continuing.

"Elly says she's enjoying nursing school, and seems to like it in Des Moines. Anna's been assigned to a staff position at the bomber training base in Wendover, Utah. Been there about three weeks." He shook his head. "Scattered to the winds," he said, almost to himself. Then he cleared his throat.

"How's your Aunt Nora feeling?"

"Better some days than others," Maggie said. "Uncle John is taking her up to the Mayo Clinic again next week."

"Doctors." Her father spat out the word. "Well, I'll be praying for her. You tell her that, now."

"I will."

Maggie slowly stirred her iced tea while she gathered the courage to bring up the subject she'd been avoiding all week.

"Dad, before I head back to Sioux City next week, there's something I wanted to talk to you about." She took a deep breath and plunged ahead. "I wanted to talk to you about going to college at the end of the summer."

"Are you asking or telling?"

"Well, I want to know what you think."

"What I think." Maggie waited while her father lit a cigarette and tossed the match into the dregs of his tea. "Well, tell me. What would you be needing with college? Have you decided to become some kind of career girl?"

"Well, I'm not sure, exactly. But that's what college would help me figure out, what I want to do and how to prepare for it."

Her father frowned.

"So, being a wife and mother's not good enough for you?"

"No. I mean, yes. I do want to get married and have children. Someday. But, it's important to have an educated mind for whatever you want to do in life."

Terrence arched an eyebrow. "Oh, it is, is it?"

Maggie felt the color rise to her face.

"I think college would be great for Maggie," Michael interjected. "She's always gotten great marks in school, and she's a really good writer. Maybe she could be a newspaper woman or something. Or a war correspondent!"

"Michael. Go out and see to the cows."

"Aw, Dad — "

"The cows, Michael."

"Cows. Cows! The whole world's aflame and I've got to milk the cows." Michael shoved his chair away from the table and slammed out the door.

Their father was quiet for a few more moments.

"Where is this college?"

"It's called Saint Mary's College. It's in Indiana. Across the street from the University of Notre Dame."

"What Order runs it?"

"The Congregation of the Holy Cross."

"Where would you live?"

"In the dormitory with the other girls. And some of the Sisters. But, I'd be back for vacations and in the summer."

"Must cost a pretty penny."

Maggie shrugged.

"Humph." He took another puff on his cigarette. "And the nuns. They'll be watching over you?"

"Yes, Dad."

"What does your aunt say about all this college business?"

"It was her idea. She said she really wants me to go." Maggie hesitated. "No matter what."

Terrence stared out the newly cleaned window at the empty farmyard.

"Well, Nora and I don't always see eye to eye on things, Lord knows. But, she's always tried to do what she thinks is best for you." He looked at Maggie. "We all have."

"I know that, Dad."

Terrence studied the smoke curling up from his cigarette for a long time. Then, he broke into a wry smile.

"What's so funny?" Maggie asked, puzzled.

"Oh, I was just thinking about your grandfather. Here's this poor, uneducated Irish immigrant, come to this country with nothing but the clothes on his back. And, now, here sits his granddaughter, planning to go off to college."

Maggie waited.

Terrence took a deep pull on his cigarette and blew the smoke out in a long, steady stream.

"Well, I guess if Patrick can plow the ocean, you can go to college."

"Thank you, Dad." Maggie reached over and touched his hand. Without a word, he crooked his index finger over hers and gave it a tiny squeeze.

Military contracts for beef and pork had business booming down at the stockyards, and Maggie spent what remained of the summer helping Uncle John in the office. The rest of her time was spent tending the family's *Victory Garden* with Louise, hauling scrap metal down to the collection site, attending farewell parties for friends and planning for college.

As best she could, Nora threw herself into the preparations for Maggie's departure. She made numerous phone calls to her friend, Mrs. Powers, to find out what kinds of things her daughter had found useful when she attended Saint Mary's. Nora and Maggie drew up long lists of items needed, items to be purchased and items to be made. In mid-August, a chatty, informative letter arrived for Maggie from her *Big Sister* at Saint Mary's, a girl from Chicago who would be a junior this coming year. The letter helped to calm the butterflies Maggie was beginning to feel as the day of her leaving neared.

Beneath the happy commotion, however, ran the ominous undercurrent of Aunt Nora's deteriorating health. Her energy waxed and waned. Many days, she was confined to her bed. But, on her good days, she shared in the excitement of Maggie's upcoming departure. On those days, her laugh sounded as it always had, and Maggie could almost forget that time was running out.

At Nora's request, Aunt Kit arrived at the end of the third week of August. She began immediate implementation of Aunt Nora's *to do* list with an efficiency that would have been the envy of any supply ordinance officer. But, she also exhibited a sensitivity that surprised and touched Maggie. Kit would sit at Nora's bedside each morning, reviewing with her the exact size, color and number of items Maggie would need to purchase that day. Then, with Maggie in tow, she was off to Davidson's or Martin's to fill the list. Kit even tried, though she did not always succeed, to overcome her own frugal leanings and mimic Nora's more extravagant style. At the end of the day, she and Maggie would display and model their purchases for Nora's approval, gradually filling a trunk with items to be kept, and making a smaller pile of items to be returned or exchanged.

Walking into Nora's bedroom after work one day, Uncle John found the three of them surrounded by dresses, sweaters, skirts, blouses, shoes, socks, hats and gloves.

"What in the name of St. Finbar is all this? Maggie, I thought you were goin' to school to study, not put on a fashion show. You do know there's a war on?"

"Oh, now, John, " Nora cajoled. "We can't send her off into the wilds of Indiana in rags. Besides, I'm just following the suggested list that the Sisters sent me, with a few extras." Nora smiled, her gaunt yet still pretty face as pale as the pillows that supported her head.

"Kit. Are you buying into this foolishness?"

"I'm just doing what Nora tells me, John," she replied archly. "*You're* the one doing the buying."

Maggie stifled a giggle.

"The story of my life," John lamented, shaking his head. But Maggie knew he would do anything to keep that smile on his dear wife's face.

The day came at last. Uncle John was outside putting Maggie's trunks in the car when she came downstairs, her overnight bag in hand. Aunt Nora, who'd been feeling stronger of late, sat in a chair in the parlor. John had refused to allow her to ride along to the train station with them, and Nora was not happy.

"This is silly. I feel fine. There's no reason I can't go with you to the station."

"You know Uncle John when he gets his mind made up," said Maggie.

"Big stubborn Irishman," Nora grumbled. "Well, let me take a look at you."

Maggie twirled in a little circle, showing off her new blue traveling suit and the straw hat with the matching blue grosgrain ribbon.

"Oh, Maggie. You're a picture. So smart and well turned-out. I do hope we were right about the length of that skirt, though."

"The saleswoman said all the hemlines are shorter now, Aunt Nora, to save on material for the war."

"Hmm. Sometimes I think they just make up those regulations so the soldiers can stare at a little more leg. But, I have to admit, you look ... well, you just look wonderful." Aunt Nora took a handkerchief out of her pocket and dabbed at her eyes. "What happened to that little girl with the freckles and the skinned knees?"

"Well, I still have the freckles." Maggie began to tear up a little herself.

"Glory be. The waterworks have started already." Uncle John, stomping in from the porch, looked from one to the other in mild exasperation. "Come, come. We've no time for that, now. We've to be off or we'll miss the train."

"I know." Nora sniffed, trying to compose herself. "Well, now, Maggie. You be careful on the train."

"I will."

"Do you have your ticket?"

"Right here in my purse."

"And a nickel for the telephone in case you have any problems?"

"I have a bag of nickels."

"Nora — " John attempted to hurry her along. She ignored him.

"Call us when you get there to let us know you arrived safely."

"I will."

"And don't forget to write. Do you have your new stationary?"

Maggie nodded.

"Did you get some stamps from my desk?"

"Yes, Aunt Nora."

"Nora! We have to leave." John pointed at his watch.

"All right, John!" she snapped. Did he think that she, of all people, didn't realize that time was running out? She closed her eyes for a moment to collect herself. She knew she was babbling, stalling. Why, after all these years, was it still so hard to say the words she really wanted to say? This might be her last chance to tell Maggie what was in her heart, to explain to her … so many things. But, if she did, would Maggie understand — and forgive?

Nora's arms trembled as she reached for her niece. She enfolded the young woman in a tearful embrace. She had to speak now or never.

Pressing her lips to Maggie's ear, Nora whispered, "All those years ago … I'm sorry. I just wasn't strong enough to let you go."

Maggie drew back, stunned. Restrained by culture and fear, she'd never asked, nor had her aunt ever revealed the reasons for their lives together. They'd lived within unspoken boundaries, not quite mother and daughter, maintaining a delicate balance between love given and love withheld. Why now, when she was about to walk out the door, had her aunt cracked the lid on that Pandora's box? For what purpose? Did she really think that by this one cryptic statement, this admission of weakness, she could justify the years of secrets? That a childhood darkened by loss and abandonment could be made right by some vague last minute confession?

Maggie looked deep into her aunt's pale blue eyes, eyes that now looked to her for absolution.

"Goodbye, Aunt Nora," she said, her voice breaking. She turned and stumbled toward the door.

Chapter 14

Autumn 1942

The University of Notre Dame Du Lac, established in the wilderness of Indiana in 1842 by the French Catholic Congregation of the Holy Cross, found itself at an important crossroads as World War II approached. Notre Dame, like many other colleges, suffered from a severe decline in enrollment during the Depression years, a situation made worse by military mobilization and conscription in 1941 and 1942. In an effort to keep the University afloat, then Notre Dame President J. Hugh O'Donnell, C.S.C., offered University facilities to the armed forces. The Army, which had had some minor presence on campus during the Civil War and World War I, showed little interest now, but the Navy took advantage of the opportunity and established a unit of the Naval Reserve Officers Training Corps (NROTC) at Notre Dame in September of 1941.

When war was declared after the bombing of Pearl Harbor on December 7, 1941, the campus quickly took on the look of an armed camp. A small number of civilian students remained, but the majority of the student body was made up of members of the NROTC program, the V-7 program, also known as the Midshipmen's School, and the V-12 program, a group chosen for special training from among high school graduates or from the fleet. Trained in the traditions of both the Navy and of the University, these young men were sent forth to do their duty "for God, Country, and Notre Dame."

Just across the highway from Notre Dame stood Saint Mary's College, an all-women's Catholic school run by the Sisters of the Holy Cross. Long dedicated to Our Lady and to "the ideal of intelligent womanhood," the faculty and

*students of Saint Mary's also devoted themselves to the sup-
port of the war effort. Now, in addition to the regular
areas of study, Saint Mary's offered courses in first aid
and nursing. The students sold war bonds and stamps,
began knitting programs, packed kits for the Red Cross,
and ran scrap and paper drives. And they prayed.*

*For the young men and women of these two schools, it
was an exciting, bittersweet time. They lived each day
intensely, reveling in being young and, for some, being in
love. For who knew what tomorrow might bring.*

Maggie peered up at the huge, square bell tower as the taxi-
cab turned into the main circle in front of Le Mans Hall, the
main college building of Saint Mary's College. Two wings of
the massive stone building extended like protective arms around
the sides of a main quadrangle, both fronted by long covered
walkways with brick arches and iron railings. As the driver
unloaded her bags, Maggie stepped out of the cab, attempting
to smooth her wrinkled suit. The trip had involved a long series
of train rides from Sioux City, through Chicago, and then to
South Bend, and she feared she looked rumpled and unkempt.
She fumbled in her purse for the money to pay the cab driver,
then turned and stared at the building that was to be her home
for the next four years.

Suddenly, the front doors of Le Mans burst open. Two
burly young men wearing Notre Dame letter sweaters bounded
down the steps.

"Hello. Welcome to Saint Mary's," they greeted her. "We're
part of the official welcoming committee. Can we help you
with your bags?"

Without waiting for an answer, the two young men picked
up Maggie's suitcases, motioning her up the steps toward the
wooden, double doors of the ivy-covered main entrance. They
each grabbed a heavy iron handle, opening the doors wide.

"After you, Miss." They bowed in unison.

Blushing, Maggie ventured into the dim entryway.

The air inside the building was cool and smelled of floor wax, stone and faint cooking odors. A short series of steps led up from the small vestibule to a stone wall with arched doorways on either side. This wall contained a large stone carving of St. Michael the Archangel. He stood with spear poised, ready to protect his innocent young charges from the evils that threatened, two of whom were, at that very moment, carrying Maggie's bags through the doorway to the left, into a large lounge area. There, a competent looking upperclassman sat at a wooden desk bearing the sign *Freshman Registration*. The young men plunked Maggie's bags down in front of the desk, gave her a smile and a wink and headed out the door to check out the next arrival.

"Hello. Welcome to Saint Mary's. Name, please?" said the girl behind the desk.

"Maggie ... Margaret Owen."

"Owen, Owen ... yes. Here you are." She checked Maggie's name off the list in front of her. "You're in room 312. That's a double on the third floor. You take the hallway behind me to your left, and the stairs will be on your right. Or, you could take the elevator, though personally, I wouldn't advise it. It's a bit temperamental. Now, here are your keys and some information about freshmen orientation." She handed the keys and literature to Maggie. "Do you have any other baggage?"

"I have a trunk that's being sent from the train station."

"Good. They'll let you know when it arrives. After you've unpacked it, Maintenance will take it down to the trunk room in the basement for storage. In the meantime, you can head on up. Do you need any help?"

"Oh, no. I'll be fine."

Maggie lugged her bags across the lounge area past a few small clusters of girls saying goodbye to their parents. She struggled down the dark wood-paneled hallway and up the stone stairs. By the time she reached the third floor, she was hot and tired, and dearly wished she hadn't been so quick to turn down the offer of help with her bags.

Following the numbers over the doorways, Maggie at last came to room 312. The door was ajar, and she could see three suitcases and a hatbox piled on the floor.

"Hello?" she called, pushing the door aside with her shoulder.

A petite young woman with curly black hair was putting clothes into one of the dressers. She turned in surprise.

"Oh, hello. Are you in 312?"

"Yes. I'm Margaret Owen. Maggie."

"Hi, Maggie. I'm Beatrice Garrity. From Chicago. But, please, just call me *Bea*. I hate *Beatrice*. Family name. I guess we're going to be roommates."

"I guess so." Maggie set down her bags with a thud.

"Here. Let me help you with that."

Bea hoisted one of the bags onto a nearby bed.

"Good heavens. What have you got in here? I hope you don't mind, but I went ahead and took the bed near the window. I've been here about an hour, and thought I ought to go ahead and get settled."

"No. That's fine." Maggie looked around the small, bare dorm room with its high ceilings and large, double-paned windows. Bea smiled.

"Not the Taj Mahal, but not too bad. The sinks are in there. The bathrooms are down the hall. I met one of the girls from next door. Her name is Francis LaBelle. She's from Milwaukee and seems very nice." Bea returned to her own bags and began hanging up dresses in one of the closets. "Where are you from?"

"Sioux City, Iowa."

"*Ioway. That's where the tall corn grows,*" Bea sang from the popular song. Maggie grimaced.

"Sorry." Bea smiled. "I couldn't resist. Did it take you long to get here?"

"Not too long. I had to switch trains in Chicago. Then we had to wait on a side track in Michigan City to let a troop train pass, but it wasn't too bad."

Just then a series of bells sounded. Bea jumped.

"What's that?"

Maggie pulled out the orientation sheet the girl at the front desk had given her.

"It appears to be the call to lunch."

"Great. I'm starved." Bea closed the lid of her suitcase. "I don't know if I'll ever get used to all these bells, though. They make me feel like an old fire horse answering the call."

The two roommates joined the stream of girls heading down the stairs to the dining room. They found places together at a white linen-covered table beneath a statue of St. Theresa. A nun dressed in the black habit and veil, and the fanlike white headpiece of the Order of the Sisters of The Holy Cross introduced herself as Sister Marie Cecile. She led them in the praying of grace before meals. Lunch was then served by students who, Maggie later learned, were working in the kitchen to help pay for their tuition.

Following lunch, the new students were sent on a tour of the campus, led by a volunteer from the senior class. They began in the building they were in, Le Mans Hall. Le Mans housed not only the dormitory and the dining room, but almost all of the classrooms, a number of lounges and convocation rooms, the administrative offices and the beautiful Chapel of the Holy Ghost located on the third floor, not far from Maggie and Bea's room.

After having trooped up and down the wide stone stairways of Le Mans for forty-five minutes, the girls followed their guide out a side door to inspect the new Centennial Library, dedicated just that previous June. The library overlooked Lake Marian, a small man-made lake where the students could paddle canoes in the good weather and ice skate in the winter. There was a boathouse and a walkway bridge that led to a small island in the center of the lake.

Next to Lake Marian was a shady rock garden with stone benches, quiet pools of water and a profusion of late summer flowers that reminded Maggie of Aunt Nora's beautiful garden back in Sioux City. She would have have liked to linger in this peaceful spot, but the tour guide was already headed down the lane to where it intersected with the tree-lined main entrance road.

"If you go down this road to the left, you come to the main gate," the guide informed them. "A little way beyond that is the University of Notre Dame. It's not on our tour, but if you're lucky, in a few weeks someone will offer to give you your own private tour of that campus."

This information elicited a nervous giggle from the freshmen.

The forced march continued throughout most of the afternoon, ending with a walk along the meandering path by the St. Joseph River on the southern-most end of campus.

Maggie and Bea returned to their rooms to find that their trunks and other luggage had been delivered. They'd only just begun to unpack them when the bell rang for supper.

The last event of that busy day was a short post-supper convocation presided over by Sister Grace Ann, Dean of Students. Sister Grace Ann was a tall woman who appeared even taller in her starched white headpiece. When she stood to speak she appeared to be looking down at the students from a great height. She paused for a long moment, peering at the wide-eyed freshmen through her pince nez glasses. Then, in a loud, shrill voice, she began to speak, outlining for them in no uncertain terms all of the rules and regulations of life at Saint Mary's. When the girls had been sufficiently cowed, she concluded.

"I'm sure you will find life here at Saint Mary's quite satisfactory. Dismissed."

The girls slunk out of the room in silence.

"If the rest of Freshmen Welcome Week is like this, I'll never make it," lamented Bea, collapsing onto her bed that evening. "And remind me to stay out of Sister Grace Ann's path. *A Saint Mary's girl does not engage in grotesque and unlovely behavior.* Oh, brother!"

Maggie laughed at Bea's uncanny imitation of the Dean of Students. Then, she leaned back against her pillow, closing her eyes. There were so many names and places to remember, so many dos and don'ts, bells going off at all hours for meals, chapel and curfew — her head was spinning. And they hadn't even started classes yet. Well, she thought as she drifted off to sleep, at least she hadn't had much time to get homesick.

Freshmen Welcome Week culminated in the beautiful Madonna Ceremony. On a cool, clear October night, Maggie, wearing her best dress under a light tan raincoat, gathered with the rest of her class at the main door of the college. There they were each given thin, white candles. One by one, the tapers were lit, and the freshmen stepped out into the chill night to begin a winding, flickering procession around the quadrangle of Le Mans Hall. As they walked, the beautiful voices of the Schola Cantorum, a select student choir, drifted down from the bell tower. The rest of the student body and faculty watched and listened from the covered cloister porch.

After the procession returned to the main entrance, the freshmen joined the other students and the faculty in the lounge to listen to a program of sacred music. Then, with great ceremony, each *Big Sister* presented her *Little Sister* with a framed print of the Madonna.

When all had returned to their seats, Sister Madeleva, the President of the College, rose to address the students. She stood for a moment, a commanding figure, her serene face framed by her pleated white wimple and black veil. Then, in a clear, deliberate voice, she welcomed the students to Saint Mary's, and spoke of the significance of the Madonna Ceremony.

"Each of you freshmen came out of the dark to have your candle lit, symbolizing your coming to Saint Mary's and the light of knowledge and spiritual fulfillment that you will find here. With this ceremony, you are officially Saint Mary's girls with all of the honors and duties that that title conveys."

Listening, Maggie felt a true sense of belonging. She'd become part of an intellectual and spiritual family that would help to guide her toward the person she was to become. As she joined with her fellow students in a closing prayer, she realized that she was looking forward to the next four years. She was glad she'd come.

Maggie clattered down the steps of the library, her books clutched to her chest. She'd lost track of the time and now, just three weeks into the school year, risked being late for Western World History class. As she trotted around to the front of Le Mans Hall, she came upon a small gathering of students and nuns. They were watching a group of men lift the last of two old iron cannons onto the wooden flatbed of what appeared to be a cattle truck. Realizing that one of the nuns was, in fact, Sister Carmella, her own history teacher, Maggie joined the crowd of onlookers.

"What's going on?" she asked no one in particular.

"They're hauling away the old civil war cannons for scrap. For the war effort," answered a dark-haired girl without turning her head.

"That'll do it," yelled one of the men, tying the tailgate of the truck closed with a rope. He turned and tipped his hat to the silent crowd.

"Ladies."

Then he climbed up onto the bed of the truck with the other men. They waved goodbye as the overloaded truck weaved its way out to the main gate with its precious load.

The crowd began to disperse. Sister Carmella turned, and Maggie was surprised to see tears in the old woman's eyes.

"Well, hello. Miss Owen, isn't it?"

"Yes, Sister."

"Looks like we're both going to be a little late for class today." The nun gave a small smile. "Come. Walk along with me."

They fell into step together. After a few moments, Sister Carmella began to talk.

"Goodness, I hate to see those old cannons go. You probably didn't know this, but they were presented to Mother Angela, our first president, by the United States Army right after the Civil War in recognition of the dedicated work done by the Sisters of the Holy Cross in caring for the wounded soldiers."

"No, Sister. I didn't know that."

"Yes. I remember the cannons even had names. Let me see. *Lady Polk* and … *Lady Davis*. Yes, that's right. Actually, I don't think Mother Angela was ever that comfortable having those cannons displayed on campus. I can remember her speaking often of her dream to have them melted down and molded into a statute of Our Lady of Peace. How ironic that now they're to be used once again for violent purposes."

She gave Maggie a sad look.

"I had hoped your generation might be spared this kind of senseless suffering. Lord knows, I've seen too many wars in *my* lifetime."

The truth of her statement was written in the lines of the old woman's face. She sighed, then continued.

"Well, I do hope Sister Madeleva is right, and that Our Lady will understand if we send our prayers for peace to her, and those cannons to the scrap pile to help our boys end this horrible war as soon as possible."

They'd reached the entrance to the building. Maggie held the door open.

"Thank you, my dear. Well, let's go see what mischief the early Romans have been up to today, shall we?"

"Maggie, are you ready yet?"

Julie Kendall, a freshmen from St. Louis who lived down the hall, bounced into the room just as Maggie was finishing her hair. She gaped.

"Oh, Maggie, that suit is divine. You look so sophisticated."

Maggie, after much deliberation, had chosen to wear her light blue wool suit with the pleated skirt, the one that brought out the color of her eyes. Beneath it she wore a wide-collared, white silk blouse. Her bangs were pinned up in the popular *rat* style, with the sides loose and framing her face in soft curls. Around her neck she wore the beautiful string of pearls that Uncle John had given her for her graduation from high school.

Maggie turned to see that Julie was wearing a simple, long-sleeved gray dress with black shoes, and a silver cross on a chain around her neck.

"Do you think it's too dressy?" said Maggie. "It is, isn't it? I think it's too dressy. I'd better change."

Julie grabbed her arm.

"No! You look great. Really. Let's go."

"Wait. Are my seams straight?" Maggie asked, craning her neck to check the back of her silk stockings.

"Yes. Now, come on, before all the cute ones are gone."

The freshmen class of Saint Mary's was hosting its first Sunday afternoon *Tea Dance* for the students and servicemen stationed at Notre Dame. For many of them, it was their first opportunity to actually meet the boys from across the road, having only had a glimpse of them from the Saint Mary's section of the stadium at the first few football games. In preparation, the girls had been dressing and grooming themselves since just after morning Mass.

When Julie and Maggie arrived, the lounge was already almost filled with girls and a large number of young men, most of whom were wearing the uniforms of the Navy or the Marines. Stationed among them were the ever-vigilant nuns.

"Maggie. Julie. Over here."

Bea motioned to them from the middle of a circle of men dressed in Navy blue.

"Where have you been? Gentlemen, I'd like you to meet my roommate, Maggie Owen, and our friend, Julie Kendall."

"How do you do?" the boys responded with interest.

"Now, let me see if I've got this right," Bea continued in a singsong voice. "Jim and Terry, here, are freshmen, Louis is a sophomore, and Joe and Henry are juniors. Is that right, boys?"

Just then the music began to play.

"What good timing," Henry said, smiling at Maggie. "Would you care to dance?"

"Uh … sure."

Maggie could have used a little more time to get her bearings, but she soon found herself in a swirl of couples on the dance floor.

They exchanged the usual pleasantries — where they were from and how they liked school so far — when someone tapped Henry on the shoulder.

"Mind if I cut in?"

Henry grimaced, but gallantly handed Maggie over to the stocky young midshipmen who waited behind him. He was soon replaced by a thin engineering student from Philadelphia, then a tall blonde Marine from Cleveland. The Marine was a very energetic dancer, tough to keep up with, and Maggie found herself trying to think of a way to excuse herself to take a breather. But, before she could make a graceful exit came the inevitable tap on her partner's shoulder. Fixing a smile on her face, she turned to greet her new partner.

Maggie found herself looking up into the bluest eyes she'd had ever seen. Her new escort, dressed in the navy blue dress uniform of the NROTC, was tall, thin and handsome in a not-quite-finished way. He had dark, wavy hair, a strong chin with just a hint of a cleft in it, and a small bump in his nose that hinted of some previous athletic encounter. The young man smiled as he stepped toward her. His smile broadened when the swing selection that had been playing was replaced by a romantic ballad. He took Maggie's hand in his, placed his other hand firmly on the small of her back and maneuvered her to the center of the dancers, as far as possible from the hopefuls prowling the perimeter of the floor.

"I hope you don't mind, but I've been waiting for a chance to dance with you for the last fifteen minutes. I'd like it to last for more than ten seconds." She's even prettier up close, he thought.

"Well, it's just that there's so many more boys than girls

here," Maggie demurred. Hmm. He's quite good looking. And a good dancer.

"Oh, is that it? Well, my name is Jack. Jack Koerner."

"I'm Margaret Owen."

"It's very nice to meet you, Margaret. Where are you from?"

"Iowa. Sioux City, Iowa." She liked the dimple on his chin.

"Really? I've never met anyone from Iowa before." She didn't look like any farm girl he'd ever seen.

"Oh? You must not get out much." He probably thought she was just some little farm girl.

"Oh, I get out once in a while. I've just never been that far west. I'm from Lancaster, Pennsylvania. My Dad owns a drugstore there. I'm in the NROTC. Second year." He gave her a little dip. "Are you a freshman?"

"Yes."

"I thought so. If you'd been here last year, I'd have noticed you." He gave her a wink. "So, what brings a pretty girl like you to Saint Mary's?" Such beautiful eyes. What color were they? Blue? Gray?

"A family friend recommended it," she said, a bit unsettled. "How is it you came to Notre Dame?" *Pretty girl,* huh. He certainly wasn't shy. Or original.

"Well, like most Catholic kids, I grew up listening to the football games on the radio, and one of the nuns at my high school had her whole classroom decorated with Notre Dame paraphernalia. But, really, it was my mother's idea. I've got three older brothers who were called in the peacetime draft back in '40. My mother was pretty undone. She was afraid I'd be next. When she heard that ND had an NROTC program that would keep me in school while they trained me to be an officer, she pushed me to apply. I figured it'd be a few years yet till we got into the war, so to make her happy, I did. By the time Pearl Harbor got hit, I was safely tucked away here."

"It must be hard for you," said Maggie, who'd heard the frustration behind his words.

He frowned, certain she was mocking him. But her eyes

were filled with empathy.

"What do you mean?" he said in a guarded tone.

"Well ... you know ... being torn between wanting to spare your mother pain and doing what you really want to do." Maggie bowed her head, fearing she'd said too much to this boy she'd just met.

Jack looked at her in surprise, his bravado pierced for a moment by her gentle insight. "Yeah. It is hard," he said in a quiet voice. He shrugged. "Well, the way things are going, I guess there'll be enough war to go around."

"Where are your brothers now?" asked Maggie.

"One of them joined the Marines and the other two are in the Army. They're all overseas."

Suddenly, Jack twirled her beneath his arm. When she looked back up at him, the cocky smile had returned to his face.

"So, how do you like Saint Mary's so far, Margaret?" *He* was liking it better and better.

Maggie blushed under his unwavering gaze. He had a way of looking at her that made her feel that she was the only person in the room.

"Maggie. I'm only called Margaret when I'm in trouble." Like now, she thought.

"Maggie it is."

Just then, Jack noticed the blonde Marine making his way toward them. He decided to take evasive action.

"Thirsty?" Jack asked suddenly.

"What?" said Maggie. "Well, I guess so."

"Me, too. Let's get a drink."

Jack grabbed Maggie's elbow, guiding her swiftly through the crowd to the punch bowl. While the young woman stationed behind the table ladled out a drink for them, he observed the Marine continuing to close. Jack snatched the cup from Maggie's hand before she could even take a sip, setting it down on the table.

"On second thought, I think what I'd really like is a breath of fresh air. Let's go out onto the porch for a moment."

"But, I — "

Before she could say another word, Maggie was propelled out the French doors to the cloister porch. A few other couples were already there, engaged in close conversation, many of the young men wearing the same navy dress blues as Jack. Jack hustled her across the porch and, grabbing her by the shoulders, positioned her in the shadow of one of the stone pillars.

"Hey!" she protested.

"Sh!"

He stood very close to her, shielding her from the Marine who now stood in the doorway, scanning the gathered couples.

At just that moment, Sister Grace Ann came out onto the porch by the other doorway. She began patrolling in their direction, clearing her throat in warning to those couples that appeared a little too involved. Faced with the imposing figure of the approaching nun, and unable to locate his quarry, the Marine withdrew.

Jack glanced over his shoulder to make sure the coast was clear before releasing his grip on Maggie.

"That's better," he said, giving her a triumphant smile, proud that the Navy had, once again, out-maneuvered the Marines.

Maggie, shivering in her thin suit, folded her arms across her chest.

"Oh, you think so, do you? Well, I may just be a naïve farm girl from Iowa, but I won't be treated like that." The trembling of her voice belied her forceful words.

The smile quickly left Jack's face.

"Oh, hey, I hope you don't think ... I mean, I'd never ... You see, there was this guy, this Marine — "

Suddenly, he noticed she was shivering.

"Gee, you're shaking. Here. Take my coat."

"No. I think it'd be better if we went back inside." Maggie's voice was icy.

"But, you don't understand," he said, reaching for her arm. "I was just trying to — "

Maggie brushed his hand away.

"I know what you were trying. On second thought, why don't you stay out here and cool off."

She stepped around him and flounced into the building.

Before Jack could go after her, Sister Grace Ann swooped down on him, a suspicious look on her face. Jack turned toward her, making a graceful, sweeping bow.

"Good afternoon, Sister. You're looking particularly lovely today."

Giving her his most winning smile, he straightened, saluted and escaped through the door. The thwarted nun glowered after him.

Inside, he searched the crowd for Maggie, anxious to apologize. To his dismay, he saw her heading straight towards *No Man's Land*, the door that led to the main part of the building, strictly off-limits to ND students. As she opened the door, Jack stopped, defeated.

To hell with her if she wasn't even going to give him a chance to explain, he thought. There were plenty of other pretty girls there.

He was about to turn away, when he saw her hesitate. For a brief moment, Maggie looked back at him, her blue eyes bright with tears. Then she was gone.

"Damn," he breathed softly. How come he felt like such a heel when he didn't even do anything?

Shaking his head, Jack went to rejoin his friends. But before he did, he pulled a pen and paper out of his pocket. *Maggie Owen, Sioux City, Iowa*, he wrote. He folded the note and tucked it in his pocket.

"Maggie." Francis from next door stuck her head into the dorm room. "The front desk just called. There's a telephone call for you downstairs."

"Thanks, Fran."

Maggie had been so engrossed in her French assignment, she hadn't even heard the phone in the hallway ring. She glanced at the clock. 8:50 P.M. Who would be calling at this hour? It couldn't be her aunt or uncle. She'd just talked to them yesterday. Perhaps it was someone she'd met at the Tea Dance?

As she headed down the stairs to the phone in the lobby, Maggie ran through the faces of the young men she'd met the past Sunday. It could be that tall red head from Indianapolis — Tom somebody. Or Robby, the determined Marine from Toledo who kept calling. Or maybe it was Jack Koerner. Despite herself, her heart gave a little leap.

After their ill-fated first meeting, Jack had sent her a note of apology, explaining his reason for dragging her out to the cloister porch. He'd followed the note up a few days later with flowers and another note that said,   *I'm sorry. How about a second chance?*

If it was him, she thought, she'd accept his apology. But, she wouldn't encourage him. Of course, she wouldn't *dis*-courage him, either.

The girl on duty at the desk in the lobby handed the phone to Maggie, mouthing the words, *It's a man.*

Taking a deep breath, Maggie raised the receiver to her ear.

"Hello?" she said, her tone cool.

"Maggie." The voice was heavy and tired.

"Uncle John?" Maggie's feigned sophistication vanished.

"Yes, Maggie. It's me." He paused and cleared his throat. "I'm callin' because .... ah, Maggie. It's your Aunt Nora. She's gone." Maggie strained to hear him over the rushing sound in her ears. "This afternoon. There was no time to call you, it happened so sudden. Just yesterday she said she was feeling stronger. Then, late this mornin', she said the pains were back. Before the doctor could even get there, she went into a coma and — " His breath caught in his throat.

Maggie felt as if someone was squeezing the air from

her own lungs.

"Oh, Uncle John," was all she could manage.

Her uncle gave a small cough.

"The funeral is to be held Monday morning. I've already notified the Sisters there, and I've arranged for your train tickets. They'll be waitin' for you at the station in South Bend tomorrow morning. You'll change in Chicago, and be in to Sioux City by late tomorrow afternoon. Can you get yourself to the station?"

"Of course, Uncle John." Maggie's eyes filled with tears, but she kept her voice steady. "Don't worry about me."

"That's a fine girl. Well. I'll see you at the station, then. Good bye, Maggie."

"Good bye, Uncle John."

In slow motion, Maggie hung up the phone. The girl at the desk gave her a curious look. Without a word, Maggie walked out the front door into the darkness of the November night. Oblivious to the cold, she hurried to the rock garden, praying it would be empty. She lowered herself onto a stone bench beneath the cover of a rustling pin oak tree. Wrapping her arms around herself, she sat, too stunned to cry.

She was gone. Aunt Nora was gone. Maggie knew she was very ill, even suspected she was dying. But, dead? It was too soon, too soon. The fact of it left her reeling. All the feelings that had defined their relationship tore at her heart — the gratitude, the betrayal, the anger and the love. Maggie had viewed her aunt through the prisms of a little girl's eyes and an adolescent's emotions; judged her against a memory and found her wanting. *Mother Nora*. Uncle John had called her that, but Maggie never could. She'd never allowed herself to be the daughter her aunt had hoped for. Maybe if there'd been more time. Maybe, after experiencing for herself a woman's joys and sorrows, a mother's hopes and desires, she'd have come to understand the choices her aunt had made. Maybe then Maggie could have forgiven her for taking her away from her family — and forgiven herself for loving her anyway.

Maggie began to sway as sob after sob fought its way free from her stricken heart.

The outpouring of grief from the Sioux City community at Nora's death was heartfelt. Friends from all around paid their respects at the wake and the funeral. Both sides of the family came in from Boru. The relatives knew, but did not speak of the bad feeling that existed between Terrence and John over the adoption of Maggie, and the two men, united by their mutual grief, managed to maintain an uneasy truce through the official days of mourning. Still, Maggie saw the hardness return to her father's face when well-meaning mourners sought to console her on the loss of her *mother*.

Exhausted and numb with grief, Maggie sat between her uncle and her father at the funeral Mass in Blessed Sacrament Church. As the organ chords of the Mass of the Angels swirled around her, the awful irony of her situation hit her. For the second time in her life, she'd lost a mother. Now she had no mother, and too many fathers. And those two fathers hated each other. Maggie hid her face in her hands, her shoulders shaking as she fought to control the sudden fit of hysterical laugher that threatened to overwhelm her. Observing this, the other mourners touched each other's sleeves, commenting on the grief stricken young woman.

When it was all over, John took the body of his beloved wife back to Boru to be buried. As her last wish, Nora, who'd left the world she knew to follow the man she loved, had wanted to go home.

In the days after the funeral, many letters of sympathy arrived at the house in Sioux City. Anxious for something to keep her busy, Maggie took over the job of responding to them. She came across a plain white envelope with the return address of Walsh Hall, Notre Dame, Indiana. She was surprised to discover that it was a note of condolence from Jack

Koerner. How he'd learned of her aunt's death, she didn't know — from Bea, she guessed. But she was touched by the fact that he'd gone to the trouble to obtain her address and write to her. She wrote back the obligatory thank you note. Then, as an afterthought, added a postscript. *About the mixup at the dance — apology accepted.*

Maggie stayed in Sioux City through Thanksgiving, wanting to be with her uncle during this first holiday without Aunt Nora. They attended Mass together and lit a candle, then went home to a quiet dinner, prepared and served by Louise. They ate little and quickly, eager to be away from the sight of the empty seat at the end of the table.

The next day at breakfast, Maggie informed her uncle of her decision to quit school and get a job in Sioux City. This announcement elicited the first real emotion she'd seen from him since the funeral.

"Margaret, I won't hear of it," he thundered, setting his coffee cup down on the table with a bang. "Your place is back at school. It's what your aunt wanted, what she lived on these last few months. You'll not be breakin' your promise to her by quittin' now."

"But, Uncle John. Things are different now."

"Not for you. You're going back to school and that's final."

Further argument proved useless. With reluctance, Maggie returned to Saint Mary's the first week of December.

Being back at school was hard for Maggie. She found that she missed her aunt more than she could've imagined, missed her concern and her advice and the fact of her just being there, only a phone call or a letter away. On top of that, Maggie worried about her uncle. She called and wrote him so often that, at last, he felt compelled to admonish her to tend to her books.

Always a conscientious student, Maggie now buried herself in her studies. Her friends understood. They continued to invite her to go places with them, but were not surprised when she declined.

Jack called not long after Maggie returned. She thanked him again for his kind note, but told him she didn't feel ready to go anywhere or see anyone just yet. He didn't pressure her. But every few weeks thereafter, he would call just to see how she was doing. Maggie appreciated his kindness, and always felt somewhat cheered after they spoke.

Finally, in the midst of a dreary, gray February, Maggie accepted Jack's invitation to get a soda over at the *Huddle,* a little snack place on the Notre Dame campus. She regretted her decision at once, but could think of no graceful way out of it.

On the day of their date, she changed her clothes three times, wanting to look nice, but not too nice. Then she paced until Jack called for her from the phone downstairs.

Maggie and Jack rode the campus shuttle bus to Notre Dame. As they took their seat about halfway back, a voice called out.

"Jack. Hey, Jack."

A young man a few rows in front of them, dressed in a Navy pea coat identical to the one Jack was wearing, swiveled around to face them.

"How ya doin', Nick?" Jack answered with a wave of his hand. "You over here breaking hearts again?"

"Nah. I was just visiting my kid sister. My mom told me to keep an eye on her. Say, I heard you aced that Chemical Engineering exam. Is that true? Man, half the class flunked that thing."

"Don't believe everything you hear."

"Yeah, well, I heard it from Lieutenant Commander Price," Nick shouted as the bus lurched forward, "and he doesn't go in for jokes. Say, do you think I could get a look at your notes sometime? I'm dying in that class."

"Sure, Nick. Later, okay?" Jack said pointedly.

"Oh, yeah. Sure," Nick replied, focusing on Maggie for the first time. He touched the brim of his hat and grinned.

"Watch out, Miss. He's not quite as stupid as he looks."

"Thanks for the warning," Maggie replied. She gave Jack a surprised look.

"What? You thought I couldn't be handsome and smart, too?" Jack asked in mock indignation.

Maggie burst out laughing for the first time in what seemed like ages.

As the bus bounced along the road to Notre Dame, Jack regaled her with tales of his NROTC training, and funny stories his brothers had written from overseas. By the time they neared the end of Saint Mary's Lake on the Notre Dame campus, she realized she was enjoying herself.

Suddenly, she reached out and placed her hand on Jack's arm.

"Jack. Can we get out here?"

"Sure," he replied, signaling to the driver.

Jack helped Maggie down from the bus, walking beside her down the windswept pathway that led to the Grotto, the outdoor shrine to the Blessed Mother, tucked beneath the shadow of Sacred Heart Cathedral.

Built as a small-scale replica of the shrine to Our Lady of Lourdes in France, the Grotto was a favorite place of prayer for Notre Dame students. On this late winter Saturday, the ivy that clung to the large gray, snow-blotched boulders of the shallow cave was as leafless and bare as the trees overhead, but the light from hundreds of candles glowed with the petitions of those who'd come here to pray before the statue of the Blessed Mother.

Maggie knelt at the iron railing in front of the shrine. Jack stood a few steps behind, staring at her bowed head.

From their first inauspicious meeting, he'd been unable to shake this girl from his mind. He knew girls that were prettier, girls that were smarter, certainly girls that were more adventurous and worldly. But there was something about Maggie, a strange combination of vulnerability and strength that intrigued him. She was a puzzle it might be fun to solve.

"Jack. Jack!"

He started. Maggie was staring at him, a quizzical look on her face.

"Oh, sorry. I was … praying."

"You were grinning," she observed in amusement.

"Was I? Well, that's because she winked at me."

"Jack! That's sacrilegious."

"What can I say? All the ladies love a man in uniform. Come on." He pulled her to her feet, tucking her arm in his. "I'm starved."

He strode off down the sidewalk with Maggie clinging to him to keep up.

After that, every so often, Jack would invite Maggie to go for a walk or take in a movie downtown. Maggie knew she wasn't the only girl Jack was seeing, and that was fine. She didn't have the emotional energy for anything more than a casual friendship. Her mind was on other things.

Adjusting to life without Aunt Nora's guidance and support was difficult enough, but her death had also removed whatever constraints existed on the rivalry between her uncle and her father. Uncle John's grief was evident in his letters, his despair lifting only when he wrote with happy anticipation of Maggie's return to Sioux City for the summer. Her father's letters, meanwhile, had become more insistent that she spend more of her time with him in Boru, a request she knew her uncle would vehemently oppose. Once again, Maggie felt torn between the two men she loved most.

Maggie stared down at the scribbling on the page in front of her. After an hour and a half of writing and rewriting, she was still having no success with her English assignment on Ralph Waldo Emerson. Her paper was a muddle of crossed-out sentences and disjointed paragraphs. The words simply refused to take any coherent form. In frustration, she ripped the page from her notebook, crumpling it into a ball. The young nun seated at the library reference desk flicked a mild look of disapproval in her direction. Maggie grabbed her jacket and hurried from the building.

The minute the cool air hit her face, she felt her troubles ease. It was a beautiful clear Indiana spring day, all the more wondrous for its rarity. The rain clouds that had pressed down upon the school and the spirits of the students for the past two weeks had blown to the east, leaving everything fresh and glistening in the unaccustomed sunlight. Maggie leaned over the railing at the top of the stairs and took a deep breath. She could smell the turned earth of the cornfields that wrapped around the Saint Mary's campus like a shawl. Her father used to say that on a spring day like this, if you listened hard enough, you could actually hear the plants and trees growing. And there at her feet, in front of the as yet dormant plantings at the foundation line of the library, stood a cluster of purple and gold crocuses, proof that the miraculous cycle of growth had indeed begun once again. Nature was renewing itself, the bleak winter giving way to new life.

Spring. In a little over a month, Maggie would be back in Sioux City. What would her life there be like now that Aunt Nora was gone? When she'd been back over Christmas break, Uncle John seemed to have aged a great deal, moving without purpose through each day. Previously an active man, he now spent long hours reading or just sitting by the fire. And he worried endlessly if Maggie so much as coughed or sneezed or came in a few minutes late. Only when she was right by his side did he seem at all like his old self. After the funeral he'd told her, *Now, you're all I have.* Did she dare leave him to return to school at summer's end, or even for a short time to visit her father in Boru?

Maggie's thoughts were interrupted by a drop of cold rain on her face. From nowhere clouds had appeared overhead, blocking out the sun. She ducked under the stone awning of the library just as the heavens opened. In amusement, she watched as two of the Sisters, caught in the unexpected downpour, deftly flipped their veils up over the top of their heads to protect their starched wimples, and scurried with impressive speed toward the safety of Le Mans. Maggie was struck by how much she had come to feel at home here with these talented, devout women. Not only had they given her a spiritual grounding, but they'd also sparked her intellectual curiosity, opening her mind to the world and all of its possibilities. That she might not be coming back here was hard to imagine. But, then, if there was anything she'd learned, it was that life didn't always work out the way you had planned.

Maggie pulled the collar of her coat close around her neck and watched the rain blow across the campus for a few more minutes. Then she turned and went back to work.

Chapter 15

June 1943

In 1938, the city of Sioux City, Iowa purchased two hundred and forty acres of farmland and a small existing airstrip just south of the city near Sergeant Bluff. With the help of labor and funds provided by the New Deal's Works Progress Administration (WPA), the facilities were improved and expanded, and the Sioux City Airport was dedicated in 1940.

Not long after the attack on Pearl Harbor, the U.S. Army leased the Sioux City Airport and some adjoining acreage as a training base for Army Air Corps bomber crews. By June of 1943, hundreds of officers, enlisted men, and WACs were being trained there as a last step to combat assignments in Europe, North Africa and the Pacific.

Maggie dropped her fare into the coin box and followed Patty down the aisle of the streetcar to an empty seat at the back. Flopping down as the streetcar began to move, she lifted her hair off her damp neck, taking advantage of what little breeze there was on this sticky, June day.

"I can't believe you talked me into this."

"Oh, come on, Maggie. It'll be fun." Patty pulled a lipstick and compact out of her purse, and began touching up her makeup. "Besides, it's our patriotic duty to see that our boys in uniform are entertained."

"I'm not going to entertain them. I'm just pouring coffee."

"Oh, I get it," said Patty, giving her a knowing look. "You're still mooning over that druggist you met at school."

"He's not a druggist. His father's a druggist. And I'm not

mooning over him. He's just a friend."

"A friend who writes you an awful lot of letters."

"Look," Maggie replied, changing the subject, "all I'm saying is that I didn't volunteer at the USO just so I could pick up boys."

"Me, neither." Patty snapped the compact closed. "I'm going to find some men!"

"Patty, you are so bad."

"That, my dear, remains to be seen." She smoothed her now platinum blonde hair into place. "Oh, here's our stop."

The two girls jumped off the streetcar at the corner of Pierce and Sixth Street. They walked to the middle of the block where a converted office building bore a red, white and blue banner announcing it as the site of the local USO. On one side of the doorway, the window displayed a poster of Uncle Sam proclaiming, *I Want You ... to join the USO*, while the other bore a homemade sign saying, *Welcome United States Army Air Corps*. They opened the door, entering a large, dimly lit room. Two paddle fans spun lazily overhead, and if the air was not exactly cool, at least it was moving. There were some mismatched couches and chairs scattered in groupings, and tables piled with magazines and stacks of playing cards. A small library of donated books was set up in one corner. In another was a ping pong table and a dartboard. The strains of *That Old Black Magic* emanated from a large radio console along one wall. Next to it, an uncarpeted area of the floor had been left clear for dancing. Along the opposite wall was a long table filled with cups, plates, napkins and the ubiquitous coffee and doughnuts. As it was not quite 6:00 P.M., there were only a few soldiers about, reading newspapers and smoking.

The girls hesitated just inside the door. An officious, matronly looking woman bustled over. She stopped in front of them, casting a disapproving look at the amount of leg showing from beneath Patty's skirt.

"May I help you ... ladies?" she asked in an acerbic voice.

"Yes. I'm Patty Maloney and this is my friend, Maggie

Owen. We've come to volunteer our time. I believe Mrs. Coonan phoned ahead about us?"

"Oh! Mrs. Coonan. Yes. Yes, she did. *You're* Patricia?" With an effort, the woman regained her composure. "Well, I'm Mrs. Phillips. I'm in charge here. Thank you for offering to come down and help out. There are so many officers and enlisted men at the base — more every day — we need all the help we can get. It's early yet, so things are fairly quiet. Why don't I give you a quick tour of our facilities?"

Mrs. Phillips led the girls toward the back of the room, past two soldiers who watched their progress with undisguised interest over the top of their newspapers.

"Now ladies, our purpose is to make the servicemen and women who come in here as comfortable as possible. Most of them are very far from home, often for the first time, and we want them to look upon this place as a kind of refuge, a place where they can relax and have fun. In essence, a home away from home."

Mrs. Phillips began to walk around the room, indicating the various amenities with a fluttering hand.

"As you can see, we provide food, reading material, activities and music. And, every Saturday night, we have a dance. Sometimes we are fortunate enough to obtain a live band, but usually, we just tune in Glenn Miller or Tommy Dorsey on the radio."

Mrs. Phillips stopped, turning to consider the girls over the top of her bifocals.

"We encourage our volunteers to dress in an attractive yet … discreet manner. You may talk and dance with the soldiers if you wish, but we strongly discourage any romantic involvements. This is the USO, not a matchmaking service.

"Now, do you have any questions?" she asked in a tone that precluded any.

"No, Ma'am."

"Good. Now, why don't we start you two off at the coffee and doughnut table?"

After demonstrating to them the intricacies of pouring coffee and serving doughnuts, Mrs. Phillips handed them each an apron, leaving the girls stationed behind the table.

"Well, she's a laugh a minute," Patty snorted as soon as she was out of earshot. "*Home away from home.* Sure, if your home happens to be a convent!"

"What did you expect, an alphabetical list of the most eligible bachelors?"

"No, but I didn't expect to be watched over by Mother Superior, either."

"Oh, she's not that bad. Besides, once it gets busy she probably won't have time to bother with us."

"I sure hope not," said Patty, resting her head on her hand.

The next hour dragged with just the occasional serviceman wandering in or out. By 7:30 P.M., however, the foot traffic picked up. So did Patty's mood.

"Now this is more like it!" Patty whispered to Maggie as she gave a young Army Air Corps lieutenant a cup of coffee and a smile. "Maybe it's just the uniforms, but have you ever seen so many good looking guys in one place before? Ooh, Maggie! Quick. Look over there by the door."

Maggie turned her head to find three young men staring at them. They wore the tan summer uniforms, soft crusher caps and swaggering air of a B-17 crew.

Embarrassed, Maggie busied herself straightening the doughnuts on the tray in front of her. Within moments, the same three men were standing by the table.

"Well, hello there. Does that coffee taste as good as you look?" the tall, dark haired one asked with a sure smile.

"I doubt it. It's even older than that line," Patty parried.

He laughed in a good-natured way.

"I guess I deserved that. Let me start again. My name's Jimmy Taylor. I'm a pilot with the 244th squadron. This is my meter reader, Tom Bedell, and my navigator, Eddie Connelly. And you're . . . ?"

"Patty Maloney. And this ... " she pulled Maggie toward

her, "is Maggie Owen."

"It's very nice to meet you, ladies."

This time Jimmy flashed his smile at Maggie. When her only response was a shy nod, he returned his attention to Patty.

"Say, do you think you might take pity on a poor flier, far from home, and give him a dance?"

"Well — "

Patty gave Maggie a hopeful look.

"Go ahead, Patty. I'll take care of the table."

"Thanks, Maggie. I promise I won't be too long."

Patty untied her apron and scooted out from behind the table.

"What's a meter reader?" she asked, taking Jimmy's arm.

"A copilot," Tom answered, claiming her other arm. "Which means, he goes nowhere without me at his side."

Patty laughed as the two steered her in the direction of the dance floor.

"Coming, Eddie?" Tom called over his shoulder.

"No. That's alright." Eddie waved them off. He gave Maggie an apologetic look. "I'm not much of a dancer."

Maggie smiled but said nothing. Eddie just stood there sipping his coffee and surveying the room, showing no signs of moving on. Maggie began to feel uncomfortable at the extended silence. She supposed she ought to say something to this young man. He seemed harmless and probably was far from home. She cleared her throat with a small cough.

"So, where are you from?"

He turned and gave her a crooked smile. "Iowa."

"Iowa?"

"Yup. Ida Grove."

"Ida Grove! Why, that's just down the road. How did you end up getting stationed so close to home?"

"Just lucky, I guess."

"What do you do in Ida Grove?"

"Farm. With my dad and brothers. We raise hogs, mostly. A little corn and oats. I'm the youngest of three boys, so when the war came, I wasn't considered *essential* to running the farm. So, here I am."

"Why the Air Corps?"

"Well, I guess like all little boys, I wanted to be the next *Lucky Lindy*. And I look really swell in the leather jacket." He grinned. "Actually, the guy on the next farm over was a barnstormer. He had a rickety old biplane, a Jenny. I'm not sure what was holding it together. Anyway, he used to take me up sometimes. I just liked the way things looked from up there, like it was all planned out, neat and orderly." He pulled out a cigarette. "Do you mind?"

Maggie shook her head, sliding an empty cup toward him to use as an ashtray. As he lit his cigarette, she studied his profile. He was not handsome in a movie star way, but he had a strong chin, a kind smile and warm brown eyes. He was thin and tall with sandy brown hair, and the permanent tan that came from years spent working out in the open. She guessed his age to be about 22, not quite an *older man*, but someone to be wary of, just the same. Still, his direct manner and quiet way made her feel at ease.

"What about you?"

"What?" His question startled her from her reverie.

"What brings you here?" Eddie motioned to the USO room in general.

"Patty, actually. She thought it would be a good way to meet men. Oh, dear. I shouldn't have said that. I didn't mean … I mean, that's not why I … Oh, dear!"

She sputtered to a halt, mortified.

"It's okay." He chuckled. "Jimmy and Tom kind of dragged me here, too. I'd planned to spend the night at the base writing a letter to my folks. I've only written them once since I got here two weeks ago. But, they kept at me, called me *farm boy*. They told me I needed to get out and experience life in the big city."

Maggie bristled.

"What's wrong with being a farm boy?"

"Nothing. In fact, that's what I plan to go back to when this is all over. I'm going to buy a farm of my own somewhere in Iowa. Something little at first, but I'll add on as I can. Then I'm going to try out some new ideas I've been reading about. Put more of the land to corn. They've come up with some new hybrids and techniques that will almost double the yield per acre. And good quality corn, the finest. You know, there's nothing quite like bringing in your own crop that you planned for and sweated over and — " He became self-conscious. "I'm sorry. I get a little carried away."

"You sound like my dad."

"Oh? Is he a farmer?"

"Yes. He has a farm in Boru, in the northwest part of the state. He raises corn and oats. Some hogs and cows, too."

"How is it that you're here in Sioux City, then?"

Maggie hesitated. "I live here part time with my uncle. He and my aunt helped raise me after my mother died when I was little."

Maggie waited for the obligatory expression of sympathy, but Eddie just took a long draw on his cigarette.

"Yeah, my Mom died when I was ten. It's rough." He tapped the ashes into a cup. "Do you go back to the farm much?"

"Yes. Some holidays, and for a long visit in the summer. I miss it. I feel closer to … well, closer to things there." Why was she saying these things to a total stranger?

Eddie just nodded as if her statement was the most natural thing in the world. He extended his coffee cup toward her.

"Can I have a refill?"

"You're kidding, right?"

"Us Iowa boys are tough to kill," he said with a wry smile. "So, what do you do when you're not pouring coffee for lonely fly boys?"

"I'm on vacation from college."

"College. Wow." His voice was envious. "Where?"

"Saint Mary's College in Indiana. It's a women's college

right across the street from the University of Notre Dame."

"*The Fighting Irish*. My dad listens to all of their games on the radio. He thinks Coach Leahy's almost as good as Rockne was. I'm partial to Iowa Pre-flight, myself."

"Hey, Eddie! Come on. The night is young, and we've got a lot of places to hit yet!" Jimmy and Tom motioned from the doorway. With reluctance, Eddie set down his cup of coffee.

"I'd better go with them to see that they make it back to the base."

He hesitated, then gave her that shy, crooked smile once more.

"I've enjoyed talking to you, Maggie. Maybe I'll see you here again sometime?"

It was not a line, but a sincere, hopeful question.

In spite of herself, Maggie smiled back.

"Maybe you will."

Maggie did see Eddie again at the USO Club. He came in whenever he got a pass and always made a point of coming over to talk to her. He was never pushy or needy. He just seemed to enjoy her company. Sometimes they'd dance, but usually they just talked — about farming, life at college, movies and music. Maggie began to look forward to his visits, finding herself disappointed on those evenings when duty kept him away. She felt comfortable with him as she hadn't felt with anyone in a long time. Their backgrounds were remarkably similar. There were so many things that he seemed to understand innately. So when, three weeks after they met, he asked her to go to an early movie, she agreed, feeling only a twinge of guilt. After all, her correspondence with Jack Koerner was just platonic. And, Eddie was a lonely soldier, soon to go to war.

Maggie arranged to meet Eddie at the theater, letting Uncle John think she was going to one of her regular volunteer nights at the USO. She knew Patty would back up her story. She hated lying to her uncle, but, since Aunt Nora's death, he was so protective of her. She just didn't feel ready to run the gauntlet of his questions.

They went to see *Casablanca*, a very sad, romantic movie starring Ingrid Bergman and Humphrey Bogart. Maggie wasn't sure if she was relieved or disappointed that Eddie hadn't tried to hold her hand or put his arm around her during the movie.

Afterwards, she and Eddie walked the eight blocks home rather than take the streetcar, talking and laughing about the film. When they got to her corner, Maggie asked that they say goodbye there, lest her subterfuge be discovered. For an awkward moment, they just stood there. Then, drawing courage from the fading evening light, Eddie asked permission to kiss her. She was so touched by his deference she said yes without hesitation. His lips were gentle but his arms as he held her were strong and steady. When she stepped back, he reached out to guide a stray curl of her hair back into place. The intensity of his gaze made her lower her eyes.

"Goodnight, Eddie."

"Goodnight, Maggie."

Maggie hurried away down the street to her house. She turned just once only to discover that he was still watching her.

When she slipped in the front door, she found a letter from Jack waiting for her on the entry hall table.

Louise secured her favorite blue straw hat to her head with a hatpin while she addressed Maggie's petulant image in the front hall mirror.

"Maggie, you know your uncle is having those people from the Livestock Exchange over for dinner tonight. I have to go to the market right now if I'm to have things ready in time. He'd have my head if I were to let that young man in the house with no one else home. And didn't you promise your uncle that you'd have those windows cleaned before you went anywhere?"

"Yes, but, Louise, Eddie has to be back at the base by 4:00 P.M. Can't he just come in for a little bit? I'm sure Uncle John wouldn't mind. You know how much he likes Eddie. He always calls him *that fine lad*, and tells me I should invite him over for dinner more often."

Unmoved, Louise shook her head, pulling on her gloves. Maggie threw up her hands in exasperation.

"This is ridiculous! I can't believe that I can't let him in the house just because some people have dirty minds. After all, we're just good friends."

"Good friends who've been out together every time he can beg, borrow or steal a pass. And dirty minds or no, you have your reputation and your uncle's reputation to think about, not to mention my job. Now, my instructions were that he was not to come into the house while I'm gone. And you are not to leave the house until those windows are done. Do you hear me?"

"Honestly, you'd think I was a child. I'm almost nineteen!"

"If you were a child, there wouldn't be a problem. Now, where did I put that ration coupon book? Ah, there it is. I don't know how I'm supposed to make a decent meal for people with the shoe leather they're passing off as beef these days. You'd think with your uncle being a high muckety-muck at the stockyards, he could arrange to bring something decent home, but no — "

Still grumbling, Louise stuffed the book in her purse. She marched out of the house, past the bemused Eddie and down the street towards the streetcar stop. Maggie came out onto the front porch.

"Well, I guess you heard her."

"I heard her say we can still be together as long as the windows get cleaned and I don't go in the house."

"Eddie, do you have any idea how many windows there are in this house? It will take me an hour and a half to do them all. You have to be back at the base in two hours."

"But, if we share the work, it will only take half as long, and you and I will still have almost a full hour to be together."

"But you can't come in."

"Not a problem. There's a ladder by the garage, right? Go get two buckets and two rags. I will reveal my great plan."

For the next forty-five minutes, the residents and passersby on Twenty-seventh Street were treated to the unusual sight of Maggie cleaning the inside of all the windows of the house while Eddie, scurrying up and down the ladder, followed her from window to window like a mirror image, cleaning the outside. Together, they worked and laughed till every window in the house shone.

When at last they finished, they collapsed on the front porch steps, hands wrinkled and sleeves damp, to enjoy some well-earned lemonade.

"I've got to hand it to you, Eddie. You're a genius."

"Yeah. I can be pretty creative if it means I get to spend some extra time with you."

"I don't know why you'd want to spend time with someone who looks like a wet dishrag." Maggie tried in vain to smooth her wavy hair into place.

"I think you look beautiful," said Eddie.

Pleased yet uncomfortable with the compliment, Maggie changed the subject.

"When's your next leave?"

"I don't know. They've scheduled some of us *old-timers* to fly lead crew for a series of training flights starting tomorrow morning. We'll be taking some of the new bomber crews through high altitude formations and practice bombing runs, that kind of stuff. It could be a few days, it could be a week. It just depends on how long it takes us to get it right."

"You've only been training for seven weeks. I hardly think that qualifies you as an *old timer*."

"It does in this war. They ship us out after nine weeks."

Maggie suddenly found it hard to breathe. She placed her hand on his arm.

"You will be careful, won't you?"

They both knew she wasn't talking about the training mission, and they both pretended she was.

"Of course. These are just training runs. There's no danger as long as we make it through the ack-ack over South Dakota," he said with a chuckle. "Besides, there's no safer plane than a B-17. They don't call them *Flying Fortresses* for nothing. And Jimmy will be at the controls."

Maggie made a face. "Jimmy is a nut case."

"True, but he's also the best pilot in the squadron. If our plane so much as hiccups, he knows why. I've known him since primary training at Hawthorne Field in South Carolina, and I trust him. The whole crew trusts him — completely."

Eddie looked at his watch.

"Damn. What happened to the time? I've got to get back to the base."

Setting down his lemonade, he took Maggie's hands in his.

"Maggie, I've been trying to work up the courage to ask you something. I know we haven't known each other very long and there's a lot we haven't talked about — my leaving for Europe, and that sailor who keeps writing you from Notre Dame, for starters."

Maggie felt the color rise to her face.

"I've seen the envelopes sitting out on the front hall table," he explained, not unkindly. "But, that doesn't matter. Maggie, these past six weeks we've been together have been the happiest of my life. I feel like I've known you forever. We come from the same background and we care about the same things. The truth is ... look, I know this is kind of sudden, but ... I've fallen in love with you."

He put his finger to her lips as Maggie tried to speak.

"No, don't say anything. Let me get this all out." He took a deep breath and plunged ahead.

"I don't want to be one of those guys who pressures a girl into marrying him just because he's getting shipped out, but I think we could have a wonderful life together, farming, raising a family. I'd take good care of you. And you'd be near your uncle, and not too far from Boru, either. I know it's a lot to ask ... that you wait for me, but ... will you at least think about it?

Marrying me, I mean?"

"Oh, Eddie. I don't know what to say — "

"Don't say anything yet. I know I kind of sprung this on you. You take some time."

He glanced down at his watch and grimaced.

"Oh, geez. I've really got to go or they'll mark me AWOL. Just promise me you'll think about it?"

Stunned, Maggie nodded.

"The second I get done with this training mission, we'll talk, okay?"

Eddie pulled her to him.

"I love you, Maggie," he said, and kissed her, hard, right there on the porch in front of all of Twenty-seventh Street. Releasing her suddenly, he leapt from the porch and sprinted in the direction of the streetcar.

Maggie just sat there, staring after him.

On Tuesday morning, just before 11:00 A.M., Maggie walked up Douglas Street on her way home from Toller's Drug Store with some liniment for her uncle. She blessed herself with the Sign of the Cross as she passed in front of the huge Cathedral of the Epiphany, beautiful despite the two truncated spires that awaited completion on either side of the main nave. She was almost to the corner when a large black car with government plates careened up to the curb. Even before the car had come to a complete stop, an army officer jumped out and ran into the church. The car sat idling at the curb. In these days of gas rationing, that was enough in and of itself to draw attention. But the people of Sioux City had learned that whenever the Army sent a car for the priest, it usually meant a plane had crashed during training. A crowd began to gather.

In less than a minute, the officer reappeared, followed by Father McCafferty, the assistant pastor, his black sacramental bag in his hand and his cassock flying out behind him.

"Father, has something happened?" a woman called out.

"Yes. There's been an accident at the base. A plane crash."

"Is it bad?" shouted someone else.

"I'm afraid so, God help us. I'm sorry. I must be going." The priest gathered his skirts into the car and shut the door. As soon as the officer jumped into the passenger seat, the car sped off.

Trying to control the fear that gripped her, Maggie returned to the cathedral, slipping in the side entrance. As the heavy wooden door closed behind her, Maggie was enveloped by the cool darkness of the empty church. She made her way to the little side chapel dedicated to the Blessed Mother, taking comfort in the familiar smell of incense and candles burning, and the quiet presence of God in this place. Maggie knelt down in front of the statue of Mary and closed her eyes.

"Oh, Dear Lady, I know this is a selfish prayer. I wouldn't wish this tragedy on any of the boys or their families. But, please, Most Blessed Mother, I beg you. Don't let it be Eddie. I'll do anything. Just please, don't let it be Eddie!"

How long she stayed there she wasn't sure, but when she left, she knew she had to find out what was happening or go crazy. She ran the four blocks home and burst into the empty kitchen.

"Louise! I need the car!"

Maggie grabbed the keys to the Ford without waiting for a response. Within minutes, she was speeding towards the air base south of the city.

Maggie hadn't heard from Eddie in four days, but that was not unusual. She knew, as all Sioux City knew, that training was ongoing by the contrails crisscrossing the sky and the constant drone of bomber engines above the occasional cloud cover. Her mind raced. There were so many B-17 crews training at the base, not to mention P-51 fighter planes. So many men. What were the chances that it was Eddie's plane that had crashed? What were the chances that he would've been among the injured? Still ... suddenly, her heart froze in her chest. There was a column of dark black smoke rising from the direction of the airstrip. She increased her speed, trying to clear her mind of any thoughts but brake-clutch-shift as she wove in and out of traffic.

When she reached the base, an MP in full regalia stopped her at the gate.

"I'm sorry, Miss. The base is off-limits to civilians. You'll have to turn your car around."

"Please. Please help me. The plane that went down. Do you know which one it was?"

"I'm not at liberty to give out any information, Ma'am."

"Please, I have to know. Was it a Fortress? Was anyone … hurt?"

Seeing how distraught she was, the young man dropped his military demeanor for just a moment.

"I'm sorry, Miss. No one knows very much right now. The only thing I know is that it was a B-17. Some kind of training accident. You'll just have to wait until they release the rest of the details."

"How long will that be?"

"I don't know. I'm sorry. Now, please. You have to move your car."

Maggie wasn't sure how she managed to drive home. Uncle John met her at the door. He'd heard about the accident and had already contacted everyone he could think of that might have any information, but he'd had no more success than Maggie. He repeated the words the MP had said, *We'll just have to wait.* But for how long, Maggie wondered? When would she know if he lived or died? If the unthinkable had happened, would anyone even know to contact her? For, after all, she wasn't family. She was … what? A close friend? A sweetheart? — A fiancee?

For the rest of the day, Maggie jumped each time she heard the telephone ring, but it was always for Uncle John. He cautioned her that in accidents such as this, it took a long time to sort everything out. It could be days before they heard anything definite. But, he tried to keep the line clear, just in case.

Finally, at 10:45 P.M., the phone rang, much too late for

any of Uncle John's friends to call. Maggie stared at the receiver, desperate yet afraid to hear the voice on the other end. In slow motion, she made her way to the phone and raised the receiver to her ear. Before she could even say hello, she heard him.

"Maggie? Maggie! It's Eddie."

"Eddie," Maggie whispered. She sank to the floor. Uncle John appeared at the top of the stairs in his bathrobe.

"Maggie?" he called.

"It's okay, Uncle John. It's Eddie."

Tears streamed down her face as she relayed the happy news. "Thank God."

Uncle John blew her a kiss, discreetly returning to his bedroom.

"Oh, Eddie, I was so afraid!"

"I know, Maggie. I'm so sorry. I knew you'd be worried. I called you as soon as I could. They herded us into the ready room and wouldn't let any of us contact anyone until they'd finished their investigation. I had to punch out two guys to get to the phone first."

"But, you're all right? You're not hurt?"

"No. I'm fine.

"What happened?"

"I'll tell you about it when I see you. They're giving us leave at 1300 hours tomorrow. I'll explain everything then. There's other guys waiting in line here. I've got to go."

"Goodbye, Eddie. I'm so glad you're safe. And Eddie?"

"Yes, Maggie?"

"About the question you asked me ... before you left. I ... I have an answer for you."

"Wait, Maggie. Wait till I get there."

Seated on the davenport in the parlor the next afternoon, Eddie told his story.

"We'd been up for almost three hours, nine crews, practicing formations and bombing runs. It was pretty windy and we were having trouble with the drift — that's how the wind affects the path of the bomb. Anyway, we finally got the order to return to base. Our crew was fourth to land. We were taxiing in on the far runway when we heard the distress call on the radio."

"What happened?"

"A wheel jammed. It happens sometimes. The crew tried to crank it down by hand. They even tried to bounce the plane off the runway a few times to jar it loose. I'll tell you, that rookie pilot was a pretty cool customer. But the wheel wouldn't budge, and they were running out of fuel. So they decided to try to land belly-up, without any landing gear at all. By this time, all of the other crews had landed. We just stood there on the apron of the other runway, watching. At first, it looked like they might make it. But, then, the plane tipped over onto one wing, spun and broke up." He lowered his head. "Four of the crew were killed — the navigator, both waist gunners and the radio man. The tail gunner was badly burned."

"Oh, Eddie. I'm so sorry. Did you know them well?"

"Not real well. They'd only been here a little over three weeks. But they were good guys. Good flyers. They just had some really bad luck."

Maggie put her hand on his.

"Are *you* all right?"

"Me? Yeah."

He paused, meeting Maggie's eyes. She saw something there she'd never seen before.

"It's just that … it made it all so real, you know? Before, it was almost as if we'd been given this big expensive toy to play with. Like playing at war when you were little. We'd go up in our fancy jumpsuits and fleece jackets, make wisecracks to each other over the radio, drop our bombs on pretend targets and be back in time for mess hall. But, now … well, it's like they tried to tell us at the beginning. It's not a game. People are going to die. You just don't know who or when."

Maggie began to put her arm around him, but he stood up abruptly and walked over to the window.

"Maggie, four days ago — " He gave a small, sad laugh. "Gee, it seems a lot longer than that. Anyway, you might remember, I asked you to marry me. Well, standing out there on the apron, watching the guys on the crash truck trying to make their way through the flames to save those poor guys, knowing it could easily have been me ... I had a lot of time to think."

He turned toward her, and Maggie realized that what she'd seen in his eyes was not something new, but something missing. The innocence was gone.

"I love you, Maggie. That hasn't changed. But I realize now that I wasn't being fair to you. I said I didn't want you to feel pressured because I was going to be going across soon, but how could you not? And now, with this accident — "

He came back to the couch and took her hand.

"Maggie, the last thing in this world I want is for you to say you love me or that you'll marry me because I'm going away ... and you're afraid I might not come back."

"Oh, Eddie, that's not why — "

"Isn't it? Are you sure?" His voice was gentle, his eyes, searching.

Involuntarily, Maggie lowered her gaze. Eddie's smile was understanding, if sad.

"The funny thing is, Maggie, I think you do love me, at least a little. And, maybe if we had more time — " A muscle in his jaw twitched. "But time is the one thing we can't count on right now." He squared his shoulders. "So, I think we should wait."

"Do I get any say in this?" Maggie challenged, tears streaming down her face.

"No," he said in a firm voice. "You don't. Not now. When I come back, when I've finished my twenty-five missions, we can pick up where we left off. Then we can take our time and be sure how we feel."

Eddie raised her hand to his lips.

"I promise, Maggie. When I come back."

In late August, Maggie got a letter from a Mr. Joseph Connelly of Ida Grove, Iowa. That's how she found out that Eddie's plane had been shot down on a bombing run over Gelsenkirchen, Germany on the twelfth of August, 1943. There were no survivors.

Chapter 16

September 1943

Use it up, wear it out,
Make it do or do without.
          —homefront slogan during World War II

"Bonds! Stamps! Buy your War Bonds or Stamps. Give Hitler a shellacking and send Tojo packing. Buy your Bonds and Stamps here!"

Bea chanted her pitch over and over to the girls heading through the lobby of Le Mans Hall on their way to dinner. Maggie rolled her eyes, but couldn't help smiling.

She and Bea had volunteered to man a table for the Saint Mary's Student War Council's Defense Bond and Stamps Drive. They sat in front of a large bulletin board filled with snapshots of boyfriends, brothers and even fathers who were currently serving overseas. Over the pictures was a homemade sign that read, *These are our fighting men. Back them up! Buy Defense Stamps. Today!* The idea of using the photos had been Maggie's, and, together with Bea's fervent pitch, they'd tugged at the heartstrings and loosened quite a few purse strings.

"Bea, you sound like a barker at a circus," Maggie teased.

"Well," Bea replied, "if their sense of duty doesn't talk them into buying, maybe we can annoy them into it. Besides," she said, picking up the metal box from the table in front of them and shaking it, "it appears to be working. This is the most money we've taken in so far on any one shift."

"Well, it's also possible that the Allied invasion of Italy this past week had something to do with it, don't you think?"

"Coincidence. Pure coincidence. I tell you, when this war is over, I'm going into sales."

"What kind of sales?"

"It doesn't matter," Bea replied. "If I can get these tight-wads to shell out, I can sell anything to anyone."

Just then, three girls came walking out of the dining room, chatting and laughing loudly. One of them was raven-haired Mary Louise Gabriel, a sophomore classmate of Bea and Maggie's. Mary Louise was from New York City, and had made it her mission to bring *high fashion* to what she saw as the couture-deprived girls of Saint Mary's. Although the demand for material for the war effort and the subsequent rationing of civilian apparel had put a damper on all of the girls' wardrobes, Mary Louise always seemed to rise to the challenge with innovative ways to wear and reuse items she already owned. She was frequently written up in *The Clothesline* fashion column of *The Static*, the Saint Mary's newspaper, for her stylish and sometimes outlandish outfits. The other girls sought to imitate her natural flair, with limited success.

Mary Louise waved her manicured fingers at Maggie and Bea as she walked by their table, gabbing with her friends.

"Miss Gabriel," a shrill voice called out.

Sister Grace Ann stood at the edge of the lobby, her steely eyes riveted on Mary Louise.

Casting sympathetic looks over their shoulders, the girls with Mary Louise scurried away. She walked over to the nun, greeting her with an innocent smile.

"Yes, Sister?"

Sister Grace Ann took a few slow, measured steps closer to Mary Louise, giving her a thorough once over.

"Young lady, do you really think your attire is appropriate for a Saint Mary's girl?"

As if seeing it for the first time, Mary Louise looked down at her clothing. She was wearing a simple, white cardigan sweater with no blouse, buttoned to the top, and a slim black skirt that, it could be argued, reached just below the knee. On almost anyone else, the outfit would have been unremarkable, but on a girl with Mary Louise's lush figure and long legs, it's understatement only added to the overall allure.

"Why, Sister, it's just a sweater and a skirt," said Mary Louise.

"A very *small* sweater and a very *short* skirt," Sister countered.

"But, Sister, I'm just trying to conserve material in accordance with the U.S. War Production Board's Rule L-85 which states that no skirt should be wider than 80 inches or longer than just below the knee. For the war effort, you know. And this sweater belonged to my mother. I thought it made sense to reuse it."

"Your mother must be a very tiny woman," Sister observed wryly.

Maggie managed to stifle a giggle.

"Miss Gabriel, while I applaud your patriotic adherence to cloth rationing, in the future, I would suggest that you choose clothing that does not over-emphasize your obvious ... good health. And I hope that your facility for memorizing government rules and policy stands you in good stead for this afternoon's American History exam."

"Yes, Sister," Mary Louise replied.

With a grunt of displeasure, Sister Grace Ann turned in a flurry of robes, marching down the hallway to her office.

Mary Louise looked at Maggie and Bea.

"I still got it," she said with a wink. She sauntered off on her long legs.

"She's unbelievable." Bea's voice was filled with admiration.

"I'll say," Maggie agreed. She reached over to place another War Stamp payment in the moneybox. As she did, her eyes were drawn to the poster displayed on the wall to the left of the dining room entrance. The picture was of a determined young soldier, waving goodbye from an airplane. The caption underneath read, "*So we'll meet again ...*" BUY WAR BONDS. Unwittingly, Bea had put it up to encourage bond sales. Maggie, unwilling to reveal the reason behind the pain it caused her, had said nothing.

For how could she begin to explain? It had all happened so fast. No one here at Saint Mary's even knew that Eddie had ever existed. At times she wondered herself if it had all been a dream. But then she would hear the sound of a plane overhead, and the reality would hit her so hard she'd be left gasping for breath. Staring at the poster, Maggie's mind raced unbidden back to the bad period right after Eddie's death.

Upon receiving the letter from Eddie's father, Maggie had been inconsolable. She ate little and slept less, spending most of the time in her room, weeping and praying. Maggie knew it was irrational, but she couldn't shake the feeling that if she'd only agreed to marry Eddie when he'd first asked, he would somehow still be alive. But, Eddie had been taken from her life as had so many others. Had he been taken because she didn't love him enough — or because she'd dared to love him at all?

After ten days of this, Uncle John knocked on the door of her room.

"Maggie?"

He cracked open the door. She lay huddled beneath a chenille blanket, facing the wall. He walked to the side of the bed and sat down.

"Maggie, I think it's time we had a talk."

"Not now, Uncle John. I'm not feeling well."

"And it's no wonder with the little bit you've been eatin'. Not enough to keep a bird alive. Now, sit up and listen to what I have to say."

With effort, Maggie did as she was told. Her eyes were red and puffy, and her dirty hair hung limply about her face.

Uncle John took a gentler tone.

"Maggie. I know this has been hard on you, what with Eddie dyin' so soon after we lost Mother Nora. You never said as much, but I gathered that you and Eddie had reached some kind of understandin'. You've a right to grieve. He was a fine young man."

He gazed out at the gently swaying leaves of the oak tree

outside her window.

"I don't know why God takes the people He does when He does. Maybe it's a test of our love for Him, or maybe He has other plans for us. But, whatever the reason, it's His will, and we've just got to trust in Him, no matter how hard it may be."

Looking back down at Maggie, he continued.

"Your young man fought for what he believed in, and died bravely. You have to accept that and honor his memory. And you can't do that by stayin' here locked in your room, hidin' from life."

He handed Maggie a handkerchief to wipe the tears that had once more begun to stream down her cheeks.

"Now, I realize that I haven't set a very good example for you. When your aunt died, I wanted to hide, too. The world seemed too much to face without her. But, life goes on, whether we want it to or not. And so must we."

He walked to the window and lifted the sash, letting some fresh air into the stuffy room. Then, turning to face Maggie, he folded his arms across his chest.

"So, I've decided to make some changes. First, I'm goin' to sell this house." He held up a hand to stay Maggie's protest. "No. It's too large with you away at school, and there are too many memories here. I'm going to get a smaller place, maybe somethin' overlookin' the park. Louise has agreed to come along and cook and keep house for me, God bless her, so I won't starve.

"Second, I'm goin' to spend more time on stockyard business. The government is buyin' up meat for our soldiers as fast as they can, and we're hard pressed to keep up with the demand. Keepin' busy," he said with an emphatic nod of his head, "that's the best thing for a broken heart. Time and prayer will do the rest.

"Which is why you're going back to school. Immediately. I told the Sisters you'd be arrivin' a few days late. Don't worry, I didn't tell them why," he added in response to her panicked look. "You're goin' back to school to study and learn, and find your place in the world. You need to be with people your own age. Then, maybe in time — ”

Maggie shook her head fiercely, and began to cry again. Uncle John sat down beside her, hugging her to his big barrel chest.

“Ah, Maggie, Maggie. I know it hurts, but, don't close yourself off from life. You're young, so you may not believe it now, but it is true what they say, *It's better to have loved and lost than never to have loved at all.*”

She snorted.

“Is it?”

“That's somethin' you'll have to find out for yourself.”

“Maggie. Yoo hoo, Maggie.”

With a jolt, Maggie returned to the present.

“Oh, Julie! I'm sorry. I guess I drifted off.”

“I'll say. You were a million miles away. They sent me over from the reception desk. There's someone waiting to see you in the lounge. I think it's that *Jack* fella you used to go out with last year.”

Maggie felt her heart sink. She'd never told Jack about Eddie. She'd just stopped writing him after Eddie died. He'd want to know why, and she wasn't ready to deal with his questions, much less his attentions.

“Bea, can you take care of the table for a while? I'll be right back.”

“Sure,” said Bea, noting Maggie's strange reaction. “Don't hurry back on my account.”

Jack stood as Maggie entered the lounge. She couldn't help but notice that he'd grown and filled out in the three months they'd been apart. He looked tall, tan and incredibly handsome in his summer khaki uniform. But, there was something else about him. An air of maturity and confidence seemed to have replaced his adolescent brashness. And the look in his eyes as she entered the room made Maggie blush.

“Maggie.”

Jack wrapped his arms around her in a spontaneous embrace. She stiffened. Puzzled, he stepped back, searching her face.

"How are you?" he asked with concern.

"I'm fine, Jack," she said, avoiding his eyes. "It's nice to see you again."

"Here." He indicated some chairs huddled in the corner. "Why don't we sit down for a while?"

Jack escorted Maggie across the room, uncharacteristically oblivious to the appreciative glances some passing girls threw his way.

"I would've gotten here sooner, but the battalion had Saturday morning inspection. Gosh, it's been a long time. So, how've you been?"

"Fine. Busy. I worked at the stockyards with my uncle right up until the last minute. Since I got back a few days ago, I've been getting my room in order, going to class, getting my books … you know, the usual. How did your second cruise go?"

"Great. It was nice to put some of our theory into practice, even if it was just on Lake Michigan. I'll tell you, though, learning to load and fire small caliber guns on a cruiser is nothing compared to standing on the catwalk of the *USS Wolverine* going at flank speed when they're doing the pilot qualification tests. Man, the fliers landing those fighter and torpedo planes onto that carrier have some kind of guts." He paused. "But, then, I told you all about this stuff in my last two letters … which you never answered."

Maggie dipped her head.

"I know. I'm sorry. I went back to the farm to visit my dad for awhile. Then, when I got back, we had some bad news. A close friend of mine … and my uncle's … was killed. His B-17 was shot down over Germany." She fumbled with the cuff of her blouse. "I'd really rather not talk about it."

"Sure, that's okay."

Jack rested his elbows on his knees, twirling his hat between his index fingers. After a few moments, he cleared his throat.

"Well, Maggie, would you like to go get something to eat or maybe see a movie with me tonight? We could kind of catch up."

"Gee, Jack. I don't think I can."

"Well, I know it is kind of short notice."

"It's not that. It's just that, well, I've signed up for a lot of activities this year, the newspaper and the yearbook and the War Council. With all that and my studies, too, I just don't think I'm going to have much time to do any dating."

"What? You mean ... at all?" he asked, taken aback.

"No. Not at all."

"Now, Maggie," he cajoled, "you know what they say about all work and no play."

Maggie just shrugged and looked down at her hands.

Jack frowned.

"Maggie, what's going on? Did something happen? Did I do something?"

"Of course not."

"But, I don't get it. After last year ... your letters ... I thought you and I — "

"Jack, please don't take it personally. I'm just really going to be too busy."

"Too busy. Or just too busy for me?"

Maggie jutted her chin at him.

"Is it so hard for you to believe that someone could actually have something more important to do than date the great Jack Koerner? I told you. I need to concentrate on my studies. I'm sorry."

"Yeah," he replied. "Me, too. Sorry I bothered you."

Maggie stood up and held out her hand.

"I do thank you for coming over, Jack. It was good to see you."

Jack took her hand, but did not release it. He forced her to meet his gaze.

"Jack, please." Maggie's voice trembled as she tried to pull her hand away. Stunned by the look of pain in her eyes, he let her go.

Jack stood watching as she hurried away. Something had happened, he was sure of it. All this business about being too busy. He suspected it had something to do with this *close friend* who'd died. Obviously, he'd been much more than that to Maggie.

Well, if she preferred her memories of a dead man to him, then fine, he thought. She could have them. There were plenty of other fish in the sea.

Jack jammed his hat on his head and left the lounge.

Maggie saw Jack only once after that, by accident, at a Saturday morning Bond Rally. The Saint Mary's War Council had sold enough War Bonds to purchase a jeep, and to reward the Council's hard work and encourage future sales, the U.S. Military had sent a WAAC over in an actual Army jeep to give the top sellers rides around the campus. In the crowd of students and faculty gathered around the vehicle that October morning, Maggie spied Jack standing over by a tree talking to a pretty girl from the junior class. Without meaning to, Maggie found herself staring. Suddenly, Jack looked up, and their eyes met. When he turned away with careful indifference, Maggie was surprised to feel a slight pang of guilt. And jealousy.

"Come on, Maggie. It's our turn," Bea called.

Maggie climbed into the jeep beside her roommate. When she looked back, Jack was gone.

Weeks passed. Maggie filled her days with studies, deadlines and meetings. At night, however, the thoughts and memories of Eddie came to her in the darkness, mingling with thoughts of her mother and Aunt Nora. She could only close her eyes and pray, pray that time, with it's legendary powers, would heal her broken heart.

Uncle John wrote often. His letters were filled with information on the livestock commission and the stockyards. He'd accompanied other stockyard and meat packing industry lead-ers to Washington, D.C. to advise a Senate Committee on the most expeditious methods for producing and providing meat for the armed forces. While there, he'd even met with President Roosevelt, whom he pronounced, *an inspiring leader and a fine, robust man, despite the wheelchair.* Uncle John ended each letter with words of encouragement for Maggie, often including a ten dollar bill for Maggie to spend on *what-nots.* She spent it on war bonds.

Maggie, in turn, wrote him about her studies, her work on the school newspaper and the War Council. But, there was no mention of friends or dates or even the football games Maggie had so enjoyed attending her freshman year.

"Good afternoon, Maggie."

Maggie turned to find Sister Lenore standing in the middle of the empty dormitory hallway, holding a large stack of folded linens and a bucket of cleaning supplies.

"Hello, Sister."

"I'm surprised to see you here on a Saturday afternoon. I thought you'd be at one of the football parties with your ear glued to the radio broadcast from Soldier's Field. The game should be an exciting one. Army has a tough team again this year."

"I have a deadline on a story I'm working on for *The Static.*"

"I see. Well, do you think you could spare just a few minutes to help me out? I need to change the altar cloths and do some cleaning in the chapel."

Maggie, who wanted nothing more than to go to her room and be left in peace, replied, "Of course, Sister."

"Wonderful." She handed the bucket to Maggie. "Come with me."

Maggie followed Sister Lenore's swishing black skirts down the hall to the carved wooden doors of the Holy Ghost Chapel. *Chapel* was a misnomer, for it was larger and more ornate than many full size churches Maggie had been in. The chapel had a soaring vaulted wooden ceiling and was illuminated by seven

pairs of stained glass windows flanked by ornate iron chande-
liers. Two rows of wooden pews led up to the stone communion rail that separated the sanctuary from the body of the church.
There were two small side altars to either side of the large main
altar. The main altar was flanked by carved stone statues of
worshiping angels, and contained a beautiful golden tabernacle that towered above the candelabras used for the high and
low Masses. On the wall behind the main altar, there was a
large mural depicting the crucifixion.

Sister Lenore dipped her hand into the holy water font,
crossed herself and led Maggie up the center aisle of the empty
chapel. The air still smelled of candle wax and incense from
morning Mass. The afternoon light streaming in through the
violet, stained glass windows threw multi-colored patterns across
the pews and the tile floor.

Maggie jumped at the sound of Sister's voice in the silence.

"I'll hand the soiled linens to you, then you can begin folding them."

Maggie was not allowed to go into the sanctuary itself.
Even Sister Lenore was only allowed beyond the Communion
rail to perform the necessary jobs of cleaning and changing the
altar cloths. So Maggie waited on the congregation side of the
rail while the nun removed the old cloths, laid new ones in
their place and checked the candles and flowers. Each time
Sister passed in front of the golden tabernacle holding the Holy
Eucharist, she genuflected with great reverence.

When she finished, Sister Lenore joined Maggie in the first
pew and began helping to fold the linens.

"How have you liked your sophomore year so far, Maggie?"

"It's been fine. Busy."

"Yes. I've noticed that you've signed up for quite a number of committees and activities this year. That's admirable, but
I do hope you're not overdoing it. You need to have a little
fun, too, you know."

"Yes, Sister." Maggie folded the last altar cloth.

"There. Now, if you could just help me wipe down these

pews and pick up any stray missals or papers, I think we'll be done. Here's a clean rag. You work that side. I'll work this."

Sister Lenore went to the front of the left hand row of pews and began working. As she worked, she talked.

"You know, Maggie, your approach may be the better one. When I was your age, I had a little too much fun." She chuckled. "Don't look so surprised. I wasn't always a nun, you know. You're what, nineteen years old?"

Maggie nodded.

"Let's see. I was nineteen in 1925. Oh, yes. That was my *flapper* stage."

"You were a flapper?" Maggie asked, incredulous.

"My, yes. I had the bobbed hair, the short dresses, the make-up, the whole thing. I even won the Charleston contest back at my high school in St. Louis. Gave my parents fits. And I was in love with the most wonderful young man." She sighed. "Andrew Reston."

Sister Lenore didn't see Maggie's mouth drop open for she was lost in reminiscence, dangling the rag she was holding back and forth.

"He was so handsome," Sister continued, "and so charming — funny and kind. We were going to be married as soon as he finished college." Her expression became wistful. "But, he was killed in a car accident. Went off a curve into a tree. He did love to drive fast." She resumed dusting the pews.

"Is that why you became a nun?" Maggie asked after a moment.

Sister Lenore smiled.

"Oh, no. You don't become a nun because your first choice didn't work out. You become a nun because you realize it's what God has put you on earth to do."

"Then how did you end up at Saint Mary's?"

"Well, to be honest, at the time I thought it was just one more of God's punishments. When Andy died, I thought my life was over. I didn't want to do anything or see anyone. I barely spoke. My parents were very worried. Then a friend of my mother's suggested that a change of scene might do me good. She told her about Saint Mary's. My parents were a little nervous about how their *wild child* would take to the idea, but they were desperate. They needn't have worried. I didn't put up a fuss. I didn't really care what happened to me at that point." She stopped speaking to rub at a particularly stubborn spot on the wood.

"Then, little by little, I began to notice the Sisters here, the dedication they put into their teaching and the joy they found in prayer and worship. And I saw what a wonderful, vibrant community they had. I started talking to one of the Sisters I was most comfortable with, asking her about her life and the choice she'd made. The more I learned, the more I wanted to know. It was like my heart had come alive again. I came to believe that God was calling me to that same life of service." She chuckled. "I don't think my parents believe it to this day."

"But, if your boyfriend had lived, do you think you would have married him?"

"I don't know. But, that wasn't God's plan. It was Andrew's fate to die young, and my fate to move on and find my place with the Sisters of the Holy Cross." She came to the end of the last pew. "There, I think we're finished."

Sister Lenore looked up to find Maggie standing at the other end of the pew, an accusatory look on her face.

"My uncle talked to you, didn't he?"

The nun had the good grace to look sheepish.

"He told me only that a young man you cared for very much was killed just before you returned here, and he asked me to keep an eye on you. I have to confess, when I looked at you, I saw myself in those months after Andrew died. I remember the pain. The what-ifs. I just wanted you to know that it will get better. God will bring you out of this dark time, just as He did me."

Maggie looked at Sister Lenore in dismay.

"You mean, you think God is calling me to be a nun, too?"

"Oh, good heavens, no! I mean, He *could*, but I doubt

He'd use an ex-flapper as His vehicle. I just meant that we can't know what plan God has for us, and when bad things happen in life — and they do — we have to trust in Him and go on. You have to keep yourself open to what life has to offer, good and bad, so you'll hear His call when it comes. It's the only way to find true happiness."

Maggie stood with her eyes downcast. Sister Lenore walked over and took the rag from her hand.

"I'm sorry if you feel I've pried into your life, Maggie. It's just that sometimes it helps to hear from someone who's gone through something similar. Anyway, thank you for helping me clean the chapel."

Maggie nodded and turned to go. As she opened the door, she paused.

"Sister Lenore?"

"Yes, Maggie."

"Thank you."

"Hold still," Mary Louise scolded, her brows knit in concentration. She was attempting to draw a *seam* down the back of Bea's leg with an eyebrow pencil, a ticklish process that had Bea squirming as she steadied herself on the back of a chair. Bea had already applied a generous amount of *Cyclax Stockingless Cream* to color each leg, and the seam was needed to complete the effect. Maggie walked in just as Mary Louise finished.

"What do you think?" Bea asked, turning her legs this way and that for Maggie's perusal.

"Truthfully? I think they're a little too orange. And aren't you afraid the seams will rub off the first time you sit down?"

"Not if I sit on the very edge of my chair."

Bea looked down at her bare legs.

"Well, they may not be perfect, but it's the best I can do. I ran the last of my hose last week, and I'd rather die than wear bobby socks to the Crossroads Club tonight." She sighed. "I certainly hope our boys in uniform appreciate the sacrifices I'm making so they can have nylon for their parachutes and flak jackets."

Walking over to her closet, Bea selected a long-sleeved, deep blue cocktail dress. She pulled the dress over her head, shimmying it down over her slip so as not to smudge Mary Louise' handiwork.

"Why don't you come along with us, Maggie?" said Mary Louise. "The Crossroads Club just opened and it's supposed to be great. A bunch of us are going right after dinner."

"Thanks, but I've got a ton of work to do tonight." She plunked her pile of books down on her desk as evidence.

"On a Saturday night? Come on, Maggie. You've had your nose to the grindstone all semester. You need to have a little fun once in awhile," Bea urged.

"Yeah, come on," said Mary Louise. "There's a new band playing tonight. They're supposed to sound just like Glenn Miller. Well, almost. Come on. It'll be good for you."

Maggie looked down at the pile of books and writing assignments on her desk, then out the window at the darkening December sky. The past week had been long and hard, and she was tired. Not just physically tired, but tired of the self-imposed frenzy, tired of feeling empty and alone. She'd tried to shut off her feelings and fill up her life with busy work and noise, but it was no good. Eddie was dead, and no amount of self-denial could change that fact. Nor could it change the fact that she was alive, with all of the desires and dreams of a young woman. With sudden clarity, Maggie realized that, although she would never forget Eddie, she needed more than a memory. She needed to get on with her own life. And as she watched the first few stars begin to twinkle in the winter sky, she felt quite sure that Eddie would've agreed.

Suddenly, Maggie felt a slight easing of the grief that had weighed upon her heart for so long. Maybe it was time to take that first step. Nothing big. Just a night out with the girls. Yes. Maybe it was time.

Maggie turned to Bea, a new light in her eyes.

"You know, you're right. I could use a change of pace. Can

you give me fifteen minutes to get ready?"

"Really?" Bea's look of surprise changed to delight.

"Hallelujah," said Mary Louise. "I'll go tell the other girls. We'll meet you downstairs."

Heads turned to check out the new arrivals as the girls paused inside the doorway of the Crossroads Club. The place was already crowded with boisterous young people either gathered around the bar, or eating and drinking at the white cloth-covered tables surrounding the dance floor. There were some couples, but the crowd was composed primarily of groups of single men, many in uniform, who'd come to check out the groups of single girls who'd, in turn, come to eye them. A smoky haze hung over them all.

"Come on. I see a table over there," said Bea, leading the five girls through the noisy throng to a table along the wall.

"Bea, no guy's going to be able to find us way back here," Janey Nash protested, plunking herself down in one of the chairs. Janey, a petite junior from Cleveland, Ohio, who was very determined not to return there, had made it her goal to become engaged by the fall of her senior year to someone from a warm and sunny area of the country.

"Well, it's the only table that's open," Bea replied as she took her seat, mindful of her leg make-up. "You'll just have to lure them over here with your charms."

Mary Louise managed to flag down one of the beleaguered waiters. The girls ordered rum & cokes, feeling reckless and sophisticated when he didn't bother asking them for proof of their age.

"Wow. There's quite a crowd here tonight. I guess word got out about this place," commented Connie Marko. Connie was a tall, thin attractive girl who exuded a practiced air of ennui in the belief that it made her appear more sophisticated. She scanned the room, brushing her blonde hair from her face with a graceful sweep of her hand. "It certainly seems to have attracted some handsome young men."

Maggie followed Connie's gaze. A table of midshipmen in their khaki uniforms was looking their way with interest.

"Connie, that hair of yours is like a beacon."

"Yeah, and it only costs two dollars and eighteen cents a bottle," Mary Louise added. Connie glowered at her.

"Now, ladies. Your conduct is becoming *grotesque and unlovely*," Bea teased, taking a sip of her drink. "Oh, good. The band's coming back."

The Harvey Caswell band, dressed in white dinner jackets and ties, returned to the stage and began tuning up their instruments.

"Ooh. The drummer's cute," gushed Janey.

"You think anyone in pants is cute," said Connie.

Janey's retort was interrupted by a loud drum roll.

"Ladies and Gentlemen. Once again, I'd like to welcome you to the Crossroads Club. I'm Harvey Caswell, and these are the boys in the band."

The band members stood and bowed, while the audience applauded with enthusiasm.

"Let's get things hopping," the band leader yelled.

The band swung into a credible rendition of *Little Brown Jug*, and couples began to take the dance floor. Despite Janey's fears, a number of young men did find their way to the girls' table and asked them to dance. Maggie found it was good to be out dancing and laughing again. Bea caught her eye over her partner's shoulder, and winked.

After a few more songs, the band leader rapped the podium with his baton, holding up his hands to quiet the crowd. The winded girls were glad to return to their table.

"Ladies and gentlemen," he began. "During the break, it was brought to my attention that we have something of a minor celebrity in the crowd. A young man who sang with the famous Red Nichols Band in the Philadelphia area before enlisting in the service of his country. I think if we all ask him nicely, we can get him to sing for us tonight. Ladies and gentlemen, I give you Mr. Hank Hogan. Where are you, Hank?"

There was a commotion of clapping, whistling and jovial shoving at a table of sailors across the dance floor. They bullied the reluctant vocalist to his feet. Maggie and her friends joined in the general applause, encouraging the young man to take the stage. The spotlight honed in on him as he made his way through the crowd toward the bandstand.

"Oh my gosh."

"What's the matter, Maggie?" asked Connie, still applauding.

"It's Jack."

They all stared as the young man shook hands with Harvey Caswell, and turned to face the crowd. Bea gasped.

"It *is* Jack."

"Jack, who?" demanded Janey as the crowd began to quiet.

"Sh. Jack Koerner. He's a friend of Maggie's from ND."

"But, I thought they said his name was Hank Hogan?" Janey whispered back.

"They did. Sh."

The lights came down and the music began to swell. Looking out over the darkened room, Jack began to sing.

> *You'll never know just how much I love you,*
> *You'll never know just how much I care ...*

Mary Louise elbowed Maggie.

"Hey, he's good. And good looking. You never told us he sang with the Red Nichols Band."

"He didn't," Maggie replied, a bemused look on her face. She had to hand it to Jack. He looked every bit the part of the band singer — handsome, soulful — and while he was no Frank Sinatra, he did have a beautiful voice. And more gall than anyone she'd ever met.

> *If there's some other way to prove that I love you,*
> *I swear I don't know how*
> *You'll never know if you don't know now.*

Jack held the last note, his arms opened wide. The audience applauded wildly. With exaggerated humility, he refused the request for a second song, thanked the band leader and made his way back to his table of cheering buddies. Within moments, the table was surrounded by people, many of them young ladies, congratulating him and offering to buy drinks for him and his friends.

"Can you believe him?" Maggie said, shaking her head.

"Are you going to go over and say something to him?" said Bea.

"Oh, most definitely. But, I'll wait till the worshippers thin out first."

Maggie sipped her drink, biding her time while she watched Jack accept the adulation of his fans. When the band resumed playing, he excused himself from his admirers, and started to make his way across the room. Maggie got to her feet, eager to intercept him. Just before she reached him, however, a young woman with flaming red hair piled in curls on top of her head grabbed his arm.

"Oh, Mr. Hogan," the young woman yelled over the noise of the band, "I just had to tell you how much I enjoyed your singing. You know, I can't believe I've never heard you sing before. I'm from Philly, and I'm such a big fan of The Red Nichols' Band."

"Well," Jack stuttered, "maybe you just forgot."

"Oh, no," the girl replied with a flutter of her false eyelashes. "I'd remember you. Anyway, I think it's just wonderful how you gave up such a brilliant career to fight for our country. I just wanted to thank you ... in person." She held his eye while the invitation hung in the air.

"Well, thank you, Miss — ?"

"Chastity."

"Really? Well, you're very kind ... Chastity. And I'm very tempted. But, you see, we've got early morning maneuvers tomorrow. And it's my job ... as captain ... to make sure all of the men get back to the USS Walsh safely. The demands of war, I'm afraid. But, I do appreciate hearing from such a big fan. I'll be sure to tell Red about you."

She pouted, batting her eyes at him one last time.

"Oh, well. If it's for the war, I guess I understand. Goodbye, then."

She gyrated her way back through the crowd.

Jack gave a low, appreciative whistle — a whistle that died on his lips when he turned and found himself face to face with Maggie.

"Hello, Jack." She watched the color creep up his face.

"Maggie! Wh-what are you doing here?"

"Well, I heard that the famous Hank Hogan was singing, and I just had to come."

"I can explain."

"Uh huh."

"Not here. Step outside with me for just a minute, okay? Please?"

People were beginning to stare. Maggie let him squirm a few moments more before agreeing.

Once outside, Jack led her out of earshot of the couples near the front door. Then he turned to her with a sheepish grin.

"You're not going to turn me in, are you?"

"Maybe. Maybe not." She folded her arms, but couldn't keep the smile off her face. "Tell me something, Jack. Why in the world would you pretend to be a singer with a famous band? Aren't you afraid you'll get caught?"

"Well, as far as I know, there's no law against impersonating a band singer. Besides, no one around here would know whether I really sang with Red Nichols or not. And, thanks to my years of training as a choir boy, I have a decent enough voice to carry it off, if I do say so myself."

"You are many things, Jack Koerner, but a choir boy isn't one of them," Maggie replied. "But, I still don't understand why you do it."

"Two words, Maggie. Free drinks."

"Free drinks?"

"Yes. Every time I do this — "

"You've done this before?"

"Well, once or twice. Anyway, when I'm done singing, people always come over and buy drinks for me and my friends."

"By *people*, you mean *girls*."

"Well, I have to admit, girls do go crazy over singers. But, here's the way I figure it. The girls from the Bendix plant in South Bend have a lot of money to spend, but with most of their guys overseas, no one to spend it on. Me and my friends are right here, but we don't have much money. *Hank Hogan* brings the two groups together. So, when you think about it, what I'm doing kind of provides a public service."

"Jack, back on the farm we used a shovel to carry around an explanation like that."

Jack shrugged his shoulders and grinned. Then the grin faded.

"Actually, Maggie. I'm surprised to see you here." He raised an eyebrow. "I thought you were spending all of your time hitting the books."

She blushed.

"I know. I was. Look, Jack. I'm sorry about the way I acted the last time I saw you. Something happened over the summer, and I needed some time . . . " She stared at the ground, her voice trailing off.

"And now?"

"Now?" She hesitated, then looked up into his blue eyes. "Now, I think it's been time enough."

The smile returned to his face.

"Good." He paused. "Are you here with someone?"

"Just Bea and the girls."

"Great. Why don't you all join me and the fellas at our table?"

"Can't. Got to catch the bus. 10:30 P.M. curfew. Besides, don't you have to shove off for the *USS Walsh, Captain*?"

"You're never going to let me forget this, are you?" said

Jack with a chuckle.

"Probably not."

"Well, then, maybe I could give you a call sometime? If you're not too busy, that is," he teased.

She opened her mouth to make a smart comeback, then stopped.

"Yes. I think I'd like that."

Chapter 17

October 1944

I'll be seeing you in all the old familiar places
That this heart of mine embraces all day through.
In the small café, the park across the way,
The children's carousel, the chestnut tree, the wishing well.
I'll be seeing you in every lovely summer's day,
In everything that's bright and gay,
I'll always think of you that way,
I'll see you in the morning sun and when the night is new.
I'll be looking at the moon, but I'll be seeing you.
              -by Irving Kahal and Sammy Fain.
              From the 1938 musical, <u>Right This Way.</u>

Maggie crawled on her hands and knees across the slick tile roof just below the second floor dormitory windows, trying not to look down. She was grateful for the darkness, not only because it obscured the steep drop-off to her left, but because the October breeze kept lifting her skirt in a scandalous fashion. As she came abreast of Mary Louise's window, a pale arm shot out into the night.

"Grab my hand."

Maggie reached up, grabbing the proffered wrist just as she felt her feet begin to slip. Mary Louise yanked her through the open dorm window, sending them both sprawling onto the wooden desk on which she'd been kneeling.

"Maybe we should just use the hallway next time," suggested Maggie, rubbing her sore shoulder as she sat up.

"And risk getting caught after hours by Sister Jean Marie?" Mary Louise exclaimed, hopping down to the floor. "Not on your life. If I get campused one more time, I'm likely to get kicked out of school. Besides, scaling that roof between your room and mine keeps us physically fit, just as we promised when we signed the *Civilian Defense Pledge*." She gave a mock salute and plunked down in a chair. "So, what did you find out?"

Maggie sat on the desk, swinging her legs.

"It's all set. Julie Frasier is going to let us in the basement door near the tunnel at 11:20 P.M. tomorrow night."

"Julie Frasier?" said Mary Louise. "How did you get that goody-two shoes to agree to that?"

"Oh, Julie's not so bad. Besides, she owed me one. I tutored her in French. She got an eighty-seven percent on her last test, I'm proud to say. Anyway, she promised she'd be there. Only don't be late. Sister makes her rounds at 11:30, and she's got ears like a beagle."

"I'll be there. The movie ends at 10:20 and the bus gets us back to the main gate before 11:00. Where are you going with Jack?"

"Oh, no place special."

On the contrary, the willow tree by the lake where she and Jack would meet on these stolen nights had become one of the most special places in the world to Maggie. They'd arrange for friends to cover for them, sign out for their respective libraries and head for the far end of Lake Marian. Maggie's heart always skipped a beat when she parted the curtain of leaves to find him waiting. They'd talk, hold hands and kiss. Maggie was careful to keep things under control, and Jack was a reluctant gentleman. Still, she was finding it harder and harder to say goodnight to him, lingering in his arms until they were both dizzy with frustration.

On this early autumn night, she entered their leafy hideaway to find Jack already there. He was standing with his back to her.

"Jack," she whispered. Her smile faded when he turned around. Even in the fading light she could see the tears in his eyes.

"Jack. What is it?"

"My brother," was all he could choke out. Then he dropped his head to his chest, and his shoulders began to shake with his silent weeping.

Maggie rushed to his side. Taking both of his hands, she pulled him down with her until they sat together on the ground, her arms around him and his head resting on her breast like a child's. She stroked his hair while he cried.

Finally, with a last shuddering sigh, he sat up, wiping his eyes and nose with his handkerchief.

"My father called today. He got a telegram from the War Department. My brother, David, was killed on the twelfth of October, near some town called Aachen in Germany. They said a sniper got him." He shook his head. "He was supposed to be coming home on leave at the end of the month."

The war. For a time, they'd been able to keep it on the periphery of their lives, an unreal backdrop to their romance. But, now, it had reached into their world with its horror and death — again.

"Oh, Jack. I'm so sorry."

He nodded, but he wasn't really listening. He was twelve years and six hundred miles away on the grassy banks of old Mill Creek outside of Lancaster, Pennsylvania.

"You know, Davie used to take me fishing all the time. He actually seemed to enjoy being with me, even though I was just a little snot-nosed kid. I remember I'd always get mad when the fish wouldn't bite right away. I'd blame it on the kind of bait we were using or the time of day. Davie would just sit there on a rock and smile. *You know, Jack,* he'd say. *There's one thing you gotta have to be a good fisherman. You gotta have more brains than the fish.*" Jack's smile trembled. "God, I'm going to miss him." He took a deep, steadying breath.

"They're shipping his body home this week. I got permission for a week's leave to attend the funeral and spend some time with my mom and dad."

"How are your parents taking it?"

"Dad's pretty stoic, but I can tell he's torn up inside. Mom's taken to her bed."

"Jack, I don't know what to say." Another young man dead, another life of promise cut short.

"Yeah." He got to his feet, pulling her up, too. "Anyway. I leave tomorrow morning, so I won't be able to take you to the dinner/dance Saturday night."

"Don't worry about that, Jack."

"Yeah, but I know you got a brand new dress and everything — "

"Look. You just go home and be with your parents. Is there anything I can do?"

"Maybe light a candle for Davie at the Grotto on Saturday? That's the day of the funeral."

"Sure."

"Well, I've got some packing and some paperwork to fill out before I can leave, so I'd better go." Jack bent down and kissed her. Then, picking up his Navy cap from the ground, he turned and parted the curtain of leaves. He stopped and looked back.

"I'm really sorry about the dance. I'll make it up to you. I promise, Maggie. When I come back."

Then he was gone.

She sat alone beneath the willow tree for a long time, Jack's words ringing in her ears — *I promise, Maggie. When I come back.*

Eddie's gentle face flashed before her eyes. She shuddered.

Rain poured down the day of Private David Koerner's funeral. Jack, in his dress blues, stood between his father and mother throughout the funeral mass at St. Anthony's Church and the service at the Catholic cemetery. His mother, clutching the flag that had been on her son's coffin, broke down anew every time she looked at Jack in his uniform. As soon as they returned home to South Marshall Street, he went up to his bedroom to change into civilian clothes.

While the quiet voices and melancholy laughter of the

mourners drifted up from downstairs, Jack lingered a moment
to sit on his boyhood bed and re-read Maggie's letter. She'd sent
it to him separate from the formal letter of condolence and
Mass card she'd sent to his parents. Her gentle concern showed
through each beautifully scripted word. With a sigh, he tucked
the letter into his breast pocket and returned to the gathering
downstairs.

When at last everyone had left, Jack wandered from room to
room. His brothers had all gone to war, one of them never to
return, and the very house seemed to be listening for the sound
of their voices. His mother and his older sister, Betty, were busy
in the kitchen, taking what wordless comfort they could from the
rhythmic routine of washing and drying the dishes. Reluctant to
disturb them, he drifted into the parlor.

There he found his father, standing at the front window, hanging a gold star banner next to the three blue stars already displayed there. Jack watched as he adjusted the little pennant with
meticulous care until it was perfectly aligned with the others.
Satisfied at last, his father paused. Then he reached out and traced
the outline of the gold star with trembling fingers. When at last
he turned around, Jack was dumb struck by the mixture of grief
and pride he saw in his red-rimmed eyes — and at how old his
father had suddenly become. His father acknowledged him with
a quiet nod of his head, patting his arm as he left the room.

Jack stood there a moment, uncertain what to do. Finally, he
sank down into one of the velvet armchairs. Lighting a cigarette,
he leaned his head back against the antimacassar, blowing wispy
curls of smoke into the air as he contemplated the small constel-
lation that bespoke his family's dedication and personal sacrifice
in a world threatened by darkness.

Despite the tragic circumstances that precipitated his visit,
Jack's father, mother and only sister were thrilled to have him
home. His mother cooked all of his favorite foods, and his father
shared his best cigars and stories with him. No one said it aloud,
but they all knew that this might be the only time they'd have to

be together before he shipped out at the end of the school year.

On the last Sunday of his leave, Jack was sitting at the dinner table, telling a story, when he realized that his father and sister were staring at him in an odd way. His mother was frowning.

"What?" he demanded indistinctly, a piece of his mother's Sunday pot roast in his mouth.

"Nothing," replied his father with a wry smile. "It's just that's the sixth time — "

"Seventh," corrected Betty.

"Seventh time that you've mentioned this girl, Maggie, just at dinner today. I take it she's someone special?"

"Special?" The color rose in Jack's face. "No, not really. I mean we do go out once in awhile. She's nice. But, it's nothing serious. Besides, once I get my commission, I'll be off to who-knows-where. And she's got another year of school left after this one." He shrugged. "We just have fun together, that's all."

"Oh." Betty gave him a knowing smile.

He glared at her.

"Well, I'm certainly glad to hear that," said his mother, slapping another helping of mash potatoes onto his plate. "You're much too young to be getting serious about anyone yet, much less some girl from Idaho."

"Iowa."

"Wherever. Getting involved at your age is just foolishness. Besides, when you do decide to settle down, there are lots of wonderful girls right here in Lancaster who would be thrilled to have your attention. Now, eat!"

Jack looked from his glowering mother to his father and sister, both of whom were smiling into their plates. Shaking his head in exasperation, he took another huge bite of potatoes.

"My, don't we look nice. What's the occasion?"

Connie leaned against the door jam of Maggie's dorm room, munching on an apple.

"I'm meeting Jack at the train station this afternoon," Maggie answered, straightening the jacket of her gray tweed suit.

"You two are getting awfully chummy," Connie said. "You've been dating him pretty steady for what, the last nine months? And, I saw the two of you sharing a soda downstairs at *The Oriole* a couple of weeks ago. The way he looks at you …!"

"Connie, you are so nosey," said Bea. She was sitting on the bed, tissue between her toes, waiting for the *Flamingo Pink* polish on her nails to dry.

"Jack and I are just good friends, Connie," said Maggie, arranging her gray felt hat just so.

"Yeah? Well, maybe somebody better tell him that. See you later, gals." Connie sauntered off down the hall.

"Really, Maggie. You kinda like this guy, don't you?" Bea ventured.

"Yeah, I guess so. But, he'll be going overseas as soon as he graduates in June, so there's no sense in getting too serious. We're just enjoying the time we have together."

"Well, just be careful."

"I will, Bea. Don't worry."

On the bus on the way to the train station, Maggie thought about her roommate's warning. She *had* come to care about Jack more than she liked to admit. He was unlike anyone she'd ever met. Smart, handsome and funny, he approached life with an eagerness that was infectious. He had big dreams that stretched far beyond the places and people of his childhood, dreams that attracted Maggie even as they frightened her. Jack was open and honest, and for some reason, he cared about her. Maggie was tempted to trust in him, trust in them being together. But she knew better. She knew how it would end. The way it always ended. She'd let herself forget for a little while, but the death of Jack's brother had brought it all rushing back. As the bus pulled up in front of the train station, she made a promise to herself. She would be more careful. She'd let him close. She mustn't let him any closer

"Jack! Jack Koerner!"

A pretty, young woman with chestnut hair and very red lipstick skittered across the floor of the train station, her arms flung wide. Her conservative blue traveling suit did little to conceal her well-endowed figure, and a number of servicemen looked on in admiration as she wrapped Jack in a warm embrace.

"Ruthie? Ruthie Gemmel?" Jack sputtered, returning the hug. "What are you doing here?"

Maggie, a smile frozen on her face, watched from just behind Jack's shoulder.

"Didn't your mother tell you?"

"Tell me what?"

"Well, of course. I'm sure she forgot with the funeral and all." She placed her white-gloved hand on Jack's arm. "I was so sorry to hear about David."

"Thanks, Ruthie."

"Well, anyway, the reason I'm here is that I've transferred to Saint Mary's. Can you believe it? You see, Bill and I broke up. The details are just too gruesome to go into. But, it's for good this time, and I really needed a change of scene. I was tired of Immaculata College, and you raved so about Saint Mary's in your letters. So, I thought, why not? I applied, they accepted me and here I am. Isn't it great?" She beamed up at Jack, her hand still on his arm. "They didn't want to accept me this late into the semester, but Daddy pulled some strings. He's such a dear. Anyway, how lucky I ran into you first thing! It must be fate."

Finally noticing Maggie there, Ruthie cocked her head. "Oh, hello."

"Hello," said Maggie. His mother? Letters?

"Oh! Maggie!" Chagrined, Jack grabbed Maggie's elbow, propelling her forward. "Ruthie, this is Maggie Owen. A ... a friend of mine. Maggie, this is Ruthie Gemmel. An old friend of the family. From back home."

"How nice to meet you," Maggie managed.

"My pleasure." Ruthie smiled sweetly, but her eyes narrowed ever so slightly as she looked Maggie over.

"Maggie goes to Saint Mary's," Jack continued. "She's just starting her junior year, there. Hey, she could probably show you around when you get settled, couldn't you, Maggie?"

"Sure." Maggie wondered when would be the best time to strangle him.

Ruthie, as unenthused about the idea as Maggie, gave her a noncommittal smile in response. Then she turned her attention back to Jack.

"You know, Jack, if it wasn't for the picture of you in your uniform that your mother gave me, I might not have recognized you. You look so handsome and grown up. But, then, you always were a heartbreaker."

"Well, you could dress a tree stump up in these dress blues and it would look good," Jack protested.

"You're much too modest," Ruthie assured him, squeezing his arm. "Isn't he too modest, Maggie?"

"To a fault," she agreed. If he said, *Aw shucks*, she was going to throw up.

"Jack," Maggie prodded, "it's getting late. Don't you think we'd better get a cab back to campus?"

"Oh, yeah. Say, Ruthie, would you like to ride with us to Saint Mary's?"

"I'd love to." She batted her eyelashes at him. Then, glancing at Maggie, offered, "But I can take another cab, if it's an imposition."

"We wouldn't hear of it, would we, Maggie?" Jack insisted, not waiting for a response. "Besides, we've got to conserve gas. There's a war on, you know."

Ruthie giggled.

"Oh, Jack, it's so great to see you again. I was nervous about coming out here all on my own, but, running into you like this, I just know everything's going to be all right." She linked her arm through his. "My bags are right over here," she purred, drawing him toward the train siding.

Just then, a large burst of steam filled the air. Whether it came from the train or Maggie was hard to tell.

"Gee, wasn't it something running into Ruthie like that?"
Jack had escorted Ruthie right up to the reception desk of Le Mans, sending her off with a hug and a promise to call her soon. Now he stood in the lounge with Maggie, an innocent smile on his face.

"Yes, it was *something*, alright. Had I known she was going to be on the train, I wouldn't have bothered coming down to the station." Maggie thrashed around in her purse for her room key.

Jack gave her a quizzical look. Then it dawned on him.
"Wait a minute, Maggie. You don't think Ruthie and I — ?" He started to laugh.

Heads turned in their direction.

"Sh! Keep your voice down. Do you want everyone to hear?" Maggie glanced around in embarrassment.

"Well, then, let's go outside," he whispered.

Head high, Maggie led the way out the front door. She found an empty bench well out of earshot of the girls heading back to the dorm for dinner, sat down, and folded her arms. Jack stood before her, a bemused smile on his face.

"Maggie, really. Ruthie and I grew up together on East Petersburg Street. She's like a little sister to me."

"Well, she seems awfully fond of her *big brother*."

"Oh, that's just her way. Really, she's just an old friend from back home."

"Oh, a *friend*. Like I'm your *friend*?"

Jack sat down beside her.

"Maggie, I had to say that. If I'd called you anything else, she would've written to my mother immediately. I told you my mother was a little shaky right now about losing any more of her boys."

"Jack, are you equating dating me with losing a son in the war?"

"No, of course not. But, my mother might in the state she's in right now. She's still trying to adjust to David being gone, and if Ruthie were to tell her there was something serious going on between you and me, she might get the idea that she's about to lose me, too."

Maggie frowned as she tried to decipher Jack's answer. Did that mean that he thought there *was* something serious between them ... or that there wasn't? And why did his careful ambiguity bother her so much? Remembering her earlier pledge, she shrugged her shoulders with careful indifference.

"What's to tell? There is no *you and me*. You were right the first time. We *are* just friends."

Jack leaned closer, slipping his hand around Maggie's waist. "Close friends, I hope."

Maggie picked his arm up by the sleeve as if she were removing a loathsome bug. "No, just friends. And I think it's best if we keep it that way."

Jack held up both hands in mock surrender. She waited for him to argue, but he just sat there looking at her.

"Well ... it's late. I guess I'd better head in," said Maggie.

"Yeah, I guess you'd better," he agreed, remaining seated.

"Goodbye," she said with an expectant tone.

"Goodbye." He just stared at her.

Maggie stood and stomped toward the dorm. She was almost to the steps when he called after her.

"Say, *friend*."

Maggie turned a pouty face towards him. Jack was standing with his hat in his hand.

"Thanks for coming to meet me."

"You're welcome," she answered, grudgingly.

"And thank you for the note you sent. It meant a lot to me."

"You're welcome, again," she said. Her voice was kinder this time.

"You really are a good friend, you know. More than a good friend."

There was no mistaking the look in his eyes. She fought the urge to run into his arms.

"Goodnight, Jack."

She fled into the safety of the dorm.

Maggie and Jack walked home through the cold November night with their arms around each other. They'd lingered a little too long at Rosie's Restaurant, talking and laughing about nothing in particular over two plates of spaghetti and a bottle of cheap red wine. They'd almost missed the last bus back to Saint Mary's. Now, with Maggie's 10:30 P.M. curfew fast approaching, they hurried down the long sidewalk to Le Mans.

All of a sudden, up ahead they spied one of the Sisters gliding in and out of the pools of light cast by the street lamps. She was headed straight for them. Maggie and Jack dropped their arms and put a respectable distance between themselves at once. As the nun's face was illuminated by the nearest lamp, they realized with trepidation that it was none other than Sister Madeleva, the president of the college.

"Good evening, Margaret. Good evening, Mr. Koerner," she said as she passed.

"Good evening, Sister Madeleva," they chorused. Jack touched the brim of his cap. They continued on with studied nonchalance.

"Oh, young man."

Her voice stopped them in their tracks. Jack and Maggie turned to face her.

"When you return to campus this evening, you might want to avail yourself of a clothes brush before retiring."

With just the slightest of smiles, Sister Madeleva continued on her way.

Confused, Maggie and Jack stared at her, then at each other, then down at Jack's coat.

"Oh, no!" Maggie gasped, bringing her hand to her mouth.

Clinging to Jack's navy wool dress uniform in all their accusatory glory were fine white hairs from the angora sweater she was wearing. Jack started laughing.

"It's not funny, Jack. What must she think?" Mortified, Maggie started trotting toward the dorm.

"It's actually very funny, and you know exactly what she thinks," he said, chuckling. He bounced along beside and in front of her like an overeager puppy. "Oh, come on, don't worry. If Sister Madeleva wanted to call us out on the carpet, she would have done it right then. I think she approves of us. She even remembered my name."

"Still, it's embarrassing. I have to face her at Mass tomorrow morning."

"Well, I have a feeling we're not the first couple she's caught returning from an evening of necking."

"Jack, sh! Someone will hear you."

"Hey, I don't care who knows I'm kissing my girl. I'd like to tell the whole world."

"You do and that will be the last kiss you get. And who says I'm *your girl?*" Maggie stood at the side entry of Le Mans with her hands on her hips.

Jack just gave her a devilish smile. He reached out to pull her close, but Maggie scooted out of his reach and through the door. Pulling it shut behind her, she stood on tiptoe, peering through the leaded, glass window of the door. Then she stuck her tongue out at him.

Defeated for the moment, Jack tipped his hat and sauntered off in the direction of Notre Dame, absentmindedly brushing at the white hairs that clung to his coat.

As he walked, Jack thought back to the day he first arrived at the University of Notre Dame, his one suitcase in hand. He'd never been west of the Allegheny Mountains before, yet there he stood, just off the bus, staring up at the Golden Dome. He remembered thinking at the time, *What in the world am I doing here?* Now, three years later, he wondered if, just maybe, this shy, pretty Irish girl from Iowa, with the quick temper and the loving heart, was the answer.

Jack retrieved his bicycle from where he'd left it leaning

against the trunk of an old elm tree. Lost in thoughts of romance and destiny, he pedaled down the main avenue of Saint Mary's in the dim moonlight. Even the clanging of the back fender did not disturb his reverie. He crossed the highway without slowing, there being almost no traffic at this time of night, and continued along the quiet back road that ran next to the Holy Cross Community cemetery.

"Halt! Who goes there?"

A member of the Shore Patrol, almost invisible but for the white S.P. on the armband he wore, stepped from the shadows. He'd been headed back to the dormitories, his watch almost ended, when he heard the approach of a bicycle. He correctly surmised that it was yet another sailor returning from an after hours rendezvous at Saint Mary's. They were a slippery lot, these late night Romeos. The S.P. was not about to let this one get away. He took his stance in the direct path of the bicycle.

Jack blanched. Being caught out of the dorm after lights out was punishable by, at the very least, numerous demerits on your permanent record and, at the worst, expulsion. Talk his way out of it or make a run for it? He had only a split second to decide. He slowed and sat up a little straighter on the bike, as if preparing to stop, taking care that the brim of his hat shielded his face from view. Then, so fast he surprised even himself, he turned the wheel of the bike sharply to the right. Crouching low, he pedaled with a strength and speed achievable only by one faced with the possibility of sudden and immediate assignment to active duty in the Pacific.

"Hey, sailor! Stop! I SAID STOP!"

The S.P. lunged and missed. He began to give chase. The sound of his boots grew louder and louder until, at any moment, Jack expected to be wrenched from the bicycle and thrown to the pavement. Suddenly, the bike gave a violent jerk. Somehow, Jack managed to stay upright, even increasing his speed. Behind him he heard a loud thud and clanging.

"Goddamn it!"

Jack glanced over his shoulder. He could just make out the S.P., pulling himself up onto all fours. His hat was gone, and he was clutching something shiny in his hand. Too relieved to even smile, Jack sped on into the concealing darkness.

"GODDAMN IT!" he heard again, followed by the sound of something whistling past his ear, landing with a harmless clank in the bushes by the side of the road.

Jack pedaled the rest of the way back to campus on shaky legs. He returned the bike, now minus its rear fender, to the spot behind the NROTC building where he'd *borrowed* it earlier that evening. Keeping to the shadows, he made it back to Walsh Hall, slipping unseen through the basement window his room-mate had left unlocked for him.

When, at last he reached the safety of his own room, he vowed never again to let any girl endanger his future as an offi-cer in the United States Navy.

His vow was forgotten the very next time he heard Maggie's voice.

"Hey, Maggie." Mary Louise stuck her head in the door. "They just called from downstairs. Jack's waiting for you in the lobby."

Maggie glanced at the clock. Exactly 7:30 P.M. Right on time. She made one more check in the mirror. This was the night of her Junior Prom, which she'd spent months helping to plan. She wanted everything to be perfect.

For once, her hair had turned out just right, her bangs turned back and held in place by an antique silver clip. She wore mascara and deep red lipstick, and had concealed her ever-present freckles with a skillful application of powder. Her silver drop earrings coordinated with her hair clip, and around her neck she wore the silver heart locket Jack had given her for Christmas. Her dress was from Carson Pirie Scott in Chicago and was the most glamorous thing she had ever owned. The bodice was black velvet with a heart shaped neckline and thin halter straps. The silver moiré skirt was full, accentuating her tiny waist. To finish the look, she wore black gloves that reached just above her elbows.

Maybe the neckline was a little too low, Maggie worried, tugging at it just a little. The dress showed off her graceful shoulders and just the barest hint of the swell of her breasts. No, it was just right. If ever she was going to wow'em with a dress like this, now was the time. She pirouetted once on her black velvet sling-backs, pleased at the way her skirt caught and reflected the light.

Maggie picked up her beaded bag from the dresser. She took a deep breath, then laughed at herself. What was she so nervous about? She was about to have the night of her life with a guy she was crazy about. Still, she gripped the carved wood railing firmly as she descended the two flights of stairs in a perfumed rustle of silk.

Jack, cooling his heels in the lounge with the other young men waiting for their dates, jumped to his feet when Maggie glided into the room. All heads turned and not a few mouths gaped as she hesitated, searching for him amidst a sea of Navy uniforms. The smile that lit up her face when she saw him took his breath away. He rushed to her side, folding her arm in his with a proprietary air.

"Maggie, you look spectacular."

"Why, thank you, Jack. You look pretty wonderful your-self."

She meant it. While all of the young men seemed to grow in stature while wearing their uniforms, Jack made the uniform look good. He'd continued to grow since they'd met her fresh-men year, and was now 6'4" tall with broad shoulders and a trim waistline. His dark hair was wavy despite the regulation haircut, and the dress blues accentuated the blue of his eyes. The bump in his nose he'd gotten from high school football kept him from being too movie-star handsome, and for Maggie's money, made him that much more wonderful to look at. What she most liked about him, however, was the fact that, beneath his fun-loving demeanor was a serious, sensitive young man, a man whom she was having great trouble keeping at an emotional arm's length.

"Oh, I almost forgot. This is for you."

Jack handed her a small florist's box containing a single white orchid tinged with pink.

"Oh, Jack. It's beautiful."

He took the flower out of the box, hesitating as he tried to decide where on the rather skimpy top of her gown he might permissibly pin it.

"Here. Let me do that."

Maggie took the flower from him. Turning to the large gilt mirror in the lobby, she pinned it in her hair over one ear.

"Hey, that looks great ... although I was rather enjoying figuring out where to pin it myself," said Jack.

Maggie blushed.

"Shall we go?"

The prom was being held in the Louis XVI ballroom of Le Mans Hall. Maggie and her classmates had spent weeks planning, and most of that day working, to transform the large ballroom into something magical. Now, with the addition of the lights, the music and the elegantly dressed young men and women, Maggie thought it'd turned out even better than they'd hoped.

The theme of the prom was the popular song, *I'll Be Seeing You,* a bittersweet theme given the war and the uncertain future of so many of the attendees. The ballroom had been decorated so as to illustrate various lines from the song. At the entrance to the ballroom, a wishing-well held dance programs. *The park across the way* was depicted by drawings of park scenes at either end of the wooden dance floor. In one corner of the ballroom, a small *children's carousel,* complete with pastel horses with plumes on their heads, revolved under a blue and white striped canopy. In another corner, refreshments were served in *the small café* with candlelit tables covered with red and white checked cloths. Behind the tables on the wall were drawings and signs from *all the old familiar places,* such as Rosie's, the Ramble

Inn and the football stadium — all favorite haunts of the girls and their dates. With the low lights and the music, the effect was wonderful.

By the time Maggie and Jack entered the ballroom, it was already half-full of men in their dress service uniforms and Saint Mary's girls in silk, tulle and chiffon. Jack spied some of his classmates, and he and Maggie joined them and their dates at one of the tables. Soon the band began to play. Couples poured onto the dance floor to Lindy, two-step and slow dance. Jack was a good dancer, and Maggie followed his lead with no fear for her new shoes. The room began to heat up. After a few more dances and a stop at the refreshment area, Jack and Maggie escaped to the fresh air of the cloister porch just outside the ballroom.

Even the weather seemed to be cooperating this evening. Although it was late January, it was not bitter, and the sky was full of stars. There were already a few other couples out on the porch, for it was the only place that provided at least the illusion of privacy for couples who wanted a few moments to talk or steal a quick kiss. Jack and Maggie walked over to lean against the stone railing.

"Cold?" he asked, putting his arm around Maggie's bare shoulders.

"A little, but it feels good. Boy, it's warm in there." All of a sudden, she giggled.

"What's so funny?"

"Oh, I was just thinking about the first time you brought me out here. I thought you were some kind of wolf."

"And now?"

"Now, I know you are."

Jack glanced down the length of the porch. The Sister patrolling had ducked inside to warm up. He bent down and gave Maggie a long, hungry kiss.

"Jack," she protested. "Sister will see."

"No," he assured her, pulling her close and breathing in the perfume of her hair. "I checked. They're changing the guard."

Maggie slipped her arms around him underneath his coat. She could feel the muscles in his back and smell the intoxicating fragrance of him — wool, skin and cologne. The warmth and strength of his arms around her made her feel safe and dangerously out of control at the same time. Jack lifted her chin and kissed her again, gently at first, then harder and more passionately. Amidst the swirl of her emotions, some far off corner of Maggie's mind observed in amusement that she was actually getting weak in the knees. No one had ever kissed her like this, made her feel like this. Everything and everyone fell away — the cold, the music, the other couples. All that existed was her, Jack and this endless kiss.

At last, gasping for breath, Maggie pushed him away.

"Jack, we'd better stop."

Jack looked down at her with eyes clouded with desire.

"Maggie. I don't ever want to stop. I've never felt this way about anyone before in my life. You're all I think about, all I dream about. It seems like nothing that happens in my life is real until I've shared it with you." He took a deep breath. "Maggie, I'm in love with you."

Maggie felt as if someone had dashed cold water in her face. She drew back in alarm.

"No, Jack. You mustn't say that."

"Why not? It's true. I'm in love with you. I think I have been for some time." His smile was almost shy as he took a step closer to her. "This can't come as much of a surprise to you. After all, I've spent almost every free moment of my life with you for the past year."

In desperation, Maggie searched for the right words, trying to keep things light.

"Jack, this past year with you *has* been wonderful. But, you can't make more of it than it is. I know you care for me. I care for you, too. But, you're not really in love with me. You're just a little frightened because you'll be leaving soon to go overseas."

Jack frowned.

"Frightened? Hell, yes, I'm frightened, but that has nothing to do with how I feel about you. I love you. I'd love you no matter where I was or what I was doing." He searched her face. "I think you're the one who's frightened."

"What do you mean?" Maggie avoided his gaze.

"You're afraid to say it. Everything you do, everything you say shows that you love me. You just can't bring yourself to say the words."

"You're wrong, Jack." Maggie fought to keep her voice steady. "Don't misunderstand, I am fond of you — "

"Fond of me? Maggie, do you really expect me to believe that after all this time, all the things we've talked about and shared ... do you really expect me to believe that you're just *fond* of me?"

Maggie pulled free of his arms, turning away from him.

"Yes, Jack. I'm sorry if I misled you."

Jack stared at her, dumbfounded. Then his eyes narrowed. "Maggie, you're not a very good liar. Tell me what's really going on."

"Nothing is going on," she insisted. "I just don't feel the same way you do. You knew from the start that I wanted to keep things casual, what with the war on."

"I know, but I thought things had changed. I thought we — "

She turned to face him.

"Well, I'm afraid you were wrong."

Jack studied her face, a look of disbelief on his own.

"Maggie. What's going on here?"

Not trusting her voice, Maggie just shook her head. She brought her hand to her chest to still her racing heart, and felt the locket hanging there. Trembling, she reached behind her neck and undid the clasp. She placed the necklace in Jack's hand.

"I'm sorry, Jack," she said quietly. "I shouldn't have let it get this far."

Jack stared down at the necklace. He closed his hand into

a tight fist.

"Just like that?" His face darkened. "So, this has all been just some kind of game to you? Just have your fun till I get shipped out, then pick up with someone else, is that it? Well, isn't it lucky you told me now, rather than wait till the end of the semester. It gives you time to get started on your next conquest."

He spun on his heel, then stopped, shoulders heaving. When he faced her again, the anger on his face had been replaced by pain.

"Maggie," he pleaded, "don't do this. Don't push me away. What we have together is too special."

Before she could respond, he grabbed her by the shoulders, pulling her to him. He crushed her lips in a desperate, longing kiss. Despite her resolve, she felt herself yielding to him, her lips betraying her words.

Suddenly, he pulled away.

"Look at me, Maggie," he demanded, his voice hoarse. "Look at me."

She met his eyes, almost undone by the desire she saw there.

"Now, tell me you don't love me."

She bowed her head, helpless to stop her tears. She'd tried to keep her distance, tried not to let him too close, but he wouldn't be turned away. So, he wanted the truth? Fine. Then she'd give it to him.

Maggie looked up at Jack, her expression fierce, and spoke to him from the agony in her heart.

"Do you know what happens to the people I love, Jack? To the people who love me? They die, Jack. That's right. They die. They die, or they leave, and they never come back. And I can't, I *won't* go through that again. So, no, Jack, I don't love you. I will never love you."

Maggie brought her hand to her mouth and ran from the cloister porch, leaving him in shock, standing alone.

Maggie took the train to Sioux City at the end of March for

Easter vacation. She was never so glad to get away from school. The last two months had been agony. She hadn't seen or heard from Jack since the night of the dance. Although she'd tried to maintain the façade that everything was all right, things had never been so wrong.

She managed to keep her composure during the trip on the South Shore Line from South Bend to Chicago. She even managed to hold it together in the midst of the departing soldiers and sailors saying goodbye to their sweethearts at Union Station. But when, at last, Maggie found herself alone in a compartment of the Milwaukee Road for the last leg of the trip from Chicago to Sioux City, her resolve crumbled. Hot tears streamed down her face as she tried without success to stifle her sobs in her handkerchief. At one point, the concerned porter came by to check on her, but she could only wave him away, unable to stop her weeping.

She knew it was her own fault. Jack was right. She did love him. But, she was afraid. She'd been afraid all of her life. So she'd done the only thing she dared to do — send him away before he could leave her. Like the others.

Now she had to live with the choice she'd made.

Maggie and her uncle returned from the Easter Vigil service at Blessed Sacrament Church at 9:00 P.M. Maggie still had trouble getting used to his little white stucco house on the edge of Grandview Park. Once already she'd turned into their old street out of habit, then driven slowly past the red brick house, wondering how it could adapt to new lives after all that had gone on there.

As they entered the house, Uncle John removed his raincoat and hat, and Maggie set her dripping umbrella in the rack of the coat tree by the front door. Louise was with her family for the Easter weekend, and the house was silent but for the chiming of the grandfather clock in the alcove next to the stairs.

"Why don't I build a fire to take off some of the chill? I swear, that cold rain gets right into my bones."

Uncle John knelt to the task of stacking the wood in the fire-place.

"That'd be great. Are you hungry? I could fix us some-thing to eat," Maggie offered, unpinning her hat from her head.

"A little soup would be grand."

Maggie went into the kitchen, flipping on the light switch. She was standing there, trying to remember which cupboard held the pots and pans, when the doorbell rang.

"Ah, that'd be Louise with the ham," Uncle John called from the other room. "I told her not to bother, with all she has to do for her own family, but she insisted on bringin' it over tonight so we'd have it to put it in the oven before mornin' Mass. Would you get that, Maggie? I've got my arms full at the moment."

Maggie opened the front door.

There on the stoop stood Jack, rain dripping from the brim of his navy cap and rolling off the broad shoulders of his coat.

"Jack!" Maggie's heart leapt to her throat.

"Hello, Maggie." He did not smile.

"What are you doing here? How did you get here?" she stammered.

"I hitchhiked."

"The whole way? Oh my goodness! Well … come in out of the rain."

"No. I may not be here that long. I've got something to say, and I want you to listen."

Dumb struck, she could only nod.

"Maggie Owen. You're a damned coward."

She gasped, indignant.

"Yes, a coward. I've spent the last eight weeks thinking about what you said to me the night of the dance, and you know what? It's all bullshit. Superstitious bullshit."

"Jack!"

"I'm not finished," he barked, ignoring her injured sensi-bilities. "Now, I know you've had some rough breaks in your life, maybe more than your share. You've lost a lot of people you've loved, and it hurts, and it's scary. But, I'm here to tell you that if you let it stop you from living, you may as well be dead yourself.

"Now, I can't promise you I won't get killed in this war. Hell, I can't even promise I won't get hit by a bus crossing the street. But, I *can* promise you that I will spend the rest of my life with you, and if that means one minute or sixty years, to me, it'd be worth it. I love you, Maggie, and whether you're willing to admit it or not, you love me, too. So," he jutted his chin at her in challenge, "I'm only going to ask this once. Will you marry me, or not?"

He stood there in the cold, hands jammed in his pocket, waiting.

Maybe it was the truth of his words, or the vehemence of his proposal. Or maybe it was just the fact that, as he stood there, an earnest, almost combative expression on his face, there was a little droplet of rain hanging from the end of his nose. In any event, Maggie felt a sudden falling away of the protective shell that had encased her heart for so long. Here, standing before her, was the love she'd looked for all of her life — an impossible, unpredictable, wonderful love — offering her a second chance at happiness. She felt her heart reach out to his.

Maggie looked up at him, the tears bright in her eyes.

"I will." She almost whispered it.

"You will?" Jack sputtered.

"Yes. I will." It'd been so easy to say. And it felt so right.

Jack just stood there a moment. Then, with a cry of joy, he swept her up into his arms, twirling her in a circle.

"I take it this is Jack." Uncle John stood in the doorway of the living room. Maggie managed to nod yes. "Well, for heaven's sake, you two. Close the door and get in out of the cold. Pneumonia's no way to start an engagement."

"Maggie! I just heard. Let me see, let me see."

Mary Louise, at the head of a small cluster of girls, ran up to where Maggie sat at the dining hall breakfast table and grabbed her left hand.

"Oh, it's just beautiful. Look, isn't it beautiful?"

The girls oohed and aahed as they jostled for position, trying to get a better look at Maggie's engagement ring. They'd all just returned from Easter break the evening before, and word had spread like wildfire. Maggie blushed under the glare of her sudden celebrity.

"Janey, did you see?"

Bea thrust Maggie's hand at the older girl passing by.

"Oh, yes. It's ... cute. Congratulations, Maggie." Janey gave her a pained little smile, and left the dining room.

"Oh, don't mind her, Maggie," said Connie. "She's just jealous. If she doesn't catch a man in the next two months, it's back to Cleveland for her."

"I don't care," Maggie assured her, and meant it. Nothing could dampen her happiness. She loved Jack with all of her heart and, wonder of wonders, he loved her, too. Life was full of excitement and promise.

The mood in general on campus was hopeful this spring as the war in Europe appeared to be drawing to a close. The Allies had crossed the Rhine and were closing in on Berlin, steady advances were being made in the Pacific, and more and more people were beginning to speak of their plans for *after the war*.

The following week, right after supper, Maggie, Bea and Mary Louise trudged to the library together to study.

"I can't believe Sister Jerome set the science test for tomorrow," Bea moaned. "Friday the thirteenth! As if I'm not having enough trouble in that class."

Although it was mid-April, winter hadn't completely surrendered its hold on northern Indiana. The girls clutched their coats to their throats as they hurried between the buildings.

Suddenly, they heard the distant tolling of the bells in the tower of Notre Dame's Sacred Heart Church. Within moments, the bells in the Le Mans Hall tower joined in the mournful tribute. Everywhere students stopped and looked up as if the answer was to be found in the bells themselves.

Connie Marko came clattering down the steps of the library without so much as a sweater to protect her against the chill. She rushed up to them, out of breath.

"Have you heard the news?"

"What news? What's with the bells?" Bea asked.

"President Roosevelt's dead. I just heard it on the radio."

"Dead! When?" Maggie gasped.

"Just a few hours ago. He was on vacation in Warm Springs, Georgia and had a stroke, or something. Anyway, he died."

"Oh, my daddy will be so happy."

Maggie, Connie and Bea stared at Mary Louise, their expressions incredulous.

"Mary Louise!" Bea reproached her, horrified.

"Well," Mary Louise defended herself, "I mean, I'm sorry the man died, but my daddy said he was a horrible president. He absolutely stole money from the upper classes to finance his programs. And it was his bumbling that got us into this war to begin with."

The girls, dumbfounded by the news, as well as Mary Louise' outburst, continued walking toward the library. No one spoke for a long time.

"What are we going to do now? Who's going to run the war?" Connie's voice betrayed the sense of bewilderment and fear they all were feeling.

"Well," said Maggie, "we still have Eisenhower and MacArthur. And Vice President Truman will take over as President, God help him."

"God help us all," Bea added.

"Gee, Roosevelt's been the President since I was eight years old. I can't imagine having someone else as President," Connie mused.

"You know," Maggie said, "I think I'll go over to the church and say a few prayers before I go to the library."

"Good idea," Connie agreed. Bea nodded. All three girls

looked at Mary Louise.

"All right, all right. I'll go, too," she acquiesced. "I guess we'll need everyone's prayers if that little Truman is going to be in charge now."

In the next few weeks, it seemed that the entire face of the world began to change. On April 28, Benito Mussolini, the *Father of Italian Facism*, was tried and executed by partisan Italians, and his corpse hung upside down for viewing in the streets of Milan. On April 30, Adolph Hitler, the maniacal German despot who'd brought so much suffering to humanity with his dreams of Aryan supremacy, robbed the world of its revenge by committing suicide in his bunker beneath the city of Berlin, even while the remains of his army fought the advancing Russian soldiers in the streets above.

Germany formally surrendered on May 8, 1945. The announcement was met with great jubilation in the United States. People danced and cheered, bells rang and whistles blew. And joyful loved ones waited for the soldiers to come home.

Maggie and Jack rejoiced with the others, but their happiness was tempered. The war continued in the Pacific theater. Despite steady Allied victories, there was no sign of surrender by the Japanese. If anything, the fighting had become fiercer as the Allies pushed ever closer to the home islands of Japan. While the rest of the world celebrated the defeat of Nazi Germany, Allied troops were fighting a horrific battle for the island of Okinawa, just three hundred fifty miles from the Japanese home islands. By the time the battle ended on June 21st, twelve thousand, five hundred Allied troops had died in the fighting. Approximately one hundred ten thousand Japanese died, including a large number of civilians who chose to commit suicide rather than surrender to the Allied forces. Kamikaze attacks on the American fleet at Okinawa sank at least thirty ships, damaging more than three hundred fifty others. The Japanese army and its people appeared determined to fight to the death.

While the firebombing of Japanese home cities, begun in January, continued, American Naval Forces prepared for the invasion of the home islands of Japan. *Operation Olympic,* involving an invasion force of 15 divisions, larger than the one that had invaded Normandy, was tentatively set for November of 1945. Estimated death toll of the invasion: one million American lives.

On June 16, 1945, NROTC candidate Jack L. Koerner received his commission as an Ensign in the United States Navy and was shipped out for duty in the Pacific.

Chapter 18

May 1946

Where the Fleet goes, we've been.
—wartime motto of U.S. Navy Mine Force

Maggie sat cross-legged in the grass, resting the cardboard box on her knees. The sheltering curtain of the willow tree provided much more privacy than she could ever hope to get in the dorm. Right after supper, she'd signed out for the library and hurried here to the far end of Lake Marian to be alone. She removed the lid of the box and took out the first of seven packets of letters. Leaning back against the rough trunk of the tree, she pulled the ribbon that bound the letters together. She lovingly ran her fingers along the familiar scrawl on the outside of the top envelope. She really didn't need to even open it. She'd read each of the letters so many times she could have recited them by heart. But, she took comfort in this ritual, depended on it to ease the pain and uncertainty of such a long separation.

With undimmed anticipation, she removed a well-worn sheet of paper from the first envelope and began to read, once more letting the words transport her into the heart and thoughts of the man she loved.

August 13, 1945

Dear Maggie:

  V-J Day! Can you believe it? I was waiting at the Navy Yard in San Diego for the arrival of my ship, the USS Thompson, *when word came down. You could hear the roar go up all over the base. Reports are that we dropped some kind of super bomb on two*

Japanese cities and that's what forced them to surrender. Probably didn't hurt that the Soviets invaded Korea, too.

The ship is expected to dock by the eighteenth. After six weeks at destroyer school in Norfolk and three weeks cooling my heels here in San Diego, I'm anxious to get aboard.

The Thompson was originally a destroyer. In fact, she was part of the naval force that bombarded the shore batteries on D-Day in Normandy. But now, she's been converted and reclassified as a destroyer/minesweeper (DMS). I've been assigned duty as Deck Officer in charge of a seventy-five man deck crew that maintains and operates the mine sweeping equipment. Not bad for someone who had trouble keeping track of his room key, eh? She'll spend some time in port to take on new crew members and make a few repairs. I expect we'll get underway sometime in the first week of September and head west with the Fleet.

Some of the new fellas are disappointed that we didn't get into at least one battle before the war ended. I'm not sure how I feel about it. I would have liked to have tested myself in combat, but I'm also relieved that no one's going to be taking shots at us on our Pacific tour. And, as my CO points out, the mines don't know that the war is over.

This letter should reach you just before you leave for Saint Mary's. Senior Year — wow. It seems like only yesterday I saw you across the room at that first Tea Dance.

You were the prettiest girl there.

I wish I could be with you at school to take you to the dances, the football games and dinners at Rosie's. I can't tell you how much I miss just talking with you and going for walks. And other things! I'll be thinking of you every moment, and the way your face looked in the moonlight on our last night together. Have fun, but don't forget whose ring is on your finger! As the song says, "Don't sit under the apple tree with anyone else but me."

All my love,
Jack
P.S. Write me c/o USS Thompson DMS 38, FPO San Francisco.

Maggie stared down at her left hand and smiled. Did Jack really think she could ever forget the wonder of that moment when he first slipped the diamond ring on her finger? Every time she looked at it she thought of him and the promises they'd made to each other. Even during Mass she found herself gazing in fascination at the way the facets of the diamond reflected the colors of the stained glass windows of the chapel, and daydreaming about Jack and their future together. Her return letter had sought to reassure him of her love, as had every letter thereafter.

Maggie carefully slipped the letter back into its envelope, choosing a couple more at random.

September 15, 1945

Dearest Maggie,

I'm writing this letter in my cabin at 0445 — I had the 2400 to 0400 watch — but I'm wide awake and feeling great because I just finished reading the letters you wrote me. The mail was loaded onto the ship late yesterday afternoon just before we left Pearl. I was the happiest guy on the ship when I saw that there were six letters from you. That happens a lot. We'll get no mail at all for a while, then when it finally catches up with us, there'll be a whole bunch. We all live for mail call. It really picks up morale. I saved your letters to read until I got off watch just now so I could concentrate on every word.

Don't ever worry about boring me with details about classes and goings on at school. I love to hear about everything you're doing and picture where you are at different times of the day. It makes me feel a little closer to you and to home.

I miss you so much. It's hard being away from you, not even able to call you on the phone. Being stuck on a ship in the middle of the ocean with a hundred and fifty ugly fellas doesn't help. About a third of our crew is regular Navy — career men. The rest are reserves like me. Most of them are pretty good joes, but, there are some real derelicts, too.

Thanks for the newspaper clippings about the football team. We get the scores of most of the games over Armed Forces Radio, but not much else, so I'd really appreciate any additional info you can send. Looks like Coach Devore's going to have a pretty good team this year, despite the fact that so many of his experienced players are still in the service. I have a little wager going with the Gunnery Officer on the Illinois game — he's a Fighting Illini grad. Any money I make I plan to put aside for a nest egg for us. Besides, where am I going to spend it out here in the middle of the Pacific?

Not much else to report. One day's pretty much like the next. Go to the Grotto and light a candle for me that I'll do my job well and come back to your arms as soon as possible.

Love,
Jack

October 2, 1945

Dear Maggie,

Just finished reading your latest letters. Congratulations. I know you'll be the best newspaper editor Saint Mary's has ever had. Send me some issues of The Static *so I can brag about my fiancée, "the newspaper woman." Actually, the fellas are jealous enough of me already. I get the most mail of anyone on the ship — including the Captain!*

We arrived at Okinawa a few days ago and dropped anchor in Buckner Bay to await orders. I took advantage of the delay to go ashore and look around this morning. You can still see the effects of all the heavy fighting that went on here from last April through June — trees leveled, giant craters left from the shelling, vegetation burned. Many of the native people were left homeless by the fighting and are still living in makeshift shacks.

Okinawa's only three hundred fifty miles south of Japan and they say the battle here was one of the bloodiest of the war — over twelve thousand Marines killed. And the naval force off-shore suffered incredible damage from kamikaze attacks. Looking around at the devastation, I can't imagine what it must have been like to live through it, if somehow you did.

Maybe that partially explains something that happened to me while I was "sightseeing." I ran into a couple of Navy and Marine officers who'd been hanging around the BOQ — that's Bachelor Officers' Quarters — for the past few weeks, waiting to catch a ship home. They asked me if I wanted to go hunting with them. It turns out there are still a number of Japanese soldiers hiding out in caves on the northernmost part of the island who either do not believe our loudspeaker reports that the war is over, or who just plain refuse to surrender. A string of Marine camps, a kind of "human fence," has been set up to contain the Japanese within this area, and, periodically, patrols go in to flush them out. These officers wanted to know if I wanted to go along with them on one of these forays to shoot Japs — "just for fun." They said it with about as much emotion as if they were going rabbit hunting. God only knows what kinds of things these guys saw during the war, but still, aren't we supposed to be the good guys?

Things like that just make me miss you even more. You are so sweet and good, and talking to you always helps me make sense of things. I can't wait to get back to you and start our life together, away from all this hate and destruction. Keep writing me. You keep me sane.

All my love,
Jack

October 12, 1945

Dear Maggie,

    Sorry I haven't written in awhile, but it couldn't be helped. Right after I sent off my last letter to you, we got word that a typhoon was headed in our direction, and the entire Fleet began a mad scramble to try to get out of the way. You see, the harbor at Buckner Bay is very shallow — only fifty feet deep in many places — and in a typhoon you can easily get waves with troughs that deep. That means that if you get caught in the bay when the storm hits, you could run aground at the bottom of one of those troughs, with fifty plus feet of water crashing over your head. If the water gets down one of the stacks, the thermal shock will explode the boiler and blow out the side of the ship. Needless to say, we headed out to the deep water of the East China Sea as fast as we could.

    Once out at sea, about all you can do is turn the bow into the wind, keep the power up and ride it out, which is what we did for two very long days and nights. Maggie, I've never seen seas like that in my life. The ship was rolling and pitching, equipment was washing overboard. At one point, when I was up in the radar tower, the ship got turned sideways. Before we could get the bow headed back into the waves, we got hit broadside by a big one. The ship rolled so far to starboard, I swear I could have reached out my hand and touched the surface of the water. The Thompson *is built to withstand a roll of fifty-two degrees. Our instruments registered that roll at forty-seven degrees. I don't think I've ever been so scared in my life — even that time the Shore Patrol almost caught me sneaking back from Saint Mary's! We learned later that that typhoon had winds of one hundred ten knots with gusts up to one hundred forty-four knots. We were lucky. A lot of ships weren't.*

    As soon as the storm was over, we formed a scouting line with the other ships from Mine Division 61 to find what was left of the Fleet. We steamed about four miles apart the whole way back to Buckner, searching for life rafts, derelict ships or men in the water. I don't think I'll ever forget my first sight of Buckner Bay after that typhoon. There must have been fifty ships, large and small, all over the harbor — ships half sunk, some with only their masts sticking up out of the water, some on their sides, wreckage floating everywhere. It looked like a ship graveyard. I guess the Japanese finally got their "Divine Wind." It was just a little too late.

But, enough of that depressing talk. Tell me, how does Notre Dame look this fall? Have the trees changed color, all golds and reds? I wish I could be walking with you through the leaves along the main road to Saint Mary's, stopping by our special place, kissing you until you pretended to want me to stop. I have your picture taped to the bulkhead in my cabin so your face is the last thing I see at night and the first thing I see in the morning. If I'm really lucky, I even dream about you at night, only it's hard to wake up and remember how far apart we are. Still, no matter how great the distance between us, you're always right here in my heart. I live for the day when I can make you my wife and spend the rest of my life with you.

Until then, goodnight, my love.

Jack

October 18, 1945

Dear Maggie:

Thanks a million for the picture you sent of you standing by the lake. You look so beautiful. The Exec said that if that's what "the old ball and chain" looks like, he wouldn't mind getting married, himself.

Sorry I scared you with that typhoon story, but you did say I was to tell you everything. Besides, don't you know by now that I always land on my feet?

You asked me to describe what it is we're doing out here. It's called *"occupation sweeping." The minesweepers clear the channels and harbors of mines so that our guys can get the POWs out and the occupation troops and necessary supplies in. Then we sweep the sea lanes around and between various Japanese ports so our ships can move about freely.*

As I write this, we're on our way to the Yellow Sea, between Korea and China, to begin sweeping operations to clear an area known as "Rickshaw." This is The Thompson's *first real sweeping run since I came aboard in August, and the whole crew is anxious to get to work at last.*

I forgot to tell you - I got a chance to see Bob Hope at the USO show before we left Okinawa. It was great. He had Francis Langford and a bevy of beauties there to entertain us. One young lady caused quite a sensation. She came on stage in a very simple dress, looking like "the girl back home," except that "the girl back home" was never built like that! Except for you, of course. Seriously, Maggie, she had a figure that ... well ... talk about a morale builder! She came to center stage, threw her arms open wide, and began to sing, "I ... ain't got no-body ..." "Oh, yes you do, Sweetheart!" yelled one of the marines, and fifteen hundred love-starved men began whistling and hollering. She kept singing, but you couldn't hear another word. God bless Bob Hope and the USO.

I've got the duty at 1600, so I've got to go. Good luck on your mid-terms. I know you'll do great. Don't forget how much I love you.

> *Kisses,*
> *Jack*

October 21, 1945

Dear Maggie,

We swept our first mine yesterday, the first one swept by the entire task group, I'm pretty proud of my deck crew. They performed their duties well.

Since you asked, I'll give you a quick description of how we sweep a mine. The process is pretty simple, really. There are different kinds of mines, but my ship is equipped to find and disable moored mines, i.e. mines that are anchored by a chain to a weight on the ocean floor. The mines themselves look like large metal balls with horns all around, each of which contains a detonator. The mines sit about ten feet below the water line and, when they come in contact with the hull of a ship, watch out!

Our ship steams back and forth, towing behind it a long steel cable, or sweep wire, that can be rigged to sweep from either side of the ship. The cable extends out from the ship for about two hundred yards and has a float at the end so we know exactly how much area we've swept. The sweep wire is held about twenty feet below the water line by a weight at the end of it. An "end cutter" is attached to the sweep wire near the weight. When the sweep wire comes in contact with the chain of a mine, the chain slides along the sweep wire and into the jaws of the end cutter. The chain is cut, the mine pops up to the surface, and our gun crew blasts them out of the water with our twenty mm guns. It's exciting the first few times, but after that, it gets pretty routine.

We sweep in a convoy of three or four ships, each one staggered at an angle off of the lead ship, so that each ship, except for the leader, sails in a swept path. Even so, only during the first sweep is the lead ship in any danger. After that, it turns and is moving within the outer boundary of the area already swept.

When we finish sweeping, we set down buoys to mark the cleared channels. Then the rest of the fleet can move through in safety. See how easy? The only real problem is that sometimes the mines break loose and float around free, so our lookouts have to stay pretty sharp.

The mail boat hasn't found us for a while and I'm missing you terribly. You can't imagine how much news from home picks us all up. It's funny, but I find myself missing the strangest things — sitting in a hot bathtub, Grandma Koerner's special sticky buns, fresh milk — things I used to take for granted. Well, maybe the mail will get here tomorrow. Hope everything's going your way and that you're missing me, too? Don't forget me.

Love always,
Jack

Jack's glib description of his duties hadn't fooled Maggie. In *The Huddle* one Saturday afternoon, she'd cornered a Notre Dame senior who'd recently returned from duty on a minesweeper. He described the process to her in detail, using numerous spoons, and salt and peppershakers as props. He concluded his tutorial by proclaiming that minesweepers performed one of the most important, least appreciated, most dangerous duties in the Navy. At the stricken expression on Maggie's face, he backtracked, assuring her that Jack would be fine since, with the war over, he didn't have to contend with shelling or kamikaze hits. Just mines.

November 20, 1945

Dear Maggie,

Greetings from Sasebo, Japan!
Our letters keep crossing in the mail, so I guess I'll just tell you about what we've been doing lately and assume that your answers to my earlier letters are on the way.
We finished up the Rickshaw operation, officially sweeping the whole area of Japanese mines, and I'm proud to say that The Thompson *scored highest with sixty-four mines located and destroyed. Afterwards, we came here to Sasebo, which is the base for MineDiv 61, to get the ship outfitted, i.e., take on fuel, supplies and ammo.*
After the ship was ready, the Captain somehow got permission to steam over to Nagasaki, which is not too far to the south of us. I guess he just wanted to be able to tell his grandchildren that he'd been there. Anyway, when we pulled into Nagasaki harbor,

everyone was speechless. The city stretches back from the beach for a few miles and climbs up a high ridge — or it did. As far as the eye could see, everything was just destroyed. There were almost no buildings standing at all, just piles of rubble, and a few charred trees and telephone poles leaning at odd angles. Even three months after the blast, you could still smell the smoke from the fires. They say that thirty-five thousand people were killed instantly and many more died soon after. All from just one bomb. I saw it and I still can't believe it.

A few streets had been cleared for traffic so the Exec and I commandeered a jeep and drove around the city. The "traffic" was mostly by bicycle or foot. What little vehicular traffic we saw was American. Here and there, there were little groupings of huts or shanties that people had pieced together from the debris. They couldn't have provided much protection from the cold and rain, though. We saw a few Japs, old people and women, mostly, digging through the rubble for God knows what. They'd actually stop and bow when they saw us. No anger, no fear. Just a numb acceptance. A strange people.

Every now and then you'd come upon a pile of bricks or burned wood that must once have been someone's house, and there'd be a piece of paper stuck to it. My Exec knows a little Japanese, and he said they were notes left by people trying to find out what had happened to the people who used to live there.

Once, we got out of the jeep to take pictures of each other standing atop some ruins. Suddenly, all these little children appeared from nowhere. They kept bowing and saying, "G.I., G.I.," and holding out their hands. We gave them what chocolate bars or food we had, but it was nowhere near enough. I felt so sorry for them. It wasn't their fault that their parents started a war, but now, they're suffering for it. We took our pictures fast and got back in the jeep.

Then we drove to the top of the ridge just behind the city. The view from there was eerie. The bomb must have detonated just to the ocean side of the ridge with the ridge acting as a kind of shield, because, on the other side, there was comparatively little damage.

On Sunday, some of the guys and I went to Church in the chapel of a private Catholic girls' school run by French nuns just a couple of ridges over. I will never forget it. There we were, just a few miles from Ground Zero, listening to these little Japanese girls, with these incredibly high voices, singing "The Mass Of The Angels" in Latin, the same Mass I sang with the choir back in Lancaster. The world suddenly felt very small.

Looks like it'll be Thanksgiving dinner on board ship. The Captain managed to commandeer a few cases of good red wine from one of the supply ships, so at least we won't be toasting with sake. Can't tell you how much I'd rather be spending this holiday with you and my family — the holidays are always the hardest. Next year, I get the drumstick!

Love,
Jack

December 10, 1945

My Dearest,

We've been sweeping the waters off of Nagoya, Japan for the past few weeks as flagship of the task group. The people who say we shouldn't have dropped the atomic bomb should try spending a day on a minesweeper in Ise Bay. I've never seen so many mines. Everyone is on highest alert at all times. I can only imagine the hell it would have been trying to clear these mines with shore batteries firing at us, and kamikazes crashing into our decks. We were scheduled to be part of the Invasion Fleet and would have been the first ones in to Tokyo Harbor. I don't think we would ever have made it out. I've heard rumors that the U.S. government had over a quarter of a million purple hearts made up for the invasion of Japan. From what I've seen of the minefields and the shore defenses that are still intact, they would have needed every one of them.

Has the snow fallen in South Bend, yet? I never thought I'd miss it so much. It rarely snows here, except on the tops of the mountains — just cold and wet and gray. When I'm freezing my _____ off, standing on the bridge staring out at a steel gray sea, I like to think of you skating in the winter sunshine on the blue ice of Lake Marian, with the snow-covered trees surrounding you like a picture frame. You see — I'm turning into a poet. That's what these long, monotonous watches will do to you.

In case you need reminding, I love you more than I can say and I'm missing you horribly. Can you possibly be as beautiful as I remember? Your letters keep me close to your heart, but I could sure stand to be close to some other parts of you right now.

Ah, well. Guess I'd better go take another stroll around the bridge. Works almost as well as a cold shower.

Love,
Jack

P.S. My mother wrote to say that she got a lovely note from you at Thanksgiving time. I think you're winning her over.

The postscript made Maggie laugh every time she read it. Jack had tried to downplay it, but she knew Jack's mother was more than a little cool to the idea of their marriage.

What Maggie didn't know was that Mrs. Koerner had thrown a minor fit, wailing that she hadn't schemed and prayed so hard to keep her baby boy out of the worst of the fighting war, only to face losing him to some farm girl from halfway across the country. But Jack stood firm in the face of her tears, and his mother relented, sending a stilted letter of welcome to her future daughter-in-law.

December 31, 1945

Dear Maggie,

How I wish I could hold you and hear the sweet sound of your voice. We had a tough duty yesterday. We were on Ready Duty — the Navy always has one ship in the harbor under full steam, ready to go in case of emergency, hence, "Ready Duty" — when a call came in at 2:00 A.M. that a Minevet, steaming off of Tsushima Island, north west of Kyushu, had been hit by a mine and was sinking. We took off immediately to assist in the search for survivors. When we got there, the ship itself, which had been blown into two pieces by the mine, had already sunk out of sight. Just disappeared. Rescue boats picked up about sixty men from the water, but one of the officers and thirty of the crew were killed in the explosion or drowned before we could reach them. Everyone was very low. There was a lot of angry talk that we should have the Japs out here sweeping these waters. They're the ones who laid the mines, let their men die getting rid of them. Actually, we do have Japanese minesweepers working the waters, but they seem to have lost their "bushido" — their "warrior spirit." They're unreliable and have the tendency to sweep the same safe path over and over. And so, we sweep.

Sorry to be so down, but sometimes this is a pretty grim business.

Hope you and your uncle had a nice Christmas together and that you got a chance to see your dad, too. We had a rousing session of Christmas carols in the wardroom with "Hank Hogan" providing the harmony. We even had a Christmas tree — a stunted little palm tree decorated with shell casings and cigarette packs. Festive.

The mail boat is leaving in just a few minutes so I've got to close so I can get this in the bag. I love you, I love you.

Jack
January 1, 1946

Dear Sweetheart,

Happy New Year — our first year at peace in a long time. Let's hope it lasts. The guys set off a few rounds and flares at midnight to celebrate — made the Japs a little nervous, but that was fun, too.

I'm bored silly right now. Since Christmas we've done little more than steam around Japanese home waters showing the Flag and drawing occasional Ready Duty. Demobilization has sent home some of the best officers and crews from the Fleet, and the dedication of those who remain is questionable. No one is eager to risk his neck in peacetime. Plus, we've had quite an epidemic of "Dear John" letters onboard ship lately. It's tough with the war over and all of those "heroes" returning home, while we're stuck out here, mopping up. Everyone feels forgotten. Morale is pretty low. If it wasn't for your letters, I think I would've gone crazy long ago.

Do you realize that in a little over six months, we'll be married? That is, if you think you still want to marry a wind-burned, underweight ex-Deck Officer. There's nothing like Navy food to bring a guy down to fighting trim.

I've been giving it some thought, and I figure when I get home, I'll take advantage of the G.I. Bill and go back to Notre Dame to get the last few credits I need for my Chemical Engineering degree. I think it will mean better job opportunities for me in the long run. Would you mind living in South Bend for a while, while I finish up? I could find us a nice little place and we could move in right after the wedding. Write and let me know what you think.

About the wedding. August seventeenth should work out great, as long as the Navy lets me out on schedule. That'll give us a couple of weeks to spend honeymooning and setting up house before classes start. And, don't you worry. I'll help with all the arrangements as soon as I get back. In the meantime, you just have fun picking out your wedding dress.

I've got the duty, so I've got to go. Love you, always.

Jack

I'll help with all of the arrangements — Maggie shook her head. Men! They had no idea how far in advance you needed to plan for a wedding. There was the dress, the guest list, the invitations, the bridesmaids and groomsmen, the flowers, the

Church, the reception, the menu. So many details to be discussed and agreed upon — and one momentous problem that she hadn't yet figured out how to address, much less solve.

With an effort, she put such thoughts out of her head, selecting another letter.

March 8, 1946

Dear Maggie,

For the last few days we've been sweeping the waters around a deserted little rock in the Marshall Islands called the Bikini Atoll. The military is planning to do some atomic blasting here to determine the effect of the blast on naval vessels and we have to make sure the surrounding waters are clear before they can begin. Evidently they're going to fill the harbor here with a bunch of derelict, old ships — abandoned, of course — and set off the bomb. I guess that's one way to get rid of the old clunkers.

I've got to tell you about something that happened yesterday. It's almost funny, now that I know we're all still in one piece.

We were sweeping just east of the atoll and had our lookouts positioned as usual around the ship — one on the bow, one portside, one starboard and three up in the radar shack, including me, all with binoculars. We're all connected by radio headsets so we can communicate with each other quickly. Well, at about 1020, the ensign next to me in the radar shack sees a mine floating directly off the bow, only twenty-five yards away. Immediately, he radios the crewman positioned at the bow, "Mine! Dead ahead!" The bow lookout starts raking the surface of the water with his binoculars, trying to find it. "Where?" he screams. "Look down!" yells the radar tower lookout. The crewman in the bow lowers the sights of his binoculars until he's looking almost directly down in front of the ship, beneath him. There, about to hit, he sees the mine, a floater. Well, let me tell you, that crewman got out of there so fast he ripped his radio headset right out of the console. He set a new world's record running astern, the wires of the headset flapping behind him. If we hadn't been so scared we would have laughed ourselves silly. We braced ourselves for the explosion. Instead, all we heard was a loud, metallic "clunk" as the mine struck just off the port side of the bow. The horn failed to detonate. We held our breath as it continued, "clunk, clunk, clunk," bouncing the length of the ship, striking a different horn each time. It never went off. A dud.

There were many converts that day. I guess it's just destined that I'm to return to you safely.

I just realized that by the time you get this, it'll be around St. Patrick's Day. Wish I could be back at "the Home of the Fighting Irish" to celebrate. Still, I'm sure we'll have a little celebration here on board — the ship's cook is named Murphy, the radio operator is Fitzgerald, and the Exec's name is Rooney. So we'll hoist a glass of sake to the "Ol' Sod."

All my love to my favorite Irish lass.

Yours forever,
Jack

St. Patrick's Day. Maggie shuddered at the memory.

Maggie had gone back to Boru for a kind of mini family reunion. Anna and James had remained in the Army Air Corps after the war and were unable to get leave, but Patrick had hitchhiked up from Iowa City, where he was enrolled as a freshman at the University of Iowa on the G.I. Bill, and Elly had finagled a few days off from her nursing duties at the Veteran's Hospital in Des Moines. After the worries and long separations of the war years, it was wonderful to be together. Michael, now a senior in high school, pumped Patrick for details of his tour of duty in the Pacific, but Patrick, looking much older, was reluctant to discuss his wartime experiences. He was very helpful, however, in answering Maggie's questions about Jack's probable duties and experiences aboard ship.

Elly looked wonderful — happy and fulfilled in her work at

the VA Hospital. She confided to Maggie that she'd met a young man in the hospital who was recovering from shrapnel wounds to his leg, and they'd fallen in love. Maggie hugged her, wondering at the gentle transformation this new love had caused in her outspoken older sister.

Together, the family had traveled into town to enjoy Boru's annual St. Patrick's Day Parade. There they'd seen many childhood friends, home from the war — and mourned many who would not be coming back.

At the house that evening, they sat around the kitchen, sipping lemonade and whiskey and discussing family and friends, missing and gone, and their own plans for the future. Eventually, the talk turned to the subject of Maggie's wedding. That's when the problems started.

"I'm so excited. I've already reserved four days vacation for that week so that I can travel to Sioux City and properly perform my *Maid of Honor* duties," said Elly. "And, I just love the bridesmaids dresses you picked out, Maggie. I was so afraid you would choose something in pink. I look ghastly in pink." She turned to their father.

"Dad, what are you going to wear? You simply cannot give Maggie away in that old black suit you've had forever."

Maggie gave her sister a desperate look, but it was too late.

"There'll be no need to be spending money on a new suit that won't be getting out of the pew," her father growled, stubbing out the remains of his cigarette.

"What are you talking about, Dad?" Patrick's eyes narrowed.

"It's not me who'll be walking your sister down the aisle. That honor has been taken from me."

"Uncle John." Patrick spat out the name.

"Patrick, please," said Maggie.

"No, Maggie. It's not bad enough he takes you away from the family, now he's taking Dad's place on your wedding day?"

"Not now, Patrick." Elly, giving Maggie an apologetic look, glared at her brother. Even Michael shook his head at him in warning.

The tension in the room was palpable. Finally, their father got to his feet, picked up his glass of whiskey and drained the little that remained in one swift gulp.

"Come, Michael. It's time to check on the stock."

Michael followed their father out the door, leaving Maggie, Elly and Patrick to wrestle with their own allegiances in silence.

Maggie shook her head to rid it of the painful memory and reached for a thin letter near the bottom of the stack — her favorite.

March 10, 1946

Dear Maggie,

Only have a minute. Just got word we'll be finishing up operations here next week, then our orders are to return to San Francisco via Pearl Harbor. The good old USA! And, hold onto your hat — by then I will have accumulated enough points from active duty to be rotated out. I don't know exactly how long it will take — you know the Navy — but what it means is ...
  I'M COMING HOME!
I'll call you as soon as I get leave in San Francisco.

All my love,
Jack

The fading light was making it difficult to read. Maggie raised her eyes from the page.

Despite Jack's optimism, it'd been mid-April before the *USS Thompson* made it back. He'd called her from San Francisco on a very poor phone connection, but his voice sounded wonderful anyway. Weeks of duty and endless paperwork followed before he got his orders to report to the Philadelphia Naval Yard to be discharged from the Navy. Then, yesterday, she received a telegram from him telling her he was stopping briefly in Lancaster to see his mother and father. He'd arrive in South Bend on the 5:08 train on Thursday evening.

Thursday. Maggie sighed. This was only Wednesday. The closer it came to time for his arrival, the slower the minutes seemed to pass. She clutched the precious letters to her chest, trying to still the ache in her heart. She couldn't believe she would finally be able to see him, to touch him. Just one more day.

Stiff and cold, Maggie stood up and gathered her things. She peeked out through the curtain of leaves. The coast clear, she skirted the lake, heading for the lights of Le Mans Hall. As she approached the entrance, she observed with a twinge of jealousy the scattered couples saying their lingering goodnights outside the front door.

Suddenly, to her left, Maggie saw the flare of a cigarette in the dark. A figure emerged from the shadows, a tall man in a slightly oversized suit. He stepped into the lamplight, and his eyes, even bluer than she remembered, locked on hers. She froze. Then with a small cry, she dropped the cardboard box and rushed into his arms, tears of joy streaming down her cheeks.

Chapter 19

June 1946

An ever-growing number of young women in every walk of life are taking jobs as they finish school or college, but the main job of the average woman in our country still is to marry and have a home and children.
—*"Woman's Place After the War," by Eleanor Roosevelt, originally published in* Click 7 *(August 1944)*

Maggie frowned at the paper in front of her, chewing on her pencil.

"There's just no way this is going to work. We need to trim at least ten people off this guest list. Do you really have to invite all of these fellas from your ship?"

"Maggie, those guys are like brothers to me."

"Even this one whose last name you can't remember?"

Jack smiled and shrugged. He chucked a small pebble across the surface of St. Joseph's Lake, causing the reflection of the Golden Dome to shimmer in the resulting ripples.

"And you haven't given me your answer on the kind of chicken to serve."

"Well, I'm not sure. But I definitely think it should be dead. And cooked."

"Jack, come on. You're not helping at all. You're leaving right after my graduation tomorrow, and we still have all of these decisions to make. The wedding is less than two months away, I've got a million details to take care of as soon as I get back to Sioux City, and you're treating it all like it's just a big joke. This is supposed to be the most important day of our lives … "

Maggie's voice tapered off, and she began to cry.

"Whoa, whoa! Maggie, take it easy." Jack sat up from the blanket on which he'd been reclining in a post-picnic stupor. "I'm not treating it like a joke. Really. I just didn't realize you had to have all of the answers right this second."

He reached out to take her hand, but she pulled it away, continuing to cry. He frowned.

"Hey, Maggie. What's wrong? This isn't just about sailors and chickens. Say, you're not having second thoughts, are you?"

She shook her head.

"Then what?"

"Oh, Jack. It's Uncle John and my father. I didn't tell you about it in my letters — there didn't seem much point with you being so far away — but they had a horrible fight."

"About what?" he said, handing her a napkin to wipe her nose.

"About the wedding. About me." She sniffed. "Last February, Louise — you know, my uncle's housekeeper — she overheard a phone conversation. Actually, I think she listened in on the extension, which is a horrible habit of hers, but this is one time I'm glad she did because she wrote me about it right away, thank heaven.

"Anyway, my father called Uncle John with a question about the wedding, and it came out that my dad was expecting to be the one to give me away. Uncle John said, no, *he* was my legal father and he'd be the one walking me down the aisle. My dad got angry. He said it didn't matter what the law said, he was still my father and it was his right. Then Uncle John got mad and said *he'd* raised me, *he* was paying for the wedding and *he* was damn well going to walk me down the aisle. Then my dad started shouting, which he almost never does, and … and … he called Uncle John a kidnapper."

Jack gave a low whistle.

Maggie blew her nose. She continued, her voice ragged.

"Uncle John told him that if that was the way he felt, maybe he shouldn't come to the wedding. Then Dad said fine, maybe he shouldn't, and hung up on him.

"As soon as I got Louise's letter, I called Aunt Bid. She was able to smooth things over and get Dad to agree to come. Louise worked on Uncle John. Now they're just back to hating each other.

"I asked Aunt Bid if she thought they might agree to walking me down the aisle together. She turned white, and made me swear that I wouldn't even mention the idea to either of them.

"I don't know what to do. I love them both, but they're both so stubborn and proud. And I'm so tired of being caught in the middle." Maggie's voice trembled. "Your wedding day is supposed to be a happy day, and mine is turning into a blood feud."

She began sobbing anew. Jack put his arm around her.

Jack knew that the animosity between Maggie's father and her uncle had been a source of great pain to her over the years. The reason for it remained a mystery. Maggie had explained to Jack as much of it as she understood, which wasn't much. He'd urged her to confront her father and uncle, and demand to know what happened, but Maggie refused. The abject fear in her voice kept him from ever pressing the point again. Now, on the eve of her wedding, she was once more torn between these two men she loved so much. And he felt powerless to help her.

He stroked her hair, wondering for the hundredth time at the emotional tightrope she must've been walking all of these years.

"Listen, Maggie. Whatever the trouble is between your father and your uncle, it's their problem, not yours. We're going to be married and spend the rest of our lives together. That's what's important. Just try to focus on that."

Maggie opened her eyes to sunlight streaming in through the lace curtains of her bedroom. Her heart knew before the thought had fully formed in her head. Today was her wedding day. She closed her eyes again, holding the realization close like a secret she was not yet ready to share. Savoring the anticipation, she lay there in the early morning quiet, the whole of this dreamed-of day stretching out before her. At last, all of the planning, the lists, the endless details — over. All that was left was to let events unfold as they would.

Then, despite her best intentions, Maggie felt the apprehension begin to creep in. So far, a major confrontation had been avoided, but she feared the stresses and emotions of the day might ignite the bitter fire that smoldered between her father and her uncle. Everyone assured her the day would go beautifully, but Maggie was worried. With good reason, if the rehearsal dinner the night before was any indication.

The rehearsal dinner had taken place in a private room of the Warrior Hotel in downtown Sioux City. Hosted by Jack's parents, the attendees included Uncle John, Terrence, Jack and Maggie's siblings, Aunt Bid, Bea Garrity, Maggie's roommate from school, Aunt Kit and Patty Maloney, her childhood friend. A last minute addition to the group was Mr. Stroebel, Mrs. Koerner's elderly father. Though well into his eighties and practically deaf, he'd insisted on making the long trip west to attend the wedding of his favorite grandchild. The older generation sat at one table of ten with Jack and Maggie, while the rest of the wedding party sat at another.

The seating of the four major powers at the Potsdam Conference in Berlin had involved less diplomatic maneuvering than had the seating arrangements for this dinner. Aware of the ill-feelings between Uncle John and Maggie's father, Mrs. Koerner had followed Jack's suggestion that she place Maggie's aunts at strategic intervals as buffers in hopes of keeping the conversation on neutral ground. The plan almost worked.

"How was your trip out from Lancaster, Mr. Koerner?" Uncle John asked as they waited for a round of drinks to be served.

"Please, call me Paul. It was quite enjoyable. I've never seen this part of the country before."

"Yes," said Jack's mother. "Our people have always stayed in the Lancaster/Philadelphia area. We're a very close family." She looked pointedly at Jack.

"By the way, Jack, have you and Maggie decided where you're going to live after you're married?"

Jack's smile was noncommittal.

"No, Mother. We won't decide that until after I graduate from Notre Dame next spring and find a job."

"Well, if I can help you in that regard, Jack, just let me know," Uncle John offered, reaching for a breadstick from the basket in front of him. "I have some well placed friends in the Chicago area who might be able to put you on to some good leads."

Both Terrence and Mrs. Koerner gave him baleful looks.

"What did he say?" Grandpa Stroebel bellowed.

"Chicago, Papa," said Mrs. Koerner, leaning over to speak directly into his ear. "He said he has business friends in Chicago."

"Chicago? I thought that place burned down."

Maggie hid a smile behind her hand.

"Mrs. Koerner," said Aunt Bid, gently turning the conversation, "I saw the beautiful handkerchief that you gave to Maggie as the *something old* to carry with her tomorrow. It's just lovely."

"Yes." Mrs. Koerner looked wistful. "It was my mother's. I carried it at my own wedding. I thought Maggie might want to carry on the tradition."

"Oh, yes, Mother Koerner. Thank you so much," said Maggie, doing her best with the unaccustomed appellation. Jack squeezed her hand.

Mrs. Koerner looked across the table at Maggie's father.

"Speaking of needlework, Mr. Fahey ... Terrence ... I had a chance to take a look at some of the wedding gifts at the house today, and I saw that you'd given Maggie an exquisite lace tablecloth made by your late wife. She was quite gifted with a needle."

"Thank you, Marie. That she was," Terrence said.

"I remember Lizzie worked on that cloth for months and months," said Aunt Kit. "I think she was prouder of that table-cloth than of anything else she ever made. She used it only on the most special of occasions."

"Who's busy?"

"Not *busy*, Papa," said Mrs. Koerner. "*Lizzie*. Elizabeth. She was Maggie's mother."

"Is that her?" Mr. Stroebel asked, pointing at Aunt Bid with a gnarled finger.

"No, dear. She passed on many years ago."

"Looks fine to me."

Uncle John raised his napkin to his mouth and coughed. Even Maggie's father had a twinkle in his eye.

"You did receive a number of lovely gifts, children," said Mr. Koerner, ignoring his father-in-law. "You have a wonderful start on your household."

"Yes, Dad. People have been incredibly generous."

Jack avoided looking at Uncle John. He still didn't know how to respond to the wedding present that Mr. Owen had given them — a brand new Chrysler automobile. Such an extrav-agant gift made him uncomfortable. But Jack knew how Mr. Owen doted on his niece, and could think of no gracious way to refuse. Maggie assured him that Uncle John just wanted to help them get started in life, but Jack could tell that she, too, was worried that such an expensive gift would be seen by her father as another attempt at one-upmanship. Fortunately, Mr. Owen had presented the keys to them in private and hadn't mentioned the gift to anyone.

Just then, a group of waiters arrived with the meal — a lovely salad, fresh vegetables, whipped potatoes and big thick steaks, so appreciated after years of meat rationing. Mr. Stroebel's booming comments were stilled as he chewed with great care each minute piece of beef his daughter painstakingly cut up for him.

As the meal was winding down, Mr. Koerner instructed the waiter to fill the champagne flutes. Standing, he raised his glass.

"If I could have your attention, please," he said in a loud voice.

The gay, young crowd at the other table stilled.

"This is a very special evening, not only for Jack and Maggie, but for their families and friends. Their love and commitment to each other is a symbol for all of us, having recently lived through such dark times, that life does indeed go on, and flourishes.

"Jack, you were always a dear boy and you have grown to be a fine man. Your mother and I are very proud of you. And Maggie, now that we've gotten to know you, we can certainly understand why Jack loves you so much. Here's to many, many wonderful years together.

"To Jack and Maggie."

Glasses clinked around the room as everyone toasted the engaged couple. Jack leaned over and gave Maggie a kiss, to the raucous applause of the younger table. Mrs. Koerner smiled through her tears. Only her husband heard her mumble, *My poor baby*.

Mr. Koerner sat down. There was an expectant lull. Maggie felt a wave of panic. This was the point at which the father of the bride traditionally made a toast. She'd been so busy anticipating any possible points of friction connected with the wedding ceremony, she'd forgotten about this particular problem posed by the rehearsal dinner. As the seconds ticked by, she looked down at her place. Then she heard the scraping of a chair.

"I'd like to thank Mr. and Mrs. Koerner for hostin' this lovely dinner tonight."

Maggie looked up to find her father standing, glass in hand, his nervousness betrayed only by the slight brogue that'd crept into his voice. Across the table, her uncle sat with an impassive expression on his face.

"This is indeed a wonderful occasion. Maggie is the first

of my children to be married. Hopefully, not the last."

Everyone chuckled. At the next table, Patrick elbowed Elly.

"And she has found herself a grand young man. I only wish her mother could be here to share this day. But, on her behalf, and that of the entire Fahey family, I wish Jack and Maggie a happy and blessed marriage. To Jack and Maggie."

Glasses were still being clinked when Uncle John came to his feet. The room went silent. Aunt Kit and Aunt Bid exchanged worried looks.

"I would like to add my thanks to Mr. and Mrs. Koerner for bein' our gracious hosts tonight. This is a time to celebrate the love between Maggie and Jack, a love which they will declare before God, family and friends tomorrow. I know that my late wife would join me in wishin' our daughter and her future husband all the joys that life can bring. To Maggie and Jack."

Maggie sipped at her champagne, not daring to raise her eyes, so she was spared the sight of Aunt Kit with a vice-like grip upon her father's arm, or the look of defiance Uncle John wore as he lifted his glass and drained it.

Shaking her head to rid it of such troubling thoughts, Maggie got up and put on her robe. She tiptoed down to the kitchen. Despite her nervous stomach, she forced herself to eat some toast and juice. The wedding wasn't until noon, and it was just 6:30 A.M. She wondered how she'd last until then. Settling into the window seat in the parlor, she watched as the milk truck rattled by, Mrs. Edsall from across the street tiptoed out to pick up her morning paper, and Mr. Peterson from a few doors down passed by with his fussy little Pomeranian dog on their morning walk. She was amazed that these people could go about their normal lives, unaware of the momentous event that was to take place this day. She, herself, had such a feeling of pre-science, as if she stood on the edge of a great, exciting journey, one she'd been preparing for her entire life. She didn't know what the future would hold, but she knew that, whatever it was, she and Jack would face it together. If she could just make it through the next few hours.

"My, you're up early."

Uncle John shuffled into the kitchen in his slippers, heading straight for the coffee pot.

"Too excited to sleep, is it?"

"I guess," Maggie blushed. He joined her at the window.

"Looks like it will be a beautiful day," he commented, sipping from his cup.

"I hope so."

"Don't worry, Maggie. Everythin's going to be perfect. I'll see to it."

By 9:30 A.M., the bridesmaids began arriving at the house, carrying their long dresses in garment bags and lugging suitcases full of make-up and hair supplies. Terrence drove Aunt Kit and Aunt Bid over to help Maggie with her final preparations. Elly, Anna, Bea and Patty took over one upstairs bedroom while Maggie and her aunts took over the other. Uncle John retreated to a secluded corner of the parlor, out of the way of the giggling, excited women and the clouds of perfume and powder they exuded. Terrence chose to wait outside.

While her bridesmaids helped each other dress, Maggie stood in the center of her bedroom while her two aunts circled around her, making final adjustments to the beautiful satin wedding dress she'd chosen. The gown was simple and elegant with long sleeves, a slim skirt, a scooped neckline and a four-foot train.

"All right, Nugget," announced Aunt Kit, who'd been helping Maggie fasten the long row of pearl buttons down the back of her dress, "I think we're ready for the veil."

Aunt Bid went to the closet door and lifted the long tulle veil from its hanger. She held the satin and pearl encrusted headpiece in one hand, draping the rest of the lace trimmed fabric over her other arm. She carried it, almost reverently, to where Maggie stood in front of the full-length mirror.

"Turn towards me, now," Aunt Bid instructed. She placed

the headpiece on Maggie's head, careful not to muss her hair, and secured it with the attached combs. Aunt Kit fanned the veil out over the skirt of her dress.

"There," said Aunt Kit. "Let's have a look at you."

Maggie turned toward the mirror. For a split second, she saw, not a young woman in her bridal gown, but a little girl with her mother's eyes, dressed in a white Communion dress and veil, hand stitched by another's loving hand. The pang of longing she felt was strong.

"You look beautiful, Maggie," whispered Aunt Bid.

The vision in the mirror transformed itself into that of a graceful, young bride. Maggie stared in wonder. She did look beautiful — and a little scared. Her eyes filled with tears for the two women who should've been there to share this day with her.

"Ah, now. Don't be ruining your make-up," Aunt Kit handed her a tissue, dabbing at her own eyes with another.

Uncle John knocked at the door.

"Maggie. It's time to be leavin' for the church. Are you ready?"

"Get away from the door, John. Don't be rushing the poor girl on her wedding day," Aunt Kit barked.

Maggie took a last look in the mirror and smiled.

"It's all right, Aunt Kit. I'm ready."

At the sound of the screen door opening, Terrence looked up from the porch swing where he'd been enjoying a smoke away from the frenetic preparations. He froze, his cigarette halfway to his mouth.

"Oh, Maggie," he whispered.

She stood before him in a graceful swirl of satin, a hopeful look on her face. Aunt Kit and Aunt Bid stood just behind her, ready to accept accolades for their handiwork. Terrence stood, his eyes misting over even as a smile crossed his lips.

"How I wish your mother could be here to see you. You look just like she did on our wedding day. So beautiful."

He kissed Maggie on the cheek. But when he stepped back, his expression had darkened.

"Dad, what's the matter?" Maggie asked in alarm.

Terrence turned away, fighting for control of his emotions. The sight of Maggie in her wedding dress — the beautiful daughter he couldn't claim as his own, not even on her wedding day — was too much. He'd kept his silence all these years, watched while another man usurped his rightful place, but this, at last, was just too much to bear.

"Kit. Bid. I'd like to talk to Maggie alone, please."

"Terrence, I don't think now is a good time — " Kit began.

"Kit. Go to the car. You too, Bid."

The look on Terrence's face precluded any argument, even from Kit. With worried expressions, the two older women left the front porch, hurrying down the walkway to where Uncle John, dressed in a new suit with a white boutonnière in his lapel, stood leaning against one of the cars, watching.

"Margaret, there's something I need to tell you," her father began in a portentous voice, his hard eyes on his brother-in-law. "Something I should have told you long ago."

Maggie stared at her father's stern profile. What could it be, she wondered? Just a moment ago he seemed so happy.

Suddenly, she knew. She held her breath, afraid to move. Was this it, then, at last? Was she to learn the answers to the questions that had plagued her since she was a scared little girl huddled in the backseat of her uncle's car? Over time, she'd reconciled herself to the fact that she'd never know what transpired in those years just after her mother's death. She'd even made herself believe that it no longer really mattered. But now, as she watched her father's face, the voice of that frightened little girl, never really silenced, welled up within her.

Why, Daddy? Why did you send me away?

She waited, afraid yet desperate to hear the truth.

Terrence took a long, last drag on his cigarette. He'd waited a long time for this, his chance to reveal the betrayal and the heartache, to redeem himself in his daughter's eyes and reassert his rights as her father.

He flicked his cigarette butt over the railing and turned toward Maggie. But as he looked upon her face framed in its white veil, so lovely, so innocent, he realized it was too late. The time for explanations and recriminations had long since passed. Breaking the silence now would only cause her more pain, and quite possibly destroy the love she felt for Nora, John … and himself. Besides, what grounds did he have to assert his *rights* as a father, anyway? Had he not, in reality, given her away long ago? No. No good could come of speaking his mind on this, her wedding day, of all days. He'd failed her in so much. The least he could do was to give her this day.

Terrence's face softened. He reached out and gave his daughter's hand a gentle squeeze.

"I just wanted to tell you … I love you, Magpie. Now go. They're waiting for you."

But Maggie had seen the fire flare, then die in her father's eyes. Poised on the brink of revealing to her all that had happened, he'd stopped and turned away. For whatever reason, he'd decided not to open the doorway to the past. She realized this, and felt dizzy with confusion, disappointment … and relief. The questions of her childhood would remain unanswered, as much a mystery as the father she loved.

Without a word, Maggie swept the train of her dress into one arm. The tears of the little girl mingled with those of the young woman. She wiped them away with a white-gloved hand and descended the porch steps.

The organist was playing the *Ave Maria* as Maggie and the wedding party entered the vestibule of the church. Through the small leaded windows of the inner doors, she caught a glimpse of the congregation, fanning themselves in the August heat. Some small part of her mind thought how nice it was to see the women in their full-skirted silks and gabardines and their fanciful hats, an orgy of color and fabric after the somber tones and utilitarian styles of the war years.

Jack's parents had already been seated. Maggie could pick out his mother's wide-brimmed lavender hat. Standing on tip-toe, she tried to catch a glimpse of her father. She knew he was seated somewhere in the front of the church. Uncle John stood behind her straightening and re-straightening his tie. She felt her nerve falter, and wished she could talk to Jack for just a minute. She longed for his reassurance, his support for what she was about to do. But she was on her own.

Suddenly, the music swelled, the signal for the bridesmaids to line up for their measured walk down the aisle. The inner doors opened. Maggie's senses were assailed by the perfume of flowers and candles, and the sight of many faces turned toward her in happy expectation.

Elly gave her a quick embrace.

"This is my last chance to hug you before you become an old, married lady," she whispered. Then she turned and fol-lowed the rest of the bridesmaids already processing down the aisle.

When Elly got halfway to the altar, the organist made a smooth transition into *The Wedding March*. Maggie felt her heart skip a beat.

Uncle John offered his arm to her for the walk up the aisle. She didn't move.

"I can't," she whispered.

"Come now, Maggie, you're just a little nervous. It'll be fine."

"No, Uncle John, you don't understand. I can't walk up the aisle with you."

"What?"

"Uncle John, I love you. I will be forever grateful for every-thing you have done for me, and for this beautiful wedding. But, I can't walk up the aisle with you. I can't do that to my father."

The organ continued to play while the guests craned their necks toward the back of the church.

"Maggie, don't be ridiculous," Uncle John hissed. "It's all been decided."

"Not by me. If I walk down the aisle with you, it'd look as if I'd chosen you over him. And I won't do that. I love you both. I won't be made to choose between you — not even by you."

"Margaret, everyone is waitin'. Stop this nonsense right now, and take my arm."

Maggie's eyes were bright with tears. Her chin quivered, but she stood firm.

"I'm sorry, Uncle John. I have to do this on my own."

He stared at her, his expression thunderous.

"Then, go."

He turned and walked away.

The confused organist was just beginning her third run through of *The Wedding March* when Maggie took her first tremulous step. She concentrated on putting one foot in front of the other, trying to ignore the shocked whispers of the wedding guests and the disapproving look on the face of Father Brennan standing at the end of the long aisle. She'd never done anything so rebellious, so unconventional in her entire life, and she feared she might die of shame and embarrassment before she ever reached the altar.

Then, suddenly, he was there. He met her halfway, reaching out to her, his eyes filled with love and pride. Smiling through her tears, she took the hand he proffered. Jack folded her arm through his, and they walked the rest of the way down the flower-trimmed aisle of the church, together.

Jack hopped into the car and closed the door. Inside, it was blessedly quiet, the only sounds the muffled goodbyes of the guests and the ticking of the rice against the windows.

"Whew!" Jack laughed, brushing a few grains of rice from his sleeve. He leaned over, threw his arms around his bride and gave her a big kiss.

"Jack!" Maggie protested, blushing. "Everyone is watching."

She smoothed the skirt of her pink gabardine going-away suit and readjusted the brim of her matching hat.

"After what you did today, do you really think a little kiss is going to shock them?"

Jack started the motor and pulled away from the curb, honking the horn in farewell as the cans that Michael and Patrick had attached to the back bumper banged along behind them. As the well-wishers disappeared in the rearview mirror, he glanced over at his new bride.

"Well, you certainly gave the matrons of Sioux City something to talk about for the next few weeks."

"Oh, Jack. Don't tease me. I don't think Uncle John is ever going to forgive me," Maggie said in a pitiful voice.

"Sure he will. After all, he didn't leave the church. And he came to the reception."

"I think he did that because Louise and Aunt Kit threatened him."

"Well, he made a nice toast as father of the bride."

"'To the bride and groom'?"

"Okay, maybe not eloquent, but a toast, nonetheless. And your dad never challenged him."

"I think even he thought I'd crossed the lines of good taste."

"Actually, once they got over the shock, I think both your uncle and your father were proud of you."

Maggie looked skeptical.

"No, really. For the first time in your life, you stood up to them. That took guts. I think, down deep, they respected that. I think that's the reason they were able to share the *father of the bride dance* without coming to blows."

"It doesn't solve anything, though. They still hate each other."

Maggie felt a sudden overpowering fatigue as the adrenalin rush that had sustained her through the excitement and tension of the day drained away. Jack reached over and patted her knee.

"Maggie, there are some things in life you just can't fix. Sometimes, you just have to accept that fact, and move on."

They drove south out of town along the road that paralleled the Missouri River. After a few miles, Jack pulled over onto the shoulder. He detached the cans and the *Just Married* sign, tossing them into the trunk. Pausing for a moment, he looked out over the endless fields of corn that stretched for miles along the stretch of land between the road and the river. Darkness was beginning to fall, and in the slight breeze that rose off the water, the tasseled stalks whispered and waved their farewells.

"There, that will make the ride to New Orleans a little more pleasant," he said, getting back into the car. He reached over, taking his young bride's hand.

"You know, with all the excitement and well-wishers, this is the first time all day that I really feel like I have you to myself," he said.

Maggie bowed her head. A tear ran down her cheek.

"Hey, what's the matter, Mrs. Koerner? Change your mind?"

She shook her head.

"Not homesick already?"

"No," she whispered. Then she looked up at him with eyes so full of love it took his breath away.

"I was just thinking that, right now … here with you … is the first time in my whole life that I've ever really felt like I *was* home."

Jack felt a lump rise to his throat. He stared at his young bride in wonder, feeling both honored and humbled. He leaned over and kissed her with great tenderness, praying that he could live up to the trust she placed in him. Then, without a word, he put the car in gear and pulled back onto the highway. With his arm around her and her head on his shoulder, they drove south together, while the darkness of the Iowa night closed around them.

photo by Michael Good, M. Photog., CPP

Mary Frailey Calland grew up in Elmira, New York, and is a graduate of the University of Notre Dame and Notre Dame Law School. She lives in Pittsburgh, Pennsylvania, with her husband and five children. *Barefoot In The Stubble Fields* is her first novel.